SPARES

SPARES

Caroline Gray

·PARRALLEL·

4 Spares

This title first published in Great Britain in 1993 by
Severn House Publishers Ltd.
This edition licensed by Severn House Publishers Ltd,
produced by Magpie Books Ltd, and published by Parragon
Book Service Ltd in 1995.

A copy of the British Library CIP data is available
from the British Library.

ISBN: 0 75251 279 X

Printed and Bound in Great Britain

This is a novel. The characters and events are invented and are not intended to portray real people or actual events.

“Sweet is the lore which Nature brings;
Our meddling intellect
Misshapes the beauteous form of things:-
We murder to dissect.”

William Wordsworth

CHAPTER 1

Sirens screamed, and the squad car jerked violently from side to side as it avoided the people crowding the street. "Fucking ghouls," Chief Detective Inspector Lampson growled.

"They don't know what's happened yet, sir," Detective Sergeant Parton reminded his superior.

"Neither do we," Lampson said, and cracked his knuckles. "The bastards should be in church." Lampson was a big man, with hunched shoulders and a weatherbeaten nose. His black hair was streaked with gray and his suit was crumpled; his tie was a piece of multi-coloured string. His hands were enormous, made more so by what Sergeant Parton considered his detestable habit; each time Lampson cracked a knuckle it sounded like a pistol shot.

Chief Detective-Inspector Lampson was a much-feared policeman, by his own men no less than by the underworld; Sergeant Parton was one of the few who refused to be browbeaten by the waves of aggression Lampson could so easily emanate – he had worked with the Inspector long enough to know that the instinctive brilliance with which his superior was credited was merely meticulous attention to detail, that the aggression was cover for an often painful uncertainty.

The car screeched to a halt, and the Inspector got out. Three constables waiting on the pavement saluted; others were holding back the crowd which was attempting to get closer. Lampson looked up at the building rising above his head. It was a typical old London house on a typically quiet London street – even if at eight o'clock on this May Sunday morning the street was no longer quiet. Like so many large, old London houses this one had been converted into flats just after the Hitler War. That meant, Lampson reflected grimly, that there would be no lift, and the despatch girl had said something about the top floor. A police sergeant opened the street door. "Nasty, sir," he commented.

Lampson raised his eyebrows. There were several people in the hall, presumably other tenants, muttering, pausing to stare at the police officers; some were fully dressed, others in dressing gowns. A small dog sniffed at his boots, from somewhere in the interior a baby was wailing. The hall itself was surprisingly bright; it had a well-cared for look, and was scrupulously clean – despite the dog. "Nobody leaves," Lampson said, and climbed the stairs with Parton, hatchet-faced and dapper, at his heels.

On the top floor landing – the fourth – a woman police constable knelt, vomiting into a bucket. "What in the name of Christ . . .?" Lampson demanded, panting from the speed with which he had climbed the stairs.

"She saw the victim, sir," the policeman at the door told him. He was looking green himself.

Lampson thrust him aside and stepped into the living room of the flat; the lock had been forced and the door hung open. A glance left and right told his practiced eye that it was definitely a bachelor establishment, with a cleaning woman coming in perhaps twice a week: the flowers in the vase on the table by the window were at least two days old. The room itself was comfortably and even expensively furnished, but there was evidence of a struggle, in that a couple of chairs had been knocked over and one of the rugs was gathered into a heap. There was also a peculiar smell, which Lampson could immediately identify: death. A police sergeant waited at the closed bedroom door; his hands were trembling. "What is the name of that girl?" Lampson demanded.

"WPC Williams, sir."

"And you?"

"Sergeant Cray, sir."

"Who gave the alarm?"

"One of the other tenants felt that something was wrong and called 999. WPC Williams and PC Morton . . ." Cray nodded to the young man at the outer door, "were nearest and took the call. They could get no reply so they broke the door. Williams was first into the bedroom." He hesitated. "It's not very nice."

"No corpse ever is," Lampson reminded him. "Open up."

The sergeant drew a long breath and pushed the door inwards. Lampson stepped inside, and checked. His first impression was blood. There was blood everywhere; the bedclothes were a deep red-brown, and there were huge pools of dried blood on the floor and soaked into the rugs – there was even blood on the walls, and scattered across the dressing table. Then there was the smell. Although it was a warm spring morning, the windows were tight shut and the murder had clearly been committed several hours before. The room stank of dead humanity. Lampson took a step into the room, found he had to tiptoe round and between the bloodstains; there were other shoemarks to be seen. Made by the policeman and woman, or the murderers? Because instinctively he knew there had been more than one.

Cautiously he approached the bed, felt a hardness in his throat. The victim had been stripped naked and spreadeagled, wrists and ankles tied to the four posts, and so far as Lampson could see, had then been cut to pieces. The head was intact, and so were the legs from the thighs down. But the torso was just a mass of flesh and skin and bones . . . and blood. The face was absurdly, disturbingly, relaxed – the dead man had not known, or cared, what was being done to him. Lampson frowned, and leaned over the head. But there was no blood up there, no indication that he might have been hit on the head and rendered unconscious.

"Mad," the sergeant suggested. "Whoever did this must have been stark, raving mad."

Lampson found he was drawing long breaths, but each breath was less pleasant than the last. He swallowed, made himself speak just as he was making himself think. "They, sergeant. It would have needed more than one man to do something like this. Unless he and his killer were playing games and something went wrong. So, they should be easy to find, with all this blood."

"Not necessarily, sir. They used the bathroom."

Lampson made his way between puddles of dried blood across the room and looked through the open bathroom door. Here again he saw nothing but blood; there was a dried pool of it, diluted, in the tub as well as in the basin, and stains were scattered across the floor. "I estimate he . . . they stripped before carrying out the murder," Sergeant Cray said behind him. "Left their clothes in the living room. Then bathed when they had finished, got dressed, and walked out." He pointed at the two bloodstained towels, lying on the floor just inside the bedroom door. "Whoever did it will have no blood on them."

"Shit!" Parton had arrived. "Talk about Texas chain saws!"

"Gays?" Lampson asked.

"Doubtful, sir. The flat belongs to Douglas Openshaw, the shot putter. Got a bronze at the last Olympics."

"Being a world class shot putter doesn't tell us anything about his sexual habits," Parton objected.

Cray scratched his head. "That him, Openshaw, on the bed?" Lampson asked.

"I think so, sir."

"Well, that's something to start with. Famous man, might have had enemies, estranged boy friends . . ."

"Or girl friends," Cray suggested, stubbornly.

"This was a man's murder," Lampson declared. "It could even be described as a ritual murder." He pointed. If what had happened to the dead man's torso was difficult to determine without a detailed examination, it was simple enough to see he had been castrated – and the testicles and penis were gone.

"Or a gay one," Parton put in.

"Or both. Where the hell is the surgeon?"

"On his way, with the photographer. You got here very quickly, sir."

"I was about to leave for church, sergeant, when I received the call. No one else is to come in here, understood?" Lampson went to the outer door. WPC Williams was on her feet, but leaning against the wall, mopping her face with a handkerchief. "First corpse?" Lampson asked.

"No, sir." She was a handsome young woman, and not all that young, either, Lampson realised. She'd been around some time, and looked tough enough. Now she inhaled, her nostrils flaring. "But I've never seen anything like that."

"Well, keep mum about it," Parton told her. "We don't want any Jack the Ripper stories getting about."

"Two Jacks the Ripper," Lampson corrected. "At least. But two men, with a bag . . ."

"Sir?"

"They had at least a couple of surgical scalpels, and we don't know what else, and they took something away. Oh, yes, I think they'd have a bag. Two men, with a bag, entering and then leaving the building, walking up and then down the stairs, not to mention the scuffle in the living room. Let's have a chat with those people downstairs. The ones who called 999."

* * *

"Forty-fifteen," said the umpire.

"Hurrah!" shrieked the crowd.

"Quiet, please," the umpire said, and looked disapprovingly at the rustle amongst the spectators as a large man made his way along the benches surrounding the tennis court to a seat which had been vacant all afternoon. The girl about to serve also glanced at the crowd, and raised her eyebrows, then concentrated. Three rapid bounces, a high toss, and a full swing – just long. The second service went into the net.

"Forty-thirty," remarked the umpire, and the crowd hummed.

"You'd have done better to stay away," Anne Moresby commented. "That's her first double, and at what a time! Where have you *been*, anyway?"

"Slept late," Jonathan Rudder replied. "Serving for the match, is she?"

There was a flurry of rallies, lithe sun-tanned legs and arms scything across the afternoon, short skirts flaring in the self-created breeze. "Deuce."

"You slept until after lunch on the day your girl friend is playing in a final? She said you weren't feeling well." Anne's somewhat cold features were rigid with disapproval; she was her younger sister's mentor in all things, and had to reflect that but for her initial approval, Angela would never have taken up with this enormous layabout in the first place.

But she *had* approved. Jonathan Rudder might be in every sense a drop-out, and he could not be described as handsome – he had the features of a retired boxer – but there was something infectiously attractive about him, from the wide shy grin to the shock of dark hair, the curiously flat blue eyes to the deep, relaxed voice, the way he scratched his ear when embarrassed – as now – and even the flare of his nostrils when he was about to be aggressive, which was fairly often. And he had the body to be aggressive with, six feet four inches of solid bone and muscle, however much he seemed to be trying on occasions to drink it into fat. Naked, he was superb. Anne had more than once reflected that if she was more into men she'd have grabbed him for herself. As he draped his blazer over the back of the seat she had kept for him – it was a warm, sunny May afternoon – the muscles in his arms rippled deliciously.

But his habits could be tiresome, as could her sister's determined loyalty. "She was more than half right. The lads had a bit of a party," he explained. "Oh, good shot!"

Angela had just put away a volley. "Advantage Miss Moresby!"

"She should do it now," Anne said with satisfaction. "And then, do you know what? She's qualified for Wimbledon. You are going to be here for Wimbledon, Jonny?"

"I shall try. I'm not quite sure how many races Bruce has lined up. I know there are a few. He wants us all in top shape for the Newport-Bermuda."

"Grown men, messing about in boats," Anne commented.

Jonathan gave his twisted grin. "Grown women, playing with balls. Soft balls, anyway. There it is."

The crowd rose to applaud the winning shot, and continued to clap as Angela was congratulated by her opponent, and then faced the dignitary who was presenting both the trophies and the cheques. "Another week's rent," Jonathan observed.

Anne glanced at him. "I don't suppose you ever contribute."

"Oh, but I do, after my fashion. Let's go get the girl."

* * *

"Did you see any of it?" Angela asked, as she got into Jonathan's dark blue Mercedes coupe.

"The last game. But that about summed it up, didn't it?"

Angela sighed. Twenty years old, and thus three years younger than her sister, she was a tall girl, whose slim body concealed a good deal of muscle and superb physical fitness, necessary for someone who dreamed of climbing the lucrative ladder of the professional tennis circuit. She wore her yellow hair severely short, in a fringe just below her ears and scattered across her forehead. She was not really pretty, with her face, with its snub nose and rounded chin, was attractive and far softer than Anne's, and she possessed a glow, which was always much in evidence just after winning a match. She also possessed a most even temper and a great deal of patience, which she needed; on the day of the most important match of her career, so far, she had last seen her lover in bed with the duvet over his head, groaning.

"Can we drop you somewhere?" Jonathan was asking Anne.

"Yes, home." She got into the back. "Now, Angie, I think an early night, and then some light practice tomorrow morning. We'll lunch together. And when I'm away, I want you to practice every morning for a couple of hours.

"Leaving, are we?" Jonathan inquired.

"Mother has her hay fever, and I've promised to go down to Hastings till Friday. You won't forget what I've said, Angie?"

"Right," Angela agreed, and glanced at Jonathan. "Right?"

"Well, tonight will be as early as can be. The lads are giving me a farewell bash at the Marquis of Granby."

"Oh, no," Anne said. "Oh, no, no, no. Anyway, you said you were out with the lads last night."

"Those were a different set of lads. Come on, Angie, I'm going to be away for the next month at least."

"Oh . . . well . . ." Angela looked over her shoulder.

"Home by midnight," Jonathan promised.

"And I won't touch a drop," Angela added. Anne looked as if she would have argued, but then changed her mind. "I won't, you know," Angela said, when they had dropped Anne at her flat. "You and me have things to talk about."

The flat they shared was on the first-floor of a custom-built block in Barnes, close to the river although the water could only be seen from the fourth level. Being custom-built, every spare inch was utilised for some purpose or another, and the two bedrooms were both small. By the time Angela had dumped her tennis gear in the one chair, the room was already crowded. Jonathan stretched out on the bed. "Come here," he said. She went willingly enough, stood beside him as his hand slid up the back of her thigh, under her dress and into her knickers to caress her bottom. "The sight of you leaping around like a gazelle always turns me on."

"Me alone? Don't you think the reason Barbara lost was because her boobs kept getting in the way of her service?"

"Absolutely." He pulled her down for a kiss, and then laid her on top of him.

"I don't want a fuck. Not right now. I want to talk."

"Make it quick. What's the subject matter?"

"Pregnancy."

She found she was holding her breath. Although Jonathan had been her live-in mate for nearly a year now, Angela understood that she knew very little about him. His reactions always took her by surprise. And she was afraid of his temper, which could be almost maniacal when he was really aroused – or when he had had too much to drink. He had never in any way been violent to her, or treated her with other than the greatest respect, but then, they had never shared a crisis before.

As always, he took her completely by surprise. "Then surely you shouldn't have been charging about a tennis court."

"Well, obviously, it's early days." She frowned, rolled off him, put her feet on the floor and sat up. "You mean you're not mad?"

He grinned. "That's what women are for."

"Pig!" She got up, walked to the window, and stared at the lawn beneath for some seconds. "It makes one think."

"Absolutely." He sat up as well. "Like, how?"

She bit her lip. "I was finding last year that the pill was making me a bit lazy on court. At least, I supposed it was the pill. So, for this year's first tournament, I stopped taking it."

"I think you should have told me."

"I know. I'm sorry."

Jonathan scratched his ear. And frowned. "That tournament was six weeks ago. So you've only missed one period. So you're speculating."

"I just feel it."

"Well, the first thing to do is find out for sure."

"Yes. Trouble is, I'm registered with Mumsy's doctor. For her, the world stopped moving when Churchill died. She still has those standards."

"She knows about me, doesn't she?"

"Not exactly. That's why, when she comes to town, I always go round to Anne's for the duration."

"What a deceitful lot you women are. Does Anne know about this?"

"God forbid! With the tennis season just starting? She'd go stark, raving mad."

"Point taken. Okay. You'll go to a friend of mine."

"Friend?"

"He's a doctor. We were at medical school together, but where I dropped out, he went on to qualify. James Colley. He should be there tonight. I'll introduce you. You go along to see him tomorrow and he'll tell you what's up. If anything."

Angela came back to the bed, moving slowly. "Supposing the test is positive . . ."

"Then we'll start to think, seriously."

"Jonny, you do know the baby is yours?"

"It bloody well ought to be."

"Well . . . I'd really hate to abort."

"Who said anything about abortion? If you want the little fellow, you have him. Mind you, you'll miss Wimbledon."

"Um. It's only a month off . . . but Jonny, what about us?"

"If you're pregnant, I'll marry you. I can be old-fashioned too."

She sat beside him, threw both arms round his neck. "I was so afraid . . ." she pulled away. "Won't your uncle be furious?"

"That is one of the things we have to consider. I might have to get a job."

"Oh, Jonny!"

He raised his eyebrows. "I'm sure your sister would approve of that, at least. But let's cross that bridge when we come to it. Now, do I get that fuck? And then, we're going to celebrate!"

"I'll enjoy that." She undressed, then undressed him. As she did so, she frowned. "Just what were you doing last night?"

"Would you believe I have no idea?"

She sighed. "Meaning, you got blind drunk and had a fight. One day you're going to be arrested and sent to prison for GBH."

"Now, how can you say I had a fight?" he demanded, raising his hands. "Not a bruise on my knuckles."

"You must have used something else. There was blood on your shirt this morning. You're sure you're all right?"

He grinned. "You're welcome to look, all over. If I'm damaged, I never felt a thing."

The Marquis of Granby public house was packed when Jonathan and Angela arrived: it was seven o'clock on a warm Sunday evening, and the crowd of happy drinkers had overflowed into the beer garden at the rear; the noise could be heard even above the din of traffic on the London streets outside, and at the bar men, and women, were standing three deep.

"Over here!" someone shouted as Jonathan pushed his way through the doors in front of Angela, and they saw his friends, who had taken up a strategic position in a corner of the bar close to the darts board. Angela had discovered over their year together that Jonathan had several sets of friends, those whom he had accumulated at medical school, and those through rugby and sailing. These were apparently the medical and rugby group. There was only a smattering of women, and none that Angela knew very well, although she had of course met several of them, and their boy friends, at other parties she had attended with Jonathan.

She felt distinctly nervous. He had promised not to tell anyone that she might be pregnant, and he had seemed to take the news entirely in his stride . . . but she could tell he had a lot on his mind. That could be just concern over his relationship with his somewhat mysterious uncle, who lived in a vast house in the country and whose allowance was very necessary if Jonathan was going to continue his pre-1940 lifetsyle – and who apparently did not care for itinerant young women, not even if they came from a good family and were potential tennis champions. The old boy, whom she had never met, seemed to be in every way a bastard, but Jonathan hated work and loved sailing . . . and was now getting drunk just as rapidly as possible. "G and T for the girl," he told the barman.

"No, really, Jonny," she protested. "I don't think I should."

"You're damned right. I'm a fool. Champagne!" he announced. "Champagne for everyone." He drank his brandy and soda at a gulp.

"Champagne!" The shout was taken up.

"What's the occasion?" someone asked.

"Angie is celebrating."

"Jonny!" Angela pulled at his arm. The first cork flew with a pop, and glasses were filled. "Please, Jonny, you promised," Angela begged.

He winked at her, raised his glass. "This afternoon, Angie qualified for Wimbledon. How about that, then?"

Toasts were drunk, and Angie was hugged and kissed, while relief seeped through her system. He hadn't let her down after all. But the evening wasn't over yet. His arm was round her shoulders as he escorted her away from the bar to where a man of approximately his own age, just past thirty, sat at a table drinking beer. "That's not right," Jonathan said, picking up the mug and emptying the contents into the nearest potted plant. "Watch them droop." They didn't, but he summoned some champagne, and retained the bottle. "Jim," he said, "I want you to meet Angie."

Angie was pushed into a seat beside Jim. She gave him a nervous smile. He was slim, of medium build, and quite good looking in an intense sort of way. In contrast to the blazers and sports jackets around him, he wore a dark suit, and a neatly knotted tie. He smelt of good tobacco, and there was a pipe in his breast pocket. A friend of Jonathan's, tidy, and not obviously some kind of Corinthian? Jonathan sat down as well, and placed the bottle between the three of them. "Hello," Jim said. His voice was quiet.

"Dr Colley," Jonathan explained. "We were friends, once."

Jim Colley raised his eyebrows. "Once?"

"Don't see much of you nowadays," Jonathan pointed out, and turned to Angela. "Jim doesn't approve of me any more."

"I just hate to see talent thrown away," Jim remarked, as quietly as ever. "This great hulk could have been the finest surgeon in the world, if he'd stuck with it, Miss . . .?"

"Angie. Angela Moresby."

"The tennis player!"

"That's what we're celebrating," Jonathan said, refilling their glasses. "In a manner of speaking."

"Would you really have been a great surgeon?" she asked. He had always refused to discuss his brief medical career, or his reasons for giving it up, and she found it difficult to reconcile his size and often violent movements with the delicacy needed to carry out successful surgery.

"Probably not. Jim, old man, I wonder if you'd do me a favour. In the strictest confidence."

"If it's not illegal."

"I don't think it is. Angie has a small problem, and would like you to give her a couple of tests. There are various reasons why she doesn't want to go to her own GP."

Colley's rather solemn gaze shrouded Angela, and she gave a little gulp; obviously he entirely understood the situation. "It'll be a pleasure," he said. "When?"

"How about tomorrow morning?" Jonathan asked.

"Short notice. I'm afraid I'll have to check with my appointments diary."

"Jim is a specialist," Jonathan explained.

"A gynaecologist?"

Colley smiled. "Not exactly. What Jon means is, I'm in private medicine."

"Entirely," Jonathan added.

"Are you allowed to do that?"

"As long as he's paid enough, he's allowed to do anything."

"No one is ever paid enough," Colley commented. "I'll squeeze you in, I promise. May I give you a ring . . . Angie?"

"Yes, please. I'll write down my number."

"And I'll give you my card."

"And I'll get another bottle," Jonathan announced, and pushed his way through the throng back to the bar.

"It's an awful imposition, approaching you like this, at a pub," Angela said.

"Not really. And Jonny was a very good friend, once. I'm assuming it's nothing serious?"

She gave a little shrug; there was too much noise for anyone to overhear them, and besides, he'd surely already guessed. "I need a pregnancy test."

"Is Jonny the father?"

"Yes."

"How'd he take it? Or was it planned?"

She grinned. "No, it wasn't planned. Actually, it's a damned nuisance. It'll mean I'll have to miss Wimbledon." She looked at him. "Won't it?"

"That's up to you. Do you really expect to get beyond round one?"

"Depends who I'm drawn against."

"Then perhaps it might be possible. We'll talk about it tomorrow. But . . . Jonny is quite happy?"

"Oh, yes."

Colley pulled his nose. "I wouldn't really put him down as possessing the father mentality."

"He wants me to have it," she said defiantly.

"People do change. It's eight years since I knew him at all well."

"Why did he give up medicine?"

Colley gave her a sideways glance. "I imagine he found better things to do."

"I can't believe that. People don't give up things like medicine unless they're forced to."

Colley considered. "Yes, you're probably right."

"So tell me."

"Have you and he never discussed it?"

"Not really."

"Then perhaps I would be telling tales out of school."

"Look, this man is the father of my child. He's going to marry me. Don't you think I should know, if there's, well . . . anything I should know?"

Colley grinned. "Don't panic. Jonathan gave up medicine because he wanted to be a great surgeon, and found out that he couldn't."

"Oh, what a shame. I know he would have made a great surgeon if he'd been allowed to. But . . ." she frowned. "You said just now he *would* have been a great surgeon if he hadn't quit. So it wasn't just a matter of failing exams, was it?"

"No. Something more serious than that."

"Please tell me?"

Colley hesitated again, then shrugged. "You won't believe this of a great lug like Jonathan, but . . . he can't stand the sight of blood."

Angela turned her head to look at the bar, and Jonathan, and the people around him. One in particular, wearing an open-necked shirt and no jacket, was leaning on the counter. He was a big fellow, and from the colour of his face" no less than his demeanour had had a great deal to drink. "Whose party?" he inquired in a loud voice.

"Mine," Jonathan told him.

"Getting married, are we? Who's the unlucky bride?" The intruder looked around the suddenly anxious female faces.

"Oh, lord," Angela muttered, and got up.

"Can you stop him when he gets going?" Colley asked, laying a hand on her arm. She looked down at him, and bit her lip. She couldn't, she knew.

"The only unlucky person in here is you," Jonathan said evenly. "Now listen to me, friend, clear off before I break both your legs."

"You and who else?" the man demanded, standing straight and revealing that he was actually the taller of the pair.

"What's the trouble, gents?" The barman hurried along the counter.

"You want to pick your clients more carefully, Syd," the man said. "We don't take to lager louts in this area."

"Look," Jonathan said. "My friends and I were having a quiet drink, right? Now, Syd, if you don't get rid of this bloke I am going to do it for you."

"Now, gents . . ." Syd was interrupted as the threw a punch. To his astonishment, however, Jonathan merely caught the fist, in both hands, gripping hand and wrist and twisting with such violence that his assailant gave a scream of pain and spun round, thudding into the bar counter. Jonathan continued to hold the fist and gave it another jerk before letting it go, while the man slid down the counter to the floor, shrieking with pain.

Colley was thrusting his way through the onlookers, who had now been joined by everyone else in the bar; there was a great deal of noise. He knelt beside the injured man. "His elbow is dislocated," Jonathan told him.

Colley acted promptly, seizing the man's wrist, putting his foot into the armpit, and pulling very hard. The man gave another scream of agony, but the arm came straight. "You could have done that," Colley remarked.

"I'm an amateur," Jonathan reminded him.

"Jonathan!" Angela grabbed his arm.

"You'd better get out of here," Syd recommended. "I'm going to have to call the police."

"He's not going anywhere," said an aggressive looking woman. "He attacked our Bill, he did."

"Now, really, madam," Jonathan said. "He tried to hit me."

"Broke his arm, you did," said another of the regulars.

"We'll have the law on you," said a third. "Harry, go get a copper."

"I'll call them," Syd announced, obviously balancing his regular trade against Jonathan's occasional visits.

"We'd better be off," muttered one of Jonathan's group.

"You just stay there," said the aggressive lady.

The young men looked at Jonathan. "Jonathan," Angela begged.

"You people going to try to stop us?" Jonathan inquired.

"God, send for an ambulance," moaned the man on the floor.

"You'll be all right," Colley told him. "Just take it easy for a day or do."

"Bleeding bastard," the injured man muttered.

"Gaol," said the woman. "That's what you need. Gaol."

"We'll say goodnight, Syd," Jonathan said.

"Well, I don't know, Mr Rudder." Syd's hand was hovering over the telephone. "They'll want to talk to you."

"Then you give them my address. It's that or your bar gets wrecked."

Syd took the point. "No trouble, now," he bawled. "You let these gentlemen out, and I'll call the police. Like he said, I know where he lives."

The regulars reluctantly backed out of the way, and the farewell party left. "Bit early," someone complained as they reached the street.

"Absolutely," Jonathan agreed. "Why don't you all come round to our place?"

"No," Angela snapped. "You promised me an early night." Once this crowd got stuck in they'd be there for hours.

Jonathan scratched his head. "Look," Colley said. "Maybe this wasn't meant to be. I'm for bed." He squeezed Angela's arm. "I'll call you first thing tomorrow, and we'll set up a meeting."

"Honestly," Angela grumbled as they drove away; in the distance they could hear the wail of a siren. "I can't take you anywhere."

"He began it. I thought I was very restrained."

She realised he was right. He could easily have hit the fellow and done him a nasty injury. "What do I say when the police come calling?"

"Tell them I've fled the country. Always tell the police the truth."

"They'll be waiting for you when you come back."

"I'll worry about that when I come back." He glanced at her with his shy smile. "You're not really mad?"

"Yes, I am. There is absolutely no need for you to take on everyone who challenges you. As for what your uncle is going to say . . ."

"I'd better tackle that before I go," he said thoughtfully.'

"You're flying at eleven-thirty tomorrow morning."

"He lives within a couple of miles of Heathrow; I'll have breakfast with the old trout. He's always best at breakfast, gets progressively more grouchy as the day goes on. It's his arthritis or whatever." He pulled to a halt before the block of flats. "So maybe an early night was a good idea after all. Don't worry, everything is going to be all right."

He always said that. But she kept thinking of what Jim Colley had told her. There had been blood on Jonathan's shirt last night. Not a lot, but more than could have been caused by careless shaving. And it hadn't seemed to bother him in the least.

Blessop Manor was in Berkshire, some ten miles north of Ascot. Fortunately it was not in the direct flight path to Heathrow, but it was still fairly noisy. Time was when the Manor had owned a great deal of the surrounding country, including the nearest village. This had been in the eighteenth century, when the Rudder family had been earning a fortune from their West Indian sugar plantations. Emancipation had changed all of that; the last plantation had been allowed to return to bush and squatters long before any socialist-minded ex-colonial government had determined to nationalise the sugar industry.

Then it had been a matter of living off rents, and when those proved inadequate for expensive tastes, of selling off land. Now Blessop Manor was reduced to five acres surrounding the house itself, just as the immediate family had been reduced to one ageing uncle and two itinerant nephews. Last of the breed, Jonathan thought, as he drove at speed through the twisting lanes behind Blessop Village. Last of a good many breeds. But for his size and the fact that he was good at games and enjoyed them – and that he could not afford a valet – he could have been a reincarnation of Bertie Wooster.

He had always rather gloried in being such an anachronism, even if deep down inside he knew that it was basically immoral, in this modern world. Perhaps it had been immoral in Wooster's day as well, but people had been less sensitive, then. Perhaps that was why he drank so much; he knew he was on a course with self-destruction written all over it. He had always intended to go out in a blaze of glory. But that had been before Angela's announcement. And before the night before last, as well. Drinking had always come easily to him: he could hold more than most. And when he indulged in an outburst of apparently maniacal violence, it had always been a concious decision – let everything go and the hell with the consequences. He had always known what he was doing, felt certain he could halt the proceedings whenever he chose.

The night before last had been disturbing. As Angela, the night before her important final, had determined to stay home after some practice at the club, he had gone out on his own, telephoned a few friends, joined them at a pub and got happily drunk. And had then, for the first time in his life, passed out! At least, he presumed he had passed out. He could remember nothing after about ten o'clock, until he had awoken just after midnight, sitting behind the wheel of his own car, outside the block of flats. That had been a miracle to begin with, that he had got home without being done. Such a miracle wasn't uncommon; he drove very well when drunk and gave no cause for alarm to any watching policeman. But not to remember where he'd been, or even who he'd been with . . . Because the friends he had first met up with had left quite early on. He could remember that. But nothing after. Yet he had certainly had a great deal to drink.

Angela had been very understanding. But clearly it couldn't be allowed to happen again. And now there was the matter of her pregnancy. He had mixed emotions about that. On the one hand, he resented anything which would interfere with his lifestyle. On the other, he was exhilarated at the thought of becoming a father. And marriage? To Angela? She was a deliciously attractive, earthy girl. Sex during this last year had been a joy. But did he love her? He had never even considered that side of it. They turned each other on, and that was all that had ever been necessary, up to now. Then, did she love him? Oddly, he realised, she had never said so. Not even yesterday. As if it mattered. She didn't want her child to be a bastard. He would go along with that, if he could persuade old Eric it wasn't the end of the world.

And then, maybe, a new leaf. He was going to be a father.

The gates were electrically operated, but the gardener had either quit or was not being paid regularly; the hedges needed clipping and the shrubs appeared like something out of a prehistoric movie. It had rained during the night, and although it had been light for several hours, at half past eight in the morning a thick mist lay over central southern England, and there had not been sufficient warmth to burn off the damp; everything was dripping, loudly. The Mercedes scraped to a halt outside the ornate front doors. Jonathan always felt that he was somewhere in Transylvania when he came here. Even Caunt, tall and thin and slightly cadaverous, could have been Dracula's butler. Save that Caunt would have run away from his own shadow. He and his wife were all that were left of a staff for the Manor House, but they were at least faithful retainers, who greeted Jonathan with affection; he had telephoned to let them know he was coming. "Doesn't look too good, for flying," Caunt remarked.

"It looks bloody awful," Jonathan agreed. "Uncle Eric up?"

"Breakfasting, sir."

Jonathan followed the butler-cum-valet into the great hall, beneath the huge chandelier and past the suits of armour, walking on priceless Persian rugs scattered across the parquet floor, and up the main staircase, a huge double, down which it was easy to imagine bustled and over-bosomed beauties descending in rustling evening gowns a hundred years ago. Off the first floor gallery there opened the small parlour, and here Eric Rudder was seated before his breakfast tray, at a table which looked out through french windows, presently closed, at the croquet lawn and the maze – which was as unkempt as the front garden, and, shrouded in mist, even more prehistoric. "Uncle!"

Eric Rudder gestured at a chair. He was a large man, and had once been heavily-built, like his nephew, but had recently been dieting; he was sixty-eight. He had no hair on his head, but a bristling white moustache which on occasion seemed almost to meet his equally bristling eyebrows, leaving him peering through a mass of hair. But he remained remarkably alert and even sprightly, although his handshake was less firm than usual. His problem, and Jonathan's, was that he had been a lifelong bachelor, and believed that only fools ever got married. "I thought you were off to America today."

"I am. Thought I'd stop by to see you on the way to the airport."

"Broke, are you?"

Jonathan waited while Caunt poured coffee, and nodded towards the sideboard where breakfast waited. The butler left the room, and he helped himself to bacon and eggs. "I'm always broke." Eric Rudder snorted. "But this is a serious matter," Jonathan went on. "I would like to get married."

Carefully he placed the plate on the other place setting at the table, and sat down. "Some bimbo after my money, eh?" Eric commented.

"I doubt it. This bimbo may be carrying my child."

Eric Rudder leaned back in his chair. "May?"

"Early days. But she should know in a week or so."

"And you think it's yours, naturally?"

"We've been living together for the past year, and I

have no reason to doubt that she has been faithful to me in that time."

"No woman is ever faithful."

"You must tell me the unhappy secrets of your youth, some time," Jonathan suggested. "Maybe things have changed."

"For the worse."

"I see you're still taking the *News of the World.* Angela is a very decent young woman who aspires to be a tennis champion."

"Tennis! God Allmighty! And you have allowed yourself to be taken in."

Jonathan's temper, never very far beneath the surface, began to surge. "I came here to find out your reaction to my marrying, not to have you insult the mother of my child."

Eric pointed. "You don't know she is the mother of your child. If she is not, do you still intend to marry her?" Jonathan chewed some bacon, drank some coffee. "Exactly. You are being blackmailed into marriage."

"If Angela is not pregnant, then we will reassess the situation," Jonathan said, aware that he had just weakened his position irretrievably.

"Then come back to me when you have done so."

Jonathan finished his coffee. "I would like a decision now."

"A decision? You mean as to whether or not I will continue your allowance after you have allowed yourself to be sucked into this mesalliance? I have said, come back to me when *you* have made a decision."

Jonathan stood up. "You know, one day, someone is going to strangle you."

Eric smiled. "It won't be you, dear boy. When I go, so does your allowance."

Jonathan was aware of that situation. His uncle, although possessing a very substantial income, had no stake in the estate; his dissolute youth – which included being sent down from Cambridge and at least one paternity suit – had determined his father to make sure what was left of the family fortune could not be dissipated. Thus when Eric Rudder died, the interest in the estate and the income, went to Jonathan's cousin, the son of the second brother, who lived in Australia. The third brother, Jonathan's father, had also fallen out too severely with his father ever to be included in the old man's arrangements. Thus, as he had reflected earlier, he would in any event have to find himself a job in the not too distant future; Uncle Eric was not going to live forever. The question was, what at? "Good luck with the yacht racing," Eric commented.

"If I ever get there," Jonathan muttered, looking through the window at the mist, which had accumulated into fog.

"I'm sorry, sir, but there appears little chance of any flights getting away before this afternoon," explained the booking clerk at Heathrow. Terminal Three indeed looked like a ghost town.

"You mean I can't even check in?" Jonathan demanded.

"I'm afraid not, sir. If you give us a number, we'll call you just as soon as we can say when your flight will be."

A number! He could of course go back into London. But he had mentally severed himself from London and his current problems, and was already thinking only of the blue waters off Newport, Rhode Island, where he would be racing with Bruce Hardy and his crew for the next few weeks. He had no real desire to go home to Angie and the world of competitive tennis . . . or prospective babies. Time enough to worry about that when Jim Colley delivered his verdict.

His meeting with Uncle Eric had in fact left him decidedly out of sorts; he had not supposed the old bastard would be so difficult. He had not even given a straight answer, and his uncle was so moody and bad tempered it was quite possible that the answer, when it came, would be no. Jonathan felt he needed time to think. "I'll be at the Sheraton," he said.

There he could get drunk in quiet comfort.

When Angela got up and looked out of the window she decided that she was not going to have the peaceful day she had anticipated: London was shrouded in fog, the sort of thing which had been supposed to have become history twenty years before she had been born. That meant it was extremely likely that a very bad-tempered Jonathan would be back in her midst by lunchtime. Just to make sure, she telephoned Heathrow, and heard what she had feared: there was no prospect of any flights taking off before that evening at the earliest, and incoming traffic was being diverted. "Hell!" she commented.

She had been looking forward to a rest from Jonathan. Of course she loved the big lug, and he could be the most stimulating company . . . but that was part of the trouble: he could be just too stimulating, at times. Added to which was the sudden feeling that she knew him far less well than she had supposed. Yet he was the father of her child, and he was going to be her husband.

She had an urgent need to discuss her situation with someone, and it could not possibly be Anne, who moved through life on very straight lines. Anne's reaction to news of the pregnancy would be to command abortion, immediately, before it interfered with her tennis – and especially if Jonathan Rudder was the father. As for marrying him! Anne, a good player herself but with never a suggestion that she could go beyond club level, wanted her sister's success more than Angela herself. What she was going to say when she did find out . . .

The telephone buzzed. It would be Jonathan, of course,

cursing and swearing and announcing that he was on his way back. "Yes," she said resignedly.

"Miss Angela Moresby?"

"Yes?" This time she frowned.

"James Colley. We met last night."

"Oh . . . yes, of course." How on earth had she forgotten?

"Jonathan get off all right?"

"He's gone to the airport, but I'm not sure he's going to be flying anywhere before this afternoon. They seem pretty pessimistic about this fog lifting."

"It does look a little grim. Now, when are you going to come to see me? I can fit you in just before lunch today. Twelve thirty. Will that suit?"

"Of course. I'm very grateful." She had had no intention of practising today anyway, despite Anne's instructions.

"Twelve-thirty," Colley said again. "You're sure you can find us? It's fairly well up the Edgware Road."

"No problem," she assured him.

Angela had a bath, and predictably, before she was out of it, the phone rang again. She had placed the cordless handset by the tub, so it was merely a matter of stretching out her arm. This time it was Anne. "Jonathan get away?"

"I have no idea. He hasn't called."

"Then he must have. What time can you lunch?"

"I won't be able to make it before one fifteen."

"Why not? You know Mother likes me there for tea."

"I have something to do," Angela said, and switched off.

She put on clean underwear, aware of a certain sense of excitement. It was some time since she had been to a doctor: both in herself and because of her tennis she was an extremely healthy young woman. And this was an extremely attractive doctor. She made herself some breakfast, and read the paper, more in hope than expectation; she didn't really expect to be in it. But she was, in the fine print of *Other Sporting Events*: *At Mallingham*, *Women's Final*, *Miss A Moresby bt Miss B Smart*, *6–4*, *6–3*. That was all. But it was an item for her scrapbook.

There was nothing exciting in the news. The usual crisis in the Middle East, the usual gloomy comment on the economy, the usual scandal involving someone who had once entertained royalty, and the usual murder. The murder at least was mildly interesting; she had watched Douglas Openshaw on TV putting the shot at the last Olympics. And now he was dead, brutally stabbed to death, according to the newspaper, in his own bedroom. She supposed no one really knew anything about anyone else's private persona. To admit someone to your bedroom, you had to know him or her pretty well. To admit someone you thought you knew pretty well, and then discover you didn't know him at all, that indeed he had come there to kill you . . . or her, as the case might be, was a terrible concept. Angela gave a little shudder. She had admitted Jonathan Rudder to her bedroom under the supposition that she knew *him* very well.

She drove her Mini to the north London address on Jim Colley's card, and found herself outside a large, new building situated down a quiet street off the Edgware Road. There was nothing about the building's exterior to suggest hospital or clinic, but when she took the driveway to the rear, she found herself in a good-sized car park, less than half full, and faced rather more conventional double glass doors into a lobby, where an efficient-looking middle-aged woman sat behind a desk. "Dr Colley? Ah, yes . . ." she flicked the page of a desk diary. "Twelve-thirty. You're early."

"I didn't know how long it would take me to find you," Angela explained.

"The doctor will see you in a few minutes," the receptionist said. "Wait through there, please."

Angela opened a door on her right, and found herself in an unusually pleasant waiting room, where the magazines were recent and the chairs comfortable. She was the only person there, which was a relief. She began to relax. The dragon had been irritating, but no doubt all institutions needed dragons to protect them from the public, and she enjoyed both the quiet of this place and the total absence of any of the smells she associated with hospitals or doctors' surgeries. She wondered if this was, actually, a hospital.

The door opened and a uniformed nurse smiled at her. "Dr Colley can see you now, Miss Moresby."

Another pleasant surprise; she had hardly flicked the page of the first magazine. Angela followed the woman, not very much older than herself, she estimated, and quite attractive, with auburn hair and good legs beneath her blue skirt, along a corridor and up a short flight of stairs. On the first floor there was another corridor, and off this Jim Colley's surgery was situated. The nurse opened the door, and Angela stepped into a large, airy room. "This is a pregnancy test," the nurse checked. "I'll just take down some particulars." She sat at her desk, and pulled a form in front of her. "We use both biological and serological tests," she remarked. "As I'm sure you know, false results are not uncommon in pregnancy tests, and Dr Colley likes to cover every possibility."

"Yes," Angela said, not really knowing what the woman was talking about.

"So, if you'd like to go into that room . . ." she pointed, "and give me a urine sample, it'll save time."

Angela obeyed. "What shall I do with it?" she asked when she returned.

"Just put it on the table over there. Now, sit down. I shall need your full name and address, age, occupation, medical history."

Angela obliged. "What exactly do you do, with . . . well, that." She gestured at her bottle.

"If you are pregnant, your urine should contain an excess of chorionic gonadotrophin. In the old days, we used to inject it into mice, and see if any changes resulted. If they did, the test was positive. With modern methods, of course, we can discover the excess by our own tests. Now, if you'd like to push up your sleeve, I'll take a blood sample. This is called the leokocyte alkaline phosphatase test. If you are pregnant, the amount of alkaline phosphatase in your white blood cells should have measurably increased."

Angela watched her remove her blood sample, with total expertise; she didn't feel a thing. "But you said neither of these are foolproof."

"That is correct. On the other hand, if they both prove positive, then I think we may assume that you are pregnant, Miss Moresby."

She returned behind her desk, and Angela rolled down her sleeve. "Don't you want to know the name of the father?"

The nurse looked surprised. "The father is your business, Miss Moresby."

"Oh." She tried another approach. "Do I see the doctor?"

"Normally, it's not necessary. But as a matter of fact, Dr Colley does wish to see you." She completed writing up her form, and got up. "Through this door."

She opened it, and Angela stepped into an even more airy and pleasant office; the windows looked out at the carpark, and the sounds of London were very far away. James Colley had been seated behind his desk, writing up some notes, but he rose as she came in. "Angela. How good to see you. All well?" He glanced at his nurse.

"Yes, doctor."

"Good. We should have the results in a couple of days.

Now, I'd like to give you a thorough physical examination, if I may."

Angela raised her eyebrows. "I've heard about people like you," she said, smiling. She thought the idea of being examined by Jim Colley rather attractive.

But he took her seriously. "Nurse Welldon will stay. Would you go behind that screen and undress."

Angela glanced at Nurse Welldon, whose face was expressionless. "Everything?"

"If you would be so kind."

Once again, Angela did as requested. "Do I come out, or do you come in?" she asked when she was naked.

"We will come to you."

The last time she had had a physical examination had been at school, and she hadn't enjoyed it. This was far more detailed, and she enjoyed every moment of it, despite the clinical presence of Nurse Welldon; Colley had delightfully soft hands – his touch was quite erotic. "You are an amazingly healthy specimen of womanhood," he said when he was finished and washing his hands.

"You may get dressed," Nurse Welldon said.

Angela dressed herself; her heart was pounding and she knew she was flushed. "But then, I suppose that's not to be surprised at," Colley went on, drying his hands. "Thank you, nurse, that will be all." Nurse Welldon left the room, and Colley sat behind his desk, gestured Angela to the seat opposite. Angela sat down, uncertain what was coming next. "I really am very pleased," Colley said, ticking off a list on a sheet of paper. "Heart, lungs, kidneys, liver, genitals, all superb."

Angela didn't know what to say in reply to that. She had never had her genitals tested for health before. But presumably this time was because she was pregnant. "Tell me about yourself," Colley invited.

"What about myself?"

"Family?"

"My mother is the widow of an army officer. He left her quite well off, I suppose, so Anne – that's my sister – and I went to a good school, and have been able to indulge ourselves to a certain extent."

"Playing tennis. Where does your mother live?"

"Hastings. Well, St Leonards, actually."

"Very wise. Warmest place in Britain. Does your sister play tennis?"

"Oh, yes."

"But not up to your standard, obviously. Do you live with her?"

"No, I live with Jonny." She grinned. "That's how I got pregnant."

"Point taken. So right now you're alone."

"I imagine so. Jonny hasn't telephoned, so he must be sitting it out. Or he's managed to get away."

"Does it bother you, being alone?"

"I've been alone often enough. Jonny is inclined to live his own life. I mean, he was out nearly all Saturday night, only staggered home about two in the morning. Covered in blood." Colley raised his eyebrows. "Well, not really covered," Angela explained. "But there were bloodstains on his shirt, as if he had hit someone, torn his knuckles, and rubbed them on it, you know."

"And had he?"

"Well, no. His knuckles were unmarked."

"Then what was the cause?"

Angela shrugged. "He got drunk, and doesn't remember a thing about it. Maybe it was the sight of blood made him lose his memory. But he didn't seem upset about it."

"As we agreed last night, people change. Angela, I hope you won't think I'm prying, but are you sure Jonny is the right father for your child?"

"It's not something we can change, now, is it?"

"Not genetically. But you don't have to marry him, you know. You don't even have to have the child."

"But I want to have my child. And Jonny wants me to have it."

"Okay. It's not my place to advise you. I just want to be sure you know what you're doing. Well, as I say, we'll be in touch in a day or two. You know, I'd offer to take you out to lunch, but I'm afraid I haven't the time, today."

"That's all right. I have a lunch date anyway." Again he raised his eyebrows. "With my sister. Thanks, anyway."

Colley waited for Nan Welldon to come in again. "Let's have a look at that form," he said.

She placed it on his desk. "She came up very well," she remarked.

"Superb." He raised his head to look at her. "I've seldom come across a more splendid specimen."

"You're not serious?"

"Of course I am. With Rudder away, she's made to order."

"I think we'd be sticking our necks out. There's a link."

"There was a link with Openshaw. It's not something anyone is ever likely to connect. And if they do, what can they prove? That they were both patients of mine? Beyond that, nothing."

Nan Welldon considered. "I'm still unhappy about it. I mean, well . . . isn't Jonathan Rudder your friend?"

Colley shrugged. "He's a total layabout who's trying his damndest to drink himself to death. Marriage to him for a girl like that would be a disaster; next thing she'd be drinking as hard as he does." He picked up the telephone. "Come to think of it, I'm not sure I ever even liked the fellow."

Angela was late, and Anne was huffy, and even more so when Angela confessed that she had not practised that morning. "In this fog? You must be joking."

So they went their separate ways, and Angela returned

to the flat. She called Heathrow, and was told no traffic had moved as yet, and in fact, none was expected to move, now, before tomorrow morning. "Can you tell me if a Mr Jonathan Rudder has checked in?" she asked.

"We have not opened the check-in desk, madam. If Mr Rudder was flying with us this morning, he would have been requested to leave his telephone number, so that we may call him the moment we know when flying will again be possible." Angela switched off. If he had given a telephone number, it certainly wasn't this one; he was off again on one of his jaunts. Well, bugger him, she thought.

She spent a totally relaxing afternoon, reading and napping. She didn't even bother to dress that evening, but padded about the flat in a silk kimono Jonathan had given her. She wrote up her diary – there was a lot to record about her visit to the Clinic – then watched the seven o'clock news, which was mainly concerned with the fog, prepared a boil-in-the-bag dinner, and settled down with a video. She had finished her meal, and the film was halfway through, when the phone buzzed. She answered with the number.

"I'd like to speak with Mr Jonathan Rudder, please," said a male voice she did not recognise.

"I'm sorry, he's not here."

"Can you tell me when he'll be back?"

"I would say, six weeks. Can I take a message? I'll probably be speaking with him on the phone in a couple of days."

"No, thanks all the same. I'll be in touch when he comes back. Good night."

Angela replaced the phone, wondered who that was, and found herself unable to concentrate any longer on the film. Someone out of that part of Jonathan's life of which she knew nothing. The man who she was going to marry. James Colley was against that. He hadn't said so, because Jonny had once been his friend. But she could tell what he had been thinking.

But she loved Jonny, that was the trouble. With every moment she was feeling more sure of that. Oh, why didn't he call to tell her where he was and what he was doing? It would be so reassuring. But Jonny always did his own thing.

The film clicked to a halt and she realised she hadn't taken in the climax. She considered rewinding and looking at it again, then decided against it; the time was half past ten, and she felt like bed. She got up, and the street bell rang. Suddenly she was excited. However late, it would be Jonny, no doubt utterly contrite. How she wanted to see him. "Is that you?" she inquired.

"Miss Moresby?"

"Yes." She frowned. It certainly wasn't Jonny's voice. Then who, at this hour of the night?

"I'm sorry to trouble you at this hour, Miss Moresby, but Mr Rudder . . ."

"What about Mr Rudder?"

"There was this accident, miss . . ."

"Accident?! You'd better come in." She released the door, and opened the flat door as well, watched two men climbing the stairs, one quite tall and powerfully built, the other much smaller in every way. Both were in dark coats and hats; the tall men carried a black briefcase, the smaller a large black carryall, which, from the way he carried it, appeared to be empty. Angela gave a little gasp of relief; for a moment she had thought they might have brought Jonathan's effects.

"Miss Moresby?" The tall man raised his hat. "This is a sorry business."

"Are you from the police?" she asked.

"Do you think we could go in?" he asked. "It's a little public out here."

"Yes, of course. Come in." She stood back and the two

men entered the flat. Angela closed the door, turned to face them. "Tell me what's happened."

The tall man smiled. "Why, nothing has happened, yet, Miss Moresby. It's what is going to happen that matters, at least to you."

CHAPTER 2

Before Angela really grasped what he had just said, the tall man made a quick movement, and from his coat pocket produced a small automatic pistol, already fitted with a silencer. "Don't make a sound," he said. "Or I will shoot you. If you behave yourself, I promise you won't feel a thing."

For the first time she noticed that they were both wearing skin tight black gloves. Burglars! And she had just let them in. Of all the foolish things to have done. "You won't find very much to take here," she panted, trying to think. "We don't keep anything of value in the flat."

"Oh, but you do," said the man with the gun. "Yourself." He gestured at the bedroom. "Inside."

My God, she thought, I am going to be raped! Me! In my own bedroom! It was not a possibility that had ever occurred to her. And there was nothing she could do about it. She went into the bedroom. "I'm pregnant," she said, her voice beginning to tremble.

The two men followed her. "No one would ever know it," said the one with the gun. "Strip."

Angela drew a long breath. She wanted to scream. She wanted to turn and strike at them both with her nails. But she knew that would achieve nothing more than a beating – or worse. Above all, she wanted Jonathan to walk through the door. She released the sash of the kimono and let the garment slide from her shoulders to the floor.

"Get on the bed, and lie on your back," said the man with the gun, behind her.

Trembling with a combination of fear and outrage, Angela lay on the bed, on her back, as instructed. That meant she had to look at them, and she didn't want to do that, so she closed her eyes. And opened them again as the small man knelt beside her . . . and she inhaled a whiff of perfume. She also saw that "he" had several lengths of cord in "his" hands. "I'm not going to fight you," she protested. The idea of being tied up made the thought of rape so much more revolting, especially if one of her attackers was a woman.

"Can't have you moving about," the woman said. Her voice was low and husky, and now that Angela looked more closely, she saw that she had a crisply attractive face. She looked neither the least aggressive or violent. But she was certainly efficient. There were no bedposts, only the short legs beneath the mattress base, and so the woman extended Angela's right arm, looped a length of cord around the wrist, and then carried the cord down to the leg and tied it there. Then she did the same to Angela's left wrist, and to each ankle, so that she was effectively spreadeagled and quite unable to do anything more than inflate her lungs and stomach.

While the woman was tying her up, the man stood above her, the gun still in his hand, looking at her. Angela was equally surprised to see there was no suggestion of lust in his face; he merely looked thoughtful. The woman was panting a little by the time she had finished securing Angela's left ankle, and stood back to survey her handiwork. "Don't you ever get the urge?" she asked. "Jim used to."

"Jim is a monster. I don't get the urge, for them," the man said. "Let's get it done."

"There's an air-conditioning unit," the woman said. "What do you reckon?"

"Might be an idea. It'll confuse the time factor."

The woman walked around the flat, closing every window before turning on the air-conditioning system, while Angela strained ineffectively against the cords and gazed at the man, who ignored her, as he undressed, as did the woman when she returned to the bedroom. She took off her hat to reveal dark hair, cut short, and then displayed a slender, small-breasted body. Like me, Angela thought. But she was more concerned to see that the man remained totally unaroused, and certainly incapable of penetration. She tried to think about the name Jim. She knew only one person named Jim – but there had to be thousands of men in England named James.

The woman carefully folded their clothes and took them into the other room. Then she brought in the two bags and laid them the floor, just inside the bedroom door. From the valise she took a pair of clippers and an electric razor. "Oh, God, no," Angela protested.

"It's necessary," the woman said, and proceeded to shave Angela's pubic hair. "If you knew how many germs are contained in these hairs!" Just as if I were about to undergo an operation, Angela thought, pink with embarrassment. "There we are," the woman said. "Wasn't that fun?"

She went to the bathroom, returned with a wet towel, which she further soaked in some liquid she took from a bottle in her valise, and washed the shaved groin. And still the man watched, dispassionately.

"Now we'll just put you to sleep." The woman reached into the valise and took out another small bottle and a hypodermic needle, which she proceeded to fill. Then she knelt on the bed beside Angela. "No," Angela begged. "I'd rather stay awake."

"But you can't," the woman explained. "You wouldn't enjoy it, really." Gently she inserted the needle into

Angela's forearm, and injected the liquid. Angela gasped, and tried to concentrate. "I promised you," the woman said. "You won't feel a thing."

"You are a pervert," the woman said, as the man stood against her in the shower.

"I have feelings. Is it wrong to have feelings?"

"Yes," she said. "Now. You had none before."

"She was a pretty girl," he said, and took her face between his hands to kiss her, savagely, on the lips.

Whatever her criticism, she didn't resist him; she was hardly less affected by what they had just done. "When we get home," she promised him, and slipped out of his embrace.

They had taken towels from the airing cupboards, and with these they dried themselves, then wrapped and tied them round their feet as they padded through the bloodstained bedroom to the living room door. Neither of them looked at the mutilated thing lying on the bed.

The bags had been carefully repacked before they had showered. Now they stripped off the wet gloves, dropped them into the briefcase, and pulled on a fresh pair. Then they kicked off the towels round their feet, stepped into the living room, and dressed themselves. The man zipped and picked up the carryall, now heavy, as it was packed with plastic containers, all full. The woman took the briefcase, and they let themselves out, carefully switching off all the lights, and closing the door behind them. They went down the stairs and walked out of the building.

Their car was parked two blocks away; they passed one or two people, but no one even looked at them twice. When they reached the car, the two bags were placed, very carefully, in the back seat; the man drove, at a steady speed, until they reached a garage set in the wall of a narrow street. The woman leaned out of the window and flashed a torch, and the doors opened.

The man drove in, to darkness, and the doors closed behind him. Lights immediately came on, illuminating a large area; there were three other cars, and a row of deep freezes against the left hand wall. There were also three men and a woman, waiting for them. The man and the woman got out. No one spoke. They walked to another car, opened the boot, and took out a suitcase. They began to undress.

One of the men and the woman removed the bags from the back of the first car, and carried them to the deep freezes. There they began to unload the carryall, handling each plastic container with great care, attaching identifying tags, before storing it in the appropriate freezer. One of the other men drove the first car to a corner of the garage. There he was joined by the third man, who immediately began preparing the car for spray-painting, while his companion began unscrewing the number plates for replacement.

The man and the woman who had carried out the assignment had meanwhile finished undressing to their underwear, and were now dressing again, the man in a suit, the woman in a dress. They got into the waiting car, and drove towards the back of the garage. Here another signal with the flashlight opened another door, at the same time as the interior lights went off. They drove out into another street, and the door closed behind them.

"Annabelle's, I think," the man said.

"Briefly," the woman agreed. She stared down the path of the headlights. "She *was* pregnant."

"So her womb was useless. Can't win them all," the man said. The woman shivered.

* * *

"So tell me what you've got." Lampson sat at his desk with his arms spread wide, and regarded the police doctor as a child might regard a lollipop. And then frowned. "You all right, Fred?"

"That was at once the easiest and most unpleasant post mortem I have ever carried out," Fred Mayhew replied. He was a small man, whose sharp nose and sandy moustache – it matched his hair – made him look like a ferret which, mentally, he was. Lampson had a great deal of respect for Fred Mayhew's analyses. "Did you take a close look at the body?"

"I leave that to you blokes. If you mean, did I see that he'd been castrated, yes, I did see that."

"That was the least of his troubles," Dr Mayhew said. "He had also been gutted."

"Come again?"

"All you saw was a welter of blood and bone. Because that was all there *was* to see. Douglas Openshaw had been opened up like a fish, about to be filleted. Only they didn't take his backbone and ribs; they left those. But they took everything else."

Lampson's hands came together and a knuckle cracked. "What do you mean, took?"

"What I said. The victim's heart, lungs, kidneys, liver, and stomach, had all been removed, as well as his penis and testicles."

"Shit!" Lampson commented. "That doesn't tie in with our information." He glanced at the sheet of paper on his desk. "Two men called to see Openshaw, at about eleven-fifteen on Saturday night. The people in the ground floor flat heard the street door open, and looked out of their window in time to see the men going in. They had obviously called on the street phone, and been admitted, so it seems likely that Openshaw knew them."

"Or they had a convincing reason for making him let them in," Mayhew suggested.

"We'll leave that for the moment. The point is, the two men went up to Openshaw's flat, and were admitted, just after eleven-fifteen. The people on the floor underneath Openshaw heard a slight noise above them, at around eleven-twenty. Not enough to disturb them; that's a solidly built house. But the people on the ground floor saw the two men leave again at five to midnight. In that time, we know, they stripped Openshaw, tied him to his bed, stripped themselves, killed him, bathed to wash off the blood, and dressed themselves. Now you are telling me they also took out his guts? Sorry, Fred, the timescale is wrong. They weren't in the flat more than half an hour."

"Once I had you unconscious on the table, Bill, I could open you up and whip out any of your organs in seven minutes. Four minutes if I wasn't bothered about putting it back, or if you were going to survive. And once you were open, I could take out anything else I wanted to at roughly two minutes a time, again, if I wasn't bothered about your health. With two of us going at you, the whole job could be done in under fifteen minutes."

"That's all very well, but you're a doctor."

"Quite. The murder weapon, or weapons, I would say, were surgical scalpels."

Lampson frowned at him. "What are you trying to tell me?"

"That this murder was carried out with surgical precision, and by two men who knew exactly what they were doing. The victim was even shaved, although why they should bother to use any antiseptic methods is beyond me."

"Surgeons?"

"Certainly men who had been to medical school."

Lampson stroked his chin. "Are we right in assuming that the victim was alive when he was, er, dissected?"

"I'm afraid so. But unconscious, due to the anaesthetic."

"What anaesthetic?"

"A pre-med jab. Very simple. But again, indicating medical knowledge, and possibly even access to medical equipment. It's not very easy to buy that stuff at your corner chemist."

"Then what exactly did he die of?"

"In the circumstances, it's difficult to say. He could have been stabbed in any one of several vital organs, and that organ removed. Or it could simply be blood loss. They didn't waste any time in tying up arteries. All thirteen pints just flowed out."

"I saw it. And at least they didn't drink it." Seeing no glimmer of humour in the doctor's face, Lampson went on. "What you have just said confirms my theory that it was a ritual killing. They probably wanted those innards to burn to some heathen god."

"Oh, really, Bill."

"All right, you tell me? First count is, this man Openshaw doesn't seem to have had any enemies. We thought maybe it was some kind of gay revenge, but he appears to have been straight as a pole. He even has a fiancée."

"Have you spoken with her?"

"Not yet. She was out of town over the weekend. Parton is bringing her in now."

"You going to tell her what happened?"

"And have her puking all over my desk? I've been through that with one of my WPCS. And . . ." he pointed, "not a word of this report is to go any further until I say so. Just try imagining what the tabloids would do with a story like this."

"I'd rather not. What about other family?"

"Mother dead, father lives alone. He came in yesterday to identify the body."

"Does he know what happened?"

"No way. Openshaw was covered with a sheet and we

let him see only the face. Anyway, he was in such a state of shock I doubt he noticed too much. Kept muttering, it can't be true."

"I'm inclined to mutter that myself. By the way, you say the killers were seen both arriving and leaving. Were they carrying anything? They should have had a couple of bags."

Lampson checked his notes. "Yes. One was carrying a large kind of hold-all, the other, a small black valise . . ." he gulped. "Like a doctor's bag."

"I'd say it *was* a doctor's bag. And when they left, the holdall contained most of Douglas Openshaw's guts."

Lampson took out a large blue handkerchief and wiped his forehead and neck, then cracked a couple more knuckles.

"There are a few other points I think you need to consider," Mayhew went on.

"Tell me." Lampson was never averse to receiving competent advice.

"Number One, have you given any thought to a Jack the Ripper type character? Jack didn't know any of his victims personally. And the murder of Openshaw does bear some resemblance to the Ripper killings: the surgical way in which it was carried out, and the removal of various organs."

"What are you trying to do, make my day? The Ripper was one man. Here we have two, working together."

"That's not impossible."

"Jesus! Two deranged medical students! Another thing, the Ripper only removed one or two organs, not the whole bloody lot, and he left them by the body."

"So this could be an over the top Ripper. Or Rippers."

Lampson glared at him. "You said something about more than one point."

"Simply that it's all very well for you to want to keep what really happened from the press, but the body has to be released for burial, some time."

"No way. We're holding on to it."

"For how long?"

"For as long as we can. Certainly until the killers are caught. It's evidence, isn't it?"

"You'd better have a chat with the family. Keep in touch."

Mayhew left the office and Lampson again wiped his forehead and neck with his handkerchief. He had spent twenty-three years as a detective, rising from constable to chief inspector, but he had never encountered anything like this before. He pressed his intercom. "Sergeant Parton back yet?"

"Just in now, sir, with a lady."

"Tell him to bring her up."

"The press would like a statement, Chief Inspector."

Lampson sighed. "I imagine they would. Very well, I'll see them first."

The office became very crowded with reporters. "I have simply to tell you the dead man is Mr Douglas Openshaw, the shot putter," Lampson said. "He was murdered in his flat during last Saturday night."

"How was he killed, Chief Inspector?"

"We have already released that. He was stabbed several times." Lampson had chosen his words with care; there were times when lies were necessary

"Have you made any progress towards an arrest?"

"We always make progress," Lampson asserted.

"Is an arrest imminent?"

"No."

"Mr. and Mrs. Avery say they saw the killers arrive. They gave you descriptions."

"They did. We will be putting out what we have today.

But it was dark, and the Averys caught only glimpes of the men."

"But there were more than one?"

"The Averys saw more than one," Lampson said, carefully. "Thank you, ladies and gentlemen. You'll appreciate these are early days."

There was a brief hesitation, then the journalists began to shuffle towards the door. They did not look very happy. But they had accepted what he had told them. Or had they? A young man with a moustache suddenly turned back. "Is it true, Chief Inspector, that Douglas Openshaw was mutilated?"

Lampson glared at him; there was one in every crowd. "I am not answering any questions about the condition of the corpse."

"Then it *is* true," the young man persisted. "Is it also true that he was left to bleed to death, that there was blood everywhere in the flat?"

"I have said, I am not answering any more questions," Lampson snapped. "Good day to you." He watched them file out, muttering to each other. He wondered who the hell had leaked that. When he found out . . . but the investigation had to continue. He pressed his intercom. "Tell Parton to bring this Brand woman up."

Lampson hadn't made up his mind what to expect of Jennifer Brand. He already knew she was American, and that she had been engaged to be married to Openshaw. But it had been an old-fashioned relationship, in that they hadn't been living together. Maybe if they had . . . He was surprised. Jennifer Brand was small and dark, slender and handsome; her neat features indeed were rather lovely, dominated by deep green eyes and dark brown straight shoulder-length hair, and the figure concealed by the pale blue pants suit was promising. She was also very positive, and not the least weepy.

"I want to see the body," she said as soon as she had been introduced, "And this . . ." she gave an embarrassed Parton a scathing glance, "person, says I can't."

"Why don't you sit down, Miss Brand. Murder isn't a nice business. Mr Openshaw has been identified, by his father . . ."

"I know. It was a shock for poor Alex. I don't know he'll get over it. Why didn't you wait for me instead?"

At least she had sat down. "We didn't know where to find you, Miss Brand."

"Don't give me that bullshit. You'd have examined everything in Doug's apartment. My name is in his diary, on his telephone list . . ."

"Of course it was, Miss Brand. So were a whole lot of others. There was nothing in the first instance to indicate that you were someone special; we only learned that you were the dead man's fiancée when we spoke with Mr Openshaw senior. Anyway, you were out of town, weren't you?"

She refused to be put out. "Sure I was. But I was back in this morning."

"And you didn't immediately call your fiancé."

"Why should I? I knew where he was. Or I thought I did. It was only when I read the papers . . ."

"That you contacted us."

"And I've been kept waiting damn near four hours."

"I'm afraid we were pursuing other avenues of investigation. Where were you visiting?"

"Some friends of mine in Cornwall. I gave your sergeant the address."

Lampson glanced at Parton, and received a quick nod. "And these friends do not have television?"

"As a matter of fact, they don't. That's one of the reasons I go to stay with them when the pressure gets a bit much."

"The pressure being your job, I take it?" He glanced

at the information sheet. "You are personal assistant to Richard Ebershaw of Consolidated Business Associates."

"You got it. Now, are you going to tell me what happened?"

"Very simply, Miss Brand, two men were admitted to your fiancé's flat just before midnight on Saturday, and once inside, murdered him. They then left."

"Just like that? Nobody saw them?"

"Indeed. They were seen entering and leaving."

"Then you have descriptions."

"None that are likely to do us a lot of good."

"The newspapers said something about it being nasty."

"Mr Openshaw was stabbed to death, Miss Brand. That is always nasty."

"Is that why you won't let me see him? We were going to be married, for Christ's sake."

"You are welcome to see the body in due course, if you wish. When our investigations are completed. We are also hoping you can help us apprehend the murderers."

"Tell me how."

"As I said, Mr Openshaw admitted them to his flat. Therefore the odds are that he knew them. Can you tell us if he had any enemies?"

"Doug? Everyone loved Doug."

Lampson nodded. "That certainly ties in with what we have learned. But *somebody* didn't love him, Miss Brand, or he would be alive now." Her face puckered up most attractively, as she thought about that. "How long had you known Mr Openshaw?"

She shrugged. "About a year. We met at a party just after I'd come over to work for Richard. Richard is big on sport. He's always having receptions for athletes and tennis players and footballers, you name them. Well, we met, and we clicked, I guess, and, well . . . one thing led to another."

"Do you know anything of his life before you met?"

"Everything that mattered."

"Did he have any vices?"

"Vices? He's been an athlete all his life. Physical fitness was a religion with him. Sure he had a vice: getting up early to go jogging."

"Is that why you weren't living with him? Your habits were incompatible?"

"I wasn't living with him because I have a place of my own," Jennifer Brand said evenly. "Incompatible? We were going to be married."

Lampson cracked a knuckle, thoughtfully. Jennifer Brand looked pained at the sound. But he liked this girl; she appeared sensible, and very tough. And he had no leads at all. "Miss Brand, I'm going to be honest with you, and tell you something nobody else knows. I'm relying on you to keep it absolutely quiet, because if you don't, then our chances of catching these people become appreciably less. You want them caught, don't you?"

"Of course I want them caught." She was irritated by his condescending tone.

"Well, then, I can tell you that there is a suggestion that Mr Openshaw may have been the victim of a ritual murder." He paused to let that sink in.

"Come again?"

"Our observations and the medical report lead us to believe that he may have been executed, rather than just murdered."

"You have got to be joking. Executed? For what? By whom?"

"That is what we are going to have to find out."

She was frowning. "What makes you think it was a ritual killing?"

"Certain things about the body."

"What things?"

Lampson glanced at Parton, who shrugged; he had also formed the opinion that this was no shrinking violet. "Well, Miss Brand, I'm sorry to say that Mr Openshaw was castrated."

Jennifer Brand's eyes were very wide. "When he was dead?"

"I'm afraid it may have been while he was still alive." He paused, waiting for some violent or perhaps hysterical reaction, but Jennifer Brand sat absolutely still. "So you see, Miss Brand," he continued. "Mr Openshaw may have been a much liked fellow, but someone doesn't seem to have liked him at all. Can you tell us if he was mixed up in any weird religious sects?"

"Doug? That's nonsense."

"What kind of religion do you practice?"

"I don't, nowadays. But I was confirmed in the Presbyterian Church, if that's important."

"And Mr Openshaw?"

"He was an Anglican."

"So there is nothing you can tell us which might have any bearing on either his murder or his mutilation."

"No, there isn't. It must have been . . . God, I just want the bastards caught."

"We all want that, Miss Brand. But we need to do more than want. And until we do find them, there are two very nasty customers roaming about out there. I'd bear that in mind, if I were you."

"When is the body to be released?"

"As I have said, I'm afraid the body cannot be released, permanently, at this time."

"What?"

"It is evidence."

"Are you trying to tell me Doug can't be buried?"

"There can, of course, be a funeral. But we will attend

to the casket, which is not to be opened, and we will have to return it to the morgue, afterwards."

"Until when?"

"Until we have caught the murderers. Not very long, I hope."

"You hope." She got up.

"Miss Brand, I'm very sorry."

"Sure you are."

"Will you please remember my request. Don't immediately call a press conference, if you want us to catch your fiancé's murderers. What I have told you today is absolutely confidential."

Jennifer Brand gazed at him for several seconds, and then left.

Jennifer Brand returned to her flat in Chelsea; when he had heard what had happened, Richard Ebershaw had given her the entire week off. Jennifer had always been very proud of her flat. It had only one bedroom, but was on the first floor and had a pleasant outlook. She had furnished it with great care, shipped over a lot of her personal treasures from Connecticut when she had realised that her job with Ebershaw might occupy her for some time. Her bedroom walls were covered with banners and pennants from her college days, and with posters of her favourite pop groups, as well as a large print of Chopin – she was a romantic. Today she hated them all.

She made herself a cup of coffee and sat with her elbows on her knees and her shoulders hunched, holding the mug in both hands and staring at the wall. There was a hell of a lot to be done. Top of the list was going to see Alex. Speaking to him on the phone had been traumatic enough; he needed the support of her company. In the oddest fashion she had grown closer to Alex Openshaw than the son she had been going to marry. He was such a charming man, and not even so very old; he was only in his fifties, and she, at twenty-seven, had been two years older than Douglas, who, in any event, had been young for his age. She had seemed to bridge a gap between the two men; Alex had from the first been delighted with his prospective daughter-in-law.

While she . . . she wished she could be sure of her emotions, even now. Being such a small woman herself, she had always gone for large, powerful men. For all the feminine independence which she cherished so fiercely, she knew nothing so comforting as to feel inordinate strength flowing over her and into her, especially when it was a gentle strength. Douglas had been very gentle. He had also been absurdly old-fashioned. Jennifer had never thought too deeply about relationships before. One drifted in and one drifted out. Children and or marriage had always seemed a long way in the future, an unthinkable limiting of one's own ego, a necessity to compromise . . . there was so much to be done with one's life. Internationally equipped with languages, talent and qualifications, she had worked in Tokyo and Buenos Aires, Paris and Rome before coming to London. London, the suggestion of permanency emanating from Richard's offer of employment, had been the first anchor she had ever put down, even mentally.

She had never intended to consider any additional permanency. Douglas had just happened, and in his gentle adoration had changed her mind, aided of course by his international fame as an athletic strong man. And even, dared she admit it, by his old fashioned approach. He had asked her to marry him, after some half-dozen dinner dates, before suggesting bed! She had been so surprised she had said yes, and only then considered what she had done. But to hurt Doug would be impossible. And surely, where there was so much love, and so much real perfection, her own love would have to grow.

Over the near year they had been engaged, only her doubts had grown. Had they married right away, perhaps it all would have flowed, but Doug had not wanted to take the plunge until after the next Commonwealth Games. Now he would never take the plunge at all, and she was left with angry bitterness, rather than sorrow. And her anger was not at losing the man she had loved, but at the manner of his end. The very thought of castration made her shudder. And if he had been alive . . . wouldn't he have screamed? He must have been bound and gagged. But the thought . . . and why? How could anyone in this modern age be so savagely inhumane? Who on earth could have hated Doug to that extent?

Hardly less traumatic was trying to decide what she should do with her information. That great lump of a policeman had told her it was confidential. She could understand his point of view. He didn't want to sensationalise the killing, and he didn't want the killers to know how much he knew. But that was absurd. They would have to know that whoever found the body would have seen the castration. And did his stricture include Alex? Alex had a right to know what had happened to his son. But she knew she wasn't the person to tell him.

The street phone rang. Without thinking she picked it up. "Miss Brand? John Cunningham, *Daily Echo*."

She supposed she should have expected this. "I'm sorry. I'm not speaking to reporters right now."

"We'll pay you handsomely for your story, Miss Brand."

"What story?"

"There's a rumour going round that the police aren't telling the whole truth about Douglas Openshaw's death."

"Then why don't you ask the police?"

"Ten thousand pounds, Miss Brand, for what really happened to your fiancé . . . exclusive to the *Echo*."

Jennifer hung up.

* * *

"Thought you weren't coming," Bruce Hardy said. He was a small man, whose weatherbeaten face revealed that he spent as much time as possible on the water, just as his weatherbeaten clothes entirely concealed the fact that he was a millionaire who could afford to indulge his hobby.

"Fog," Jonathan told him. "Lost a whole day."

"Well, the guys are ready to put to sea. This is Phil."

"Hi," Phil said. She had a deep, husky Southern drawl, and a strong sun-tanned body as well, amply displayed by her T-shirt and shorts; red-headed and freckled, five foot ten and powerfully built, she looked like a gorilla – in the yachting sense of the word, meaning those members of the crew whose business is to handle the winches at great speed. Actually, she was a handsome woman.

"Well, hello," Jonathan said. "Are you special?"

"You betcha," Bruce said. "She's the cook. Let's go."

It was one of Bruce Hardy's many idiosyncracies that he entirely separated his working lifestyle from his playing lifestyle. For some forty weeks of the year he sat in his chrome, steel and glass office high above Fifty-Fourth Street, attended by a bevy of secretaries and yesmen, and with a chauffeur-driven limousine awaiting his command in the basement garage. For the remaining twelve weeks, he raced his yacht, and totally changed his persona. Thus he had driven down from Newport himself to meet his principal helmsman at Kennedy, the only obvious concessions to his wealth being the Cadillac and the computer fitted into the dashboard, so that he was in constant touch with how the markets were moving. And the redhead, of course. But maybe she *was* the cook. "Mind if I make a phone call before we leave?" Jonathan asked.

"Be my guest."

"Wife?" Philippa asked.

"Fiancée."

"Ah!" She looked disappointed.

Jonathan's feeling of irritation had dissipated on the flight over, helped by the hangover he had accumulated at the Sheraton the previous night; having checked with Heathrow and discovered there was going to be no flying at all, he had taken a room and put away the better part of a bottle of scotch while watching in-house movies. He remembered absolutely nothing about the movies, and in fact he could not even remember what he had had for dinner, courtesy of room service. But at least he had woken up in the same place he had gone to sleep, which made a change from last Saturday night. Now he was feeling guilty. He should've called Angie; she would have known all flights had been suspended and would be wondering where he had got to.

He put in his card and punched the numbers, listened to the dialling tone. And again and again. He looked at his watch; he had adjusted it on the plane and it read three-fifteen. Eight-fifteen in London. He knew Anne was away for a couple of nights, so where the hell was Angie? Well, fuck her, he thought. But maybe someone else was doing that.

"All correct?" Bruce asked when he returned to the car.

"It would appear so." Jonathan got into the front seat, squeezing Philippa between them. "Tell me what you do besides cook?" he invited.

"Come on, come on," Bruce Hardy bellowed at his foredeck hands. "Get that fucking spinnaker down. Now's your time, Jon," he added in a lower tone.

"Ready about!" The marker buoy was close on the port bow. Jonathan put the helm hard down and the forty-two foot sloop *Halcyon* scythed through the water, rounding the can almost close enough to touch it. Instantly she was back on course and creaming close-hauled through the smooth seas of Long Island Sound for the next marker as her genoa was set and filled, following two opponents who were only a few seconds ahead.

Behind her, the low coast of Long Island itself fell astern; just visible ahead was the hardly higher outline of northern Connecticut; the sun dominated a cloudless sky and drew facets of brilliant light from the wave crests. Bruce was not interested in the beauty of the afternoon, was instead glaring at his stop watch. "Seventeen fucking seconds," he said. "To change a sail? What are you, crippled old men?"

These early races around the cans on the Sound were really only practices, to kick the new members of the crew into shape. But in Bruce Hardy's vocabulary, the word kick was taken literally. Now that the yacht was on a long beat the three chastened foredeck hands came aft to sit on the weather deck above the cockpit and keep the ship as upright as possible. "Wind's freshening," Bruce commented. "All hands."

The two gorillas joined the other three, and even Philippa came out of the saloon to sit with them, dangling her shapely legs above the foaming water streaking away from the yacht's hull, while Jonathan strained on the wheel to keep the sloop as close to the wind as he could without pinching her. Philippa looked back at him, and winked as her auburn hair flowed across her face. It was Hardy's way that they all slept on board during racing week, and there could not be anyone unaware of Phil's presence, her long legs and thrusting breasts, her scent and her persona, not to mention her very good cooking. But she didn't obviously have any favourites. Or was he elected? Because he was English? Or because he was the biggest of them all?

Bruce grinned at him. "We'll get a crew together, yet."

* * *

The trial ended at five, and once ashore, Jonathan called Angela again, and again got no response. He was now definitely annoyed: it was past ten in London and she was not going to be out on her own at that hour. The little rascal had taken off someplace, without even telling him. And he didn't even know if he was to be a father! Next morning, Thursday, he was ashore at the crack of dawn, before anyone else was awake, and called Jim Colley; it was mid-morning in London. "Did you see Angela on Monday?"

"Yes, I did. Where are you?"

"Newport."

"Isle of Wight?"

"Rhode Island, asshole. So what was the verdict?"

"Just come in. Negative, I'm afraid. I'm sorry, old man."

Slow waves of relief began to seep through his brain. "Have you told her yet?"

"I'm sending her the report, yes. I imagine she'll be in touch about it."

"If she's there. I can't raise her."

"Perhaps she's gone away."

"Perhaps." But would she have done that, while waiting for the result of her pregnancy test?

The same thought must have occurred to Colley. "Would you like me to go round and see her?"

Jonathan was tempted. But he didn't want Angie to think he was spying on her, or so wildly in love with her he lost his cool simply because she didn't answer her telephone. "No," he decided. "She's probably got something on. She'll call me when she gets the result of your test." Or will she, he wondered as he hung up. Just what sort of game was she playing, anyway?

"Fi-an-cey givin' yuh the runaround?" Philippa inquired. She pronounced each syllable of the word "fiancée" with distinct and equal emphasis.

He was surprised to see her ashore so early, and looking good enough to eat in very short shorts and a loose shirt. "Isn't that what fiancées do?" he asked.

"If they cain get away with it, Ah guess."

"Where are you off to at this hour?"

"The fish market. It's a fishy lunch today. Yuh comin'?"

"Why not." They walked into the town. Newport was always a hubbub during the yacht racing season. There were already a lot of people crowding the quaint old streets while a constant stream of traffic moved across the bridge linking the island to the mainland. The market was busy, the fishing boats having just returned. Jonathan watched in admiration as Philippa selected half a dozen specimens, revealing a great deal of knowledge, and placed them in her basket before heading towards the beach away from the dock. "Planning a barbeque?" he asked, following.

"Must haive these gutted and cleaned by the time the boss gaits up," she said. "And he doesn't like the smell so they haive to be done well away from the ship. Yuh cain give me a haind."

"Gutting fish is not my strongest point," Jonathan confessed. "Those look still alive."

"They are, just." She placed her basket on the sand, knelt beside it, and from her waistband drew a wicked looking knife. "But a quick slash . . ." she decapitated the first of her victims. "Puts them out of their misery. Yuh do laike to eat fish, don't yuh?"

"Properly cooked, yes." He knelt beside her. "Where'd you meet Bruce? You weren't here last year."

Philippa was removing various pieces of gut and bones from the first fish, and putting it back into the basket before starting on the second. "Ah didn't meet him. Ah answered an ad."

"What did it say?"

"Cook wanted for ocean racin' yacht. Would suit beautiful blonde who gaits on well with main."

"That sounds like Bruce. And you went for something like that?"

"Waall," she said, demolishing her third victim. "Ah know Ah'm not exactly blonde . . . but lots of people do classify raidheads as blondes."

She raised her head and they gazed at each other. "And you get on well with men," he suggested.

"For someone who's engaged yuh ask one haill of a lot of questions, big boy. Or are yuh feelin' deprived?"

"Yes, I'm feeling deprived." And I'm no longer necessarily engaged, he thought.

Once again their eyes held for several seconds. "Can yuh wait until after the race?" she asked. "Or do yuh want somethin' on account?"

"Every little helps."

She finished gutting her fish, dropped the knife, and stood up. "Ah haive to get this stink off ma hainds."

She kicked off her sandals and walked down the beach into the water. Jonathan watched her go, nostrils dilating to the stench of fish guts, which lay scattered all around him. Then he kicked off his docksiders in turn and followed her. His affliction, if it could be called that, was something he had been working on for several years, ever since he had realised that he was never going to have the stomach for surgery. And he believed he just about had it licked. He grinned. Maybe what he should do, while Eric remained alive, was go back to medical school and qualify. If they'd have him. After eight years of doing exactly as he pleased when he pleased and how he pleased, could he possibly accept the discipline of either school or a hospital?

So what the hell? He felt like a fuck, and he'd been faithful to Angie for far too long. If she was playing him around . . . Philippa glanced at him, then stood up. "Nothin' laike an empty beach, at dawn."

He stood behind her and put his hands round her waist,

then let them slide up inside her shirt to cup her breasts. If they had been good to look at through the thin shirt, they were even better to hold. "Mmmm," she remarked, and nuzzled her cheek against his, while putting her hands behind her to fumble at the crotch of his shorts. "Ah laike yuh too."

She turned in his arms for his kiss, and they rubbed against each other. "Will that hold yuh until tonaight?" she asked.

"You have to be joking. That'll hold me for the next ten seconds at the most."

"So Ah get saind up ma ass."

"There's some soft looking grass up there."

"Saind, or aints, or poison ivy, the things we girls do for main." She walked up the beach to the grass beneath the trees, unbuttoned her shirt, slipped her shorts and briefs down to her ankles and stepped out of them, and was in his arms again, removing his shorts herself. He had never known anyone quite so tumultuous. She had him on his back and he was in her and she was surging against him long before he was properly ready, and if her climax was a fake he hadn't encountered anything better there, either. Then she lay on him, smiling as she kissed him several times. "What *do* you do when you're not cooking on small boats?" he asked.

"A bit of this, an' a bit of thait." She rolled off him, went back down to the sea. He joined her, and they washed each other. "Good?" she asked.

An insecure love goddess! "Excellent."

"Not all big main are big all over," she said seriously, standing up to let the morning breeze dry her; he could have spent the rest of his life looking at those nipples.

"I'm glad you approve."

"Yuh're a great hunk of man," she said. "Ah wish Ah was the Quain of Sheba, or Cleopatra, or somethin'. Ah'd have yuh as ma slave."

"And you'd beat me when I didn't perform?"

"Oh, no," she said, taking him in her hands and rolling him as an expert might have rolled a cigar. "Ah'd cut it off, pickle it, and mount it."

"Charming. Wouldn't that be to cut off your nose to spite your face? In a manner of speaking."

"Oh, Ah wouldn't do it until Ah'd found a replacemaint." She released him, reluctantly, and pulled on her pants. "We'll talk some more, tonight."

"I'm not sure it'd be safe."

"Well, yuh cain tell me what yuh'd like to do to me, were Ah completely in your power."

"I've just done it."

She grinned. "One guy Ah knew waill said he'd like to dissect me, slowly, bit by bit. He was a medical student."

"That figures. They're a depraved lot. Dissection isn't all it's cracked up to be. Before you know it, you've nothing left to dissect, just a bloody great mess. I'd rather have you around."

"Yuh say the sweetest thaings." She kissed him.

Predictably, half-way through the race Jonathan's conscience began to trouble him. That evening he called London again, and again got no reply. "Skipper," he said to Bruce when they'd moored up. "I am going to have to bow out of the next couple of days' racing."

Bruce Hardy had a disconcerting habit of looking at one, his eyes conveying a great many messages, all of them condemnatory.

"I haven't been able to raise my girl friend since leaving England," Jonathan explained, "and there's an important bit of news I think she should want to share with me. I just have to sort it out."

"I can spare you for one week," Bruce said. "I thought you were old enough to be over emotional crises."

"Are we ever?"

He went to the local travel agent, got a flight out of Kennedy at eleven that night. "Ah'll draive yuh down," Philippa suggested. "If yuh don't maind, Bruce."

"Help yourself," Bruce said. "Just be sure *you're* back in time for tomorrow's race."

Philippa was not amused. "We were gonna spend the naight together. Say, how's about me comin' to London with yuh? Ah've never bin to London, England. An' on the way, yuh could join the Six Mile High Club."

"You mean you wouldn't?"

She laughed. "Silly boy. Ah'm a member already."

"Sounds a great idea. But what would I do with you in London?"

He was too preoccupied even to say a proper goodbye. He had a growing sensation that something was wrong. So the obvious answer was that Angie had taken off somewhere, but Angie wasn't the sort of person to do that, in secret. He was more concerned that the negative result of the test might have upset her. But there again, Angie had always come across as a most sensible girl, who took the ups as well as the downs of life in her stride. No doubt she supposed he would not now marry her. Well, his initial reaction to Jim Colley's news *had* been a sense of relief, of regained freedom . . . that had been the main cause for his brief fling with Phil. But he certainly didn't want to hurt Angie in any way.

Their trouble was that they lived too separate lives. He went to watch her play tennis, when he had the time, and she had come to watch him play rugby, once or twice last winter, but those apart they moved in different circles. His attempts to interest her in sailing had failed: she got seasick. Their eleven-year age gap even meant they had different tastes in pop music. He wasn't really interested in her tennis-playing crowd, and she seldom inflicted them upon him. Similarly, although she would sometimes accompany him to special nights out with the boys, she was not a friend of any of them. There was no one he could telephone and ask to check her out. He supposed he could have tried calling Mrs Moresby's flat in Hastings. But Angela had specifically told him she wasn't going down to see her mother this week – the old lady was at her complaining worst when she had hay-fever – and to call would have involved Anne in their domestic problems: he didn't want Anne to know about any of the private tensions which existed between Angie and himself, and of course he didn't know if Angie had told her sister about the baby. She had said she wouldn't.

Maybe he should have let Colley go ahead and call on her, but Colley was no longer a close friend, either. The last thing he wanted was someone like Jim trying to psychoanalyse their relationship. He hardly slept, felt like a worn out rag when the jumbo touched down just on seven-thirty. He was travelling with only hand luggage, however, and was in Central London before nine. Jetting back and forth across the Atlantic always made him lose track of days, and he had to buy a paper to remind himself it was Friday.

He parked the Mercedes, looked at Angie's mini, stooped to peer underneath. It had very obviously rained a good deal during the few days he had been away, but underneath the Mini was as dry as a bone. She hadn't been anywhere. She simply hadn't been answering the phone. He unlocked the street door. Inside the hall were four pints of milk and four newspapers, as well as several letters, stacked in a corner. He regarded these for some seconds, and the door of the ground floor flat opened. Jonathan did not care for his immediate neighbour, who was an inquisitive little man. Now he was clearly about to leave for work. "Bit of carelessness there, eh?" the man remarked. "Both of you going away and not cancelling the milk or papers. I brought them in for you."

"Why, thank you," Jonathan said. "Miss Moresby away?"

"Well, of course she is, or she'd have taken this stuff in herself. Left the air-conditioning on, too."

"Dear me." He didn't want to get into any theories with this twerp, who must have seen Angie's car outside all week. Anyway, he could not possibly get all of this stuff upstairs as well as his carryall in one go. He'd have to come back down with a basket.

He went up the stairs, listened to the street door close behind Nosey Parker. He put his carryall on the floor, unlocked the door, picked up his carryall, and stepped inside. He checked, his stomach revolving. Every window in the flat was closed, and the curtains were drawn. There was no sound except for the constant whirring of the air-conditioning – the room was quite cool. But there was an unearthly stench.

He gasped, put his hand to his nose as he crossed the room and opened the bedroom door. Here the gloom was such he couldn't see for a moment. He switched on the light, stared at the bed, gasped, and fell to his knees. It was some seconds before he could move. When he did, it was violently.

CHAPTER 3

Lampson regarded the young man with a mixture of pity and contempt. A great big hulk who had hadn't the stomach of a WPC. Of course, the stench in here must have been pretty grim when the front door was opened; it was still pretty grim and he had had every window in the flat thrown wide to the summer air. He reckoned the body must have lain on the bed about three days – even with the air-conditioning, a couple more days and the smell would have faded. "Feel you can talk?" he asked.

Jonathan raised his head, gazed at the people in the room; there were a great number, because this time Dr Mayhew and the photographers had also arrived – it was a working morning. Then he looked at the bedroom door, behind which the body still lay, as Mayhew had not yet finished his preliminary examination. Jonathan licked his lips. "Who did it?" he muttered.

"With your help, we may be able to find out," Lampson said. "We gather you were a friend of the deceased, as you had a key to get in?"

"I live here," Jonathan said.

"The flat is in the name of Miss Angela Moresby. I assume that is the name of the deceased?"

"Yes, that is her name. We were engaged to be married."

"And you lived here with her?" Lampson glanced at Parton to make sure the sergeant had got that. "Where have you been the past three days?"

"I left on Tuesday morning, for The States. I have been racing on Long Island Sound. I came back on last night's plane."

"I assume you have your ticket?"

Jonathan felt in his pocket and handed over the ticket. Lampson scrutinised it. "This is an open return ticket to Kennedy. So you were going back again?"

"Yes. I only came back to find out what had happened to Angie."

Lampson raised his eyebrows. "You knew something had happened to her, Mr Rudder?"

"Of course not. But she didn't answer my telephone calls."

"I see." He glanced around the wrecked room; there was furniture scattered everywhere, some of it smashed. "You don't have an ansaphone?"

"No need. We're neither of us working people."

"I see," Lampson commented again, disapprovingly. "And you fly the Atlantic whenever you feel like it, whenever your fiancée doesn't answer a phone call."

"Look," Jonathan said, beginning to get annoyed. "She didn't answer several calls. I was worried. There were . . . well, when I left she thought she was pregnant. When it was discovered she wasn't, I thought we should talk about it. When she didn't answer my calls, I began to worry."

"You say when you left you thought she was pregnant. Now you say you knew she wasn't. Would you explain that, please?"

"I happen to know the doctor to whom she was going for her tests. When she didn't answer my call, I checked with him."

"And he told you she wasn't pregnant. Can you tell us if your fiancée had any enemies?"

"Of course not. Angie was friends with everyone."

"Well, then, can you tell us if she belonged, or had ever belonged, to any unusual religious cult." Jonathan stared at him in total bemusement. "Do I take it that she didn't?" Lampson pressed, gently.

"I've never heard of anything so ridiculous. Why, was there something about the murder . . . you mean the way she was tied up? It was a sexual assault, wasn't it?"

"Perhaps," Lampson said. "Has she any close kin?"

"My God! The old lady in Hastings. She'll have to be told!"

"Old lady?"

"Her mother."

"Yes, she will have to be told. Anyone else?"

"Her sister, Anne. She's down with her mother this week. They'll both have to be told." Parton wrote the names down. "Will you tell Mrs Moresby, or must I?" Jonathan asked.

"Don't you get on with your prospective mother-in-law?"

"She's not my prospective mother-in-law, so far as she knows. She didn't know about the engagement."

"Neither did your fiancée, it appears. She wasn't wearing a ring, and there is no mark on her finger to suggest one was taken off by her killers."

"We only got engaged the day before I went away. I was going to buy her a ring when I got back."

"You got engaged when she told you she was pregnant?"

"There hadn't seemed any reason, before."

"Quite. So you flew out of England on the morning of . . .?"

"As I said, it was Tuesday when I flew out. I was due to go on Monday, but the flight was cancelled because of the fog. Here's my original ticket."

He gave the policeman that as well, and Lampson studied it before handing both back. "So you returned here for Monday night?"

"Well, no." Jonathan was visibly embarrassed. "I stayed

the night at the Sheraton Skyline. I had a lot to think about."

"Did you inform your fiancée of what you were doing?"

"No, I did not."

"Because it was her you had to think about, and her news that she was pregnant. Am I right?"

"That is right," Jonathan said evenly, gazing at him.

"And you can think of no person or persons who might have wished Miss Moresby dead? There is no sign of forced entry. Whoever did this was known to Miss Moresby, or had a very good reason for being admitted. But then there was this hell of a struggle."

"What struggle?"

Lampson placed his hands on his hips. "You don't see any evidence of a struggle?"

Jonathan looked left and right. "This? Oh, I did this."

Lampson looked at Parton, who raised his eyebrows. "You broke up this place, Mr Rudder?" Lampson asked. "May I ask why?"

Jonathan shrugged. "I suppose, when I saw Angie . . . I kind of flipped. I do that sometimes."

Lampson regarded him for several seconds. "But you're all right now?"

"Yes. I've worked it out of my system."

"I see. But you still can't help us as to who might have done this?"

"No. If I knew who it was . . ." again Jonathan looked around him. "I'd have given him to you by now."

"Thank you, Mr Rudder. Will you be remaining here, after the body has been removed?"

"No."

"Don't blame you, really. Where will you go?"

"I'll go and stay with my uncle. He has a house in Berkshire."

"Be sure to give Sergeant Parton the address, so we'll know where to contact you. You won't be flying back to the States in the immediate future, then?"

"There are things to be done here."

"Quite. We'd prefer you to remain in this country for the time being. Certainly until after the inquest. As for your fiancée's mother, we'll inform her. And her sister. Thank you, Mr Rudder."

He stood up to indicate that the interview was at an end, but Jonathan remained seated. "I only have overnight things with me. I'll need clothes."

"And your clothes are in that bedroom? In that case, Mr Rudder, I suggest you wait here until we have finished." Lampson nodded at Parton, and stepped into the bedroom, where Mayhew was just completing his examination of the body; the photographers had already left, but the fingerprint squad was still at work.

"Think he's our man?" Parton muttered.

"I'd say for this one, almost certainly," Lampson said. "But what about the other? We need to find a link."

"Both sportsmen? Or rather, one a sportsman, the other a sportswoman?"

"Where's the link in that? Have someone check out his Sheraton story," Lampson told him. "Well, Fred?"

"Oh, exactly the same m.o. as that fellow Openshaw." Mayhew gestured at the blood on the walls, the pools on the floor. "You can see that."

"Save that she wasn't castrated, eh?"

"No," Mayhew said wearily; Lampson's humour could be exhausting. "She wasn't castrated. But she was mutilated." He pointed to the bloody scars where Angela's breasts had been.

"Was she raped?"

"You'll have to wait for the post mortem for that. On a preliminary look, I would say not. There are no obvious signs of semen." The doctor picked his way through the mess into the bathroom. As at Openshaw's flat, this too was a mass of blood, but Mayhew ran water into the basin and rinsed his hands.

Lampson followed him. "Can you tell if she was pregnant?"

"No, her womb was amongst the organs removed, together with the tubes."

"Isn't there a test you can carry out on the blood?"

"This blood is at least three days old."

"That's something else I need to know. When was she killed?"

"Difficult to say."

"Don't you shove a thermometer up her ass and work it out from the degree of cooling?"

"Yes, where the body is still cooling. As I said, this one has been lying here for several days."

"You said at least three days?"

Mayhew opened the bloodstained cupboard, took out a towel, and dried his hands. "That's right."

"So she could have died Monday night."

"I think that is most probable."

"What about Tuesday?"

"No."

"You're very sure."

"Because of the air-conditioning. The onset of rigor mortis could have been delayed for several hours. So, as it takes about eighteen hours fully to set in before disintegration commences, we're talking about twenty-four hours after death at the earliest. I would say disintegration has been in progress for something over forty-eight hours. That gives us Monday night as the time of death. Even Monday may be a bit soon, but Monday night is the most recent possible date." He draped the towel over the basin and glanced at the Superintendent. "Any visual witnesses?"

"Not this time. But this is a different neighbourhood.

People don't peer out whenever the street doorbell rings."

"Equally, they don't report anything which might be suspicious. What about big boy outside?"

"He heads the queue, in this case. Certainly a motive: girl friend suddenly springs a pregnancy on a footloose young fellow and demands marriage. Certainly behaviour; he's violent. But why Openshaw? And where's the other killer? And, he really was upset after seeing the body. By the time we arrived he'd been puking all over the place."

"That's not conclusive," Mayhew argued. They stood in the bathroom doorway and watched the ambulance men encasing Angela's mutilated corpse in a body bag preparatory to removal. "Killing someone is easy. Coming back to view the body, especially after disintegration has set in, is another matter entirely."

"There's also the business of his cutting loose," Parton said.

"What's that?" Mayhew asked.

"I said he was violent. He seems to have gone wild when he saw the body, and broke the place up. You saw the mess out there."

"Hm," Mayhew commented.

"Let's have it," Lampson said. He could tell when Fred Mayhew had an idea.

"You only have his word for it that he created that mayhem *after* finding the body."

"True. What does that indicate?"

"Well, obviously he's a man who is subject to sudden violent rages. Remember Heath?"

Lampson frowned. "Killed several women in 1946."

"I think it was '47, actually. The point is, he seemed a very normal and indeed likeable fellow most of the time. But sex drove him mad. He'd start biting off their nipples and at least one was opened up with a bayonet. This case has a lot of similarities."

"What about Openshaw?" Parton objected. "Or do you reckon he's bisexual? Rudder, I mean."

"I really don't know. It's just something I think you should keep in mind."

"We will," Lampson promised him. "Let me know if you find anything new in the PM."

"I don't expect to. But I'll be in touch."

The doctor followed the corpse out of the room and down the stairs. Lampson looked at the bed and the blood. "Finished?" he asked the fingerprint men. They nodded; they were in a hurry to get out. Lampson went to the door. "You can take anything you wish, now, Mr Rudder," he said.

Jonathan swallowed as he got up. "Do you know of anyone who might clean this up?" he asked.

"We can recommend someone," Lampson said.

"The Sheraton story seems to be true," Parton told his chief later that morning. "Jonathan Rudder certainly checked in, on Monday. He went in quite early, left his car in their park, had a few drinks and lunch, and then took a room. Presumably by then he had heard he wasn't flying that day. He spent the rest of the day and the night in his room. But," he went on as Lampson would have spoken, "he was sending down pretty regularly for drinks, and he had dinner by Room Service."

"When?"

Parton checked his notes. "Eight-fifteen."

"Were there any calls after that?"

"None. The room service tray was collected just before midnight. There was a Do Not Disturb sign on the door."

"So any time after eight-fifteen he could have left his room, gone down to the car park, taken his car and driven away. Say half an hour to central London at that time of night. And half an hour back. The Sheraton is a big hotel. Nobody would have noticed."

"From the amount of alcohol which was sent up to his room, I think if he'd tried that we'd have had him in a cell before he could commit any murders."

"He didn't have to drink it all, Ned; he could have poured it down the sink."

"So he's still nominated?"

"He's my number one boy, at the moment, yes. Do you know we found a shirt of his in the laundry basket, stained with blood?"

"Moresby's blood?"

"It's being analysed now. But it's another pointer. What I'm trying to work out is if he did Openshaw as well, and where does the second bloke come in? We want them both. So I think we'll just keep an eye on Rudder for the time being. Put a tail on him; he's at Blessop Manor. If he's connected with the Openshaw murder as well, he'll be contacting his friend soon enough."

"Do you want to apply for a tap?"

Lampson shook his head. "Too elaborate. We'll just wait for the two of them to get together."

"And if they don't?"

"There has to be a link between the two murders, Ned. If there isn't . . . we're up shit creek without a paddle." Lampson was cracking his knuckles continually with huge snaps of sound. "Because that will mean that in addition to our violent young yachtsman, there are a couple of nutters roaming London, cutting people into little pieces for no obvious reason. Right out of the blue. I can't buy that. They *have* to be connected. I want you to check our records for any similar type murders in the past ten years, and then I want you to contact Interpol and find out if there have been any other killings to this pattern anywhere in the world over the past few months – no, make that the last few years; these people didn't just wake up one morning and say how boring, let's go out and chop someone to pieces. There has to be a pattern. And I also want you to find out if there is any link between Angela Moresby and Douglas Openshaw, Angela Moresby and Jennifer Brand, and Jonathan Rudder and Douglas Openshaw. Or Jennifer Brand."

"Thin," Parton commented, closing his notebook.

"It's all we bloody well have to go on. And this is going to bloody well break at any moment. Such as Openshaw's inquest."

"The Press are asking for a statement, now."

"So give them one. Second brutal killing, etc, etc." He pointed. "But no details. Understood?"

It was late morning before Jonathan got away from London. By then his stomach had settled down, even if his mind hadn't.

He arrived at Blessop Manor in time for lunch. Eric Rudder listened to what his nephew had to tell him. He only had to look at Jonathan's face to realise what he had been through. "Who did it?" he asked.

"The police don't seem to have any idea. Although there were mysterious remarks to suggest they'd seen something like it before. Christ . . ."

Eric rang his bell. "Caunt," he said, "fetch Mr Jonathan a large brandy. You say she'd been cut to pieces?"

"And apparently left to bleed to death. God, if I ever lay hands on who did it . . ."

"Let's hope you don't. What are you going to do? You're welcome to stay here for as long as you wish, of course."

"A few days. I'll move back in to the flat when the cleaners are finished with it. The police want me to stick around for awhile, anyway."

"Because you're a suspect?"

"I suppose I am." He told his uncle about the mix-up over the flights. "I mean, I can prove I was at the Sheraton, but I can't prove I stayed there all night."

"And you'd just found out your live-in girl friend was pregnant and demanding marriage. And . . ." Eric gave a dry smile. "You weren't getting any financial support from your uncle."

Jonathan glared at him. "Whose side are you on?"

"Yours, in this instance. I'm just agreeing with the police that you should stick around. Now you'll forgive me, dear boy, but I'm feeling rather tired. I'm going to have a lie down."

"At one o'clock in the afternoon?"

"This is as good a time as any. Don't bother about me, Jonathan. Caunt will take care of you."

Caunt was waiting in the doorway. "You will be pleased to know, sir, that the car has been returned."

"Oh, good," Eric Rudder said, walking slowly towards the stairs.

"Where has it been?" Jonathan asked.

"Just to the garage in Blessop for its thirty thousand mile service. I will see you later." Jonathan watched the old man go with some concern; he was certainly moving more slowly than usual. And now he looked more closely, Jonathan saw that Eric's face was grey – he had been too preoccupied before. He would have to find out what exactly was wrong. But he was actually relieved to have some time to himself.

He phoned America to bring Bruce up to date, but was informed by the marina office that Mr Hardy and his crew were already on the water. Bruce and the crew, including Phil!

Caunt served lunch, but Jonathan ate little, and left the table to sit on the terrace and brood. If he had been able to relieve some of the mental pressure by breaking up Angie's furniture, on the drive up from London his brain had been a raging torment, filled with the picture of her lying tied to that bed, her face already suggesting the skull it would soon become, her body a welter of dried blood. As far as he had been able to make out from his one horrified glance someone had driven a knife into her chest and then ripped right downwards to her pelvis. Some knife. And some hand wielding it.

And her flesh already rotting. He would never get that stench out of his nostrils. He had thought himself as tough as anybody. His size and his naturally aggressive nature had carried him in, and out, of numberless brawls, always the victor. But the sight of Angie, harmless, inoffensive Angie, reduced to a decaying lump of flesh had left him as weak as a young boy. He watched his fingers curl into big fists. Not again. When they caught who had done that . . . supposing they ever did. And supposing he was even allowed to see the bastard, outside of a courtroom. His whole being was consumed by another urgent desire to run amok, to break things, and people, for what had happened. To take the whole world apart. And he knew himself well enough to wonder just how long he was going to be able to suppress that primeval urge.

His anger was compounded by guilt. While Angie had been lying dead, he had been fucking Phil. God damn! But who would do such a thing? Someone Angie had admitted to her flat. Someone she knew, surely. Who, who, who? Once again he was aware of how little he knew of her background. The police thought she had been mixed up in some demoniac cult. Could she have been? She had never revealed any evidence of it during the year they had lived together. But had she been killed, so horribly, for attempting to quit?

Would Anne know anything about that? He would have to contact her. But he decided to wait until the police had done it first. The afternoon drifted by. Caunt offered him tea at four, but he refused it, while the same thoughts chased themselves round and round his mind. Someone she knew. Someone who had rung the street door and said, "Can I come up." And Angie had said, of course.

Only, from the way the police kept speaking in the plural, it had been two someones. Who?

Caunt cleared his throat. "Would you like a whisky, Mr Jonathan."

Jonathan started; he hadn't realised it was that late. "Yes, that sounds like good idea, Caunt. Uncle down yet?"

"Ah, no, sir. I don't expect him down again this evening."

"Not even for dinner?"

"He may have a tray in his room, later. I'm afraid Mr Rudder is not very well."

"How not very well?"

"Mr Rudder had a heart attack on Tuesday morning, sir."

"Tuesday? Why wasn't I informed?"

"You weren't here, sir."

"What kind of a heart attack?"

"I sent for the doctor, sir. He said it was a heart attack. He gave Mr Rudder a thorough examination, and put him to bed. He said he should stay there for some time. He really shouldn't have got up this morning. But you know what Mr Rudder is like."

"Yes." Jonathan went up to his uncle's room. He was very fond of the old boy, the only living relative who gave a damn whether he lived or died. "What's all this then?" he demanded.

Eric had been lying on his back, his eyes open, gazing at the ceiling. "I'm afraid it's the knock on the door."

"Nobody gets that kind of knock nowadays," Jonathan told him. Unless they're about to be murdered, he thought savagely. "So you've had a heart attack. Hasn't Morrissey put you down for a pacemaker?"

"No. He says it wouldn't do the trick. Seems the whole shooting match, valves, arteries, you name it, is pretty well shot. He's given me something to take whenever it gets rough." Eric gave a tired smile. "What I need is a new heart."

"Well, then . . ."

"Oh, I'm on the list. But pretty low down. Time comes when you just have to face facts, Jon. I am an elderly layabout with no family to support, except you, of course, but then, you're a layabout as well. Keeping me alive at vast expense is a waste of time and money. There are just so many spare hearts to go round, you know."

"Morrissey told you that?"

"He more or less spelled that out, yes."

"That's absolute nonsense. What about private medicine?"

"In this country, it's not on, for heart surgery of that nature."

"Abroad then."

"I believe Morrissey is checking around."

"Morrissey," Jonathan said in disgust. "And you just mean to sit there and die, because of an incompetent GP?"

"Morrissey has been my doctor for years," Eric protested. "He's a good man."

"Sure he's a good man, when it comes to migraine and ingrowing toenails. Obviously not when faced with a crisis."

Eric smiled. "You're getting excited. I mustn't get excited."

"Listen, you leave this with me. I know some people in the business. Hell, I should. I'll sort this one out." He grinned. "We'll find a spare heart lying around."

He wanted to have a chat with Jim Colley anyway. And Jim was big in private medicine. He looked at his watch: it was nearly seven. First thing tomorrow, even if it was Saturday.

* * *

Jennifer Brand frowned at the newspaper. The item was on a middle page, and could easily have been missed. Yet . . . she left her breakfast table and hunted through the pile of newspapers on the table, waiting to be thrown out – but she wasn't throwing anything out right this minute. She found the description of Doug's death. He had been "brutally murdered" with a knife; there had been "multiple stab wounds". She looked at the current edition: some woman named Moresby had also been brutally murdered with a knife – she had suffered multiple stab wounds.

Her brow puckered. Since her return to London on Tuesday she had thought of nothing but Doug, of what the police had told her. The police had actually been totally unhelpful. They had not even told her the actual cause of death, and they had not allowed her to see the body. According to Alex, Doug's face had been calm, even relaxed. But he had been castrated. Could one die from being castrated? Presumably one could bleed to death.

She had told no one of that, certainly not the reporters who kept seeking her out to interview her. In making that decision, she had been not consciously obeying the wishes of the police – why should she? She just didn't want anyone to know that something so disgusting, so humiliating, had been done to her Doug. She hadn't even told Alex about it; he had done no more than look at his son's face when identifying the body beneath the blanket in the morgue. She had felt he might have a heart attack if he knew. But that had meant there was no one she could talk to about what had happened; even if she hadn't been given the week off she wouldn't have wanted to discuss it with Ebershaw or any of her acquaintances at work; she was not a woman who made close friends easily, and she had none on this side of the Atlantic – the Holts, in Cornwall, were more friends of her mother's.

But here was a woman, murdered, in the same phraseology. Had she been obscenely mutilated too? And mightn't her murder be linked to Doug's? It was something she had to find out, and there was no point in approaching that shit of a police inspector. But there was the address where this second murder had taken place. She dressed, and ran downstairs. Her little Renault was parked by the pavement, and a moment later she was hurrying towards Barnes.

Jennifer pulled into the opposite side of the road to look at the block of flats from a distance. She was an early riser, and it was just eight o'clock. Thus there was hardly anyone around, certainly no crowd, although there was a van and several cars parked in front of the building. She left her car and walked across the road, went up the steps and studied the names on the board. Moresby was the first floor. She drew a long breath and pressed the bell. She had to wait several seconds before a woman's voice said, "Who is it?"

"I'd like to speak with someone," Jennifer said. "It's about what happened."

"I'm not speaking with any more reporters," the voice said.

"I'm not a reporter. Please. It's most urgent."

There was a brief hesitation, then the voice said, "I'm not alone."

"I didn't think you were," Jennifer said. The phone went dead, but a moment later the lock clicked, and she was able to push the door inwards. She stepped into the hall, waited to get her breathing under control, and went up the stairs.

A woman waited at the top, surprisingly young, certainly younger than herself, Jennifer realised. She was also fully dressed in what might be termed "county" clothes – tweed skirt and cashmere sweater – and remarkably well groomed, in all the circumstances. She looked perfectly composed, although there were shadows under her eyes.

"I'm Jennifer Brand."

"I'm Anne Moresby."

"Oh. Are you . . . I mean . . ."

"My sister was murdered, yes. If you are not a reporter, what do you want?"

Jennifer looked past her at the open door of the flat. Beyond there were cleaning noises, and the slurp of water. She hadn't been to Doug's flat. Although she had a key and since the police had finished with it, it had been thoroughly cleaned, she hadn't been able to force herself, and thus had no idea what it had looked like. "The newspaper said it happened in there."

"Yes, it did. Look, who *are* you."

"I was engaged to Douglas Openshaw," Jennifer blurted.

Anne looked at her for several seconds, then the penny dropped and she threw her arms round her. "Oh, my dear. You poor girl." She escorted Jennifer into what must once have been the living room. Now it was almost bare of furniture. "The kettle's on. Would you like a cup of coffee? Instant, I'm afraid; this place is a little disorganised; the cleaners started work this morning at six. Do sit down." She gestured at the one chair.

"I'd love a cup of coffee." Jennifer sat down, and looked through the half open bedroom door, where two men were busy with what appeared to be hoses on the floor and walls.

"Blood," Anne explained, from the kitchenette.

"Oh, my God!"

"That was my first reaction, too." Anne placed a tray on the bar counter. "It's my sister's blood. Wasn't it like that at your boy friend's flat?"

"I don't know. I haven't seen it. Was it out here as well?"

"No," Anne said bitterly. "Out here was broken up by my sister's flatmate."

"Oh! Did he . . . she . . . do it?"

"It's a he, and he very probably did, the bastard. Although the police haven't arrested him."

"Oh!" That rather spoiled her theory that the two crimes could be connected, Jennifer realised; she had never heard of Angela Moresby before this morning. "May I ask his name?"

"Jonathan Rudder." Anne poured coffee. "Do you know him?"

"No. No, I don't know him. His name, anyway. May I ask . . . was your sister mutilated?"

"Mutilated?" Anne frowned. "Nobody said anything . . . my God!"

"I didn't mean to distress you," Jennifer said.

Anne stared at her. "You mean . . . was Mr Openshaw?"

Jennifer bit her lip, and decided to stonewall her way out of her slip. "It was just something the police said."

"The police!" Anne snorted. "They're as much good as a fifth wheel to a coach. As for that bastard Jonathan . . ."

"Do they think he's the murderer?"

"I should think so. Only they won't arrest him because they don't have any conclusive evidence."

"But . . . do you think he murdered Doug as well?"

Anne glanced at her. "I don't know? When did it happen?"

"Last Saturday night."

"And what makes you think it could be Jonathan?"

"It's just that . . . they were both cut up . . ."

"Stabbed several times, the police said."

"Yes." Jennifer swallowed. Obviously this woman didn't know what had really happened to her sister. But then, neither did she; she was clutching at straws. "This Jonathan . . . you say he roomed with your sister?"

"According to the police, they were engaged." Anne

Moresby spat the words. "He told them that. He told them Angela thought she was pregnant, by him. My God, the filth some people spew out."

"They must have been good friends," Jennifer observed, at once naively and provocatively.

"Oh, they were lovers. I knew *that.* He lived here. Now he's done a bunk. Talk about rats deserting a sinking ship."

"Done a bunk?"

"He's gone off to his uncle in Berkshire. His uncle looks after him, pays him an allowance so he can drive a bloody great Mercedes. The swine."

"Oh. What's his name? The uncle."

"Eric Rudder. He should've been here, with her, not gadding about the world."

"This chap Eric?"

"Eric is the name of his uncle," Anne said with great patience. "Jonathan is the name of the bastard who let Angela die."

"Who killed her, you think?"

"Oh, I don't know. Who else could've?"

Jennifer realised that Anne Moresby's brain was not functioning one hundred per cent. But the meeting had raised endless possibilities. "Will you give me the address of this uncle in Berkshire?"

Jennifer was pleasantly excited. She at last could feel she was accomplishing something. What, she couldn't be sure. But this man Jonathan Rudder at least gave her something tangible to go after. Perhaps he had killed his girl friend . . . but then, had he also killed Doug? In either case, he was a highly dangerous man. Yet she was more exhilarated than afraid. He'd know the police were after him, now. He wasn't going to take any more risks, and certainly not at his own home.

However, she had seen a lot of thrillers in her time,

and she stopped at a call box and telephoned Scotland Yard. After some delays, she was put through to the right office. "I'd like to speak with Chief Inspector Lampson, please."

"I'm sorry, miss, but the Inspector isn't in today."

"Well, then, connect me with Sergeant Parton."

"The sergeant isn't in today either."

"For God's sake! They're both off?"

"It is Saturday, miss. Can I help you? Detective Constable Martin."

Jennifer drew a long breath to get her annoyance under control. "I hope so. My name is Jennifer Brand. Does that mean anything to you?"

There was a pause while DC Martin attempted to remember who she was. Then his voice sounded wary. "Yes, Miss Brand."

"Any progress?"

"The police are always making progress, Miss Brand, even if we don't shout about it until we're ready."

"Okay. Tell me about this Jonathan Rudder."

She could picture Martin frowning at the telephone, even if she didn't know what he looked like. "Do you know Mr Rudder, miss?" he asked at last.

Now she could imagine his brain working. A link between the two deaths! "I sure mean to," she said. "But I thought you guys should know about it. Right?"

"I'm not sure I follow you, Miss Brand."

"Listen. I have an address for this Rudder. His uncle's place in Berkshire." She pronounced each syllable very distinctly. "Blessop Manor. You know about that, I guess."

"Ye-es." Now his tone was guarded.

"Well, I'm going out there to have a word with him."

"I'm not sure the Chief Inspector would approve of that, miss."

"Listen, what I do is my business, right. I just wanted

you to know, and to tell you that if I don't call back in, by twelve noon, you'd better come out there and get me. Right?"

"Miss Brand, I'm afraid I have to refer this matter to my superiors. If you'll give me your number, I'll come back to you as soon as possible."

"Forget it. You remember, twelve noon. If no call by then, you come and get me at that address." She hung up. She felt quite pleased with herself.

It was a glorious day, just right for a ride into the country. She and Doug had liked to do that, whenever possible. But last weekend she had gone to visit Sue and Robert Holt down in Cornwall, by herself. Sue and Robert were Americans, and they had a lot in common. Why in the name of God had she chosen to do that last weekend?

If she had stayed . . . but if she had stayed, she might well have stayed the night with Doug; they often slept together on Saturdays, as Sunday was the one day Doug didn't train. In which case she might be lying in a police morgue now herself, evidence in a murder case. After having been . . . what did it feel like, to be castrated? In Doug's case, nothing, according to the police: he had been anaesthetised. But when they'd stripped him naked and tied him to the bed he must've known that something ghastly was going to happen to him. What had he said? Had he begged, or had he fought? He'd been a powerful man, and there had been some evidence of a struggle in the living room.

Had she been there, what would she have done? But what was she going to do now, bearding this man Rudder in his den? She had no idea, save that of panicking him into doing something stupid. To her? There had been evidence of a struggle in Angela Moresby's living room as well . . . only it hadn't been a struggle. According to Anne Moresby it had been Jonathan Rudder breaking the place up.

It was still early in the morning, and she made good time along the M4. More planes were landing than taking off at Heathrow; several of them would be the overnight flights from the States. She would have to be on one of those when it went back again, some time soon. Of course the job was still there, and when she had taken it she had given no immediate thought to a return home. But over the past year England had come to be identified with Doug. She wasn't sure she wanted to go on living here.

Mom thought she should go home right away. When she had called to tell her what had happened, Mom had been almost more upset than herself. Mom had fallen for Doug, for his health and strength and also for his international renown. The thought of him murdered, even if she hadn't known any of the details, had been more than she could bear. She had wanted Jennifer to catch the next plane home. And Jennifer had wanted to go, instinctively. Then she had reminded herself that she couldn't go until after both the funeral and the inquest – both of which were to be next week. And anyway, she wasn't going anywhere, until the police had caught Doug's killer. The trouble with the goddamed British was that they didn't have the death penalty!

Past the airport, she pulled on to the hard shoulder and got out her road atlas, before turning off to the south. Following the main routes had been easy, but now she was plunging into a world of lanes and high hedgerows; she knew she was close to this Blessop Manor place, but she could be a hundred yards away and not see it. She heard the blare of a horn, and peered ahead in alarm; there was no room for cars to pass in this lane. She watched the Mercedes coupe come round the bend, at some speed, and scrape to a stop only a few feet from the bonnet of her Renault. Predictably, the horn blared again.

Jennifer wondered if she should blow back. Before she could make up her mind, the driver of the Mercedes had leaned out of his window. "Back up!" he bawled. "There's a field a hundred yards back. You can pull in there."

Jennifer considered giving him two fingers, but he had the bigger car. She backed up; she remembered the field, and the gap in the hedge. She reversed into this, and the Mercedes drew level and stopped. The man behind the wheel grinned at her. "Sorry about that, but I'm in a bit of a hurry."

He was a very large, rather attractive looking young man. Presumably he would qualify, from certain points of view, as a great big hulk. And he was driving a Mercedes! A penny dropped in Jennifer's brain. "Are you Jonathan Rudder?" she asked before she had thought the situation through.

His smile changed into a frown. "That's right. Who're you?"

Jennifer bit her lip. She had supposed herself in no danger, because they were going to meet in his uncle's house, surrounded by servants and people who knew him . . . there could hardly be a lonelier lane in all England than this one. But she'd started the conversation. "I'm Jennifer Brand," she said. "I was coming out to see you."

"What about?" The Mercedes engine gave a little growl, to suggest that his foot had twitched on the gas pedal.

"It's about . . ." oh, what the hell! "About your fiancée's death."

"Ah," he said. "A reporter. Well, I'd love to talk to you, Miss Brand, but as I said, I'm in a hurry."

"I'm not a reporter."

"Then who are you?"

"I'm Douglas Openshaw's fiancée. I mean, I was Douglas Openshaw's fiancée."

"Douglas Openshaw. Douglas . . . the shot putter! He was murdered last week."

"That's right."

"Small world. Why do you want to see me about it?"

Jennifer got out and went to stand beside his car. Presumably she was increasing the risk factor, but oddly, she felt in no danger from this man. "I think both murders were done by the same people. The police think so too."

Jonathan Rudder frowned at her for several seconds. Then he said, "Get back in your car and follow me."

"Where?"

"Look, just do as I say, will you."

She glared at him, but reflected that she did want to speak with him, and he hadn't jumped out of his car and attacked her. She got behind her wheel, and followed him down the lane. He turned a couple of corners and arrived at a village, and pulled in to park behind the pub. "It's shut," she pointed out.

"Well, we're a bit early. But you can leave your car here. Park over there, and get in."

"With you?"

"You said you wanted to talk with me, and I have somewhere to go. Don't worry, I'm coming back here afterwards, and you can pick your car up then."

To go along with him would be really sticking her neck out. But she just couldn't see this rather gorgeous hunk of manhood cutting his fiancée open. She parked, and sat beside him. "Where are we going?"

"To see a friend of mine."

"Someone involved with the case?"

"Could be." He drove very fast, but with complete assurance; she felt much happier when they were on the motorway. "So tell me about it."

"It wasn't very nice."

"No. Did you find the body?"

"No, I was away. Did you know the police think it could be a ritual killing?"

Jonathan half turned his head, then concentrated on the road again. "Didn't they say that to you?" Jennifer pressed.

"They asked me what religion Angela belonged to. I wondered about that. Why should they think it was a ritual killing?"

"Doug was . . . castrated."

Again his head started to turn. "The police told you that? My God! You've been through it."

"That's why I came to you. Was your Angela mutilated?"

"Yes. I don't know how badly. I didn't look very closely. I just flipped."

"So I heard."

"The police tell you that, too? How did you get on to me, anyway?" Jonathan asked.

"Not through the police." Jennifer told him about meeting Anne. "She seemed very unhappy about the whole situation. Well, that's understandable. But she seemed to think . . . well, that maybe you'd done it."

"That's Anne." He grinned. "And you thought maybe I'd done them both."

"Of course not," Jennifer snapped; she had never been a good liar. "I think there has to be some connection. Nobody has any idea why Doug should have been murdered. He had no enemies, no vices, nothing. Ditto your fiancée, from what I have been able to gather. But they're both dead. And I want to find out who did it and see that they go away forever."

"Snap!" They glanced at each other, and Jennifer flushed. "Why do you keep saying 'they'?" Jonathan asked.

"Doug was done by two men. They were seen arriving, and they were seen leaving."

"Holy shit! Then the police have descriptions."

"Apparently nothing that's worth a damn. It was night,

and nobody was taking too much notice. You don't think it was two people did for your Angela?"

"Now you come to mention it, it probably was. The police kept talking about them, and it was too slick to have been done by one. But hell . . . do you know what they did?"

"If it's anything like what happened to Doug, they stripped her and tied her up, then they stripped themselves, then they cut her about, then they showered to wash off the blood, dried themselves, and left, with their little bags."

"Bags?"

"The police said they were carrying bags. They also left with Doug's testicles and penis."

"Are you as tough as you sound?" he asked.

"I mean to be." She looked around her; they had turned off the motorway on to King Street through Hammersmith. "Say, where are we going, anyway?"

"To see a doctor friend of mine. Names of James Colley. He works in a private clinic. Just up the Edgware Road."

"Did you say, James Colley?"

"Do you know him?"

"It's one hell of a small world. No, I don't know him. But I do know he was Doug's doctor."

"What did Doug Openshaw need a doctor for? I thought he was one of the fittest men in the world?"

"Well, he is. Was. God, I keep getting mixed up. But last autumn he began to get pains in his right knee. He didn't want anyone to know about it; he was afraid he might get sidelined when it was time for selection for this year's team. So he went to see this fellow Colley. I think he was recommended by his own doctor."

"And Colley cured him?"

"I don't know. He had a preliminary examination, then

he was going to see him again Friday before last. You say this doctor is a friend of yours?"

"We were at medical school together."

"You, were at medical school?"

"Why shouldn't I have been?"

"You just don't look the type."

"It was a few years back. Jim and I drifted apart after I left. But I would say we're still friends."

"And what is he treating you for?"

Jonathan pulled into the carpark behind the surgery. "He isn't. He'd been seeing Angie. She thought she was pregnant. But she wasn't. You'll like him." Jonathan led the way into the reception office, smiled at the woman behind the desk. "Jonathan Rudder. Dr Colley is expecting me."

"You're to go right up." She looked inquiringly at Jennifer.

"She's with me," Jonathan explained, and led Jennifer along the corridor.

"Looks awfully plush," she remarked, glancing at the empty waiting room as they passed.

"It's a plush outfit."

"Which specialises in sportsmen?"

"I wouldn't think so. They specialise in a lot of things. Being outside the National Health, they can act as a sort of clearing house, you know; they send patients all over the world to receive the best treatment."

"Must be expensive."

"Good medicine always is." They went up the stairs and into the outer office.

"Mr Rudder?" asked Nurse Welldon. "Dr Colley is waiting for you." She knocked on the inner door. "Mr Rudder, and . . ." she looked at Jennifer.

"Jennie Brand," Jonathan said.

"Jennifer," Jennifer said. "Jennifer Brand."

"Jonathan!" James Colley was on his feet to greet them,

and clasped Jonathan's hand. "I can't tell you how sorry I am . . . sorry! I'm shattered. Have they got the man who did it?"

"No. This is Jennie Brand."

"Jennifer," Jennifer insisted.

"Miss Brand." Colley looked puzzled.

"She was Douglas Openshaw's fiancée," Jonathan explained.

Colley looked at Jennifer again. "Doug Openshaw's . . . my God!" He looked from one to the other, frowning. "You don't think . . .?"

"Don't get me wrong," Jonathan said hastily. "It's just that the only link between the two that we can find is the Freedom Clinic."

"Come in and sit down." Colley gestured them to chairs in front of his desk, sat down himself, and filled his pipe. "I'm afraid I don't altogether follow your reasoning."

"There is no reasoning. We're clutching at straws."

"The police think that both murders were done by the same people," Jennifer said.

Colley raised his eyebrows. "People?"

"It seems probable there was more than one," Jonathan explained. "And the *modus operandi* was apparently exactly the same in each case. Jennie and I have been comparing notes."

"Jennifer, for God's sake," Jennifer muttered.

"Go on," Colley invited, puffing contentedly.

"Well, it's very odd, don't you think? Why did these people murder Douglas Openshaw? He hadn't an enemy in the world. Why did they murder Angela? She didn't have an enemy in the world either. There has to be a link."

Colley smiled. "And you think I must be it."

"You're the only link we've come across."

"Well, let's see. I first saw Douglas Openshaw at the beginning of this month. He was sent to me by Bobby Enderby. You remember Bobby?"

"I should. He played fly-half for the college when I was a flank forward."

"That's right. Douglas had a knee problem which he didn't want to make public. I was able to help him."

"How?" Jennifer asked.

"I discovered that he needed an operation. It was a little cartilage difficulty. He was afraid that if news of it leaked out, he might lose his place in the British team. So I managed to arrange for him to go to a clinic in France, where it could be done in absolute secrecy."

"This was last Friday, right?"

"Why, yes. He was to go down on Monday. I had to cancel when I heard the dreadful news. But if you were his fiancée surely he told you all this?"

"I never saw him after last Friday morning. I knew he was coming to see you. But I was going down to the country for the weekend. And the next night he was dead."

"My God! You poor girl. But to get back to what we were speaking about, I had of course heard of him before. But I didn't know him. I'd never even met him, until Bobby telephoned and asked if I'd see him. I'm afraid I must confess, Jonny, that I hadn't heard of Angela before you introduced us at the pub last Sunday night; I don't go much for tennis. As you know, she came to see me on Monday morning, and we made a pregnancy test. I have not seen her since. I mailed the results of that test to her on Thursday morning, but she didn't contact me."

"She was already dead," Jonathan said through gritted teeth.

"I know that now. As I said, I am quite shattered. By both of them, so close together. The point is, I certainly didn't get the impression that they were in any way connected, or even knew each other. I can't imagine what the link could possibly be. Apart, as you say, from them both having been here, on totally unrelated matters."

Jonathan scratched his head. "I suppose it was a pretty feeble idea."

"What about this guy Bobby whatever-his-name-is," Jennifer suggested.

"Enderby? He's in general practice. He certainly was a friend of Douglas's. And he had been a friend of yours, Jonny."

"I wasn't murdered."

"Yes, but could he have known Angela?"

"I have no idea. She never mentioned him. You're not suggesting Bobby Enderby had anything to do with Angie's death?"

"You're the one who's doing all the suggesting," Colley said, a trifle wearily. "I'm just trying to help."

"I guess it all *was* a bit feeble," Jennifer said.

"I'm sure the police are getting on with it. Our police are pretty good, Miss Brand. They'll get to the bottom of it."

"Not that oaf Lampson." She stood up, held out her hand. "Thanks for giving us the time, anyway."

"I'm sorry I couldn't be of more help." Colley also got up, to shake hands.

"There's one other thing," Jonathan said. "A personal matter. What I called about."

"Oh." Colley looked at Jennifer.

"I'll wait outside," she volunteered.

"Thanks," Jonathan acknowledged. He watched the door close behind her.

"Pretty girl," Colley remarked. "Known her long?"

"About an hour." Colley raised his eyebrows as he sat down. "She came looking for me," Jonathan explained. "Because of the link, you see."

"The link you haven't been able to establish."

"It's there. It has to be there. Maybe Bobby . . ." he went into a brood.

"You wanted to see me about something," Colley said, gently.

"Oh. Yes. It's my uncle. Only living relative, well, only worthwhile living relative, and all that. He has a dicky ticker. Too bad for pacemakers and that kind of thing. He insists on going by what his GP, a bumbling old fool named Morrissey, tells him. What he needs is a new heart, but Morrissey doesn't seem able to find a hospital to take him in."

"How old is your uncle?"

"Sixty-eight, I think."

"Does he have any family?"

"Yes, me. And another nephew in Australia."

"Hardly dependents," Colley observed.

"He's been through all of that with Morrissey."

"All of these are factors which have to be taken into consideration when one begins talking about heart transplants."

"Listen, Jim, heart apart Uncle Eric is as fit as a fiddle. He could live for years if that was straightened out. And frankly, when you say he has no dependents, you're not quite right." With some embarrassment, Jonathan told him of his financial affairs.

Colley stroked his chin. "Forgive me for smiling, Jonny. What you are asking me to do seems to be to attempt to preserve the life of an ancient layabout to preserve the lifestyle of a somewhat younger layabout."

"Ha ha ha. Have your little joke. When you get down to the bottom line, all you people are interested in is money. Name your price."

Colley considered him for some seconds. "You really are serious."

"Of course I'm serious. Money apart, I'm very fond of the old boy."

"If, and it's a big if, I did find somewhere to take him in and do the job, we could be talking about six figures."

"No problem. He doesn't spend his money, anyway."

"He gives it all to you. There's another point: it certainly would not be in this country. Despite what you read in the newspapers, it really isn't on to buy treatment in front of more deserving cases in the UK."

"So we'll take him abroad."

"Is he fit enough to travel?"

"You find me a clinic to handle him, Jim, and I'll get him there."

Colley shrugged. "I'll see what I can do. Not because of your uncle, not because of you, but because of Angie. If you'd let me go to see her . . ."

"Forget it. She was already dead. She was dead Monday night. While I was boozing at the Sheraton Skyline. You don't have to lecture me about guilt, Jim. Just get my uncle back on his feet." He left the room, banging the door behind him.

"You look all hot and bothered," Jennifer remarked as they went down the stairs. "You sounded all hot and bothered on the other side of that door, too."

"Did you hear what we were saying?"

"Not really."

"Oh, yes, you did. Well, am I guilty of being a layabout?"

"I plead ignorance of the facts. Where are we going now?"

"Back to Blessop. For your car." They roared up the M4.

"You reckon that's a dead end?" she asked, slumped low in the seat.

"Probably. I'll give Bobby Enderby a ring Monday."

"And you'll keep in touch."

He glanced at her. "Would you like me to?"

"We both want to get to the bottom of this, don't we?"

He drove in silence for awhile, becoming more and more aware of her. Of course to think of her sexually, in his circumstances, or hers, was obscene. But then he'd spent his entire life doing the wrong thing. And she was a most attractive girl. "In that case we had better have dinner together. Say Monday night."

"Will you have something by Monday night?"

"I can present a progress report, Jennie."

"If you ever call me Jennie again I shall scratch out both your eyes, even if you're driving. The name is Jennifer."

"Don't you like diminutives?" He drove in silence for some more minutes. "Did you love Openshaw?"

"We were going to get married."

"Not the same thing. I was going to marry Angie. At least, I was, when I thought she was pregnant."

"You mean she wasn't?"

"Apparently not."

"So you didn't love her."

"I really don't know. We lived together. Had a good time. But when you come down it, we didn't have much in common apart from sex. Of course I'm eleven years older than her. Makes a difference, I suppose. How old are you?"

"That's my business."

"I'd put you down as late twenties. I'm thirty-one."

"That must be nice for you."

"But you loved Openshaw."

"Oh, for Christ's sake, can it!" she shouted.

He saw to his surprise that there were tears rolling down her cheeks. He braked and pulled into a layby. "You're not sure." She opened the door and got out, walked up and down; the traffic flowed past. "Come on, get in," he recommended. "It's still twenty miles to Blessop."

"I can thumb a lift."

"Don't be daft. Next thing you'd be raped and murdered yourself."

Jennifer got back into the car, slowly. "Was she raped?"

"She was tied to the bed, spreadeagled, naked, before they killed her. What does that suggest to you."

Jennifer shuddered. "I don't see how you can even think of it, much less speak of it."

"Sometimes I wonder myself. But I don't mean to forget anything about it, just in case I happen to meet up with the chaps who did it."

"I feel the same way."

He had been about to drive off, now he braked again. "Then let's do it together. You and me. Partners to the end of this thing."

"You wouldn't be propositioning me, by any chance?"

"As a matter of fact, that is probably accurate."

"With your fiancée dead not forty-eight hours . . ."

"I know. I'm a shit. But there it is. I'm going to find those people. And anyway, she's been dead five days."

She stared at him for several seconds. "I think maybe you will," she said at last. "And I want to be there when you do. But I'm not ready for bed." She gave another shiver. "I don't think I'll ever be ready for bed again."

He grinned. "I can be patient. Sometimes." They drove the rest of the way to Blessop in silence, pulled into the pub yard. "I feel like a drink," Jonathan said. "And it's open now, for sure."

"What about these tough laws you guys have about drink driving?"

"One drink isn't going to harm us. Come on." She followed him inside, wishing she could make up her mind about him. Was he truly larger than life? Or was he, as he had admitted, a shit? To proposition her the day after he'd discovered his girl had been murdered was the most crass piece of behaviour she had ever even heard of . . . but she was still here. "A pint, Ted," Jonathan said to the barman. "Jennie . . . oops, I meant Jennifer."

"A bloody mary, I guess. Lots of spice."

"One spicy bloody mary coming up," Ted promised.

Jennifer looked at the clock behind the bar. "Hell! A phone! Do you have a phone?"

"Over there, miss," Ted said.

She ran to it, ran back. "It needs coins and things."

Jonathan found some, and so did Ted. "Sounds urgent," Jonathan suggested.

"It is. Or your uncle's house is going to be crawling with cops."

He waited for her to come back, after a vigorous conversation. "Are you trying to tell me you told the police where you were going and that you might need rescuing?"

"You could have been the murderer."

"I still could be. But I hope you managed to put the fuzz off. We don't want to forget the old man has a dicky ticker."

"Oh, Jonathan, I really am most terribly sorry. When I made that arrangement I didn't know. But I did manage to catch them in time. They're not very pleased with me."

"I can believe that. Tell me how come you're on the wrong side of the Atlantic?"

"I work here. Lots of people do, apparently."

He gave his shy, good-natured grin. "*Touché*. One kind of gets side-tracked."

"But you were at medical school, you said. You had a career."

"Wasn't for me." He lifted his pint mug to her, and drank deeply.

"So what do you do?"

"A bit of this, a bit of that. I was in the middle of racing yachts on Long Island Sound when this happened, would you believe it." He finished his drink. "Lunch?"

Jennifer swallowed the last of her bloody mary. "No, thanks very much. I must be getting back."

"To what? You're not going to pretend you work on Saturdays? And you've no boy friend. Come up to the manor and have lunch. Meet my uncle, if he's still alive."

Jennifer considered. But it was past twelve, she was hungry, and it was a long drive back to her flat. Besides, she wanted both to see the manor and meet this remarkable uncle. She drove behind him, faster than she usually did in an effort to keep up, and they screeched to a halt in the forecourt. He jumped out and opened her door for her. "Some pile, eh?"

She looked at the huge iron-bound door, the mullioned windows, and then at the upper storeys and the clustered chimney pots. "Something out of history."

"Soon to be history, alas. When Australian cousin Warren gets his hands on this lot, he'll probably turn it into a nursing home. Come on in." He led her up the steps, and the door opened. Caunt stood there, and beside him, Philippa.

"When Ah heard what haid happened, Ah just haid to come across," Philippa explained.

"Who is she?" Jennifer asked.

"We were racing together . . ."

"On Long Island Sound," Jennifer remembered. "If you don't mind, I'll skip lunch."

Jonathan hesitated, as she returned down the steps and got into her Renault. "I'll be in touch," he said.

"I wouldn't bother." She grated her gears as she drove away.

"Somethin' Ah said?" Philippa inquired.

"You could just have ended a beautiful friendship."

"Shit, Ah just did that, with Bruce, when Ah told him Ah was jumpin' ship. But Ah haid to be with you in yuah hour of need, honey."

Jonathan sighed. He wasn't in the mood to tell her

that if she was rich-husband-hunting, she had backed the wrong horse.

"Does my uncle know you're here?"

"Suah thing, honey. Ah reckon he approves."

"You get all of that?" James Colley asked, leaning back in his chair.

Nurse Welldon nodded. "I told you it was far too risky, taking that girl."

"I don't see why we should be bothered. I'll admit I never expected the two fiancés to get together, but I don't think it's sinister. Jonathan Rudder has nothing between his ears but wool."

"He's a splendid specimen," Nurse Welldon said wistfully.

"Forget it," Colley advised. "He may look like a splendid speciman, externally, but you can take my word for it that every organ he possesses is pickled in alcohol, and that includes his prick. Anyway, think of *that* risk?"

"What are you going to do about this uncle's heart?"

"See that he has the op. It will be rather amusing, don't you think? I wonder whose heart he'll get? But it is something I should handle in person. Telephone Hanson and tell him to have the private jet stand by. I'll fly out at dawn tomorrow morning."

"You will see Schleyer?"

Colley nodded. "I think he should be put in the picture. Dawn tomorrow, Nan."

CHAPTER 4

"Take a look at these." Detective Sergeant Parton placed several fax sheets on Lampson's desk, selected from a sheaf he was carrying.

Lampson glowered at him. He loathed Monday mornings. He loathed them even more when his inferiors were full of the joys of summer. He picked up the sheets and studied them.

"October last year, Malaga, young man found, gutted," Parton said. "November, Alicante, ditto. Again November, again Alicante, young woman, ditto. December, nothing; they must have been celebrating Christmas. January, two in Barcelona, man and woman. Since then, nothing in Spain. The Spanish police eventually formed the opinion that the five murders were committed by the same two men, but have been unable to come up with a motive or any link other than the m.o. They believe it was the work of two madmen, and are just happy that there have been no more.

"Now look at the reports from France. February, one in Toulouse. March, two in Lyons. April, three in Paris. Six deaths, then nothing. The French are still investigating, severally. They have turned up nothing worthwhile, and were surprised by our suggestion that the murders could be connected, and still more that they might be connected with anything in Spain. So, nothing in France since last month. But now, two in London. That's some pattern. And we seem to have been the first force to try to link them up." Lampson continued to read the sheets. "Now let's analyse them," Parton went on. "The man in Malaga was a swimming champion. The one in Alicante a tennis player of some repute. The woman was a show jumper on holiday."

"It says nothing about athletics in Barcelona," Lampson pointed out.

"There's always an exception that proves the rule," Parton argued. "The chap in Toulouse was certainly a well-known rugby player. One of the people in Lyons was a cyclist."

"The other was an ordinary housewife."

"Again, the odd exception. Of the three in Paris, two were known as sportsmen. And both the victims here in London were sportspersons."

"It's a point."

Parton sat down, uninvited. "Surely it's the link we've been looking for?"

"That a couple of serial killers are roaming around Europe murdering sportsmen and women, with one or two on the side for fun?" Lampson's voice was heavy with disgust. "What leads *do* the Spanish police have?"

Parton sorted through his papers. "As I said, virtually nothing, save similarity of method. The descriptions tally with ours as far as they go: two men, one tall and heavily built, the other short and slight, carrying bags. Here's something, though: both are described as wearing moustaches."

"Because a great number of Spanish men wear moustaches. They probably peeled them off the moment they got home, or wherever it is they lurk. How were they dressed?"

"Casual gear."

"Again, because everyone wears casual gear in Spain. Here they wore dark suits and were clean shaven. Fingerprints?"

"None, I'm afraid. They're too smart for that. But there is something a little odd about the casual gear. The smaller man, despite it being damn near a hundred in the shade down on the Costas, wore a heavy sweater over his open-necked shirt."

Lampson cracked a knuckle. "Probably had a cold. What about France?"

"Same again. Four possible sightings. Bags, moustaches in two cases, jackets and ties. You reckon all of these murders . . . my God, it tallies fourteen . . ."

"Up till now," Lampson said grimly.

"You reckon they were all done by the same two chaps?"

"Doesn't matter if it was, or if they're part of a team. All fourteen murders must stem from the same source, if the m.o. is so identical. So, what have we got? A distinct geographical pattern, moving north from Malaga. Which has now got to London. According to this pattern, they will do another three or four in England before moving on. Question is, where? Maybe one more in London . . ." he brooded. "If only we had some idea where they might strike next?"

"It'll be a sportsman. Or woman."

"I can't buy that, Ned."

"Could be some bloke, or blokes, who just lost out at an Olympiad, or something like that, and is bitter and twisted."

"You've been watching too many sub-standard videos," Lampson remarked.

"Well, you suggest something. With respect, sir, a geographical pattern isn't going to do us a lot of good. There are still quite a few cities left in the UK."

"What about records?"

"They came up with the usual crop of gruesomes over the past few years, but none which correspond to this m.o., and none which make sense, if the killings began in Malaga."

"There are lots of Britishers in Spain."

"But we don't have a clue that these people are Britishers." Parton almost wailed.

"I always said the Common Market and free movement between countries was going to cause trouble," Lampson growled.

"Look, sir," Parton said. "Let's consider the absolutely certain facts we have to go on: one, the murders were carried out by someone who had a great deal of anatomical knowledge, and probably surgical training. Probably both the killers had that. Agreed?"

"Agreed."

"Secondly, we have a definite link between these murders and athletes. Even the non-athletes in the list of victims are described as having been young, healthy, vigorous people who lived an outdoor life. All right, the Olympic theory may be a little far-fetched, but what about someone who was once fit and being groomed for a major athletic career and had a severe illness or accident which ruined his chances forever, leaving him a bitter wreck of a man?"

"Who commits his murders from a wheelchair and has somehow accumulated a mate?"

Parton sighed. "The link is there, sir. It has to be. And now we have a pattern. It should be possible to track down a medical man who was in all those places on the required dates."

"That would take months, maybe years, Ned. Because we've agreed that he doesn't have to be a *qualified* doctor, only have some knowledge of surgery. Don't get me wrong. You've done a great job, and your information is certainly going to play its part in nailing these villains, but I've been staying closer to home. Jonathan Rudder."

Parton barely suppressed another sigh. "With respect, sir, Rudder is tied to only one of the murders. Agreed that he stands out like a sore thumb for that one, but even that is too obvious. If he had murdered Moresby, he would surely have covered himself better than he has. And there is absolutely nothing to link him to any of the others."

Lampson cracked a knuckle. "As I said, Ned, it is unlikely that all of these murders were carried out by the same two people, even if they dressed up to look the same. There are just too many; this isn't America, where a serial killer can drift from state to state murdering and all the time merging into the background. An Englishman in Spain stands out like a sore thumb, and so does a Spaniard in England. But I believe there is every chance that they are being carried out by the same group, or organisation, for a motive we do not yet know. The important thing, from our point of view, is to link just *two* of them. Because if we can locate *one* of these killers, and bring him in, we have a door open on the rest. You agree?"

"Entirely, sir. But I don't see how we link Rudder to any of the deaths save Moresby."

"I will tell you how." Lampson tapped a paper of his own. "Here is the report of the tail we put on Rudder, DC Dickinson. On Friday, when he left us, Rudder went out to stay with his uncle, as he said he would. On Saturday morning he left his uncle's house, drove down the lanes in the direction of Blessop Village, and made a rendezvous with . . . wait for it: a lady, whom DC Dickinson later identified as Miss Jennifer Brand."

He leaned back in his chair with a satisfied grin, while Parton drew a long breath. "With respect, sir, we knew that Rudder and Brand were to have a meeting. Brand telephoned this office on Saturday morning to tell us she was going to see Rudder, and requested us to go to Blessop Manor if she hadn't called us back by twelve."

"She's seen even more bad videos than you."

"Yes, sir. Well, DC Martin, who was on duty, passed

the message on to the Berkshire police. I gather they didn't take it very seriously. But as it happened, Brand called back just after twelve to let us know that she was all right."

"Of course she did," Lampson declared. "The whole thing was a set-up." Parton raised his eyebrows. "I don't know why, Ned," Lampson said. "Probably she was trying to hide the fact that they already knew each other. The point is, they didn't meet at Blessop Manor. They met in a lonely lane a mile away from the house. Following which they drove together to the Rose and Crown public house in Blessop, she left her car there and got into his, and they went off to London together. In London . . ." he studied the report, "they went to a place called the Freedom Clinic off the Edgware Road."

Parton frowned. "That . . ."

Lampson held up a finger. "We'll come back to that in a moment. Dickinson naturally couldn't get into the hospital while they were there, so he waited for them to come out, and trailed them back to Blessop again. On the way they stopped in a layby for several minutes, and seemed to be having some kind of an argument. Obviously he was taken unawares by the sudden stop, and had to drive by and wait for them to catch him up again, so he only caught a glimpse of them there. They then drove back to Blessop, Brand picked up her car, and they drove in tandem to Blessop Manor, where they parted, Brand returning to London." He leaned back in his chair again. "What do you think of that? Bearing in mind that Rudder denied ever knowing either Openshaw or Brand."

Parton scratched his head. "It sounds like dynamite. But this chap Rudder must be all wood from the neck up to tell a lie which could be so easily disproved."

"He has that reputation. He could also be pretty arrogant, if he's part of a group which has committed fourteen murders and got away with the lot. But the pattern fits, don't you see? Rudder had an athletic youth; we don't know what went wrong with it. He still lives a pretty athletic life, gads about the world to take part in yacht races and what have you. We also know . . ." he tapped another sheet of paper, "that Rudder was a medical student who intended to become a surgeon but dropped out for some unknown reason. Could you have a tighter circumstantial case than that? Now I want you to compile a dossier on his movements over the past year, with regard to those dates you have. I don't think you'll find they match up – as I say, he has got to be part of a group – but we will need to sift every stone."

Parton did not look entirely convinced. "And the hospital? Do you think that ties in as well?"

"You mean because Brand and Rudder went there together? It's worth thinking about."

"The Freedom Clinic is something of a maverick," Parton said thoughtfully. "It was, and always has been, outside the NHS, and is actually only registered as a nursing home, although it used to have a complete staff of doctors and nurses. But early last year it changed hands. Since then it has operated on a very limited scale. Nowadays it caters for wealthy people who don't feel they can get what they need from the NHS, but as it isn't accepted as a hospital in this country, it recommends people who need surgery to go to specific hospitals abroad. Apparently this is quite legal."

"Well, I suppose Rudder could be tied in with someone on the staff of this Freedom Clinic. Find out just what he and Brand wanted there, who they saw, anything which might be relevant."

"I'll get on to it right away." Parton got up, and stopped. "There are one or two points which still don't make sense. Such as Rudder and Brand being acquainted, and risking meeting so soon after the killings. Do you suppose they carried them out together?"

"The killings were done by two men. But the woman

could be in on the planning side. They both knew the victims just about a year. All these little things fit."

"And what about motive? We know Rudder had a motive for disposing of Angela Moresby, and indeed, for cutting her open and taking away her womb; the other organs could just have been a cover. Then he could claim that she wasn't pregnant, while all the time he knew she was and killed her because of it. And it is possible we might unearth a motive for Brand to want Openshaw dead, although for the life of me I can't think of one right now. But what about the other twelve? Where's the motive?"

Lampson shrugged. "We'll find it, Ned. We'll find it. But that's a good point about Moresby's pregnancy. Find out the name of her GP and let's get the facts on that. And . . ." he pointed, "continue to keep Rudder under surveillance, and put a man on Brand as well."

"Will do." Parton nodded and left the office.

Lampson leaned back again with a contented smile. He was getting places, as he always did, by concentrating on the essentials.

Philippa Morgan stood on the terrace of Blessop Manor and stretched. She wore a dressing gown, and as Jonathan knew, nothing else; as her long arms reached up to heaven every contour of the superb body beneath the thin material was delineated. "This place grows on me with every minute," she remarked. "Gee, yuh guys are lucky."

"You think so?" Jonathan attacked his eggs.

"Waill, haill, to laive in a place like this, so quiet and peaceful . . ." she sat opposite him; the robe flopped away from her breasts. Predictably, she was not bothered by the recurring presence of Caunt. "How's the old boy, today?"

"Improving."

"Yuh reckon this doctor fraiend of yours is really gonna be able to hailp?"

"If anyone can, it will be James. Now we have to talk about you." It was Monday morning, and he could not pretend to have had a boring weekend. Nor had it been spent in a suitable state of mourning. He had at least refused to share a bed with Philippa. She had been put out by that, but clearly regarded his scruples as temporary, and in any event, she had equally clearly enjoyed having the use of the Blue Room all to herself, nestling in the huge tester and looking at the framed masterpieces on the walls as she fell asleep. There were probably at least a million people in the United States who were far wealthier and lived on a far grander scale than Eric Rudder, but Philippa Morgan was not one of them.

The trouble was, Jonathan also knew his chastity was a temporary arrangement. He was desperate to get his hands on her again. Her arrival had been strangely gratifying, even if he was sorry about the way Jennifer Brand had taken it. But the fact was that a girl like Philippa, of tenuous background and very evident foreground, who lacked the essential vulnerability induced by the desire to love and be loved in a sacred rather than profane fashion, was what he wanted. If she was digging for gold, she was in for an unpleasant surprise: anyone who went prospecting had to accept the risks.

But having considered all of that, and well aware that he had never loved Angela and felt more anger at the fact that she had been killed and the manner in which it had been done, than the realisation that *she* was dead, he still had not bedded Philippa. He intended to, of course, but the immediate desire had been absent. Equally, although he had set out once or twice with the idea in mind, he had not got drunk since discovering Angela's body. He was obsessed with the need to think clearly, to be ready to *do*, whenever the chance arose. "Don't worry about me," Philippa told him. "Ah'm a free agent."

"And you expect to spend the rest of your life here?"

"Ah maight consider that if someone asked me. But . . ." she hurried on as she looked at his expression, "these are early daiys. Ah feel the least Ah can do is hailp yuh cope with yuah grief."

"The best way you can do that at the moment is to spend today here," he told her.

"Where are yuh goin'?"

"To a funeral."

"Say, Ah laike funerals. Why cain't Ah come too?"

"Because you are not invited," he told her.

Philippa watched Jonathan drive away with a pensive expression. From the moment she had first seen him at Kennedy last Tuesday afternoon, she had marked him as the sort of man she had been looking for, all of her life. Philippa had never had any illusions about herself. She had come up the hard way, via stripping and a massage parlour, blessed at once with a body which was superbly shaped and a constitution which could withstand almost every form of sexual buffeting; if the right man could still turn her on, sex or looks were no longer of any great importance. The only thing that mattered in this world was money, and as she had no hope of achieving any on her own, it had to be via marriage. But she understood very well that she was not suited to be the wife of a high-powered businessman like Bruce Hardy; nor did she have any great wish to enter the social whirl, where she could be put down, at least conversationally, by any sophomore from Vassar. A wealthy loner like Jonathan Rudder was ideal.

Save that, having rushed across the Atlantic to be at his side – and burned some bridges to do so, for Bruce Hardy was not a man who forgave sudden desertions – she had discovered that Jonathan was not wealthy in his own right; his money came from his uncle. Fair enough;

the great lout would probably inherit. But there was no guarantee of that, just as there was no guarantee, judging by his offhand behaviour, that Jonathan would ever consider her as more than a bedmate – whereas Eric Rudder's eyeballs had virtually popped out of his head when they had been introduced. Over the weekend she had made sure the old man's first impression had been reinforced, time and again. She had been kind solicitude itself, while wearing her most prevocative clothes and her most ingenuous mannerisms.

So Eric was very ill; everyone seemed to be straining every nerve to keep him alive. It was an enterprise in which she could profitably involve herself, with who knew what rewards at the end of the day. She had nothing to lose, and she had read enough cheap romances to know that it was not impossible for old men who were still able to appreciate a good pair of tits to marry them and go out in a blaze of glory, especially if the owner of the pair had proved herself to be an able and willing nurse and companion. She left the terrace and walked slowly across the drawing room, allowing her toes to sink into the soft pile of the Persian carpet. She stood in front of one of the suits of armour, raised the visor, and let it drop with a clang. To think that she might, just might, wind up owning all of this! Caunt appeared. "You rang, miss?"

"Just testing." She went up to the Blue Room – more luxury than she had ever known in her life before – and had a long and sensual bath. Then she perfumed herself, brushed her hair, and went along the wide corridor to Eric's bedroom, knocked, and entered. "How are you today?" she asked brightly.

"The better for seeing you," he replied. She smiled, and crossed to his bedside, leaning over to give him a kiss on the forehead, and at the same time slipping the cord of her dressing gown so that it fell open; a nipple brushed Eric's cheek. "I have a heart condition," he reminded her.

"We are gonna get yuh waill again." She sat on the side of the bed, dressing gown still flopping open. "Aren't we?"

Eric's hand moved, to rest on her thigh. "Do you mind?"

"Yuh can touch anythaing yuh laike," she assured him. "Ah'm heah to make yuh happy."

"I thought you were here to make Jonathan happy."

"Jonathan and I haive nothin' goin' for each other. Ah'm not suah he has anythin' goin' in any direction. He's not gettin' anywhere with finding you a hospital."

"I thought he was hoping for something from some friend of his."

"Ah don't thaink it's gonna come off. But Ah haive an ideah. May Ah borrow yuah car?"

"Have you ever driven in England?"

"Ah cain draive anywhere," Philippa asserted. "It's just a matter of rememberin' which side of the road yuh're on, raight?"

"And where are you going to go?"

"Ah'm gonna sort thaings out for yuh," Philippa promised. She leaned over him to give him another kiss. "Ah'll be back this afternoon. For tea."

The details of Douglas Openshaw's funeral service had been in the newspaper, and predictably, despite the rain, there was a very large turn out; not only members of the British Athletics Team but a host of sports personalities were present, as well as many other celebrities – it was clearly one of these occasions where to be seen to be present was as important as actually being there. Openshaw's elderly father, walking with the aid of a stick, was very much in evidence, as was Jennifer, spectral in black, who held his arm much of the time, and was herself escorted by a handsome middle-aged man who emerged from a Rolls and was, Jonathan guessed, Richard Ebershaw. He also surmised that the very expensively dressed woman walking on the other side of Ebershaw was his wife, but that didn't mean he might not have a considerable rival for Jennifer's affections.

Was he looking for Jennifer's affections? She was such a prickly little person . . . he would do better with just her body. But she was an interesting young woman quite apart from their joint quest. He stood at the very back of the church while the prayers were read, and felt his anger growing. He was going to have to do this again on Thursday, for Angela. It was only when the brief service was finished, and the mourners had moved into the garden to look at the wreaths – while the police surreptitiously removed the coffin back to the morgue – that he went forward.

"What are you doing here?" Jennifer asked. "You didn't know Douglas."

"I know you."

She hesitated, then turned to Alex Openshaw. "Jonathan Rudder, Alex. A friend of mine."

Jonathan offered conventional condolences, waited his moment. "I'd like to have a chat."

"Why?" Jennifer asked.

"I thought we were a team."

"My mistake."

"Look, Philippa was only trying to be sympathetic. She means nothing to me."

"Do you really expect me to believe that?"

"Yes."

She frowned at him, trying to evaluate the truth of his answer. "There's to be a wake. You can come if you like."

"I'd rather not. What about this evening? Where do you live?"

Another hesitation, then she gave him the address.

"You had better have something important to say."

He grinned. "I'll work on it."

Jonathan drove to Angela's flat, went up the stairs with the suitcase he had brought from Blessop. He hesitated for several seconds before opening the door. But there was no smell, and no sign that anything untoward had ever happened there, save that the lounge was almost empty of furniture. There was a note on the table by the door. "Whenever you decide to surface, I wish to see you. Anne." He was sure she did.

He went into the bedroom, again looked at emptiness. The bed had been removed. All the furniture had been removed. The place was spotless, and uninhabited. He opened the cupboards. All of Angela's clothing had been removed as well. A good deal of his remained; on Friday morning he had only taken sufficient for the weekend; there had been too much blood, then. He returned to the living room, called Anne's number. "You bastard," she said.

"Point conceded."

"I want you out of there, today," she told him.

"Look, I didn't do it, you know," he protested.

"You should've been there. Today!"

"I thought you wanted to see me?"

"I never want to see you again, as long as you live."

"Your decision." He hung up, opened the suitcase on the bedroom floor, and began to pack. He couldn't blame her for being angry, and Anne always had been inclined to go over the top. Presumably she was also facing the fact that the fame- and meal-ticket on which she had hoped to ride for the next few years was gone. He felt sorry for her. But then, he felt sorry for himself. When he had finished packing, he sat on the floor and stared at the wall. There was so much to be thought about, so many vague ideas hammering on the back of his consciousness, but all were overlaid with the memory of Angela.

He wondered how long it was going to take to wear off? But then, did he want it to wear off? Not until after the murderers had been apprehended. Why, why, why? The police had not seemed interested in the possibility that it might be a sex crime. Because Douglas Openshaw's had not been a sex crime? Why? Why should anyone, much less any two people, wish to tie Angie to a bed and cut her into little pieces, except as part of a sexual frenzy? Or, as Jennifer Brand had suggested, some kind of ritual. He had no idea what sort of life Angela had lived before they had got together, what peculiar sect she might have belonged to. He just couldn't figure it out. But he had to. Once he knew why, he was sure he would know who.

He frowned. Anne would know things like that. Perhaps he should beard the lioness in her den. After all, she must want Angela's murderers caught as much as he. Maybe he should do that right now. He closed the suitcase, got up, went back into the living room, and looked at the drinks cabinet. It was still full of booze. His booze. And it was after eleven. Way past his drinking time. But he didn't feel like one.

He needed to keep his brain occupied, until that evening, *without* drinking himself insensible. So what was he going to do after that evening? He did not suppose he was going to get either change or entertainment out of Jennifer. See Anne? Yes, he would do that first. And then go back to Blessop, he supposed, and Philippa. But he had to carry some news with him. He telephoned the Freedom Clinic, and after a few minutes was put through.

"Jonathan," James Colley said. "I thought you'd have called before now."

"I've been at a funeral."

"Of course, Openshaw's. I hope you don't feel I should have been there? If I attended the funeral of every one of my patients who died I'd never get any work done."

"Not a good recommendation for your healing powers,"

Jonathan remarked. "When do you hope to have news for Uncle Eric?"

"That's what I was waiting to talk to you about. I *have* something for your uncle."

"Already? That was pretty damn quick."

"We work on Sundays as well, you know. Some of us, when there's an emergency. I want you to bring him in here to me for an examination. How soon can you do that?"

"How soon can you see him?"

"This afternoon."

"I'm in town."

"Can he travel by himself?"

"I'd rather he didn't."

"Then I suggest you get back out to him and bring him in."

"I can't possibly do that before about three. I have somewhere to go, first."

"Then I'll make the appointment for three. If he's as ill as you say, we really don't have any time to spare."

"And you say you've found a hospital to take him in?"

"If we can get him there. A great deal depends on his actual state of health."

"That's tremendous. The idea that he can be fixed up, I mean. I'll see you at three this afternoon. And thanks a million, Jimmy."

"We try to help," Colley said.

The mood of despondency was gone. Something was going to be done about Uncle Eric!

"I'm afraid the blood on Rudder's shirt does not belong to Angela Moresby," Detective Sergeant Parton announced to his superior.

"Then whose is it?" Lampson inquired.

"We don't know yet, sir. Also, we've drawn a blank as regards the Freedom Clinic. But it's not all bad news. DC Dickinson called at the Clinic as instructed this morning, after tracing Rudder as far as the Openshaw funeral. They weren't very co-operative until he threatened them with a warrant, then he was received by a Dr . . ." Parton checked his notes, "Colley. Colley explained that the Clinic's records were confidential, and Dickinson again had to pull out all the stops and virtually threaten a court order. Apparently this Dr Colley got the message that we have our reasons for suspecting Jonathan Rudder of involvement in the death of Miss Moresby . . ." he paused to look at his chief. Lampson grunted. "So he was then willing to co-operate, although . . ." once again Parton referred to his notes, "he seemed more amused than concerned. Seems Rudder is an old friend of his; they were at medical school together." Another glance at his superior. "However, there is nothing sinister about Rudder's visit to the Hospital. His uncle has a dicky heart, and Colley is trying to arrange for a transplant. Simple as that."

"And Colley can do this?" Lampson asked.

"As we discussed this morning, the Freedom Clinic has contacts all over the world, to which they send wealthy patients who need something the NHS cannot immediately provide. Yes, he said they thought they could fix the uncle up."

Lampson cracked a knuckle, thoughtfully. "Dickinson found Colley most co-operative," Parton went on, "although he requested complete confidentiality, of course. But he gave Dickinson permission to interview any members of the staff he wished, and none of them had ever heard of Jonathan Rudder, or his uncle, before a few days ago. Here's an interesting point, though: Colley volunteered that Rudder sent Angela Moresby to him for a pregnancy test last Monday. The day she was killed. This was in preference to her own GP."

"Why?"

"The story given Colley was that she didn't want to go

to her own GP, in case it got back to her mother. Seems the old woman is somewhat strait-laced, and would have taken the news of an out-of-wedlock pregnancy badly."

"And was she pregnant?"

"No, but Colley didn't get the results of the tests until Wednesday. He mailed them to Moresby, of course, but by then she was already dead."

"So when Rudder left England for the States he didn't know whether she was pregnant or not," Lampton said.

"Absolutely. Colley thought they both felt she was, but he supposes that was wishful thinking."

"And you say nothing has turned up? I would say Dickinson has done very well."

"Well, sir, as I said, I am bound to report that Colley scoffed at the idea that Jonathan Rudder could have committed a crime such as the murder of Angela Moresby. Seems the reason Rudder had to give up surgery was that he threw up at the sight of a large quantity of blood."

"That was eight years ago. People change."

"Oh, quite. Colley made that very point."

"Is he seeing Rudder again?"

"Yes. He thinks he has a place fixed up for the uncle to have his operation. He was waiting for Rudder to call him."

"I assume Dickinson made it quite plain that we require his discretion?"

"Absolutely. And Colley was happy to promise his co-operation. Dickinson got the idea that Colley doesn't exactly care too much for Rudder, nowadays. Difference in life-style, I suppose."

Lampson cracked a knuckle. "And what was Rudder doing all this time?"

"Attending Openshaw's funeral. Dickinson called for support. After the funeral Rudder went back to the flat he had shared with Moresby." He paused.

"Could be significant," Lampson said. "But he was probably collecting the rest of his clothes."

"Well, he was there when Dickinson called. He'd picked up the surveillance again by then. So . . .?"

"We wait," Lampson said. "Our man will put a foot wrong, eventually."

Jonathan went down the stairs, closed the street door behind him, crossed the road and placed the suitcase in the back of the Mercedes. As he did so, he saw the small Vauxhall parked on the far side of the street. The same Vauxhall, and the same driver, he had noticed behind him on his way down here this morning, and on Saturday as well. The bastards were tailing him. He grinned. He was just in the mood to give Lampson and his crew the runaround.

Philippa reached the Freedom Clinic at just before twelve; she was unfamiliar with the roads and the one-way systems, and even with her A-Z of London got lost twice, having to stop and ask directions while motorists hooted at her, although the male drivers were usually restored to humour when she blew them a kiss. Then, when she finally arrived at the Clinic, the receptionist was not prepared to be co-operative. "I'm sorry," she said, "but you have no appointment, and Dr Colley is about to go to lunch."

"It's very important," Philippa told her. "It's about Mr Eric Rudder. Yuh do know about Mr Eric Rudder?"

The receptionist had been listening to Jonathan and Colley speaking only a few minutes before. And since the visit of the policeman she was also under instructions to report anything to do with the name of Rudder which came her way. "Oh," she said. "Well, in that case . . . I'll see if he can fit you in." She called, and Dr Colley would be able to see Miss . . .?

"Morgan," Philippa told her. "Philippa Morgan. Ah'm a fraiend of the family."

"Just go up the stairs," the receptionist told her. "Nurse Welldon will be waiting for you."

Philippa smiled at her and hurried up the stairs.

"You called about Mr Rudder?" Nan Welldon was suspicious.

"Ah'm here to see Dr Colley," Philippa insisted.

Nurse Welldon raised her eyebrows; she had not realised the caller was American. "He's waiting for you."

James Colley was on his feet, looking Philippa up and down; in jeans and a loose shirt, her feet in sandals and her hair tied up in a scarf, she was well worth looking at. "Miss Morgan," he said. "Do come in. Mrs Malcolm said you came to us from Mr Eric Rudder?"

Philippa seated herself before the desk. Nurse Welldon returned to the outer room, but left the door open. "That's corraict," Philippa said. "Mr Rudder was wonderin' if yuh-all had any information for haim."

Colley frowned at her. "We *are* speaking of Mr Eric Rudder? He sent you to me?"

"He didn't send me anywhere. But Ah know he's worryin'. Well, wouldn't yuh be, in his condition? So Ah thought Ah'd come down and see yuh for maself."

"May I ask what exactly is your relationship with Mr Rudder?"

Philippa smiled. "At the moment, doc, yuh could say Ah'm his gaiest."

"Are you acquainted with Mr Jonathan Rudder?"

"Suah. We go yacht racin' together."

"And he told you to come to see me?"

"Look," Philippa said. "No one tells me to do ainythain'. Ah'm here because Ah want to help the old man. Raight?"

"I quite understand that. But you do realise that my relationship with Mr Rudder, both Mr Rudders, must remain confidential."

"Suah, as regards the great public out theah. But Ah already know everythain' about Mr Rudder, both Mr Rudders, Ah guess, so yuh won't be breakin' any rules by tellin' me. All Ah wanna know is if yuh haive haid any luck in findin' a hospital for the old guy's trainsplant."

"You haven't spoken with Mr Jonathan Rudder this morning?"

"Not since breakfast."

Colley's frown was back. "Does he know you're here?"

"Say, what's with all these quaistions?" Philippa demanded. "No, he does not know Ah'm heah. He's gone off to the funeral of some guy whose girl he's keen on haimself, as far as Ah cain figure it. So Ah reckoned Ah'd see what's happenin' for masailf. Hell, Ah laike the old guy."

"And Mr Rudder, Mr Jonathan Rudder, told you that it was the Freedom Clinic he was dealing with?"

"Suah he did."

"But he didn't ask you to come to see me?"

"Jesus H Christ! Ah've alraidy told yuh that he didn't. Saind me to see yuh? He'd have the shits if he knew Ah was heah. He'd thaink Ah was musclin' in on his deal with the old guy. All Ah'm tryin' to do is hailp."

"I think I get the picture." Colley leaned back in his chair. "Tell me, Miss Morgan, do either of the Mr Rudders know where you are right this minute?"

"As a maitter of fact, no."

"Does *anyone* know where you are?"

"No," Philippa shouted. "What do yuh think Ah need, a nurse? Ah'm tryin' to help the old main. Thait's all Ah'm tryin' to do."

"Of course you are." Colley was suddenly sympathetic. "May I ask how you got here?"

"Ah'm draivin' the old main's automobile."

"Ah. But he doesn't know where you were going."

"Say, what are yuh? Some kaind of cop? No, he didn't know where Ah was goin'. As far as he knows, Ah've gone for a draive in the country. What the hell does he caire, so long as I come back?"

"Quite." Colley appeared to be considering. "Well, Miss Morgan, if you really are anxious to find out what we are doing to help Mr Rudder, I suggest you wait a few minutes. I'm expecting a telephone call from France at any moment, which will tell me whether there is a bed in a hospital there."

Philippa looked at her watch. "Won't be too long, will it?" She grinned; she and this doctor were at last on the same wavelength, and that being so, she no longer blamed him for his earlier suspicions. "Ah'd kaind of laike to be back at Blessop befoah Jonathan comes home from hais funeral."

"Quite. We won't be more than a few minutes, I promise you."

"Okay." Philippa smiled at him again, and allowed Nurse Welldon to escort her to an upstairs waiting room.

Colley gazed at Nan Welldon as she returned. "I don't think I have ever seen a woman built like that, in the flesh."

"She's been around," Welldon said. "She's probably pretty rotten inside."

"No one could be rotten inside and look that good on the outside. Could be a slight amount of liver damage, maybe, and I'm not suggesting her vagina will be much good to anyone, but we're not interested in vaginas, are we?"

"If you're thinking what I think you're thinking," Nan told him, "you need your head examined. The essential rule about this operation, the reason it has worked so well for so long, is that not one of the subjects has been connected to any other, so the police have always been left with the unanswerable question: what was the motive?

To take two girls, both of whom appear to have been mistresses of Jonathan Rudder, would be madness."

"It's sometimes possible to lose sight of the wood, for the trees," Colley said. "We have been given a quota of three deliveries from London. That seemed straightforward enough. But we cannot continue on our way, following Plan A, when circumstances are making that plan no longer tenable. We have to accept that Openshaw's and Moresby's murders *are* linked, thanks to this woman Brand chasing up Rudder, and between them working out that both Openshaw and Moresby were patients of mine."

"Then maybe she's the one we should use as a subject."

"That would be a real pleasure, but it would give the police too much to think about, in the wrong direction. But we do know, from that detective this morning, that right now the police aren't interested in us: they have Jonathan in their sights. Obviously they think he murdered Angela Moresby because she was about to put the screws on him to marry her. All they're trying to do is link him positively to Openshaw before they move in."

"And they won't be able to do that, so . . ."

"They are going to keep on worrying at it, because they're like that, and there's always the chance that eventually their worrying is going to bring them back to us. Now, let's take this whore Philippa Morgan. She's Rudder's mistress. Seems to me that she's also trying to become his uncle's mistress as well. She's on the hunt for the main chance. That doesn't concern us, except in so far that she's someone this earth of ours will not miss for a moment. What does concern us, and will concern the police, when she is found dead in the same fashion as Angela Moresby, is that both she and Moresby are linked to Jonathan Rudder. They're not going to look too much further."

"He will, of course, deny everything."

"He's denied everything as regards Moresby. But he didn't have a worthwhile alibi there, and he won't have one here. I have sent him out to Blessop to bring his uncle in for an examination. He said he couldn't get out and back for a couple of hours, presumably because of this funeral, so we've settled on three. But he'll be having lunch about now, and then leaving London for Blessop."

"And on the way he stops and murders his current girlfriend, and yet gets back here by three, cool as custard?"

"Whoever carried out the Moresby murder was as cool as custard," Colley pointed out. "Anyway, explaining that will be his business."

"It's still going to be a nice matter of timing."

"Something else *he'll* have to explain to the police. The important thing is that I'll bet my last cent he won't have a cast-iron alibi for the next couple of hours, and what he does have we are going to blow holes in, providing Mrs Malcolm has done her job and made a note of his car number when he was here on Saturday. And during the next couple of hours Philippa Morgan will die and be placed in a suitable position."

"That's going to be another piece of nice timing," Nan Welldon grumbled. "I don't know Marcus and Lois will be available at such short notice."

Colley smiled. "We're not going to use Marcus and Lois. This woman is right here in the hospital. We'll do it ourselves. Now." Nan stared at him with her mouth open. "Have you never wanted to carry out a dissection yourself?" Colley asked. "It's been a long time since my last one. And by God, what a subject!"

Nan blew air through her clenched teeth. "Are you doing this to incriminate Jonathan Rudder, or for spares, or because you want to get your hands on Philippa Morgan's body?"

Colley grinned. "A bit of each, I think. Now move it, there's a lot to be done." He picked up the telephone, and dialled the number of the Clinic Garage.

CHAPTER 5

Philippa Morgan idly turned the pages of her magazine. She wasn't really looking at the pictures. She was more interested in thinking about her little bit of private manoeuvering, which was going to put Jonathan's nose right out of joint, and raise her even further in the esteem of Eric Rudder. She was very pleased with herself; her decision to drop everything and come to England had been purely instinctive – it was reassuring to know that her instincts could be so accurate. The door opened and Nurse Welldon smiled at her. "Dr Colley asks if you will come back in to see him, Miss Morgan."

Philippa got up, noticed that the nurse looked a little strained. Presumably they got worked pretty hard in these hospitals; certainly it was the lunch hour, and the nurse was still here. She turned towards the office, but Welldon gestured the other way. "He's actually along here."

Philippa followed her. The nurse opened a door, and Philippa found herself in an operating theatre. Colley stood by the table, wearing a green robe over his suit – Philippa observed that he had taken off his jacket; it hung on the washroom door. There was no one else present. The room was remarkably bare, save for a large refrigerator in the far corner. "Gee," she remarked. "Ah've never been in one of these before."

"Well, let's hope you'll never be in one of these again," Colley said genially. Behind her, Philippa heard a sound. She turned, to see Nurse Welldon locking the door. "We don't want to be interrupted," Colley explained.

"Yuh guys are way ahead of me," Philippa said. "What's gonna happen now?"

Nurse Welldon was also putting on a green robe, following which she pulled on a pair of skin-tight rubber gloves. Philippa realised that Colley was also wearing gloves. "We'd like you to undress, and lie on this table," Colley said.

Philippa looked from one to the other. "Yuh guys kainky, or somethin'?"

"Why, that's probably true," Colley agreed. "Would you mind hurrying? We're a little pressed for time."

"Shit," Philippa commented. "Yuh want sex from me, yuh goddam well pay for it. And," she added, "Ah charge double for women."

"You said she was a whore," Nan Welldon remarked.

James Colley picked up a gleaming, razor sharp scalpel from the tray beside the operating table. "Now you listen to me, you little bitch," he said. "Undress and get on that table, or I am going to slit you from ass to tit."

Philippa gasped as she realised for the first time that she might be in some danger. "Okay," she said. "Keep your shirt on. Or take it off, if yuh feel laike it. Ah guess Ah can make an exception." She unbuttoned her blouse and threw it on the floor, released her waistband and let the jeans follow; she wore only a pair of briefs underneath.

"Those too," Colley said.

Philippa obeyed, and faced them, inflating her lungs. "So who gaits first go?" she asked.

"On the table," Colley reminded her. She shrugged, climbed on to the table, realised its legs were set in the centre of a large sheet of plastic, which extended some six feet on every side, and the edges of which were composed of two huge zips. "On your back, arms at your sides," Colley said.

Philippa obeyed. Then her eyes widened as Colley produced his needle. "Say . . ."

"It's my fancy," he said. "Fucking unconscious women."

"No way." Philippa attempted to sit up, and discovered herself held by Nurse Welldon, who thrust both arms under Philippa's, and brought them back up in a vicious half-nelson hold. "Hey!" Philippa shouted. "Yuh bitch! Yuh lait me go. Ow, yuh're hurtin' me."

She tried to kick, but she was being forced forward by Nan Welldon's strength as well as her grasp, and was bent almost double. Then she tried to strike behind her, but found she couldn't, while Colley took hold of her right wrist and extended her arm. "Listen," Philippa gasped. "Ah'll pretend to be out, raight? Ah'll . . ." The needle entered her flesh. "Oh, God!" she screamed. "Take it out. Let me out of heah, yuh perverts. Let me . . ." her head drooped.

Colley withdrew the needle, and Welldon stretched the unconscious woman on the table, inhaling harshly as she did so; neither had bothered with face masks. Colley stood above Philippa, stroked her hair from her forehead, and then traced his finger down the line of her jaw, down her neck, around her breasts and down her stomach into her pubic hair. "Don't," Nan Welldon snapped. "That is obscene."

"Marcus and Lois always strip when they do a job like this," Colley observed. "Or do you consider that too to be obscene."

"They have to, to protect themselves," Welldon said. "We do not have to, here. But yes, I do think it is obscene. Especially the way they tie them up. That's not necessary, once they've been given the injection."

"It is necessary, darling," Colley explained. "I thought

that one up myself. Tying them up and mutilating them maintains the pattern of ritual murder, and confuses the police. Besides, they do enjoy it so."

"Exactly. I think they are both maniacs. I wonder if we are not all maniacs."

Colley stood above the unconscious woman, scalpel in hand, considering. "Would you include Schleyer in that?"

"He's the biggest maniac of all, for thinking this whole thing up."

"He would regard himself as one of the great benefactors of mankind," Colley argued. "He destroys the uselessly beautiful, in order that others may live. And you take his money without a murmur of protest."

Nan Welldon gave a little shudder. "I don't admire myself for it. I keep wondering, what if all of these creatures are waiting for us on the other side?"

"There is no other side," Colley said reassuringly, as he made the first incision.

By the time Colley was finished, forty-five minutes later, Nan Welldon felt quite sick, and she was an experienced staff nurse. By that time too, both the body and the plastic sheet were a mass of blood; the organs which had been removed lay in special trays. Now she helped Colley roll the body off the table, so that it fell with a thump on the sheeting, causing blood to scatter like spray. Welldon wheeled the table away, leaving bloody marks on the floor beyond the sheeting, then she returned to help Colley fold the sheet up, very carefully; quite a lot of blood spilled on the floor, but most was retained within the sheet, which was then sealed with its zips. Colley unlocked the door. "Have you the body bag, Mrs Malcolm?" he called.

"Right here, doctor. Shall I bring it in?"

"I don't think you'd better. But I wish this theatre thoroughly washed out this evening."

"Of course, doctor. And Mr Bell says to tell you that both cars are ready for you. He's taken yours away as you wished."

"Thank you, Mrs Malcolm." Colley smiled at her, and returned inside with the body bag to where Welldon waited by the dead woman. While he had been speaking with the receptionist, she had been placing the organs removed from Philippa Morgan's body in the refrigerator in the corner of the room. Now she helped Colley force the plastic sheet into the body bag. The bag was then clipped shut, and the two of them went into the washroom to remove their gowns and gloves. They no longer spoke; there was nothing to say, and even Colley was a little subdued after what he had done. They left the theatre, put on fresh gloves, took the bag out the back, and placed it in the boot of Eric Rudder's car. The number plates of this car had been changed; the old, correct, plates lay on the back seat.

Colley looked at his watch; it was just after one. "I'm expecting Mr Rudder at three, with his uncle," he told Mrs Malcolm, who was watching them benevolently. "If I'm late coming back, ask them to wait, please. Tell them I've been called out on an emergency."

"Of course, doctor."

He got behind the wheel of the Honda, Welldon got behind the wheel of the other car, a dark-blue Mercedes with the same number plates as that of Jonathan Rudder's, which had been delivered from the garage a few minutes before in exchange for Colley's BMW, and they drove out of the yard. He continued up the Edgware Road until he joined the M1, increased speed as far as the Baldock exit, then through Slip End to Royston. At Royston, he turned off into the empty country south of the River Cam, until he reached the small wood he was seeking. Nan Welldon stayed behind him, her fingers playing on the wheel in nervous agitation every time they stopped at a light.

When they reached the woodland, about an hour after leaving the Clinic, Colley stopped the car. Welldon pulled alongside him. "Ten minutes," he told her; there was no point in them both taking risks, and besides, the more people who saw what appeared to be Jonathan's car in the vicinity, the better.

She nodded, checked her watch against his, and drove off. Colley turned down a lane between the trees, drove for some four hundred yards until he knew he was entirely concealed by both trees and bracken, stopped the car again, got out, and looked around him to make sure he was alone. This was actually the most dangerous part of the entire operation, and the adrenalin was pumping through his arteries. But it did him good to be back on the active side of the business; he had begun it all, a year before, on a very small scale, until Schleyer had decided to expand, had purchased the Freedom Clinic as a London clearing house, and had pulled him out to administrative duties. He had missed the old life. Now he felt exhilarated, and moved with practised speed, pulling on a pair of overalls which covered him from neck to ankle, and taking off his shoes and socks.

It was a matter of only a few minutes to unscrew the false plates and restore the real. Then he again checked that there was no one around, opened the boot, and took out the body bag. For all his slight build he was a very strong man, but he was still pouring sweat by the time he had hefted the body bag into the back seat of the car. He opened the bag and dragged out the inner, plastic sheeting, unzipped this, and literally emptied Philippa on to the seat. Some of the blood had dried, but there was still a lot around, and this immediately began to gather on the floor of the car. Colley dragged the plastic out from beneath the body, and stuffed it into the body bag. He closed and locked the car doors. Philippa lay on her face, half on and half off of the seat and Colley took the body bag away from the car into the bushes. There he removed his overalls, which were bloodstained, and put them too into the body bag, together with his blood-wet gloves. Then he put his shoes and socks back on over his bloodstained feet, and carried the bag back to where the lane joined the road.

At the appointed time, ten minutes after they had parted, Nan Welldon returned with the Mercedes. Colley threw the bag into the boot, and got in beside the nurse. Nan drove back at the same steady speed, taking the A10 now, into Central London and the firm's garage. The doors opened at the light signal, and they went inside. The mechanics were waiting for them, as was Colley's BMW, and the spray painting team to change both colour and plates on the Mercedes. Colley handed over the bag to be incinerated, got behind the wheel of the BMW, Nan beside him, and drove back to the hospital. "Do you feel all right?" he asked.

She shuddered. "I feel that I need a stiff drink."

"You shall have one, after we've seen the Rudders. Business before pleasure, my dear." Nan shuddered again.

The wake for Douglas Openshaw, organised by Richard Ebershaw, was a dismal affair, at least for Jennifer Brand. All the celebrities were there, and everyone kept saying what a great chap Douglas had been, and how *awful* that he should have been murdered . . . and not one of them knew the truth of the matter. It was that truth which kept hammering on Jennifer's mind – that and the recurring presence of Jonathan Rudder. She had liked the big man on sight. Perhaps that had been a mistake. Now he came across as a shameless womaniser, who also drank too much, and had made a complete hash of his life. But she still liked him.

And maybe he was the ultimate key to Douglas's killers,

if the same two men had murdered both Douglas and Angela Moresby. But if they had, in such a way, then it had to have been ritualistic, as the police apparently felt. And Jonathan apparently knew nothing about any involvement Angela Moresby might have had with the shady side of religion. He might not have known her as well as he thought he did. On the other hand, she hadn't really known Doug very well. Certainly she knew very little about his life before they had met, save the public side of it. He had had the reputation of being a loner, a man who did his own thing and went his own way; his decision to marry had come as a great shock and, she suspected, a great relief to his England team mates and managers.

But might he not have opted to marry, undertake such a change in lifestyle for him, simply because he had turned his back upon involvement with some sinister group and was endeavouring to normalise his relations with the outside world? And the group had taken a terrible revenge? She supposed that was pretty far-fetched. But it was at least positive thinking, supposing she had the slightest idea of how to find out if it could be true.

"You don't look happy," Richard Ebershaw said. "Well, nobody expects you to look happy. But right now you're looking downright miserable."

"Um," she said. "Richard, would it be very rude of me just to slip away? I'm finding this awfully depressing."

"I understand. No, you leave whenever you feel like it." He held her hand. "Jennifer, you do understand that I'm always here, any time you feel like help. Just give me a ring. Or tap me on the shoulder in the office."

"I understand that, Richard. And I'm grateful. See you." She went to the door, looked back into the room, and saw Roxanne Ebershaw watching her. Oh, shit, she thought. A jealous wife! But Richard wasn't like that, surely?

She drove back to her flat, parked, and went upstairs. She had more important things to think about than Roxanne Ebershaw. How to find out something about Doug's background? Alex would be no help: he and his son had been almost strangers. Nor did she suppose any of the team would have a clue. She closed the flat door behind her, and snapped her fingers. Of course: his doctor! Surely his doctor would have known if Doug had ever indulged in any peculiar sexual rites. His doctor . . . the man who had sent him to the Freedom Clinic. But she couldn't remember his name. Damnation! Jonathan would know, of course, but Jonathan wasn't coming until tonight, and she didn't know where he was, right this minute. But that nice man Colley had known. It would give her a start.

The time was twenty past one. But he might still be there. She called the Freedom Clinic. "Dr Colley, please," she said. "It's most urgent."

"I'm sorry, dear," the woman said. "Dr Colley has just gone out on an emergency."

"Oh, heck," Jennifer said. "Do you have any idea when he'll be back?"

"No, dear. But it won't be for at least two hours."

"My name is Jennifer Brand. Dr Colley knows me. Would you ask him to call me at this number . . ." she gave it, "the moment he gets back? It really is important."

"Of course, dear," Mrs Malcolm said.

"London?" Eric Rudder asked plaintively, when his nephew reached Blessop at ten past two, having lunched rather well, for all that his call on Anne Moresby had proved abortive – she hadn't been there. But his game with the detective had been hugely enjoyable, and entirely successful, although he supposed the poor fellow would eventually turn up here, looking for him. "I don't want to go to London."

"You must," Jonathan explained. "James must examine

you and make sure that you can stand the op and that you're fit to travel."

"But why is there this rush?"

"Because it's urgent. Can't you see that, Uncle Eric? Every day is vital."

"Oh . . . well." He put on his jacket. "When will we be back?"

"Depends how long the examination takes. I would say by six at the latest."

"Caunt! When Miss Morgan gets home, tell her we'll be back by six. You may serve dinner at eight."

"Just where is the fair Philippa, anyway?" Jonathan asked.

"She went for a drive. Said she wanted to explore the country."

Jonathan frowned. "In whose car?"

"My Honda. It doesn't get much use nowadays."

"And do you suppose she is capable of coping with right-hand drive, manual gears, and our roads?"

"She seems to be a very capable young woman," Eric declared, somewhat sharply.

Jonathan shrugged; he was well aware that his uncle regarded the appearance of Philippa as the best thing since sliced bread. "It's your car. Let's go."

They reached the hospital at ten past three. "Oh, Mr Rudder," Mrs Malcolm said. "Dr Colley was called out on an emergency, but he'll be back in a few minutes. Do take a seat in the waiting room."

"Typical," Eric snorted. "Have you ever been to a doctor's surgery where you weren't kept waiting?"

"Yes. Here," Jonathan told him.

And only a few minutes later the BMW pulled into the yard, and Colley and Nurse Welldon got out. Colley came straight into the waiting room. "Sorry about that, Jonny."

"Emergency, was it?"

"Emergency, my foot. This chap thinks he's ill when he's as fit as a fiddle. The ultimate hypochondriac. Trouble is, he's one of our wealthiest patients, so . . ." he grinned at Eric, held out his hand. "Mr Rudder. Come on up to the surgery."

Jonathan went upstairs with them, but remained in the outer office while Eric went in with Colley. "Would you like a cup of tea, or coffee?" Nurse Welldon asked.

"No, thanks." Jonathan smiled at her, realising for the first time what a pretty woman she was, with her red hair and pink and white complexion. More pink and white this afternoon than he remembered, she seemed to be in the grip of some strong emotion. He thought it might be rather pleasant to be in the grip of Nurse Welldon's strong emotion, then reminded himself that he had sufficient female problems already.

Colley opened the door. "Come in."

Jonathan frowned. "Don't tell me he's not up to it?"

"Actually, Mr Rudder is better than I hoped. He has a strong constitution." Colley sat behind his desk and Eric emerged from behind the screen, knotting his tie. "Now, I have booked him in at the La Croix Clinic outside Antibes. They are expecting him tomorrow."

"Can he fly?"

"Yes. I don't think it would be a good idea for him to travel alone, however."

"Don't worry about that. I'll accompany him."

"Fine. I hoped you'd say that. Very well. At the Clinic, Mr Rudder, you will be interviewed and examined by Dr Hans Schleyer. He is both the principal of the Clinic, and the man who will carry out the operation."

"Suppose he decides I am not fit enough?" Eric Rudder inquired.

Colley smiled. "He will hardly do that, as I have already examined you. It is a technical matter, that is all. However,

I must inform you that the fee will be twenty thousand pounds." He paused, looking from face to face.

"What does that cover?" Jonathan asked.

"Everything. There are no hidden charges."

"But my uncle will have to wait in the Clinic for a suitable heart to be found, will he not?" Jonathan asked. "That could take weeks."

"That is a risk Dr Schleyer is prepared to accept," Colley said. "Obviously he is sure it will not take weeks. If you wish to proceed, the fee is payable in advance."

Jonathan looked at Eric, who produced a chequebook, and wrote the cheque. He grinned at the young doctor. "What happens if I don't survive the op?"

Colley handed the cheque to Nurse Welldon. "Half the fee will be refunded," he said seriously.

Jonathan felt more exhilarated than ever, and telephoned Jennifer from the hospital, Mrs Malcolm generously allowing him the use of her switchboard. "We're finished for the night anyway," she explained.

"Listen," Jonathan said when Jennifer answered. "I'll be with you for dinner."

"I'm not going out tonight." She sounded disgruntled.

"Well, then, you can feed me."

"Forget it. I shall be in bed."

"I'll be there. I have a proposition to make."

"Forget that too. I already told you no."

"This is important. How would you like a trip to the south of France?"

"With you? You have to be nuts."

"With Uncle Eric. I'm taking him to hospital down there, for heart surgery. So I thought you might like to come along."

That made her think for a moment. "I'm sorry," she

said. "I'd love to help your uncle, but I have to be in London for the inquest into Douglas's death. That's on Friday."

"No problem. I have to be back for Angela's funeral, on Thursday. We'll fly down tomorrow, back on Wednesday afternoon. I'll see you tonight at ten, and we can sort out the details then." He hung up before she could argue further, telephoned British Airways to book three tickets, to be collected at the airport the following morning, then called an hotel he knew in Antibes to book a double room – Uncle Eric would presumably move straight into the Clinic.

"You'll like her," he promised his uncle as they drove out to Blessop.

"I think Philippa should come with us," Eric suggested mildly. "She could stay and help nurse me, if she's nothing better to do."

"Girls like Philippa always have something better to do," Jonathan told him. "As for her coming to France, that's definitely out. In fact, I'd be grateful if you didn't even mention it to her."

Eric considered that somewhat morosely for the rest of the drive, and then became quite upset when they arrived at Blessop just before five, to discover that Philippa hadn't returned yet. "She's had an accident," he said. "We must call the police."

"If she has had an accident, the police would have called us," Jonathan pointed out. "It's more likely she has got herself lost. Or absconded with your car." But he realised that was unlikely when he checked the Blue Room; all of her clothes were there, together with her credit cards. And Eric was definitely agitated, which was the last thing Jonathan wanted at this stage. "All right," he said. "I'll call the police. You go and lie down. Tomorrow's going to be a busy day." He telephoned the local station. "The lady left here at about ten-thirty this morning to go for a drive," he told the duty sergeant. "She was driving a red Honda Civic, licence number . . ." he looked at Caunt, who supplied the number. "She told my uncle she was going for a spin, and would be back for tea. But she hasn't returned. Do you have any accident reports involving a red Honda?"

"No, sir," the sergeant said.

"Well, what do you suggest we do? I mean, she's been gone pretty near eight hours."

"Well, sir, she could have intended to go somewhere, to visit a friend, and not told you where that was," the sergeant suggested.

"Hardly likely. She only arrived in this country from the States on Saturday. She knows no one here."

"Hm," the sergeant commented. "Do you wish to make an official report that this woman is missing, sir?"

"Oh, lord, I don't know. What do you recommend?"

"Well, sir, I would certainly recommend that you give it a few more hours. After all, it's just gone six-thirty. It's still broad daylight. If she's not back by dark, well, then, perhaps you should contact us again."

"Oh. Right. And your name is?"

"I shall be off duty at eight, sir." The voice sounded relieved at that. "The Duty Sergeant will be Sergeant Clayton."

"Right. I shall call Sergeant Clayton if she's not back by dark."

"You do that, sir."

Jonathan looked at Caunt. "They don't want to know, unless we make an official missing person report."

"I am sure the young woman will reappear, sir," Caunt remarked.

"You know, that sounds as if you don't entirely approve of Miss Morgan, Caunt."

"Do you, sir?"

"Snap." He went upstairs to bring his uncle up to date. "Now don't you worry," he said. "She'll be home any minute now. You've had a tiring afternoon. Have an early supper, and tomorrow we're off to France."

Jonathan had a shower and then drove back down to London, to the address in Chelsea Jennifer had given him. She had changed from her funereal black dress into jeans and a shirt, her feet were bare, and she looked thoroughly domesticated. But as aggressive as ever. "Well?" she demanded.

"It's been a long day. Do you have such a thing as scotch whisky? Or any whisky."

"I'm not going to give you one," she said. "I would be encouraging you to break the law. You are intending to drive home, aren't you?"

"As a matter of fact, I thought you might give me a bed."

"Do you know, you have more gall than anyone I've ever met?"

"You've been moving in very restricted circles." He had by now located the drinks cabinet, and poured himself a scotch and water. "You?"

"I'm on coffee."

"Caffeinated, I hope. I want you to stay awake."

"I think you should know that I am perfectly willing to call the police and have you thrown out of here."

Jonathan sat down. "I told you, I'm taking Uncle Eric to Antibes tomorrow, to a clinic which hopefully will give him a new heart and another twenty-five years of life."

At least she sat down. "That's wishful thinking,

Jonathan. The track record for new hearts is more like twenty-five weeks. Supposing the operation is successful at all."

"Oh, it will be. James has given me his word."

"Great for James. Believe me, I wish your uncle the very best."

"I shall tell him those kind words. But you'll tell him yourself. You're coming with us."

"Why?"

"Because I want you to."

"Quite apart from any reservations I might have, won't you be overloaded with women?"

"Philippa won't be there."

"Is that her name? Philippa?"

"Look, she's a broad I met in Newport. When I went over there I didn't have a care in the world. I was out for a good time. Angela knew that was what happened when the boys got together to race yachts. She wouldn't have minded. So I shagged Phil. Okay?"

"It seems to be, in your book."

He drank, deeply. "So then I telephoned Angie, couldn't get a reply, came home, and found her dead. Believe me, nobody could have been further from my mind than Phil. Permanently. Then I met you. You have a lot going for you, in my eyes, at least."

"I shall be forever grateful for such a compliment."

"Sarcasm doesn't become you. I meant it, quite apart from us sharing a bond, what with Douglas and then Angie. You know how I felt, because I told you. Getting home on Saturday and finding Phil waiting for me was the biggest surprise of my life."

"And I suppose you spent the weekend playing Scrabble."

"We didn't play anything else, if that's what's bothering you. As a matter of fact, I have a notion that Phil, having sized up the situation, reckons she might do better with Uncle Eric."

"You have got to be joking. Isn't he over seventy?"

"Not quite. And that doesn't mean he can't get it up, from time to time. As for when he gets his new heart! Either way, she's in for a bit of a surprise. Eric's income dies with him, and he has no share in the capital."

Jennifer went into the kitchenette to pour herself another cup of coffee. "Where does that leave you?"

He followed her, stood in the narrow doorway, filling it. "On my beam ends. Well, not entirely. He has a fair amount stashed away, which presumably he means to leave to me. Although a sizeable proportion of that is going on this operation."

She turned. "Is that why you're so anxious to keep him alive?"

"I'd be lying if I didn't say I had an interest in that. But would you believe I'm genuinely fond of the old buzzard?"

She gazed at him for several seconds, then nodded. "Yes. Yes, I'd believe that."

"Balm to my soul. Will you come to France?"

"I'm a working girl." She moved towards him, but as the cup full of boiling coffee was held in front of her, he decided that she wasn't surrendering – yet.

He stepped aside to let her brush by. "I'm sure your boss will give you time off, in view of everything you've been through."

She sat down, facing him, the cup held in both hands. "He might. And you genuinely feel that once you have me in a French hotel bedroom I will give you my all?"

"I genuinely feel that we may grow to know each other better, and that you may even come to like me a little."

"Chance would be a fine thing. Look, Jonathan, maybe you're telling the truth about this Philippa person, and maybe I over-reacted. It really doesn't mean a damn thing to me who you carry on with, and in what circumstances. As you said, we agreed to get to the bottom of what happened to Douglas and your fiancée, and I am still prepared to go along with that. But I can't see that we are going to get any closer to the truth by my accompanying you to Antibes, save that you are likely to get a rush of blood to the head, and I am going to have to kick you in the balls. Right? So let's leave it. I understand that your uncle has to have top priority right now. So I'll look forward to hearing from you when you get back. Maybe by then the police will have turned something up." She finished her coffee and went to the door, opened it. "Now I'd like to have an early night."

So, fuck her, Jonathan thought as he drove back to Blessop. Then he reflected that that was what he wanted to do, more and more, every time he saw her. But it was not a mutual feeling, and he had never been very good at forcing his attentions on women – it had not often been necessary – so the best thing to do was forget her. He'd take Philippa. Philippa would love Antibes.

Caunt was waiting for him. "I'm afraid the young lady hasn't come home yet, Mr Jonathan," he said.

It was just after ten-thirty, and the evening had closed in. "Shit," Jonathan muttered. "Something must have happened to her, after all."

"I am very much afraid so, sir," Caunt said.

Jonathan sighed and picked up the phone, and went through the whole story again with Sergeant Clayton. "I see, sir. Do you wish to file an official missing person report?"

"I'm afraid I do, sergeant."

"May I ask if the lady is related to you, sir?"

"Not in the least."

"Hm. I know you have stated that she knows no one in Great Britain, but are you certain of this? Are you certain this is her first visit to this country?"

"No, I am not certain. I know damn-all about her." Except that she's a good lay, he thought, but he didn't suppose that was relevant. "Are you suggesting there may be some difficulty in having her listed as missing?"

"Well, sir, the lady is presumably over eighteen. Therefore she is a free agent, and if she is not related to you, then you have no right to, as it were, call out, come in number one, your time is up." The sergeant chuckled at his own joke, while Jonathan began to feel a slow surge of anger. He kept his temper with an effort. "We don't wish to become involved in an international incident, you see, sir," the sergeant went on, genially.

"You don't?" Jonathan said. "Not even when I tell you that the young lady has taken off in my uncle's car?"

"Ah!" The sergeant's tone was suddenly brisk. "Are you saying that the car has been stolen?"

"It has been taken."

"But was it taken without permission?"

Jonathan watched his fingers beginning to curl into fists; but destroying the handset was not going to accomplish anything. "Miss Morgan had permission to take the car out for a spin, Sergeant. That was at ten-thirty this morning. She said she would be back for tea, which is normally taken at four. Thus you may say that her permission to use the car terminated at four o'clock this afternoon. That was over six hours ago."

"Then you are filing a stolen car report, is that it?"

"Yes!" Jonathan shouted. "I am filing a stolen car report."

"Very good, sir. I will just get the necessary forms. Right. A full description . . . Honda Civic . . ." Jonathan could hear the sergeant's ballpoint scraping on the paper.

"Very good, sir. We shall put out a bulletin. We shall be in touch, probably tomorrow."

"Not tomorrow, Sergeant. Tomorrow I am taking my uncle to the south of France."

"Indeed, sir? Holiday?"

"No. To put him into a hospital. I shall be back Wednesday evening. You can reach me Thursday morning. Here."

"Very good, sir. You do understand, sir, that if the young lady is apprehended and can prove that she has a right to be driving the car, there may be legal repercussions?"

"Just find her," Jonathan said. "And leave the legal repercussions to me."

Antibes was bathed in Mediterranean sunshine, as it invariably was in the summer. But the flight had not been an enjoyable one; both Eric and Jonathan had a lot on their minds. "I can't believe that girl would run off with my car," Eric kept saying.

"Well, I don't believe she did either," Jonathan agreed. "But it seems the only way we are going to get the police to go looking for her is to make her appear guilty of some crime. I'll sort it out when I get home. The important thing is that you don't worry." But he could tell the old man *was* worrying, and that worried him.

He had called ahead and booked a car at Nice Airport; it was only a fifteen minute drive to Antibes, but the Clinic was outside the town itself, reached by a winding and not very good road into the hills, with a sharp drop into a ravine on one side – which must do a lot of heart patients a lot of good, Jonathan thought. The property looked down on the sparkling blue waters from its vantage point, but was entirely surrounded by a high wire fence fronted by red notices bearing the skull and crossbones and warning of high voltage; Jonathan had to speak through a telephone next to the iron gates and ask for them to be opened. Fortunately, after a moment the receptionist turned out to speak English.

At the end of a long drive through an avenue of cypresses, they arrived at a forecourt beneath an old chateau; to either side was an inner fence, with a gate, also closed. "Is this a hospital? Or a prison?" Eric asked.

Jonathan helped him up the steps and into a very plush entry hall, panelled in dark wood to help the eyes get over the glare outside, and with a carved wooden staircase leading towards the first floor gallery. The only indication of modernity, or suggestion that they were in a hospital, was the large lift which waited in the far wall, and the nurse in a starched white uniform who sat behind a desk at the foot of the stairs. There was no one else to be seen other than a couple of gardeners trimming the topiary work outside. "Mr Rudder," the nurse said in good English. "Welcome to La Croix. Dr Schleyer is expecting you. Will you take the elevator to the first floor, please."

"Surely we can walk up the stairs," Jonathan objected.

"The elevator, please," the nurse said severely. "You may accompany your uncle."

Jonathan winked at her. "What about Mr Rudder's bags?"

"They will be taken to his room."

"You're all heart." He ushered Eric towards the lift.

"Why do you go out of your way to rub people up the wrong way?" Eric inquired.

"It stops me being bored. Here we are." The ride to the first floor took precisely two seconds, and then they faced a very long corridor, along one side of which was a moving walkway. "These people think of everything," Jonathan remarked, as they passed windows which looked out on a central courtyard; he realised the St Croix Clinic was a very large building indeed

– the original chateau was only a front. Here were square, white-walled hospital blocks and in the yard there were several white-clad nurses, hurrying to and fro.

There was also a white-clad nurse waiting at the end of the walkway, an attractive woman in her late thirties, Jonathan estimated, tall and slim, with straight shoulder length yellow hair descending from beneath her cap – she obviously had little to do with tending patients. "Mr Rudder," she said warmly. "Welcome to St Croix. I am Staff Sister Brigitte Haniff, but you may call me Brigitte." Her gaze flickered over Jonathan. "You will be Mr Rudder's nephew?"

"Spot on. May I call you Brigitte, too?"

"Of course. Will you come in, please. Dr Schleyer is waiting for you." She opened a door and they were shown into a surgery; the door to the inner office stood open, and a man was waiting to shake hands. "Hans Schleyer, Mr Rudder."

Hans Schleyer was just about the same size as Jonathan himself, well over six feet tall and built like an ox; the only real differences were in their colouring, for Schleyer was fair where Jonathan was dark, in their faces, for Schleyer's clipped features were definitely handsome, which could not be claimed for Jonathan, and in their ages: Schleyer was perhaps fifty, although he looked very fit, and if the grasp of his fingers was gentle, there was clearly an immense inert strength lurking in the huge frame. "James Colley has told me all about you." His voice was as soft as his grasp. "Now, if you'll excuse us, Mr Rudder, I would like to examine your uncle immediately. Every moment counts in things like this. I will speak with you later. Sister?"

Brigitte Haniff ushered Jonathan out of the surgery and into one of those so comfortable waiting rooms which seemed to be the hallmark of this group. "Would you like something to drink?" she asked. "Coffee?"

Jonathan looked at his watch. It was just eleven. "You wouldn't have a bloody mary by any chance?"

Brigitte smiled; in addition to her good looks, she seemed very good-humoured – another pleasant hallmark of the group. "I'm sure I can find one for you. Tabasco?"

"As spicy as you can make it."

She returned a few minutes later with the drink, and to Jonathan's surprise, sat down with him. "We understand from Dr Colley that you are your uncle's only living relative."

"Not entirely correct. There is another nephew. But he lives in Australia."

"I'll need some particulars about both your uncle and yourself." She had placed a pad and pen at her elbow.

"Shoot."

It was mainly to do with places and dates of birth, present residence, and what ailments Eric Rudder had suffered from in recent years. Jonathan sipped his drink and felt a pleasant glow creeping over him as he watched her writing; she had good hands, the fingers strong and supple. These people seemed so pleasant, and so utterly efficient, so able to take care of the old boy. "That seems about right. Ah, here is the doctor." She stood up, as Schleyer entered the room.

"I hope you have been properly looked after, Mr Rudder?"

"Oh, indeed. What is the verdict on my uncle?"

The sister left the room and Schleyer sat down. "Obviously he is a very sick man, but I think we have caught it in time. A poor heart condition, left to do its worst over any period, leads to a progressive deterioration of all those organs which depend upon a steady flow of good blood. That in turn can mean that heart surgery would clearly be hopeless. But your uncle's liver and kidneys and lungs appear to be in good shape."

"Well that's the best news I have heard in a long time. How soon do you think you will find a suitable donor?"

"Oh, suitable donors occur all the time. It is just a matter of having the right contacts. I would anticipate being able to operate within the next forty-eight hours."

"That's splendid. Should I stay?"

"There is no necessity for you to stay, although I should think your uncle might appreciate it. However, I must warn you that once we undertake surgery, it may be several days before he can communicate with anyone."

"I understand. And I am sure he will understand too. The fact is, my fiancée is bring buried on Thursday morning, and I really feel I should attend."

Schleyer frowned. "Your fiancée? How terrible. But . . . she cannot have been very old?"

"She was twenty."

"And is dead? My dear fellow, I am appalled. How did she die?"

"She was murdered," Jonathan said. Schleyer stared at him in consternation. "She was tied to her bed, raped, and then cut to pieces," Jonathan said.

Schleyer opened his mouth and then closed it again. "Have the police caught the man who did it?"

"Men," Jonathan said. "There was more than one. They think two. No, they have not caught them."

Schleyer studied him; he had regained his composure. "You must be feeling very upset. And to have your uncle so ill at the same time . . . may I say that you are handling this business very well."

"So what else am I supposed to do?"

"Agreed. But many a man would have collapsed

completely beneath two such blows. Of course you must attend the funeral. Your uncle knows all of this, I suppose?"

"Of course."

"Then he will understand." He stood up, held out his hand. "I think I can at least promise you a satisfactory outcome to your uncle's illness."

Once again Jonathan was aware of the enormous strength in those gentle fingers, as he was continually aware of the tremendous fitness of this man, the sun-browned skin, the whole aura. "I have every confidence in you, doctor," he said. "Although I must say, I wonder how you manage to concentrate, working so close to the beach and the sea."

"It was difficult once," Schleyer admitted. "And I still have a boat, do some sailing. But nowadays, I am more interested in keeping fit. I have my own gymnasium, here in the Clinic. Would you care to see it before you go?"

"Very much."

Schleyer led him down another corridor and opened the door into a very well equipped gym. "I work out here every day." He glanced at Jonathan. "You know, my friend, it would do you no harm to take more exercise, otherwise one day you could be a patient of mine. A bit of this, eh?" He bent and picked up a hundred pound barbell with the greatest of ease.

"People have been telling me that for years," Jonathan pointed out. "But I'm still around. Well, nice place you have here, doc. I must be off."

He turned towards the door, and Schleyer called, "Catch!"

Jonathan swung back in time to see the barbell flying through the air towards him. He caught it, although its force and weight made him stagger against the wall. "Is that how you get your patients?" he gasped.

Schleyer smiled. "Had you any doubts about catching it, Mr Rudder, you would merely have got out of the way, would you not? As I surmised, you are fitter than you look." He came across the room, took the weight from Jonathan's hands, and laid it on the floor, then slapped him on the shoulder. "Do not worry. I shall keep you fully informed about your uncle."

Jonathan said goodbye to Eric and was escorted into the front lobby by Brigitte Haniff. He was feeling exhilarated by the exchange with Schleyer, and thoroughly fed-up with both Jennifer and Philippa. He had an hotel room booked. A double. He had never been able to resist the challenge of a pretty woman. "I don't suppose you're free for dinner tonight?"

"Me, Mr Rudder?"

She had clearly estimated their relative ages, correctly.

"I thought it might be fun. I'm in the mood to celebrate. Uncle Eric being in such good hands, you know."

"I quite understand. But you see, Mr Rudder, I have to assist at the operation tomorrow, and so, I need a clear head and steady hands. Or they will not be good hands at all." She smiled at him. "I think you should keep your celebration until after we see how the operation turns out."

"Would that be a promise?"

Brigitte smiled. "No, Mr Rudder. It is not a promise."

I must be losing my touch, Jonathan thought morosely as he returned to the airport. But then, he had no real desire to regain it, he knew. His heart wasn't in it. Angie's death had affected him more than he dared admit. Sweet, innocent Angie, tied to a bed and torn apart. The thought kept returning, and filling his brain with a blood-red haze. "You are booked out tomorrow evening," the clerk pointed out.

"I know. I want to change it to the first available flight."

The clerk raised his eyebrows, but fiddled with his computer, and found a seat on a flight leaving at four. It was not yet noon, but Jonathan was quite happy about that. He could have a leisurely lunch, and he would arrive in England before five, thanks to the hour difference. Then it would be Blessop and Philippa; she would certainly either have returned or been found by now. Probably she was in a police cell and he would bail her out, and take her home, and smooth those ruffled feathers. He was looking forward to that. And where would that leave his determination to avenge Angela's death? He didn't know, because he had no idea where he could go from here. There was simply no reason for anyone to have murdered Angela, and in such a fashion, save for sexual satisfaction. There need be no link with her past, because it was simple enough to gain access to someone's flat with any plausible story – especially someone as essentially trusting as Angie had been. So it could merely have been someone, or someones, who had watched her playing tennis and been turned on by those long legs . . . and was also a raving maniac.

There was certainly no link with Douglas Openshaw, save the very tenuous one that they had both visited the same doctor. But as James had pointed out, neither had been regular patients. In any event, to think that James, the man who had never shown the least interest in women at medical school, and who was now part of the team engaged in saving Uncle Eric's life, could be involved in anything like sexual murder was ludicrous. James was, and always had been, totally sexless. Although, he supposed, judging by James' choice of assistant, people did change.

There was damn all he could do about Angie. So bang went another resolution. He might as well enjoy whatever he had left, and that amounted to Philippa.

* * *

"Come," Lampson grunted at the rather urgent knock on the door. He was studying one report after another, and feeling increasingly desperate. There were no links. Nothing to connect any of the fourteen murders save the modus operandi. The Spanish police had no leads, neither did the French. If there was a link at all, the word would have to be clinical. The murders had been clinical in their efficiency and their single-mindedness.

If the men had all been castrated, and all the women had had their breasts removed, there was no evidence that any of the women had been sexually assaulted immediately before death. There was no pattern of anyone, or any group of people, present at the right times in all the cities involved. And he did not even feel sure he had enough circumstantial evidence to arrest Jonathan Rudder for the murder of Angela Moresby, or, once he had him, to extract a confession from him, simply because he was still unable to tie that one in with any of the others. Except possibly with Douglas Openshaw's through the remote connection that Rudder apparently knew Jennifer Brand quite well. So perhaps it it was entirely coincidental that there had been this spate of quite horrible killings. Perhaps he should concentrate only on England and Rudder. After all, that was his job.

He glowered at Parton, who was looking quite excited. Parton was always looking excited. "Don't tell me," he said. "There's been another killing."

Parton's face fell. "How did you know?"

Lampson was on his feet. "You mean there *has* been? The same pattern?"

Parton recovered. "Almost, sir. Body gutted."

"Then what do you mean, almost?"

"Well, it didn't take place at this person's flat. She was found in the back seat of a car parked in some woodland not far from Cambridge."

Lampson sat down again. "Then it's not connected. Copycat crime."

"With respect, sir, this is not a copycat crime." Parton read from the sheet of paper he was carrying. "The dead woman has been tentatively named as a Miss Philippa Morgan, an American. The car she was found in is a Honda Civic, belonging . . ." he paused as if to say, wait for it, "to Mr Eric Rudder, of Blessop Manor in Berkshire. This car, and Miss Morgan, were reported missing at midnight last night, by . . . Mr Jonathan Rudder!" he annouced triumphantly.

"Jesus Christ!" Lampson was already on his feet.

"Having read your circular, Chief Inspector, we thought it would be a good idea to contact you," said Inspector Brewster of the Cambridgeshire police.

"You did the right thing." Lampson looked around him. The entire wood had been cordoned off, but quite a few people had gathered beyond the cordon, even if the wood was a good way from the nearest habitation. "Has your surgeon seen the body?"

"Yes. He places time of death at between twelve noon and one yesterday. He can't be more accurate – the weather has been so warm."

"And she was found when?"

"Oddly, just after noon this afternoon. She was reported missing to the Berkshire police last night, but frankly, at that time there was no suggestion of foul play, and I gather the duty sergeant felt it was something of a lover's tiff, and didn't take it too seriously. He merely warned all units to keep a look out for this car. The message wasn't extended to us until this morning. As I said, she was found just after noon today, by someone out rabbiting in the woods. I'm afraid he opened the doors. Well, all he saw was the naked body of a woman lying on her face across the back seat. He didn't really know what had happened to her. But she'd been there in a closed car for over twenty-four hours. He was violently sick, and then had to make his way back to the road where he'd left his car . . ."

Lampson nodded. Although all the car windows had been opened wide, and the body had been removed and lay on the grass beneath a ground sheet, the stench he remembered so well clung to the still afternoon air. "Have you anything to go on?"

"We've a whole collection of fingerprints . . ."

"Meaningless. The killer would have used gloves as a matter of course. Those prints will belong to Miss Morgan and whoever else legitinmately drove the car."

"We also have some bits of evidence which may be of use. My surgeon is of the opinion that she was not killed in the car, but somewhere else and then placed in the car; seems the blood had dried too much. Someone in the village just along the way remembers two cars driving through just around lunchtime yesterday. He didn't get any numbers, but one was a red Honda Civic, and the other a dark-blue Mercedes coupé."

"Now that is remarkable," Lampson said. "You have his statement?"

"Of course. *Is* this connected with yours?"

Lampson nodded. "It's connected all right. But I don't really know how." He turned to Parton. "Didn't we have a tail on Rudder all yesterday, and this morning, until he left for Nice with his uncle?"

Parton looked embarrassed. "I'm afraid Dickinson lost him yesterday, for nearly two hours."

"Good God! When was this?"

"Just after half-past eleven. Rudder had been at Moresby's flat, remember? When he left, he gave Dickinson the slip. Dickinson said it was quite deliberate. Well, he decided to return to Blessop and pick him up there, and sure enough, Rudder arrived about an hour and a half later."

"Holy Jesus Christ! You mean Rudder was out on his own from half-past eleven until two?"

"I'm afraid so, sir," Parton was now looking miserable.

"And you just let him leave the country this morning?"

"Well, sir, this business with his uncle seems absolutely above board, and then I didn't know he'd just committed another murder."

"You had better hope he comes back," Lampson growled.

CHAPTER 6

There were three police cars parked in the drive to Blessop Manor when Jonathan returned from the airport just after five that afternoon. His first reaction was thank God Uncle Eric wasn't here; Philippa must have been arrested. When he got out of the Mercedes, three constables converged on him, although they made no attempt to touch him. But a fourth policeman greeted him on the front steps. Caunt was hovering just inside the door, apparently prevented from coming out. "I'm sorry, Mr Jonathan," he said. "But it seems the most terrible thing has happened, and these people wish to speak with you."

"Terrible thing?" Jonathan looked at Detective-Sergeant Parton, standing at the drawing room door. "There's been an accident?"

"Would you come in, sir," Parton invited.

Jonathan moved towards him, brain starting to spin. He had only met Parton once, but he remembered him very well. He belonged to the wrong police force, and he was engaged in a murder hunt. Therefore . . .? He felt a slow explosion building inside him. He couldn't believe what his senses were telling him. He gazed at Lampson, and a uniformed inspector, and Inspector Carmody of the Berkshire police, who he knew already.

"We tried to get hold of you in Antibes, Mr Rudder," Carmody explained. "But were told you had already left to come home. So, instead of making a fuss at Heathrow, we thought we'd wait for you here. I believe you know Chief-Detective-Inspector Lampson of Scotland Yard?"

"You were not to leave the country," Lampson said.

"I had to take my uncle to hospital. If you knew I'd gone to Antibes, you knew that." Jonathan's tone was brusque.

"You should still have informed us of your intention," Lampson said, severely. "Now, I wish you to account for your movements yesterday."

"Yesterday when?"

"All day, Mr Rudder."

"Something has happened to Philippa?"

"You know that, do you?"

"I'm asking."

Inspector Carmody shifted his feet uneasily. "I think perhaps the situation should be explained to Mr Rudder, Chief-Inspector. Before we proceed further. He may wish to contact his solicitor."

Jonathan looked from face to face. "Very well," Lampson agreed. "The body of a young woman was found this afternoon in the back seat of your uncle's car, parked in a wood a few miles south of Cambridge."

Jonathan sat down, tried to think, tried to control the surging anger which was beginning to rack his huge frame – and knew he wasn't going to succeed. Yet when he spoke his voice was still quiet. "You are speaking of Philippa?"

"The body has not yet been positively identified," Lampson said. "We are hoping you will do that for us. But in view of the report you made to the Blessop police last evening, we are assuming the dead woman to be the woman you reported as missing, Miss Philippa Morgan, yes?"

"And she was murdered?" Jonathan raised his head, frowning, his eyes stark with horror. "Like Angie?"

"Yes, Mr Rudder. Almost exactly like Miss Moresby."

Jonathan gave a howl of mingled anger and despair,

and leapt to his feet. The policemen retreated in alarm. Jonathan picked up the sofa on which he had been sitting and hurled it at them. Inspector Brewster attempted to catch it and fell over backwards as it landed on his chest. Lampson tried to get out of the way and was hit by a corner of the settee and thrown to the floor. Parton managed to stay on his feet, as did Carmody, who flattened himself against the wall.

Jonathan uttered another roar of outrage and picked up a chair to smash it to the floor. "He's gone berserk!" Lampson shouted. "Get help!"

Two more policemen had appeared in the doorway, looking uncertain. "Bastards!" Jonathan tore a picture from the wall and hurled it at them.

"Shit!" one of them commented, taking evasive action; the picture smashed into the wall and disintegrated.

Caunt appeared in the doorway, looking like an admonitory schoolmaster. "Mr Jonathan!" Jonathan, in the act of picking up another chair, slowly lowered it. His chest was heaving, and he was pouring sweat. "Mr Jonathan," Caunt said again. "Look at the mess." Jonathan stared at him for several seconds. Then he put the chair down and turned away.

"He's escaping?" Lampson bellowed, and a tremor ran through the other policemen in the room as they moved forward.

"I am pouring myself a drink." Jonathan went to the bar, filled half a tumbler with whisky, drank deeply, and turned. As at Angie's flat, the immediate mood of desperation had passed with the outpouring of physical energy.

"Handcuffs," Lampson told his men, getting to his feet. "I want him handcuffed."

They made another movement forward, and one of them produced a pair of handcuffs. "If you try to put those on me, I shall break your arm," Jonathan said pleasantly.

"Send for a gun," Parton suggested.

"I'm not going to hurt anyone, now," Jonathan said. "Explain it to them, Caunt."

"That is quite true," Caunt agreed. "I am sure Mr Jonathan has got the mood out of his system, Inspector."

Jonathan sat down in one of the remaining chairs, while Inspector Brewster extricated himself from beneath the sofa, and the other men stared at him. "I'm afraid I don't understand," Jonathan said. "What possible connection could there be between Angela and Philippa?"

"There is only one connection, Mr Rudder," Lampson said. "You." Jonathan frowned at him.

Inspector Carmody intervened. "You have not yet been charged, Mr Rudder, but I do wish you to reflect carefully before saying anything. Would you like me to call Mr Parling?" Sidney Parling was the Rudder family solicitor.

Jonathan drank again, the glass held in both hands. "You think I killed her? You think I killed Angie? Like that? My God, do you think I'm a maniac or something?"

Parton looked at Lampson, and received a quick nod. He took out his notebook. "I am bound to say, Mr Rudder," Lampson said, "that anyone who could commit two such murders would seem to be a maniac. Or at least, capable of maniacal rages." He glanced left and right at the wrecked furniture. Jonathan raised his head. "So, sir," Lampson went on. "It would be of great help to us if you could give us your movements yesterday."

Jonathan drew the back of his hand across his eyes. Where Angie had been just sweet, Philippa had been just magnificent, at least to look at, to touch. To think of her being ripped open, those breasts cut off . . . he finished his drink. He didn't want to fly off the handle again. "Sir?" Lampson pressed.

"I'm trying to think. I left here fairly early, to attend Douglas Openshaw's funeral service."

"May I ask why you did that? Did you know Mr Openshaw?" Lampson asked.

"No. I never met him. I went because I knew Miss Brand."

"Ah. For how long have you known Miss Brand?"

"Just about a week."

"You are saying you only met her after Mr Openshaw's death?"

"That is what I am saying, yes. Do you want my movements yesterday, or not?"

"Go on."

"At the funeral, I spoke with Miss Brand, and we arranged to meet again last night. Then I went to Miss Moresby's flat . . ." Parton looked at Lampson, who raised his eyebrows. ". . . to collect the rest of my clothes," Jonathan said. "From there I telephoned a doctor, the man who was arranging for my uncle to go into hospital for heart surgery. He asked me to bring my uncle in to him later that afternoon. I then went to see Miss Anne Moresby, Miss Angela Moresby's sister, had lunch, and drove back out here to pick up my uncle."

"You also took time out to lose the man we had watching you."

Jonathan shrugged. "I was feeling exhilarated." Had he ever felt exhilarated? Would he ever feel exhilarated again?

"Very good, sir. You were feeling exhilarated. Could we have some times on those movements? When exactly did you call your doctor?"

"About half past eleven."

"And what time was your uncle's appointment?"

"Three."

"It was going to take you three and a half hours to drive

from Barnes to Blessop and back to north London? In the middle of the day?"

"I had to see Miss Moresby, and have lunch." He gave a savage grin. "And lose your boy. It didn't seem important, then. Time, I mean."

"I see. What time did you visit Miss Moresby?"

"As soon as I'd lost your man, it would have been about ten to twelve."

"She will of course vouch for this?"

"I'm afraid not, Chief-Inspector. She wasn't there."

"I see," Lampson said, keeping massively calm. "Then can you tell us, where did you lunch?"

"At a pub just round the corner from Miss Moresby's flat."

"Would they remember you in this pub?"

"I doubt it. It was very crowded."

"What time did you leave the pub?"

"I suppose about one. I don't really know. I had a hell of a lot on my mind."

"Apparently. What time did you arrive here?"

"Just after two."

"It's less than an hour's drive, Mr Rudder."

"So I didn't hurry my lunch."

"What you really mean is that you cannot account for your movements between eleven-thirty yesterday morning and two o'clock yesterday afternoon."

"From eleven forty-five, Chief-Inspector. I didn't lose your chap until then."

"What was Miss Morgan doing all this time?"

"I have no idea. She was here when I left. Then apparently she went off in my uncle's car just after half-past ten."

"To meet you."

"Eh?"

"Didn't you telephone the doctor entirely with the idea of setting up some kind of alibi for yourself, because you had planned a secret meeting with Miss Morgan?"

"For God's sake, why should I do that? If I wanted a secret meeting, as you put it, I'd have gone to her bedroom."

"You could hardly have killed her there, Mr Rudder. It would have been too obvious."

"Why in the name of God should I wish to kill Philippa?"

"Why did you wish to kill Angela Moresby?"

Inspector Carmody was shifting his feet in some agitation. "I do feel Mr Rudder should be charged and properly cautioned," he said.

"I'm quite happy," Jonathan said. He wasn't. He had an urge to cut loose again. But that was what they were waiting for, perhaps. "I didn't kill Angela Moresby, Chief-Inspector."

"Not even in an outbreak of maniacal sexual excitement?" Jonathan stared at him. "Just as you killed Philippa Morgan in such an outburst, and cut her to pieces?"

Jonathan took a long breath, then pointed. "That's where your theory breaks down, Inspector. I wasn't anywhere near Angie when she was killed, and I have already proved that."

"Not a foolproof alibi, I'm afraid, sir."

"Okay. So you say I returned there on Monday night and took her apart. In a maniacal rage. In her bedroom, when presumably we were having sex. Now you say I did the same thing to Philippa. But to have sex with her I had to make some remote rendezvous? Why? She was already my mistress. Caunt knows she was my mistress. So did Uncle Eric. If I was going to have sex with Philippa I would have done it in her bedroom. If I was going to fly into a maniacal sexual rage it would have been there. Not down some lover's lane like a sixteen-year-old schoolboy."

Lampson glared at him, and Jonathan glared back. "You do have maniacal rages, Mr Rudder," Parton said quietly. "You have just demonstrated that to us."

"How would you behave, sergeant, if two of your mistresses had been murdered in rapid succession."

Parton glanced at his superiors. He had never had two mistresses at the same time. Or even one. "Mr Rudder, you cannot supply us with an alibi for between twelve noon and one yesterday afternoon, which is when Miss Morgan was killed," Lampson said.

"No, I can't. Nothing you'd believe," Jonathan said. "So what are you going to do about it?"

"And then, after taking your uncle to the Freedom Clinic for a check-up, you returned here, and, cool as a cucumber, reported the lady as missing, having stolen your uncle's car."

"She *was* missing, Chief Inspector. And she *had* taken the car."

"Following which you accompanied your uncle to France. You purchased a return ticket for Wednesday, but you came back today. Why?"

"I got bored."

"Didn't you come back because you expected Miss Morgan's body to be found by this morning, and you to be summoned back? When there was no summons, you could stay away no longer?"

"With respect, Chief Inspector, that is balls."

"Very good. Now, I am going to ask you to come with us, Mr Rudder."

"Am I under arrest?"

"No. You are coming with us to the morgue to make a formal identification of Miss Morgan's body. And on the way, I'll tell you about a character called Heath."

* * *

Philippa's features were relaxed, as had been Angie's. Jonathan was only allowed to see her face; he didn't wish to see anything else. The police doctor was waiting by the body. "I'll be carrying out a full post mortem this evening," he said. "But taking up those points you raised, Chief-Inspector, I made a brief preliminary examination, and, yes, the victim received an injection shortly before death, and no, there is no immediate evidence of recent sexual intercourse. There are however certain contusions on her arms to suggest she may have been attempting to resist her assailant immediately before the injection was administered."

They all looked at Jonathan. "So much for your theory of sexual madness," he commented.

"It still stands," Lampson pointed out. "The madness may have arisen from an inability to erect."

"Not something I have yet started to suffer from. So, unless you mean to charge me, Chief-Inspector, I'll go home now."

"I thought you *were* going to arrest him," Inspector Brewster said, as they watched Jonathan being driven away in a police car.

"I thought so, too. It's just that, goddamit, there are too many imponderables we haven't been able to tie up. The fact that the earlier murders were committed by two men, the absence, as yet, of any link to the continental killings, the fact that we found blood on a shirt he'd worn last weekend which wasn't either Openshaw's or Moresby's . . . Besides, there's something about the man. If he's a murderer, he's the most inept murderer I have ever come across in my life. Anyway, we still don't have anything more than a circumstantial case against him. We just have to give him a little more rope and see if he hangs himself."

"Meanwhile the press are going to go wild when the

news breaks that there has been a third killing," Carmody pointed out.

"So will one or two chief constables, not to mention the Commissioner," Brewster added.

"Bugger them." Lampson turned to Parton. "As for Dickinson, I want his guts for garters."

"I'll make a note, sir."

"And I want that surveillance resumed and maintained round the clock. Understood?"

"Yes, sir."

"If he is mad," Brewster remarked, "then he would be inept, wouldn't he? During his periods of madness, certainly." Lampson gave him a dirty look. "It is also possible that he is schizophrenic," Brewster went on. "That he doesn't know, and perhaps cannot even remember, what he has done when in one of his violent moods."

"He knew what he was doing at the house just now, sir," Parton argued.

"But will he remember it, say in a few hours time?"

Lampson cracked his knuckles. "You don't know the whole picture," he growled.

"I still think he should have been formally charged and taken into custody," Carmody insisted.

"He can't come to any harm at the Manor."

"Suppose he wishes to leave, sir?" Parton asked. "Is he to be prevented?"

"You'd need half the Berkshire force," Brewster remarked.

"For the time being, we'll just keep an eye on him," Lampson said. "But if he tries to find himself alone with any other woman, I want him stopped."

"Is Mr Rudder comfortable, Mr Jonathan?" Caunt was busily restoring the drawing room when Jonathan returned.

"It seems a comfortable place." Jonathan assisted

him by replacing the sofa. "Sorry about the mess, Caunt."

"Don't give it a thought, sir. What action do you propose to take about the young lady, sir? She will have relatives, perhaps? In America?"

"Christ, I hadn't thought of that." Neither, apparently, had Lampson.

"I think they should be informed, sir."

Jonathan scratched his head. He knew absolutely nothing about Philippa Morgan's private life, save that she sailed for Bruce Hardy. Bruce! He looked at his watch. It was half-past six. That meant it was half-past one in the States. Bruce would be on the water, with *Halcyon*, and the crew . . . and almost certainly a new cook. He wouldn't be back much before six, local time. "I can't do anything about it until later tonight," he said.

"Very good, sir. Will you be in for dinner?"

Dinner, Jonathan thought. Here? He'd go stark, raving mad. "No. I am going into town. I'll be back later."

"Is that wise, sir?"

Jonathan gave a savage grin. "You mean, the police will follow me? It'll give them something to do. But Caunt, should my uncle call from Antibes, you will not tell him anything about Miss Morgan. Understood?"

"Of course, sir. Will he not find out, eventually?"

"Eventually. Hopefully when his heart is stronger."

Jennifer Brand soaked in her bath, washed her hair, and contemplated the ceiling. She had gone shopping after leaving work, late, and she had been in the bath half an hour. She was trying to relax. She felt oddly dissatisfied. Uneasy, even. Partly, the cause was Jonathan Rudder, of course. He was clearly a man who needed to be kept firmly in his place, or he would be all over one, literally. But he was also a man who exuded sexual personality.

She didn't want to think that. She didn't want to keep

reminding herself that she could have been with him in Antibes at this very moment – keeping him in his place? She had never been to Antibes, and Richard would surely have given her the time off; Richard was being quite exceptionally sympathetic and anxious to help.

But there were too many other things nibbling at her consciousness for her to concentrate on Jonathan right that minute. There was the constantly recurring memory of what had happened to Douglas: The constantly recurring thought of Angela Moresby: The constantly recurring understanding that there was at least one homicidal maniac roaming the streets of London, and the constantly returning consideration that if the only link between Douglas and Angela was the Freedom Clinic, then it was at the Freedom Clinic they should look, whatever Jonathan's reservations. And that Colley man had never called her back, while when she had tried to get him again today she had been told he was too busy to speak with her, and did she want an appointment? She had declined that, at the time, but was now inclining towards it. Because Doug's doctor was the only possible lead she had. On the other hand, Jonathan would be back tomorrow, and would undoubtedly be in touch – if James Colley didn't want to co-operate, she could do without him.

The street doorbell buzzed. Jennifer looked at her watch; it was past six. She muttered curses, got out of the bath, and padded through the living room to the phone. "Yes?"

"Richard. Can I come up?"

Jennifer raised her eyebrows. The boss had never called on her before. "Sure." She released the door, and then released the flat door as well, returned to the bathroom, hastily dried herself, wrapped her wet hair in the towel, and pulled on a dressing gown, thrusting her toes into furry mules.

The flat door opened and closed. "I'm afraid you caught

me with my hair down, literally," she said, returning to the living room.

Richard Ebershaw did not look embarrassed; but then, he was not an easily embarrassed man. He had tossed his hat on to a chair beside his umbrella – he had become very British during his years in England. "I wouldn't want to catch you any other way," he remarked. "Out of the office, anyway."

"Drink?"

"That would be very nice."

She went to the cabinet, poured them each a scotch and water. "I guess I left something undone at the office."

"You never leave things undone, Jennifer."

Little alarm bells began ringing in Jennifer's brain. She wrapped the dressing gown more tightly around herself and wished she'd made him wait while she got dressed – but she had never anticipated anything like this from Richard. On the other hand, maybe she was imagining things. "Then you must tell me to what I owe this visit."

"Well, hell, Jennifer, I'd be a pretty poor boss if I didn't worry about my staff. Some more than others. Every time I think of you, sitting alone in this flat, brooding on everything that has happened, I get real upset." You mean you get a real hard-on, she thought, realising that she wasn't imagining things after all. Shit, she thought: it had been a good job, with, up to this moment, nice people. "I mean," Richard went on, "you don't seem to go out much. I've asked the other girls at the office."

"I'm not the going out type. Unless it's something special, or the guy is."

"It's a relief to hear a girl talk like that," he said. "With my wife, it's out every night. Unless we happen to be entertaining. Gets real tiresome."

"Why don't you tell her."

"Who can tell Roxanne anything?"

"I can't imagine a relationship, where you can't tell

each other everything." Jennifer bit her lip; she might have made a tactical error, given him the chance to slip into the "my-wife-doesn't-understand-me" routine.

She *had* made a tactical error. "Yeah," he agreed. "It would be great to find a woman that understanding. Was it like that with you and Doug?"

"We were working towards it."

"And now it's gone, eh? Must be pretty tough."

"I guess I have to work back out of it. I'd offer you another drink, Richard, but if, as you say, you either go out or entertain every night, hadn't you better be getting home? It's pushing seven."

"I've given myself a night off," he said. "Told Roxanne there was some work I had to get done at the office. She's going to the theatre with some friends. Won't be home till around midnight."

"Ah," she said, and got up. "Well . . ."

Another tactical error; he caught her hand, and deposited her neatly on his lap. Her brain tumbled; she had no idea how to deal with situations like this – with one's boss. "I thought," he said, "as we seem to have a mutual problem, we might, well . . . help each other."

He still had hold of her hand. Now his free hand trickled fingers up and down the back of her dressing gown. Maybe it was a gesture of affection; more likely it was making sure she had nothing on underneath. The problem was that he was turning her on. She was lonely, and she hadn't had sex with anyone in a hell of a long time. But to have an affair with Richard was unthinkable. "What do you reckon?" he asked, nuzzling her neck, from where he could look down inside the dressing gown, sliding his lips up to her cheek.

The doorbell rang. Jennifer jumped to her feet so violently she left her dressing gown in Richard's hands, and had to snatch it back; the towel fell off her head and wet hair stuck to her neck, but she ignored that. "Yes?"

"Let me up!"

"Jonathan!" she cried in total relief. "The door's open now." She pressed the release, and turned to face Richard.

He was scowling. "Jonathan?"

"A friend. More than a friend." She was breathless. "His fiancée was murdered by the same madman who killed Doug. That's what the police think, anyway."

Richard's scowl turned into a frown. "You serious?"

"Yes. I'm serious. So, we're sort of working on it together. I thought he was in France, but he must have turned something up."

"He sounded a bit tense," Richard said.

"So, if you don't mind, Richard . . ."

The flat door opened, Jonathan filling the space. He didn't look pleased to see Richard, but then, Richard wasn't looking pleased either. "Richard Ebershaw. We met at Doug Openshaw's funeral."

"So we did." Jonathan did not offer to shake hands, but looked at Jennifer, eyebrows arched.

"Richard is just leaving. He dropped by to discuss something. From work."

Richard gave her a hard look, but she did not lower her gaze. My resignation will be on your desk tomorrow morning, she thought, and hoped he could read her mind. "I'll say goodnight then," he conceded. "Rudder." He closed the door behind himself.

"Am I glad to see you," Jennifer remarked.

"Words I thought I'd never hear. I'm pretty glad to see you, too."

He was looking well below her face, and she realised that she had not retied her dressing gown. Hastily she did so. "You really are the rudest man."

"For doing what comes naturally? It's my motto. And you have got to be the most changeable of women. Were you and he in bed?"

"No, we were not in bed. But he had ideas in that direction."

"And you turned him down? Isn't he your boss?"

"I think the word is 'was' I thought you were in France?"

"Without you, what was the point."

"You mean Philippa wouldn't go either?"

Jonathan sat down on the sofa; suddenly his good humour had entirely evaporated. "I need a drink." Jennifer hesitated, then poured him one, and took another for herself; she could tell that something was very, very wrong. "Now, come and sit beside me," he said.

Another brief hesitation. Unlike Richard, he had never made any attempt to touch her. She rather felt that touching, with Jonathan Rudder, would only happen after whatever else was going to happen was cut and dried. She sat beside him. "Tell me? Is it your uncle?"

"My uncle is fine. Well, relatively." He brooded for several seconds. "It's happened again. Philippa. God!"

She watched his fingers curl into fists, even if she couldn't quite follow what he was saying. "Philippa? You can't mean . . ."

He told her everything he had gleaned from the police, and about going to identify the body. She listened in silence, then took the glass from his fingers, went to the cabinet, and refilled it. "Have you eaten?"

"No."

"You'd better put some blotting paper in there." She faced him, biting her lip. "Jon, I'm so terribly sorry. Were you . . ."

"Oh, what the hell. She was a good fuck. And would you believe we only did it once? But Jennifer . . ." To her consternation she saw there were tears in his eyes. She hurried back to sit beside him and put her arm round him. "I ran amok," he muttered. "Broke up the happy home. What the hell for? It's them I want."

She gave him a hug, and he half turned his head. Hastily she stood up again. "You into eggs? I don't have much else." He didn't argue, so she went into the kitchenette and started breaking eggs, omelette at the back of her mind. She wanted time to think, to relate Philippa to Angela to Douglas. Because they had to be related. But Philippa had nothing to do with the Freedom Clinic!

She looked up and saw Jonathan, standing on the other side of the breakfast counter, watching her, and hastily checked that no more disasters had happened to her dressing gown. "And the police have no leads?"

"Sure they do. Me."

"You?"

"Well, as you know, they reckon I have a fairly substantial motive for killing Angela: unwanted pregnancy, forced marriage, quarrel with uncle, that kind of thing."

"None of which is the least bit true."

"There's only my say-so about that."

"So where's your motive for killing Philippa?"

"They're working on the theory that I get homicidal during sex. Ever heard of a chap called Heath?" She shook her head, using her electric whisk on the eggs. "Famous case just after the Hitler War. Big, good-looking chap who the girls found irresistible . . ."

"That surely lets you out for a start. Sorry. I couldn't resist that."

"Be my guest. Anyway, when he got turned on too hard he went berserk, bit off nipples, ripped them open with a knife, that kind of thing."

"Ugh!"

"Exactly. Sounds familiar, doesn't it?"

"Was he bisexual?"

"You know, I reckon that's the only thing that's keeping me free, at the moment. Try as they do, they can't link me to Doug. But I have an idea Lampson isn't going to worry about that too much longer, because he can certainly link me to both Angie's and Phil's deaths. I don't have an alibi, see."

"Why not?" She served the omelette on to two plates.

"Well . . ." he ate his wolfishly, still standing at the counter; she realised that he must be very hungry indeed. "It's my own fault. I called Jim Colley at eleven-thirty yesterday morning to find out what he had for Uncle Eric. He did have something in prospect, as you know. He wanted me to bring Uncle in for a check-up, so we made an appointment for three that afternoon. Well, at eleven-thirty I was thinking purely in terms of lunch. But it was too early, so I decided to play a little game with this tail . . . did you know Lampson has put a tail on me? Anyway, I dropped him, then went round to see Anne – that's Angela's sister . . ."

"I know."

"Did you? Well, she wasn't there. So I had lunch, and drove out to Blessop. I got there just after two. Well, you see, had I driven straight out from the flat, after calling Colley, I'd have been there by twelve-thirty at the outside. So what did I do for those extra couple of hours? Had lunch. But I can't prove that; it was in a pub where I'm not a regular. When I dropped that tail I still could've got there in just over the hour, if I hadn't stopped to eat. But I didn't. I got there at quarter past two."

"There's nothing suspicious about having lunch, surely? What's so important about these times?"

"I dropped the tail at a quarter to twelve, and surfaced at Blessop at two-fifteen. The police say that Phil was murdered some time between twelve and one."

"But you say she was found in your uncle's car, some place outside London."

"About an hour's drive from where I lost my copper. The police think I had a date to meet her there, got there, killed her, and then went out to Blessop. Having recovered from my homicidal rage." Jennifer made no comment, and finished her meal. "Pretty cast-iron, eh?" Jonathan said. "There's just one out, that link to Doug."

"There must be something else," Jennifer said. "Somebody must have seen something about Philippa's death which lets you off the hook?"

"Don't tell me you're on my side?"

"Of course I am, stupid."

"Well, I haven't even told you the half of it. Seems a dark blue Mercedes was seen in the vicinity of the crime, just about when it was committed."

Jennifer frowned at him. "Yours?"

"Of course not mine. I was driving mine. But it's a bit of an unhappy coincidence, isn't it? Someone even got the number. Well, not the complete number, but the first two letters are the same as mine. They think."

Jennifer put the plates in the dishwasher, loaded the coffee machine, thoughtfully. "I don't believe in coincidences, Jonny. Somebody set you up."

"Oh, really, Jennifer. Why should anyone set me up? I don't have an enemy in the world."

"Neither did your Angela. Neither did Doug. And, you'll probably find out, neither did Philippa Morgan."

"They're all dead."

"So maybe whoever is behind this reckons you'd be a little difficult to kill."

"Sounds a bit far-fetched." He yawned. "God, it's been one hell of a long day."

"But your uncle is settled in okay in this hospital?"

"Yes, it's quite impressive. But am I glad he's out of the way. He was taking quite a shine to Phil."

"You told me. You mean he doesn't know she's dead?"

"No. He was pretty agitated when she didn't turn up for lunch, and even more when she was still gone by the time we left for our appointment with Colley. If he was to find out she'd been murdered . . ."

"Colley," Jennifer muttered. "Colley."

"Don't start that again. God, I'm tired. Can you offer me a bed?"

"I can."

"But will you?"

"I don't think that would be a good thing."

"Look, right now the very sight of a woman's body would make me puke."

"You were looking at mine just now without puking."

"You're exceptional. Listen! All I want to do is sleep."

"Is that a fact. The sofa over there converts into a put-you-up. You're welcome. What the . . ."

There were heavy feet on the stairs and a banging on the door. "Open up. Open up in there, Rudder, or we'll break the door down."

"Shit!" Jonathan commented.

"Who are they?" Jennifer demanded.

"Police. You'd better let them in."

Jennifer unlocked the door, just in time, as one burly policeman was about to shoulder charge it. There were four of them, led by Detective Sergeant Parton, who stared at her in consternation. "Miss Brand? Are you all right?"

"How do I look to you, sergeant?"

Parton looked past her at Jonathan. "Evening all," Jonathan said.

Parton turned back to Jennifer. "Do you wish this man to leave, Miss Brand?"

"Why should I? I've just offered him a bed for the night. He's in no fit state to drive."

"One of our cars can take him home, miss."

"All the way out to Blessop? I wouldn't dream of putting you to so much trouble."

"Miss Brand," Parton said earnestly. "I cannot force you, but I most strongly advise you not to let this man spend the night here. If you do, we cannot be responsible for your safety."

The penny dropped in Jonathan's rather fogged brain. "They reckon that once I climb into your nuptial couch, Jennifer, and get turned on, I am going to become a raving lunatic and tear you apart."

"Correction," she said. "You are not going to climb into my nuptial couch, remember? You are sleeping in here."

"But they don't know that."

"If it's all the same to you, officer," Jennifer said. "I've decided he can stay here. Right? So if you'd like to take your big feet off my carpet . . ."

Parton looked as if he would have said something further, then he shrugged. He pointed at Jonathan. "There's going to be a man outside this flat all night, Rudder. Remember that."

"It's nice to know they have my welfare at heart," Jennifer confided, as she removed sheets and pillowcases from the airing cupboard and made up the sofa bed.

"They don't. It's me they're after."

"Well then, you'd better behave yourself. There's a spare toothbrush in the bathroom cupboard. Night night."

She used the bathroom first, then left him to it, wondering if she should lock her door. But if she was going to be afraid of him she might as well open her window and shout for that policeman. Yet she couldn't sleep. There were things on her mind, vague things which she was trying to piece together, but which didn't connect, at the moment. It was the blue Mercedes. Someone *had* tried to set Jonathan up. But it had to be someone who not only knew Jonathan very well, but who also knew exactly what he was going to be doing that afternoon, and that neither he nor his car would have an alibi. Someone . . . she rolled out of bed, pulled on her dressing gown, went into the lounge and switched on the light.

Jonathan was on his back, snoring faintly. The light disturbed him and he opened his eyes. "Thought you were never going to come to me," he said sleepily.

"Listen," She pulled a chair alongside the sofa.

He reached for her, and she pushed his hands away. "Listen," she said again. "This is serious. It could be a matter of life and death."

He sat up, rubbed his eyes. "Do you know there are times when you are beautiful?"

"If you don't concentrate I'm going to call the fuzz and have you removed. Listen! You telephoned Dr Colley at half past eleven in the morning, day before yesterday. Right?"

"Right," he said, yawning.

"And made a date for your uncle to see him at three that afternoon. Do you know I called him at a quarter after one?"

Jonathan frowned. "He never mentioned it. What did you telephone him about?"

"Never mind right now. I didn't get him. He was out."

"Even doctors have lunch, you know."

"The woman on the switchboard didn't say anything about lunch. She said he was out on a case. An emergency."

"So?"

"He was going to call me back as soon as he got in. But he never did."

Jonathan's frown was back. "He was still out when we got there at three. But he came back a few minutes later. That's right. He said he'd just dashed out to an emergency."

"An emergency which lasted from around one to after three?"

"No," Jonathan said. "This must have been a different

emergency. He told me he'd only been out a few minutes, to a hypochondriac."

"He never mentioned the earlier emergency at all?"

"No," Jonathan said thoughtfully. "Mind you, there was no reason why he should."

"You don't find it odd that the chief registrar of a clinic, which does not have an out-patients department, should have been called out twice in three hours on an emergency?"

"Just what are you trying to say?"

"That James Colley, your great friend, was the only person in this world who knew exactly what you would be doing yesterday afternoon, and that you most likely wouldn't have an alibi while doing it. He also knew that you drive a dark blue Mercedes coupé, and he probably knows the number, as well. He is also linked to both Angela and Douglas."

Jonathan considered. "Won't work, Jennifer old girl. He certainly isn't linked to Philippa. He doesn't know anything about her, not even that she existed. And even suppose he did, how the hell did he get hold of her? She left Blessop at ten-thirty that morning to go for a drive. No one knew where she was going. Probably not even herself."

"Suppose she *did* know where she was going. You say Colley didn't know anything about her. But did she know anything about Colley?"

"I don't see how she could have."

"You never mentioned him to her?"

"I may have done."

"And the name of the hospital?"

"Yes. I suppose so. I told her they were trying to help the old man. As I told you, she was getting quite interested in old Eric. Or his money."

"Right! Suppose she decided to do something about that, go and see Colley, and jog him along. It would increase her stock with your uncle."

"So she goes to the Freedom Clinic, and Colley murders her? Just like that. And to help him out, he just happens to have a dark blue Mercedes coupé with a number close to mine waiting in his park? It's a fantasy, Jennifer. Quite apart from the coincidence, why? What possible motive could he have had?"

"Something we don't know about, if it was something he's done before. More than once. You can't get around the fact that Doug was seeing Colley. Angela saw Colley at least once. And they are both dead."

"And Philippa never saw him at all, except in your imagination."

"But if she did! Suppose we can find that out? Then he has got to be either our man, or the link between the deaths and the murderers. You must see that, Jonny."

"I see that you're bending over backwards to help, Jennifer. And I'm grateful. But you'll never make that theory stick." He yawned, and fell asleep again.

CHAPTER 7

"Do you realise," Jonathan said over breakfast. "That this is the first time I have ever spent a night in a woman's flat and not fucked her?"

"Perhaps you're turning over a new leaf," Jennifer suggested. She had got up early and showered, while he still snored, and she was fully dressed. She was not in a good mood, partly because she was still resentful at the way he had pooh-poohed her theory last night, and partly because she had awakened to the realisation that today was going to be a critical one, job-wise. There were decisions to be made. Most annoying of all, she could not help wondering if her out-of-sorts mood was not at least partly caused by the sheer fact that he had *not* bedded her, or even made any serious attempt to do so. Of course, he was obviously under a great strain, but just how stressed did he get? His moods seemed to fluctuate alarmingly.

"Now," he said, "what are our plans for today?"

"Your first plan is to leave," she said.

"What have I done wrong now?"

"Nothing. But it is a quarter of eight and I have a whole lot of things to do."

"A quarter of eight! Shit!"

"Don't tell me *you* have a job to go to?"

"I meant to telephone Bruce Hardy last night, and tell him about Philippa. She must have some next of kin."

"You'll have to do it today."

"It's three o'clock in the morning over there."

"Well, you'll have to do it a little later. Not from here," she added hastily.

"You mean, you really are throwing me out? What about working together?"

"As you won't accept any of my theories, when you come up with one, you let me know. Right? Until then, I'll see you at Angela's funeral service."

She knew she was soft in the head, but she also knew that she was going to get together with him some time, if only out of pity. But some time was still a good way off. She telephoned the office. "Tell Richard I won't be in today," she said.

"You think he'll buy that, Jennifer?" asked the switchboard girl. "You had all of last week off."

"So, I may take all of this week off, as well. He'll understand." He'd better, the bastard, she thought as she hung up. Then sat down to think over a third cup of coffee. If her theory was right, and it was the only one around right this minute, what was she going to do about it?

The obvious solution seemed to be to go to the police. The British police were supposed to be more helpful than the American. Lampson? There didn't seem to be any alternative.

She took a taxi to New Scotland Yard, and after being seen by several people eventually found herself in a small bare room which contained a table and two chairs, and no windows. "The Chief Inspector will be with you in a few minutes," said the WPC. And then, disconcertingly, took up a position just inside the door.

"I haven't come to confess anything," Jennifer pointed out. The policewoman merely smiled.

A few minutes later Lampson appeared, accompanied, as usual, by Parton. "Well?"

"I have some ideas."

"Do you?" He sat opposite her. "You weren't exactly helpful to Sergeant Parton and his men last night."

"They were barking up the wrong tree. Jonathan Rudder didn't kill Philippa Morgan. Or Angela Moresby. Or Douglas Openshaw."

"He told you so, did he, Miss Brand?"

"Lampson, I am trying to help."

"So help." He nodded to Parton, and she heard the rustle of a notebook being opened. She outlined her theory, while Lampson occasionally cracked a knuckle, Parton wrote busily, and the WPC gazed at the ceiling. "Well," Lampson said when she was finished. "It's a theory."

"So what are you going to do about it?"

"Miss Brand, when dealing with a murder, a policeman has to look for three things: motive, opportunity, and weapon. Now we have a pretty good idea that the weapon that killed Miss Morgan, Miss Moresby and Mr Openshaw was a surgical scalpel. So it seems likely that their killers were connected with the medical profession."

"Right."

"But that of course could include any one of the thousands of doctors, ancillary workers, and, don't let's forget, *failed* doctors in this country. You agree with that?"

"Of course. But . . ."

"Next, let's look at opportunity. Dr Colley may have had the opportunity to kill Douglas Openshaw, and he did know him, if only as a patient. He may have had the opportunity to kill Angela Moresby, and he did know her, also as a patient. But you are suggesting he had the opportunity to kill Philippa Morgan, someone he had never met, and so far as any of us are aware, did not even know to exist."

"That was Jonathan's argument. But don't you see, Philippa knew of *him*."

"Yes, but the idea that she went to see him is totally unsubstantiated. It fits with your theory, certainly. But my business is to fit my theory to the facts, not the other way around."

"He's the only link between the three victims," Jennifer repeated. "The only one!"

"The only one that we know of at the moment. Because now let's talk about motive. What conceivable motive could Dr Colley have for murdering three widely different people, especially if two of them happened to be his patients?"

"Well, what about this sexual frenzy theory?"

"You are now suggesting that your fiancé was gay?"

"Well, no, of course Doug wasn't gay."

"Yet you are suggesting that he admitted Colley and another man to his flat, and was murdered by them in a fit of sexual frenzy."

"Well . . ."

"And let's take both Moresby and Morgan. Neither was sexually assaulted, either before or after death."

"Jonathan says you suggested he might have done it because of some kind of impotence."

"That is a possibility. But we have not yet found any links between Rudder and Openshaw's killer. That's why he's walking around free. You are now trying to link all three. It won't work, Miss Brand."

Jennifer sighed. "Then you're not going to do anything about it?"

"It's not my business to go around arresting innocent people."

"You think he's innocent. I think he's guilty. But I have to be wrong, is that it?"

Lampson leaned across the table. "Miss Brand, I *know* he's innocent."

"Know? That has to be a load of bull."

Lampson glanced at Parton, then leaned back again.

"You're an intelligent woman, Miss Brand. And you've played square with us by not giving any interviews to the press. So I'm going to tell you something. It's going to break at the Openshaw inquest on Friday anyway. Dr Colley cannot be the murderer. The deaths of your fiancé, Miss Moresby and Miss Morgan are part of a sequence of killings which began in Spain nearly a year ago and have been spreading across Europe. They all follow exactly the same pattern, and there seems little doubt that they were all committed by the same men or group of men."

Jennifer stared at him in horror. "You mean they were all . . ."

"Cut up and mutilated, yes, I'm afraid they were. This is of course confidential," Lampson went on. "Although, as I said, it will probably come out at the inquest on Mr Openshaw. Now, we have not yet considered it necessary to run a check on Dr Colley, although we will do so."

"But you've checked on Jonathan?"

"We have."

"And he is linked to the other murders as well?"

"We can't prove that, at the moment."

"Well, then . . ."

"I have said, these murders have been committed probably by a group of men, not just one or two. Our business is to find any links we can, and to uncover the motive for such senseless killings. Now, we have managed to link Jonathan Rudder to the deaths of the two women in this country. Whatever I may have said publicly, I do not believe the crimes were committed in a sexual frenzy. There was another reason. That is what we have to find out. And when we do, we'll begin to unravel the whole mystery. But you'll see how stupid you were to lock yourself away with a man like Rudder."

"If you're so sure he's guilty, why don't you arrest him before he kills someone else?"

"We simply do not have sufficient evidence to stand up in court. We're trying to make him give himself away. He's under constant surveillance, as you know. He can't do any more damage, as long as no other woman is as stupid as you, and refuses our help. This man could be one of a group of mass killers. Remember that."

"How many have there been?" Jennifer asked, keeping her temper with an effort.

"Miss Morgan brings the number to fifteen."

"Holy shit!"

"As you say."

"But where *is* this motive you keep talking about?"

"That we haven't ascertained yet."

"And where's the link between all the victims? Apart from the fact that they were all killed in the same way?"

"That too remains a mystery. We know it's there, and we will find it. The police forces of three countries are working on it."

"And while you're working, more people are going to be killed. I mean, you may be keeping tabs on Jonathan, but if he's part of a group . . ."

"I'm afraid that is a possibility. Which is why you'll see that we really have more important things to do than follow up half-baked theories developed by amateurs."

He was back to his condescending tone, and Jennifer again wanted to bristle. But she had been shot down in flames, and she knew it. She stood up. "But you will check out Colley's whereabouts on the dates of the other murders?"

"Yes, we shall. I wouldn't hold out any great hopes, if I were you, Miss Brand. Dr Colley is a reputable doctor in an established practice. And in any event, your theory has other holes in it. Colley may have been both Openshaw's and Moresby's doctor; he may even have known Morgan . . . but he certainly wasn't the doctor of any of the other people killed. Twelve of them."

Jennifer left the interview room.

"What do you reckon?" Parton asked, when he and his chief had returned to Lampson's office.

"I hate amateurs," Lampson replied.

"But you will check Colley out?"

"No. You will, Ned. When you have a moment."

Parton sat down before the desk. "We don't have much else. No one has much else."

"Well, let's see what we *do* have," Lampson said. "According to the pattern, we've had our last murder in the London area."

"You think they're going to move on from England?" Parton was hopeful.

"I didn't say that. No, they may well move to some other city. I take it the basics have been circulated?"

"Yes. But that isn't going to do anyone any good. We have no suggestion of where the murderers may strike next."

"It'll be some healthy young man or woman, probably an athlete, living alone."

"Absolutely. Let's shorten the list to the most likely ten thousand, shall we, sir?"

Lampson raised his eyebrows; he had never suspected his sergeant of sarcasm before. But he could understand his frustration. "We have more than just that," he said mildly. "I believe this group, this satanic cult or whatever it is, has branches in every country. I also believe that the murders are carried out by members of the local branch, for the simple reason that it is easier for locals to merge into the background. Thus it follows that Rudder is a member of the English branch, or cell, or coven, or whatever you wish to call it. Therefore it follows that keeping him under surveillance could well give us an indication of where the next English murder is going to take place." He grinned. "Cheer up, Ned. Something will turn up. It has to. It always does."

Parton snapped his fingers. "Here's a thought, sir. If you're right, that all the victims will be athletes or very fit people living alone, that lets out Rudder altogether."

"I'm not with you."

"Well, Moresby wasn't living alone. She was living with Rudder. If you're right about the set-up, his various international pals wouldn't thank him for killing his own flatmate and turning the spotlight on himself."

"Don't you have any bloody work to do?" Lampson growled, and began cracking knuckles.

Jennifer returned to the flat. What she had just been told was quite horrifying. If it was true. But it had to be true. No self-respecting policeman would have told her something like that if it wasn't. And Jonathan was still a prime suspect, being played like a fish . . . but she knew he hadn't committed any murders. She just knew it. Lampson was hanging on to him because the police didn't have a clue. Neither did the police of France and Spain, apparently.

All she had learned was that there was something very, very sinister going on, and apparently she was the only one who had the slightest urge to look in the right direction. Well, fuck them, she thought. She was going to find out the truth even if it killed her. There simply had to be a link between Colley and all three deaths.

* * *

She took the Underground to Douglas's flat. Alex had told her to do what she liked with the contents. But this was the first time she had come here since the police had relinquished it. When she had opened the street door, she waited for several seconds in the hall; it was mid morning, and there was nobody about; the house was quiet save for the sound of a vacuum cleaner somewhere in the distance. Slowly she went up the stairs, to the top landing, inserted the key in the lock, and realised her hand was shaking. She stepped into the living room, looked at the so familiar furniture. She inhaled, sharply, but the air was not even musty; the cleaners had thoughtfully opened a window an inch.

She crossed the living room and opened the bedroom door, bracing herself. But the bedroom was also as she remembered it, save that all the bedclothes, even the mattress, had been removed; the bed itself stood stark, metal and wood. She went closer, looking for traces of dried blood, but the work had been very thorough; the bathroom was clean. She returned to the living room, and sat at Doug's desk. Alex had told her that the police had searched the entire flat very carefully, and had then restored everything as they had found it. Jennifer opened the desk drawer and took out the contents: chequebook and bank statements, various credit cards, and, what she was looking for, Doug's diary. He had told her about his diary. His best friend, he had called it. He had never shown her any of the entries.

She opened it, instinctively turning to New Year's Day, because she had finished Old Year's Night sleeping in that bed. "Bliss," he had written. "Sheer bliss. I love this girl." And then some erotic details. Presumably Lampson had read this. Shit on him, she thought.

She flicked the pages, found the appointment with Dr Enderby, the recommendation that he got to see James Colley. Of course, Enderby: she could have saved herself a lot of hassle by coming here instead of ringing the Freedom Clinic. But because of that phone call, and what had happened afterwards, Enderby no longer seemed important; she was nearer to home than that, she was certain. She moved on to the first meeting with Colley. She had not known about it until afterwards.

"Impressed," Doug had written. "Seems to know what he's talking about. Says op. may be necessary, but not a problem. Have to be out of England, for secrecy." Jennifer turned some more pages. "Saw Colley today. Says all arranged for trip to Antibes! Sounds great. Says no one will know. Gave me most thorough physical I've ever had. I wonder why? Only looked at knee last time. Says I am wonderfully fit. Very meticulous. Checks them all out on his list: heart, lungs, kidneys, liver, even balls and prick. Says I'd be a donor's dream." That was the last entry, dated 18 May. A Friday. The day before he had died.

Antibes! He had not mentioned it to her, because he hadn't seen her; that Friday she'd already been on her way down to Cornwall. He had been going to a clinic in Antibes. Colley had been quite open about that. But he had also sent Jonathan's uncle to a clinic in Antibes, again, quite openly. Wherever she looked there were connecting links, except for the vital one: why? And also how, if Colley could not be connected to any of the murders on the continent, as the police seemed certain would be the case?

A link. She had to find a link. She snapped her fingers. Doug had been murdered a few days before he had been due to go to the Antibes' clinic for treatment. Angela Moresby had seen Colley on the Monday morning. Suppose, just suppose, he had suggested *she* go to the Antibes clinic . . . But why? It didn't make sense, when she was about to be murdered. But it might still be interesting to know what Angela had recorded in her diary about that interview. Supposing she kept a diary.

She hunted through the phone book, and telephoned Anne Moresby. No reply. Not even an ansaphone. She brooded at the phone. Jonathan had said Anne had been managing and coaching her sister, nothing else, no other job. Also, she hadn't been home yesterday. She was tempted to call him and ask for help, but he would only poop-pooh her again. Then she remembered that the Moresby girls had had an elderly mother, living in . . . Hastings. It was not a fortnight since Angela's murder. Anne would surely have returned to be with her mother.

She called inquiries and got the number without difficulty, and realised she was trembling again as she listened to the phone buzzing. "Hello."

A young woman's voice. "Is that Anne Moresby?"

"Yes." The voice was inquisitive; Anne was recognising her American accent.

"Jennifer Brand. We met last Saturday, remember? Miss Moresby, I wonder if I could speak with you again. It is most terribly important."

"You are speaking with me."

"I didn't mean on the phone. I'd like to have a look at some of your sister's effects, if I may."

"Angie's things? Whatever for."

"Could you tell me if she kept a diary?"

"Yes, she did."

"Do you think I could see it?"

"You, want to look at my sister's diary? Well, really, Miss Brand . . ."

"I think it could help to find her killer," Jennifer said. "You want him found, don't you?"

"Of course I do. But . . ."

"I only want to look up one entry."

"Well . . . are you sure it might help?"

"Positive."

"The diary is at my flat in Chelsea."

"Will you be coming back up to town any time?"

"I hadn't planned to."

"If you came up this morning," Jennifer said, as winningly as she could, "I'd offer you lunch."

She placed Doug's diary in her handbag, locked up the flat and went home. She had an hour to wait before Anne arrived, and she was wet through with her morning's exertions and the various ideas which were flooding through her brain. She had a shower, changed into a pale green pants suit with a white shirt, and then drove to Hammersmith. She was waiting on the pavement when the little roadster pulled into a parking space on the far side of the square, and Anne came towards her. "This is real good of you," Jennifer said.

"I hope it serves some purpose," Anne said. "You must know that letting you see my sister's diary . . ." she led the way up the steps and unlocked the street door. "It's all full of mush about Rudder, anyway."

So she has read it, Jennifer reflected. "As I said, I only want to look at one entry. The day before she died."

Anne frowned as she led the way up the stairs to the first floor, and unlocked the door there as well. "You think that she could have recorded something that could have some bearing on her murderer?"

"Yes. Yes, I do."

"Well, come in." Anne went to her writing bureau, a rolltop, pulled the front down, and took out the little brass-bound book. "There we are. Sit down."

Jennifer sat down, and Anne handed her the book. Jennifer turned the pages; her hands were trembling again, but now with excitement. "Sunday, 20 May: Good day for it. Feeling great. Jonathan home late and covered in blood. Can't remember fighting! Sometimes I wonder. But he must be told. Timing!

"Late PM: What a day. I've qualified for Wimbledon! And Jonny is happy about the baby! Oh, I am so proud. Then he goes and has a fight in the bar! What will Anne say?! And Mumsy?! Is it true?! Will Colley call? Such a nice man."

Anne was standing behind Jennifer, reading over her shoulder. "If only the stupid girl had told me," she remarked. "And she wasn't even pregnant."

Jennifer turned the page. "Monday, 21 May: AM: Jonny's away. Such a relief. Am I disloyal? My husband! But the flat is so quiet. Will Colley call? Anne for lunch. Brrr." Anne made a clicking sound with her tongue. "PM: What an experience! But fun! Everything! Everywhere! Nice to know I am one hundred per cent fit. He listed them all, heart, lungs, kidneys, liver, womb: he should have listed vagina! But he can examine me again any time. Thank God Jonny isn't here. But where is he? No flights. Drunk! The bastard! Anyway, Anne doesn't suspect. When she does, *fait accompli* – or nothing. Fingers crossed!"

"At least she was happy," Anne commented.

"Yes." Jennifer's thoughts were jumbled.

"What were you looking for?" Anne asked.

"Some connectiom between Doug's last entry and hers. You see, they both saw this Dr Colley virtually the day they died. Don't you think that's odd?"

"Coincidence?"

"Um. I just wondered . . . Colley told Doug he was sending him to a clinic or something he has down in Antibes. I wondered if he'd suggested the same thing to Angela. But he didn't."

"Why should he?"

"I don't suppose there is any reason. It's just that the only possible link I have been able to find between your sister and Doug is that they both went to see the same doctor."

"Yes. Well . . ." Anne reached over her shoulder to retrieve the diary. "Where shall we lunch?"

Jennifer snapped her fingers. "Wait a minute. Can I see that last entry again?" Anne hesitated, then returned the book. Jennifer laid it open on the floor, took Doug's diary from her bag, opened it to the last entry, and laid it beside Angela's. "Doug and Angela never knew each other," she said, kneeling beside the books.

"Not to my knowledge," Anne said.

"Yet here are their last two entries, and they use virtually the same words. This Dr Colley checked them out so thoroughly it was almost embarrassing: heart, lungs, kidneys, liver and genitals."

"Disgusting," Anne commented.

"But don't you see, there's the link. That has to be the link. That . . . oh, my *God*!"

"Whatever is the matter?"

"Doug's very last entry, here. He writes that Colley told him he was a donor's dream. Don't you see? Holy shit! We've all been as blind as bats. Jonathan Rudder went to his old friend James Colley to see if he could get his uncle a new heart, because the waiting list here in England is too long. Colley says, no problem, and sends the old guy off to this clinic in Antibes."

"I'm afraid I don't follow you."

"So right now Eric Rudder is getting his new heart. And you know whose heart it is? It could be Doug's, or Angela's or Philippa Morgan's."

"Are you crazy?"

"I'll tell you who is crazy: James Colley. Listen, do you know what happened to your sister?"

"She was stabbed to death."

"No, she wasn't. She was rendered unconscious, and then she was opened from her neck to her crotch, and gutted." Anne stared at her, horror-stricken. "It's a fact. All of her useful internal organs were removed. And you know why? Because they were all in perfect condition. The same thing happened to Doug, and the same thing happened to Philippa. And, the same things have happened to another twelve people who have been murdered during the past year."

Anne clasped both hands to her neck. "That's not possible!"

"Isn't it? The police know there have been fifteen serial killings, but they can't figure out why. Because they haven't seen these diaries. Figure it out for yourself. What's the big problem with spare parts surgery? There aren't enough spare parts. Aren't we always being told we should carry a card around saying we're prepared to donate our organs to people who need them? Begging us to, because there are always more people needing than there are giving. So someone gets the idea, it could be Colley but it's more likely he's just a front man: why not let's build up a bank of spare parts, keep them on ice, maybe, so that whenever anyone comes to us we can say right, you're on. Supply and demand. Big business. If you don't mind a corpse or two."

Anne had been staring at her while she spoke. Now she suddenly stooped and snatched Angela's diary from the floor. "That's the most disgusting thing I ever heard,!" she snapped. "You must have a diseased brain. Get out! Get out of my flat."

"I was going to take you out to lunch."

"Lunch with you? Ugh!"

"Well . . . may I borrow that diary? To show to the police?"

"Certainly not. I don't want to hear from you again. Get out!"

* * *

A diseased brain, Jennifer thought, as she banged the street door behind her. Somebody had a diseased brain. A whole lot of somebodies. She was sure she was right. There could be no other reason for fifteen totally unrelated murders. Yet the possibilities that were opening up in front of her . . . it wasn't just having a clinic of one's very own, it was having doctors and clinics available in at least three countries, all basically cold-blooded murderers. Of course Lampson wasn't going to find any link between Colley and Spain; there was somebody else down there doing the examining and then pointing the finger.

Who then carried out the murders? But they were irrelevant, compared with the man who had thought this up, and put it into practice. She hailed a taxi to return to her flat. She wanted to be there, alone, to think. What to do next? To go back to Lampson would be useless, and might even be disastrous. Her only proof were those two diary entries, and a policeman might not consider them proof – even if Anne Moresby would allow the police to compare them.

But something had to be done, and quickly, before there was another death. Jonathan, of course! He'd have to listen to her now. She paid off the driver, ran up the stairs, slammed the door shut and punched out the numbers of Blessop Manor.

"Blessop?"

"Who's that?"

"This is the butler speaking, madam."

"Oh, say, you must be Caunt. Is Mr Rudder there?"

"Mr Rudder is away, madam."

"Away? Oh, I mean young Mr Rudder. Jonathan."

"Mr Jonathan is not in at the moment, madam."

"Has he been in today?"

"He came in this morning, then he went out again."

"Damn! What time is he coming back?"

"I have no idea, madam. Sometimes he does not come back for several days. Shall I take a message?"

"No," she said. "I'll probably call back." She hung up, gazing at the telephone. What to do? She had the whole thing in her hand, she was sure . . . and there was nothing she could do about it. Save perhaps get some additional proof. There was only one way to do that. But she needed a backup. She made herself a light lunch, because there was always the chance that Jonathan might have returned, or might call her at home. Then she telephoned Blessop again. "Caunt," she said. "It's me again. Do you know who I am?"

"I'm afraid not, madam."

"I'm Jennifer Brand. Has Mr Jonathan mentioned me to you?"

"No, madam."

"Well, I'm a friend of his. A very good friend."

"Yes, madam?" He sounded sceptical.

"Just for starters," Jennifer said, "he spent last night at my flat."

"Indeed, madam?"

She felt like shaking him all the way along the line. "We're working together on solving these murders. So he'd want you to help me any way you can."

"If I can, madam."

"Caunt, I want you to listen very carefully to what I have to say. This afternoon, I am going to the Freedom Clinic. Do you know where that is?"

"Oh, yes, madam."

"Because they're the people looking after Mr Eric Rudder, right? Say, any word on the old man?"

"Not as yet, madam."

"Then everything must be going well. Right. I am going to the Freedom Clinic to ask some questions." She looked at her watch. "I shall be there at three. Now, I am going to telephone you at three-thirty, at four, and at four-thirty, if I have to. In other words, I will call every half an hour on the half hour until I leave the Clinic. Is that all right with you?"

"If that is what you wish to do, madam."

"When I finally leave the Clinic, I will call and tell you. But until I do, expect a call every half an hour."

"I shall do so, madam."

"Now, if I don't call, on the half hour, every half hour mind, until I give you the all clear, I want you to telephone Chief-Inspector Lampson at New Scotland Yard, and repeat this conversation to him."

"Yes, madam." Now Caunt was sounding doubtful.

"Tell him I have gone looking for evidence, and as I haven't called, I need help, fast. You got that?"

"Yes, madam." He clearly wasn't happy.

"But you're only to do this if I don't call in, right?"

"I understand, madam."

"And should Mr Jonathan come in, or contact you, I want you to repeat this conversation to him. Tell him I am sure I know what is going on, but I have to be able to prove it."

"Yes, madam."

Jennifer hesitated, but he seemed to understand. "Okay, Caunt. You'll be hearing from me at three-thirty."

"I shall look forward to it, madam. What will you say?"

"Eh?"

"Well, madam, to be sure it's you calling, and that you are all right, we should have some kind of coded signal, should we not?"

"Say, that's real smart," Jennifer said in genuine admiration. "Okay! I'll call and say I'm all right. But every time I call, I'll ask how Mr Eric is. If I don't ask that, or I don't call, you go into action. Right?"

"Right, madam. And madam, the best of luck."

"Thanks." Jennifer hung up; she felt quite exhilarated. Was she nuts? But she didn't reckon so, for two reasons. Firstly, she had never been examined and had all her organs pronounced perfect, even supposing they were – therefore she was not a prospective victim. Secondly, and far more important, if she was clearly dealing with people who thought absolutely nothing of killing, they also had to be part of a vast and efficient organisation. Organisations like that were likely to fall apart if a single spanner was thrown into the works, and if she was right, and they had done Philippa Morgan on the spur of the moment, they would know they had taken quite a risk – thus they'd be pretty cautious about any more risks. And thirdly, she intended to make sure they knew all about her precautions.

She was just leaving the flat when the phone buzzed. She dived at it: Jonathan! "Jennifer? Richard."

"Oh." She sat down.

"I gather you're not coming in today? Is it because of last night?"

"No, nothing to do with last night." She wasn't in the mood to tackle that right now. "It's to do with Doug's death. Something has come up."

"Is there anything I can do to help?"

She was tempted. The more troops she commanded the better. "Would you like to?"

"Well, of course I would, my dear girl. I thought I'd made that clear."

"Yes. Yes, you did. Well, Richard, you could help a lot, if you liked. I'd be ever so grateful." A promise she could interpret in her own way, when the time came – she was committed to resigning, anyway.

"Just tell me what you want me to do."

"I have to go to see a doctor this afternoon. But I'm short of wheels. I wonder if you could pick me up."

"Pick you up from the doctor? Is that all?"

"Well, I was hoping you'd bring me back here. I don't think we ever finished our conversation of last night, did we, thanks to the appearance of that big lug?"

Suddenly his voice was enthusiastic. "No, we didn't. Just what is Rudder to you, anyway?"

"An acquaintance. I told you, we're sharing ideas on this murder thing, because Angela Moresby was his fiancée, and Doug was mine. Nothing more than that. I'll tell you all about it later. Can you pick me up?"

"What time?"

"Four o'clock."

"Four? It'll mean leaving the office early . . ."

"No one has to know where you're going. Especially Roxanne. And you could bring me back here after, and . . . you'll still be home on time at six."

"Yes. I suppose I would be. Back to your flat. You're on. What hospital?"

"The Freedom Clinic, off the Edgware Road. It's easy to find." She gave him the address.

"Right. Four o'clock."

"On the button. And if I'm not waiting, insist on seeing me."

"I might just do that."

Jennifer replaced the phone, and found she was smiling at herself. She was a born organiser. Dr James Colley was going to find the odds just too stacked against him, if he tried anything funny.

She called a taxi, and was at the Clinic just after three.

"I'm sorry, miss," said Mrs Malcolm. "Dr Colley only sees patients by appointment. And you don't have one."

"But he saw me the other day," Jennifer said. "I came with Mr Rudder, remember? It's very important that I see him now."

"Well . . . I'll see what I can do. Would you take a seat in the waiting room, please? He shouldn't be too long."

"Shit," remarked Nan Welldon. Colley raised his eyebrows. "She's on to something."

"What makes you think that?"

"Well, she has to be. I knew taking out that American woman was too risky. I said so at the time. You just wanted to get your hands on those boobs . . ."

"Simmer down," he recommended. "I don't think it can do any harm to hear what the young lady has to say, if anything. Bring her up in ten minutes. And if we have to . . ."

"No!" Nan snapped. "Absolutely not. That would be utter madness."

He grinned at her. "I accept it would have to be handled differently. But you know, I think it could well turn out enormously to our advantage. You fetch her up." He picked up his private phone. "I may have a small problem," he said into the mouthpiece. "I can't tell you what I'll need, because I don't know yet. But have the whole team standing by. It'll be some time in the next hour, if I need you at all."

He replaced the phone, leaned back in his chair, and got up as Nan Welldon opened the door. "Miss Brand. What a pleasant surprise."

"It's good of you to see me at such short notice," Jennifer said.

"Always willing to help, if I can. Do sit down."

"Thank you." She sat in front of the desk, glanced at Nan, who was hovering in the doorway. "Do you mind if we speak in private?"

"I'm afraid I never see patients without Nurse Welldon present," Colley said. "Especially attractive young women. You must know how many molestation cases are brought against doctors, nowadays."

"You mean, if she leaves, you are liable to assault me?"

Colley smiled. "If she left, it would leave you free to say that I did. Did you come here to discuss medical ethics?"

Jennifer glanced at Nan again, then reflected that she was probably in on it as well. But if there were going to be two of them, it was even more important that she had to establish her position from the outset. "Before we start, may I use your phone?"

He raised his eyebrows, and glanced at Nan, who shrugged. "Be my guest."

Jennifer waited for Caunt to answer. He took a very long time, and she was beginning to feel a slight sense of panic when at last she heard the familier, "Blessop."

"Ah, Caunt," she said. "Jennifer Brand. Any word on Uncle Eric?"

"No, miss. It's not half-past three."

"I know. I'm early. It's just that I'd like you to repeat my instructions to this gentleman. Tell him who you are and what you do. But leave out you-know-who. Dr Colley?"

"You wish me to speak to your friend?"

"If you'd be so kind."

Colley took the phone. "Hello?" He listened to what Caunt had to say. "I see," he said at last. "It all sounds very quaint. Thank you, Caunt. I'll see she calls every half hour until she leaves here." He replaced the phone. "I think you have been seeing too many X-rated movies, Miss Brand. Unfortunately, I am not a psychiatrist. But I can recommend a very good man. He'll have you right as rain in no time at all."

"I think there is something else you should know, doctor," Jennifer said.

"I can hardly wait."

"Mr Richard Ebershaw is coming here to collect me at four o'clock. That is in just under an hour's time.

Mr Ebershaw is managing director of Consolidated Business Associates. My boss."

"I shall look forward to meeting him. But seriously, Miss Brand, much as I would like to assist you in any possible way in finding the people who murdered your fiancé, I simply cannot spend the whole afternoon chatting with you. I have a great deal of work to do. So, would you please ask me whatever it is you wish, and I will endeavour to answer it, and then you can leave, with Mr Ebershaw, whenever he arrives."

He was certainly a very confident man. "All right, Colley," she said. "I think you should understand that I know the whole story."

"What whole story?"

"I have found out," Jennifer said, "that Doug's murder and that of Angela Moresby, weren't isolated. I have found out that there have been a total of fifteen murders committed, probably by the same people, certainly by the same organisation, over the past six to nine months."

"Really? They don't seem to have reached the newspapers."

"Only three of them have taken place in this country. The others were in Spain and France."

"I see. Then how do you know they were linked?"

"The modus operandi. In each case, all the internal organs were removed."

"Good lord," Colley said. "Is that what happened to Openshaw and Miss Morseby? That was never reported in the newspapers, either."

Jennifer began to feel frustrated; he was showing not the slightest sign of alarm – she couldn't even make out any sweat on his face or neck. "That is what happened, yes. And I'll tell you something else: all the victims were chosen specifically because they were either athletes or very fit. *That* wasn't reported in the newspapers, either."

"Absolutely. I'm not sure what this has to do with me."

"Try this. Doug came to see you."

"That is correct. As I explained to you when last you were here, he had a cartilage problem which required surgery. I was going to send him to a clinic in France, so that it could be done on the QT, and the English team selectors would never know about it. But you know all of this."

"You also gave him a very thorough medical examination. Not on the occasion of his first visit. On the occasion of his second. Isn't that odd?"

"I don't understand why you should think that. Openshaw came to me about his knee. I examined the knee, and decided that he needed surgery. I had to contact the clinic in France to see if they could take him. They said yes. It then became necessary to give him a complete check-up. That is one of the rules of this particular clinic. They don't like to have patients turning up for what should be a minor operation, and then find out there is some other, serious, complaint lurking in the background. So they require the GP's, or the specialists who refer patients to them, to guarantee the general health of the patient."

She glared at him, and he continued to smile. "So you tested his heart and his lungs and his kidneys and his liver and his genitals."

"I'm afraid that is standard practice, Miss Brand. Have you never had a general physical?"

"Would you like to give me one?"

"I can think of nothing that would give me greater pleasure. If you'd like to go with Sister Welldon into her office, she'll make an appointment. But do you need a physical? Or wish one?"

"It's just that, if you did, you might discover that all of my organs were in perfect condition, too."

"I would say they probably are, looking at you."

"Worth keeping, eh?"

"Absolutely."

"Just as, when Angela Moresby came to see you for a pregnancy test, you gave her, too, a complete check-up."

"I did. It was the first time she had come to me. I had to know with whom I was dealing. She thought she was pregnant, and I wished to make sure there was no risk of complications."

"You didn't examine Doug the first time *he* came to you."

"He wasn't pregnant," Colley said wearily. "And I have just explained why I examined him at all. Miss Brand, I am beginning to find your questions, indeed, your very presence, rather offensive. I've been as patient with you as possible, because I sympathise with you over the death of your fiancé, and because you are a friend of Jonathan's. But now, I simply must ask you to leave. And I must also tell you, that if you persist in this absurd hounding of me and my clinic, I shall refer the matter to my solicitors. Good day to you, Miss Brand."

Jennifer stood up. "And suppose I asked to be shown the contents of every deep freeze and refrigerator in this building?"

"I would say you, or anyone else, is welcome to do so, the very moment you have obtained a search warrant. We are a hospital, Miss Brand. What we keep in our refrigerators and deep freezes is our concern. Now, will you leave, or shall I have you thrown out? You may, if you wish, wait for Mr Ebershaw in the downstairs lobby." Jennifer glared at him, and then at Nan Welldon, who was holding the door for her. "Oh, by the way, Miss Brand," Colley said. "Should you neglect to telephone Mr Caunt and have this Dick Tracy type arrangement of yours cancelled, and the police arrive here looking for you, I shall indeed place the matter of defamation of character in the hands of my solicitor."

Jennifer stamped through the door.

Nan returned in a few minutes. "She is waiting downstairs, for this man Ebershaw. Do you know him?"

"By reputation. He's a high-powered American-type businessman."

"Oh, my God!" She sat before the desk.

"He will know all the legal problems involved in making criminal allegations without adequate proof. I don't think anything will devolve there for a while."

"But things *are* going to devolve, eventually," Nan said, and leaned forward. "Jimmy, we are up shit creek without a paddle. That girl knows exactly what is going on."

"That girl *knows* nothing. She has managed to work things out. But she has absolutely no proof."

"If she makes enough stink, people are going to find proof. Jimmy, I'm frightened."

"It would be rather ridiculous to lose our heads," Colley pointed out. "The operation has worked like a charm up to now. There is no reason for it not to work in the future. What have we got? One maverick female, who had the gall to go charging up to Jonathan Rudder and say, whoever murdered your fiancée murdered mine as well, and has taken it from there. She is the only one who has the slightest suspicion that we are involved."

"What about that policeman?"

"He was looking for information on Jonathan."

"And that's another thing! You set Rudder up tc be arrested for the Morgan woman's murder, and nothing at all has happened."

"We don't know that. I'm quite sure the police are working on it."

"Until Jennifer Brand goes to them with her story, which she is going to be doing any minute now." She looked at her watch. “It’s ten to four. And there is damn all you can do about it.”

“Isn’t there?”

“You lay a finger on her, after everything else, and the police are going to *have* to get interested in us.”

“If it can be proved that I laid a finger on her,” Colley pointed out. “Don’t you think it strange that a man like Richard Ebershaw should pick up his secretary in the middle of the afternoon from a visit to the doctor?”

“Not if he knows why she came here.”

“If he did, Nan, he’d have come with her. No, she’s following this on her own. But that doesn’t mean she doesn’t have some outside interests. She and Ebershaw are clearly having it off, with or without Rudder’s consent. But it creates an interesting situation.” He picked up the phone, made a call. “May I speak with Mr Ebershaw, please,” he told the telephonist.

“I’m sorry. Mr Ebershaw has just left the building.”

“When will he be back?”

“Mr Ebershaw won’t be in again this afternoon, sir.”

“I see. It’s rather important that I speak with him. He’s gone home, has he?”

“No, sir. Mr Ebershaw has an appointment. Who is calling, please?”

“I’ll just have to try again tomorrow,” Colley said, and hung up. “Phone book,” he said. “Jennifer Brand.”

Nan riffled the pages. “Here we are. Moleton Close, Chelsea. Number fifty-seven, flat two. Jim, you can’t do it.”

“Do what?” He punched out another set of numbers. “Marcus? I have that very special job I mentioned earlier. I want you to listen very carefully.”

* * *

Jennifer stalked up and down the lobby, watched with great interest by Mrs Malcolm. What was so annoying was that she didn't even seem to have upset Colley, or his witch of a nurse. They had treated her inquiries with contempt. So what was she to do now? Turn to Jonathan? He needed to find out the truth even more than she did, in view of the police suspicions.

But first of all there was Richard to be attended to, because there was his town car, an Alfa-Romeo, pulling into the car park. "Mind how you go, dear," Mrs Malcolm advised, as Jennifer pushed open the glass doors.

"You look all hot and bothered," Ebershaw said as she got in beside him.

"I am all hot and bothered."

"What did you have to see a doctor about, anyway?"

"It's a long story. Good lord, it's four o'clock."

"That's when you said to pick you up."

"May I use the car phone?"

"Help yourself."

She called Blessop. "I have left the Clinic, Caunt," she said.

"Yes, madam?" Caunt's tone was expectant.

"Oh . . . ah, how is Mr Eric?"

"We are waiting on a report, madam."

"So, forget it."

"Very good, miss." Caunt's tone now suggested that he might already have done that.

"Mr Rudder back yet?"

"I'm afraid not, miss."

"Well, don't forget to put him in the picture." She replaced the handset.

"Back to Rudder, eh?" Richard asked.

"I told you, we're working on this thing together. There is absolutely nothing else between us."

"I believe you," he said, unconvincingly.

"That's why I was at that clinic," she explained. "I'm positive they're mixed up in it somehow."

"The Freedom Clinic? Mixed up in what?"

"The murders."

"That's going it a bit. Ah, parking."

She realised they were outside her flat. But she had suggested this to entice him out, and she had been so upset by her interview with Colley she hadn't been concentrating on how to get off this particular hook. But maybe Jonathan would turn up again. "Shall we go up?" Richard asked, gently.

"Oh . . . yes, of course." She unlocked the street door, led him up the stairs, unlocked the flat door, brain seething as she tried to think of some way to put him off. By being downwright rude, of course – and handing him her resignation.

She stepped into the flat, and Richard immediately stepped behind her, putting his arms round her waist to bring her back against him, while his hands moved up, under her jacket, to caress her breasts through her shirt. "If you knew how long I've dreamed of this," he whispered in her ear.

She contemplated kicking backwards, but decided against it. Must keep it civilised. Gently she held his hands and moved them away, then stepped away herself, at some speed, and gained the relative safety of the kitchenette. "What's with you?" he asked, following more slowly.

"Richard," she said. "I didn't invite you here to have an affair."

He raised his eyebrows. "What are you, some kind of a prick-tease?" He was speaking quietly, but red spots were gathering in his cheeks and she knew he was very angry.

"It's just that I'm not in the mood right now. You can't hold that against me. Douglas hasn't been dead a fortnight."

He sat down. "You mean, you wouldn't mind a get together when you're finished mourning."

"I don't know. I'd have to think about it."

"You *are* a prick-tease," he said. "You invited me here this afternoon, you know."

"I know, Richard. I'm sorry. I wanted to make sure the people at the hospital knew I was being picked up."

"Why on earth should you wish to do that?"

"It's a long story. Would you like to hear it?"

"Thank you, no. The fact is, you did call on me for help, and I gave it to you, on the clear understanding, that we would come back here afterwards, and . . ."

"You would be rewarded, is that it?" Jennifer was beginning to lose her temper. "You are a class A shit, Richard Ebershaw. Did you know that?"

His head jerked. "We seem to be in the same league. But as I am here, I think I'll have something on account, Jennifer. I don't believe you are doing any mourning for Douglas Openshaw. I don't believe you ever gave a damn for him. You just like paddling your own canoe, as the mood takes you. Well you just come over here and paddle my canoe." He unbuckled his belt. "Lips and fingers will do. I said it was on account."

"Get out," she said. "Just get up and leave."

"Do you think you can speak to me like that?" He stood up, and his pants dropped about his ankles.

"Sure I can," Jennifer said. "I'm not your secretary any more, Richard. I quit."

"You're still going to fulfil your end of the bargain," he said, stepping out of his pants. "Now, do you want any rough stuff?"

"You think you can come here and browbeat me into having sex? You . . ." the street door phone buzzed. "Oh, thank God for that!" She darted for the door. Ebershaw tried to stop her, but she ducked under his arm and reached the phone. "Yes!" she gasped. "Jonathan?"

"That shit again," Ebershaw growled, but he put his pants back on.

"Police, Miss Brand," said a woman's voice.

"Don't tell me you're still watching the apartment? But I'm glad you are. Come on up."

She released the hall door, and faced him. "I won't say anything about this, Richard, if you just walk out of here."

He finished dressing himself. "I'll do that. And I don't ever want to see or hear of you again, you little bitch."

"Believe me, the feeling is mutual." The door opened, and she turned to look at the woman who stood there. Behind her was a man. Neither wore uniform. "Well, hello," Jennifer said. "Are you from Chief-Inspector Lampson?"

The woman stepped into the room. The man followed her, closed and locked the door. The woman reached into her handbag and took out a small automatic pistol. "Just be sensible," she said. "And nobody is going to get hurt."

CHAPTER 8

"Just what the hell is going on?" Ebershaw demanded. "Let me see your badge."

"Forget the badge, Ebershaw," the woman said. "Get into the bedroom."

Ebershaw looked at Jennifer, who was trying to keep from screaming, as she watched the man also draw a pistol, and realised they were both wearing skin-tight gloves. She had no doubt that she was looking at Doug's murderers. They had been described as two men, but one of the men had been small and dark – this woman! If that was the case . . . the man was holding a large carryall in his left hand. She just hadn't reckoned Colley would dare do anything like this. It was too risky, surely. Caunt knew she had gone to the Clinic, so she would be the third person to visit him and then be found tied to her bed and gutted. He wouldn't dare!

Ebershaw was looking back at the woman. "The bedroom?" he asked uneasily.

"You came here for sex, didn't you?" the woman asked. "You don't want to be disappointed, do you?" Ebershaw licked his lips, glanced at Jennifer again, and slowly moved towards the bedroom. "You too," the woman said.

"If you think you can make us . . ."

"Miss Brand," the woman said. "I can make you do anything I like. Now move."

Jennifer hesitated, then followed Richard into the bedroom. "What the hell is going on?" he muttered at her.

"They're going to kill us," she muttered back.

"Kill . . ." he turned, in the middle of the room. Both the man and the woman had now come in.

"Draw those curtains," the woman said. Jennifer drew the curtains, slowly, staring out at the various back yards behind the building. But at half past four in the afternoon there was nobody around, nobody home from work yet, certainly nobody gardening out there. How lonely could one be, in the middle of one of the most crowded cities in the world! "All right," the woman said. "Now then, you, Ebershaw's your name, right? Strip."

"Eh?"

"You came here for sex. Strip." Richard licked his lips, looked at Jennifer again, and slowly took off his jacket. "Take your time," the woman said. "We're in no hurry." She sat down; the man stood at her shoulder. Both their pistols were unwavering.

"If you fire those things," Jennifer said. "The whole building will hear."

"Is that going to mean anything to you?" the woman asked. "If I fire at you, *you* won't hear a sound. You'll be dead."

Jennifer inhaled, slowly. She had to do something. But she couldn't think what. Richard continued to undress, slowly; he also was clearly trying to think, not too successfully. "You're running to fat," the woman said. "You want to watch it."

Jennifer looked at him for the first time. He was naked, and despite his predicament, quite aroused. No doubt it appealed to his nature to be commanded to strip by a pretty young woman; she remembered reading that outwardly masterful men were often like that. But he was, indeed, more flabby than she had supposed. "Now get into bed," the woman said. "Lie down on your back." Richard lay on the bed, on his back. "Now you have to have sex," the woman said. "I don't care with whom. Take your pick." Richard stared at her, then looked at Jennifer, then looked at the man. "Sure, if that turns you on," the woman said.

Richard licked his lips. "Tell me what's going on," he said. "What's going to happen, after. She says you're going to kill us."

"Well, if that doesn't take the cake," the woman said. "I'm offering you your pick of the three of us, and you're worrying about afterwards. Listen, you have sex, and we'll just take a few photos. How about that."

"Blackmail?" He glared at Jennifer. "You put them up to this, you bitch?"

"They're having you on," Jennifer said. "They're not interested in blackmail."

"Okay, honey, you're elected," the woman said. "Get your clothes off and get in there with him."

"You must be crazy," Jennifer said.

"Look, it's up to you. You can do it with your eyes open, or Marcus is going to give you a little jab, and you'll do it with your eyes shut. That way you won't even enjoy it. Either way your boy friend *will* enjoy it. Won't you, Ebershaw?"

Richard goggled at her. Jennifer wished she could concentrate. It would be so simple to let them give her a jab so she wouldn't know a thing. But then she would never know a thing again. They had given Doug a jab before cutting him up. As long as she was awake she had a chance. Something might turn up. Jonathan! He always had before. She undressed, got into bed beside Ebershaw. "Make it good," the woman said.

The man merely grinned at her.

"You bet I'm going to make it good," Richard said. "You little whore! If you think you are going to get one penny out of me, you're the one's who's crazy. I am going to see you in court."

"Get on with it," she begged.

He was into her before she had properly spread her legs. I am being raped in my own bedroom, she thought. Is this what happened to Doug? He was mercifully quick, rolled off her, gasping. He was a heavy man, and he hadn't troubled to hold his weight off her in any way. "Well?" he demanded. "Satisfied?"

"Not really. Very perfunctory." The woman stood up.

"So where's the camera?" Richard demanded, sitting up.

"No camera," the woman said. While they had been squirming on the bed she had been screwing a silencer into the muzzle of her pistol. Now she stepped up to the bed, put the muzzle to Ebershaw's temple, and before he could move, squeezed the trigger.

Blood and brains flew, and Jennifer gave a gasp of horror and rolled out of the bed, landing on her hands and knees. Even so there was blood scattered across her shoulders and stomach. Ebershaw fell sideways on the bed, bent double; blood dribbled away from his shattered head and soaked the sheets. Jennifer tried to speak, but her throat was absolutely dry.

The woman had turned the pistol on her, and she shrank back against the wall. But, however cold-blooded, this wasn't what they had done to Doug. Or Angela Moresby. Or Philippa Morgan. "Just sit there." the woman said. "Marcus."

Marcus placed the briefcase on the chair and took out his hypodermic. Jennifer licked her lips. "Please," she said.

"Don't worry," the woman said. "We're not going to hurt you. Promise."

Marcus knelt beside her. She wanted to strike at him, fight him, but she knew that would be useless. And yet, if she didn't she was going to die. Horribly. They would find her body ripped open and gutted. She felt the faintest scratch on her arm, gazed at him with wide eyes. Then her head drooped on to her shoulder, and Marcus caught her before she hit the floor. "What about this blood on her?" he asked.

"Doesn't matter. Let's move it. She'd have packed in a hurry. Just one bag, though."

She opened the wardrobe, began taking out clothes, throwing them on to the chair, well away from the bed and the bloodstained body. Marcus laid Jennifer on her back, then took the pistol and wiped it clean, before placing it in her hand and closing her fingers around the butt and on the trigger. He pressed each finger and the thumb to make it appear that she had held the gun tightly, then he removed it again, opening her fingers and holding only the barrel himself, left it on the floor. He stood up and reached above Lois to open the upper cupboard, from where he took a carryall. "Snap," he grinned.

"Don't forget her passport and credit cards." Lois thrust clothes into the carryall, went into the bathroom and returned with an armful of bottles and brushes, thrust them in as well. "That'll do." She looked at her watch. "Not yet five. Six hours."

"Yeah." Marcus went into the living room, sat down, and from his pocket took a pack of cards. "Gin?" Lois sat opposite him, and they played, while the evening drifted by. At six-thirty the telephone buzzed. Marcus looked at it, but Lois shook her head. They continued playing. At seven she opened her bag and took out two packets of sandwiches. Marcus found an opened bottle of wine in the drinks cabinet, and they each had a glass. When they were finished, Lois carefully washed and dried the glasses; they were still wearing their gloves. Then they started playing rummy again. At eight there was a buzz on the street door. It buzzed several times.

"Think I'd better take a look?" Marcus asked.

"Just so long as you're not spotted," Lois told him.

Marcus stood against the side of the window. "I

can't see, no, he's stopped and is walking away. Big fellow."

"Probably Rudder. Anyway, he's not the police."

"He's stopped, and is looking back."

"Be careful," she snapped.

"He's going off again. Doesn't look too happy."

"So he came for a fuck and reckons she's gone out. He won't be back before tomorrow. If then. Your play."

At half past nine it became too dark to play any more.

Marcus put away the cards, then went into the bedroom and lifted Jennifer from the floor. He carried her naked body into the living room, where Lois had opened the big carryall. "Better top her up," Lois suggested.

Marcus took Jennifer's pulse, and gave her another jab. Then between them they inserted her into the bag, having to pull up her legs to make her fit. "She's going to have a stiff neck when she wakes up," Marcus commented.

"If that's all about her that's stiff, she'll be lucky," Lois grunted, zipping the bag.

"Beats me why Colley wants her alive," Marcus said. "I mean, I understand the manoeuvre. But why we don't just do her and dump her . . ."

"Dumped dead bodies have a habit of turning up, sometimes at awkward moments," Lois pointed out. "That's why we always leave the police what they want – the corpus delicti, so that they can spin their little theories. Anyway, she's supposed to have run off after killing a jealous lover."

"One day the police are likely to spin the *right* theory," Marcus grumbled.

"How are they going to do that? We've done our last job in London. As for this one, I would imagine that Colley wants to have a little question and answer session with our American friend, some place where she can't holler for help: she's come too close to the truth, apparently. Anyway, we do what we're told, right?"

Marcus shrugged and sat down again. It grew dark outside. In the block of flats doors were banged and at some stage a baby wailed. A television blared from fairly close at hand. Marcus stood at the side of the window looking down. People went out and came in, walked their dogs, chatted, but by eleven the square was empty, and the movement had ceased. It was also dark, away from the glow of the street lamps. "Time," he said.

Lois picked up the carryall of clothes and the briefcase. "Five minutes." She opened the door, left it open, and went down the stairs. The hallway was dark, and she did not switch on the light. She stepped out of the street door, carefully leaving that open as well, and walked up the pavement with the two bags. When she reached the car, parked on the far side of the square, she put the bags in the boot, got in, started the engine, and drove slowly round the square. She watched the windows of the block of flats, but all with lights in them had the curtains drawn. She drew up, double parked, outside the street door. The door opened, and Marcus appeared. He had the carryall over his shoulder. He closed the door behind him, and came down the steps. Lois already had the back door open, and he dumped Jennifer's body on the back seat. Then he got into the front beside her, and they drove off into the night.

When he left Jennifer's that morning, Jonathan drove out to Blessop. He was there by nine-thirty, and had a second, much heavier, breakfast, courtesy of Caunt, then telephoned the yacht club in Newport and asked to be connected with *Halcyon*. Bruce listened to what he had to say in stunned silence. "Shit!" he commented at last. "Your fiancée *and* Phil? Both gone? What the hell are the police doing?"

"What they can, I suppose. I'm number one suspect."

"You? What the hell for?"
"Something about maniacal rages."
"Shit!" Bruce said again. "Listen . . ." they'd been friends for a long time. "You want me to come over?"
"With what in mind?"
"To tell your police they need their heads examined."
"Maybe you should wait until they actually arrest me," Jonathan suggested.
"Fuck that. That may be too late. I'm gonna talk to the guys. And listen, until I get there, keep your peckah up."
"That's difficult, in the circumstances. People aren't co-operating."
"Stick with it, boy." Bruce was like a breath of fresh air, and Jonathan had to admit that the idea of him over here taking Lampson by the scruff of the neck and getting things done was most appealing, and reassuring.
Meanwhile, he had a day to get through. Jennifer had clearly gone off to work in a huff, so there was nothing doing there before the evening. Sitting around Blessop seemed a fairly depressing prospect . . . he telephoned the Clinic at Antibes. "Mr Rudder has had all his checks," the nurse said. "He will be operated on this afternoon."
"How is he?"
"I think he's very cheerful and confident, Mr Rudder."
"That doesn't sound like my uncle. When can I call back?"
"Well, I should think about eight tonight we'll be able to tell you if the operation was a success, at least in the short-term. You won't be able to speak with your uncle, of course."
"I understand that. I'll call back at eight."
The day was left stretching even more

interminably in front of him. He sat on the terrace and brooded at the Berkshire countryside. Jennifer had been quite upset because he had not gone for her theory. Women were like that. If she had come up with a single concrete suggestion, a positive fact, such as that Philippa had been seen at the Freedom Clinic, it could have been more than supposition. He'd make it up to her tonight.

Sitting around had never been one of Jonathan's favourite pastimes. "I'm going out," he told Caunt.

"Yes, sir. Will you be in for lunch?"

"I doubt that." He got into the Mercedes, drove to the gate, and honked his horn. He had to honk several times before the small Vauxhall emerged from a side lane. "Detective-Constable Dickinson, is it? Just thought I'd let you know I'm going for a spin in the country. Tell you what, why don't you leave your car and come with me. It'll save petrol and bother, and you'll know I won't try to drop you again."

"Wouldn't be proper, sir."

Jonathan shrugged, and drove off. Dickinson fell in behind him. He drove into the Cotswolds, stopped at a pub and had a light but leisurely lunch, especially in the beer line. Presumably Dickinson was having a sandwich in his car. He tried to think. There had to be something, some glimmer of fact which was escaping them all. He finished his lunch, and went for a walk in the hills. That worked off the last of the alcohol. He saw no sign of Dickinson, but he assumed the detective was watching him through binoculars. He went over everything he knew about the three crimes, about Jennifer's suppositions, about James Colley and the Freedom Clinic . . . it was four o'clock before he suddenly had an idea.

He hurried back to his car, waved at Dickinson, and drove back to Blessop as fast as he could, got there at six, ran into the house, panting. "Something wrong, sir?" Caunt asked.

"Something could be right, at last, Caunt. Listen, do I remember Uncle Eric telling me last Friday that his car had just come back from a service?"

"That is correct, sir."

"Then there should be a ticket or an entry in his Owner's Manual recording the exact mileage."

"I should imagine so, sir. I have a message for you."

"Not now, Caunt." He ran down the stairs, and found the neatly entered figure against the 30,000 mile entry in the book. 31,375. He looked at the milometre in the dashboard, and made a note of the current figure: 31,513.

He went back inside with the book. "Did Uncle Eric drive the car at all after it was serviced?"

"No, sir. About this message . . ."

"Then the only person who drove it was Miss Morgan?"

"And the police constable who returned it, sir."

"Ah, yes. Right, now let's see." He sat down with his road atlas. "Blessop to the Freedom Clinic, using the M4 and the Edgware Road, which she almost certainly would have done: twenty-three miles. If she was driven from the Clinic to where the car and her body was found, that's approximately forty miles. From the wood back here, by the most direct route, sixty-three miles. That's a hundred and twenty-six miles, approximately. And the difference between the figure when the car was serviced, and the figure now is . . . a hundred and thirty-eight miles. Damn!"

Caunt was peering over his shoulder. "With respect, sir, Mr Rudder's car was not driven straight from the place where it was found back here. It was taken to a police laboratory in Westminster first, and thoroughly examined and cleaned."

Jonathan snapped his fingers. "I'd forgotten that.

So, from here to the Freedom Clinic and then the wood, sixty-three total." Once again he measured. "The wood to Westminster, approximately fifty-three. That's a hundred and sixteen. And Westminster back to Blessop . . . twenty-two! By God, we've got it. A hundred and thirty-eight."

"Got what, sir."

"Miss Morgan drove the car to the Freedom Clinic, was murdered, taken in the car out to the wood, and left there. The mileage fits."

"Let us say that it is a possibility, sir. That evidence would never stand up in court."

"It's the possibility we were looking for. Okay, she could have driven in some entirely different direction. But why did she wind up in that wood, with a mileage that exactly fits going there via the Freedom Clinic? It may be entirely circumstantial, but Miss Brand is going to be pleased about this."

"I have been trying to tell you, sir, Miss Brand called here earlier. She said she was going to the Freedom Clinic then."

"*What*!" Caunt outlined what Jennifer had told him. "And you did nothing about it?" Jonathan shouted. "Good God, Caunt . . ."

"I did what the young lady wished me to do, sir. And it is perfectly all right. She called back just after four to say that she had now left the Clinic, and that my other instructions were cancelled."

Jonathan glared at him. "It was still a bloody stupid thing for her to have done." He picked up the telephone, punched out Jennifer's number, listened to the telephone buzzing, and looked at his watch. It was six-thirty. She was probably still at work. Save that she hadn't gone to work today, if she'd been at the Freedom Clinic. He got up. "If Miss Brand calls back, tell her I'm on my way."

"Aren't you going to have dinner, sir?"

"I'll have it with Miss Brand."

The traffic was heavy, and it was just on eight when Jonathan reached Moleton Close. He parked his car, walked along the pavement, and looked up at the apartment block; there were no lights to be seen on the first floor. But it was still broad daylight. He went up the steps, and rang the bell. And again. No response. She'd gone out. Where the hell to, on her own? But of course she wouldn't be on her own. He'd never probed too deeply into her private life, but she must have dozens of other acquaintances, possible dates . . . even that creep Ebershaw might have crawled back out of the woodwork.

He pressed the bell a last time, walked out into the square, paused, and looked back, just in case she'd come to the window to see who it was. For a moment he even thought he saw movement there, but then decided he'd been mistaken, and walked on. He reached his car, and spotted Dickinson a few yards down the road. "She's not in," he shouted, got behind the wheel and drove off not very far; he was both hungry and thirsty. He found a restaurant, parked, and had dinner.

Where the hell was she? But she had made it so very clear that she was her own boss, made her own decisions, did her own thing. He was just a hanger-on in Jennifer Brand's scheme of things. He had a brandy to top his meal off. So what if he was done? He felt like being done, if only to have something to fight against. It was a quarter past eleven before he left the restaurant, staggering slightly as he reached his car. He found Dickinson beside him. "Begging your pardon, Mr Rudder, but if you try to get into that car I shall have to arrest you."

Jonathan looked at him. "Good at karate, are you?"

"Middling, sir. But right now, you aren't going to be good at anything. Look, where do you want to go? Back out to Blessop? I'll drive you, and you can pick up your car in the morning."

"I thought that was against the rules?"

Dickinson almost smiled. "I'm supposed to stop you doing anything foolish."

"That's very kind of you. As a matter of fact, I wasn't going home. I was going back to Miss Brand's flat. She'll be home by now. I don't suppose you'd care to drop me there?"

"Certainly, sir. Get in."

Jonathan squeezed his bulk into the little Vauxhall, and Dickinson drove back to Moleton Close. "The flat is still in darkness."

Jonathan peered at it, then looked at his watch. Half-past eleven. "That's ridiculous. She'd be home by now."

"Not necessarily, sir. Not if she'd gone to the theatre."

Jonathan glared at him. "All right, when do you suppose she would she be home, if she'd gone to a show?"

Dickinson shrugged. "Midnight. Maybe after, if she'd stopped for a meal."

"Well, you go on home, then, because I intend to wait until she does get in."

"Very good, sir. I am due to be relieved at midnight. I shall just call in to let my replacement know where to come, shall I?"

"Be my guest," Jonathan said, morosely; he had had this kind of runaround with Angie.

Dickinson called, and explained the situation. Fifteen minutes later another Vauxhall appeared. "You'll have to change cars, sir."

"I'll just get out." There was a small park in the centre of the square, but this was railed and at night the gates were locked. Jonathan found an outside bench and sat down, gazing at the houses opposite; it was a warm and starry night. The police car parked up one of the side streets, and the driver came to stand on the corner, nonchalantly. Midnight passed, and then half past. Jonathan got up and walked across to the policeman. "Dickinson explained what I'm doing?"

"He did, sir."

"What's your name?"

"Haydon, sir."

"Well, Haydon, I believe something is wrong. I do not believe Miss Brand would have gone out to the theatre and not returned by now. So I intend to force an entry into that flat."

"You can't do that, sir. You'll be arrested."

"By you?"

"If necessary."

"Then arrest me."

Detective Constable Haydon scratched his ear, uncertainly. This whole business, of being on chatting terms with the man under surveillance, was highly irregular. He did not care to think what the Chief Inspector was going to say if he pulled the man in just because he asked to be. "I shall arrest you, sir, if you commit a crime."

"Then you'd best come along," Jonathan said, and strode up to the house and up the steps. After a moments hesitation, Haydon followed, but remained a discreet distance behind. Jonathan pressed the ground floor bell; the flat apparently belonged to a Mr and Mrs Manly. It rang for some time before a man's voice answered. "Who's there."

"Police," Jonathan said. "Open up."

"Police?" The man's voice rose an octave. "Not again? What's the matter? What's happened?"

"Open up and I'll tell you," Jonathan said.

He listened to noises beyond the door, and a moment later it swung in. "What the hell is going on?" demanded the man in a dressing gown and with tousled hair. "Do you know the time?" He frowned at Jonathan. "You don't look like a policeman. Where's your badge?"

"Plainclothes," Jonathan said, putting his foot in the door. "My colleague is outside. You Mr Manly?"

"Yes. You can't come in without a badge, or a warrant," the man insisted.

"I am in," Jonathan pointed out, gently moving him to one side as he entered the hall. "Now you can tell me something. Where is the lady in the first floor flat?"

"Out."

"At this hour? What time did she go out?"

"About eleven."

"That's a bloody odd hour to go out. You saw her?"

"No." Manly looked down the steps at D.C. Haydon, who was waiting there. "I heard her. Someone used the steps at about eleven. Then there was the noise of a car engine, and the person drove away."

"Then you don't know it was Miss Brand at all:"

"Whoever it was came out of her flat. I heard her moving about up there, and the door closing."

"Miss Brand drives a Renault Twelve. Was it a Renault Twelve drove away at eleven?"

"How should I know?"

"Let's find it." Jonathan went back out into the square, and located Jennifer's car in five minutes. "She hasn't gone anywhere," he told Haydon, who had dutifully followed him.

"She'd hardly have taken her own car to go to the theatre, sir, unless she was certain of finding parking."

"She'd hardly have gone to the theatre at eleven o'clock, unless you know of show which is currently starting at midnight." He went back to the block of flats. "I'm going up. You coming?"

"You can't do that, Mr Rudder. The lady has gone out. This gentleman says so." Manly had remained standing in the doorway, watching them.

"This gentleman says somebody left this building at eleven o'clock. He doesn't know it was Miss Brand. It could have been anyone. Now we know it *wasn't* Miss Brand." It could even have been her killers, he thought in a sudden panic, and turned back to the flat holder. "You're sure it was just one person?"

"Come to think of it, there was a lot of movement up there. But the front door only closed once."

"Well, it would have, if two people had left together. Haydon, something's wrong up there. We have to find out."

Haydon shifted from foot to foot uncertainly. "Have you heard anything suspicious from up there?" he asked Manly. "Any unusual noises."

"No."

"What time did you come in from work?" Jonathan asked.

"Just after six."

"And you've heard nothing since then. But what about before? What about your wife?"

"She works too. She got in at four."

"May we speak with her?"

"No, you may not. She's in bed."

"I'm here, Bert." A surprisingly young woman appeared behind him, also wrapped in a dressing gown. "What's the trouble?"

"Good evening, ma'am," Jonathan said. "We would just like to know if you heard, or saw, anything suspicious with regard to the upstairs flat this afternoon."

"Suspicious? Well, there were those two coppers . . ."

"Eh?"

"At about half-past four. It was just after I got in. They rang the bell for the first-floor. Well, the window was open and I couldn't help overhearing what they said. Police, they said. Then they came in; Miss Brand must have let them in."

Jonathan looked at Haydon. "Were these people in uniform, Mrs Manly?" Haydon asked.

"No. They were plainclothes people. Like you two. Except one was a woman."

"And they went up to Miss Brand's flat, at half-past four. What time did they leave?"

Mrs Manly shrugged. "I dunno. I went and had my bath after they went upstairs. I never heard them leave."

"Until eleven o'clock tonight," Jonathan snapped. "Jesus Christ!" He started up the stairs.

"Now just hold on a moment, sir," Haydon said. "I'm going to call headquarters. It'll be easy enough to establish if two plainclothes officers were sent to interview Miss Brand this afternoon."

"You do what you like," Jonathan told him, already at the first landing. "I'm getting into that flat."

Haydon hesitated, while Jonathan ran up to the second landing. He was obsessed with a sense of something being wrong, while not daring to think about what he might find when he opened the door. Getting in was no problem; he had a credit card and there was no security lock. He pushed the door inwards and fumbled for the light switch, while inhaling. He felt his whole system start to congeal; he had smelt death before. But this was recent death. "Well, sir?" Haydon asked at his shoulder. "You realise you have just committed a felony."

"Bugger off," Jonathan said. "Jennifer? Are you in, Jennifer? It's me, Jonathan." The flat remained silent.

"It all looks perfectly normal to me, sir," Haydon said. "Not a stick of furniture out of place."

"Out here." Jonathan crossed the living room, stepped into the brief corridor which separated the kitchenette from the bathroom, hesitated, then pushed the bedroom door in, followed it, and stared at the bed. His first reaction was one of relief. His second was one of panic. If Ebershaw was dead on the bed, Jennifer might be anywhere. He looked on the far side, dropped to his hands and knees and looked under it . . .

"Jesus Christ!" Haydon had reached the bedroom doorway. "Don't touch anything, Mr Rudder. Stand up." Jonathan obeyed. At least Jennifer wasn't dead, in here. "Do you know this man, sir?" Haydon asked.

"His name is Richard Ebershaw. He's a big wig in the city."

"And he was a friend of Miss Brand's?"

"She was his secretary."

"Ah," Haydon commented. "Will you kindly come out of there, sir." He led Jonathan back into the living room, picked up the telephone, and called nine-nine-nine. The Manlys had by this time arrived at the landing. "Go back downstairs," Haydon told them. "The Chief-Inspector will wish to speak with you in a little while."

"Not Lampson?" Jonathan asked.

"Yes, sir, I should think it will be Mr Lampson, as this case may well be connected with the serial murders."

"It's going to be a long evening," Jonathan said. "What about Miss Brand?"

"Yes, indeed, sir. What about Miss Brand?"

"She has to be found, and quickly."

"Very quickly," Haydon agreed. "I would say the charge will be murder."

Jonathan decided against hitting him, but Lampson was no better. He peered at the dead man, then at the pistol, and cracked a few knuckles. He was clearly displeased at having been wakened up in the middle of the night, and had not troubled to shave. Parton, on the other hand, was his usual dapper self. Lampson sat opposite Jonathan. "If there is one thing I dislike, it is encountering the same witness at two different murders," he said.

"I feel the same about policemen," Jonathan agreed.

"So tell me where she's gone."

"I have no idea where she's gone."

Lampson glanced at Mayhew, who was emerging from the bedroom. "Time?"

"Roughly eight hours."

"Had he had sex recently? I mean, he's naked."

"I would say he'd had sex almost immediately before death. I'll confirm that when I carry out a post mortem in the morning. Right now, I'm going home to bed."

"Any similarities to the others?"

"None at all."

"Thanks, Fred. I'll see you tomorrow." He turned back to Jonathan. "Eight hours. Roughly five o'clock yesterday afternoon. She's been gone eight hours."

"She may have stayed here until after dark, sir." DC Haydon told him what the Manlys had said.

"Why the hell did she hang about for six hours?" Lampson wondered.

"She didn't," Jonathan said. "She was kept here by the murderers. Tell him about the pseud policemen, Haydon."

Haydon did so. "Have you checked them out?" Lampson asked.

"No, sir. I was going to when this thing broke."

"Do it now," Lampson said. "And while you're at it, put out an APB on Jennifer Brand. Small, good-looking, shoulder length brown hair, probably carrying some kind of suitcase. If she didn't leave until eleven, we needn't bother about the airports, but she could have gone to any number of ports for the cross-channel ferries. Get on to them. Don't use this phone. Use your car phone." Haydon hurried for the door.

"You are barking up the wrong tree," Jonathan shouted. "While you're waiting at seaports for her to try to leave the country, she could be dead, somewhere."

Lampson looked at the detectives emerging from the bedroom. "Anything?"

"A perfect set on the gun."

"Take some of Miss Brand's. The kitchen would be the best place, or the bathroom. I want those prints matched, fast." The detective looked at Jonathan. "Forget it," Lampson said. "He's thick, but not that thick. Anyway, we can account for all his movements today. Rudder, what odds are you going to give me that the prints on that gun are Miss Brand's?"

"For God's sake, do you think she's the kind of woman who goes around shooting people? Especially her boss?"

"That's exactly it. Her boss is lying there in the nuddy in Miss Brand's bed, having recently fucked somebody. Now, who do you think it could've been?"

"I am going to punch you on the nose," Jonathan threatened.

"Go ahead. You'll like our cells. So you're soft on her. You can't pretend he wasn't, too. Sergeant Parton tells me Ebershaw was here last night, and left when you came in."

Parton nodded. "Well, he was," Jonathan conceded.

"What was he doing here then?"

"Look, he wanted her, yes. But she wasn't having any."

"So tonight he comes along and forces her. Maybe. So she takes out a gun and shoots him."

"With a silencer? You can hardly call that a *crime passionelle*."

"She shouldn't have had a gun at all. Therefore why shouldn't she have had a silencer? She's a Yank, isn't she? They're all high on Arnold whatshisname over there. Guns are a way of life with them."

"Oh, Jesus Christ!" Jonathan roared. "You have it all worked out in your tiny little mind, haven't you?"

Parton signalled the two policemen waiting at the door to come inside, just in case Jonathan was about to throw one of his explosions. "All right, Rudder," Lampson said, remaining perfectly calm. "If your little friend didn't shoot Ebershaw, tell me why he's lying starkers in her bed? Tell me why he's in her flat at all? Tell me why her fingerprints are on the gun? Because they are going to be her fingerprints, you can bet your last cent on that. Tell me why she didn't call the police just after five, when he was dead, if there was any possible explanation for him *being* dead? And most of all, tell me why she's done a bunk, having half emptied her wardrobe, and taken her passport, mind."

"Inspector," Jonathan said, keeping himself under control with a great effort. "Jennifer didn't do any of those things voluntarily. She was made to, by those two pseud policemen. Who then kidnapped her."

"Why, Rudder? If she was here when they shot Ebershaw, why didn't they shoot her too? They could have made it look like murder and suicide. Very simple. But they didn't. Tell me why?"

Jonathan's shoulders slumped, then he sat up again. "Of course. They were from the Freedom Clinic. Jennifer was sure that some people from the Freedom Clinic were responsible for the serial killings. She even suspected Jim Colley . . ."

"Don't start that all over again. She was on at us about it this morning."

"But she was right, don't you see?"

"The only thing I don't see is where you fit in," Lampson said. "According to Dickinson and Haydon they've had you under their noses all day. But you can't deny you slept here last night."

"On the sofa."

"Maybe. When a man sleeps in the same flat as a woman, they have to have something going for each other."

"You're incredibly old-fashioned, Chief-Inspector."

"So," Lampson went on as if he hadn't been interrupted.

"You had motive and opportunity to kill Angela Moresby, motive and opportunity to kill Philippa Morgan, both of whom you admit were mistresses of yours, and now your new mistress, who may or may not have known what was going to happen to *her* official boy friend, goes and pumps a bullet into the head of another boy friend."

"Ebershaw was not her boy friend!" Jonathan shouted.

"So, was she copy-catting you, or just turning into a murderess by association, would you say?"

"You give me a pain in the ass," Jonathan said. "Suppose I told you I can prove that Philippa Morgan was at the Freedom Clinic on the day she was killed, and that she was driven from there to the wood where she was found, either already dead, or certainly going to her own execution."

Lampson blinked at him. "So prove it."

Jonathan glared at him, and knew it wasn't going to work. He had proved it to his own satisfaction, but as Caunt had said, it was entirely circumstantial. His mileage figures were not going to jerk this ox of a man into action. And besides, right this minute, only finding Jennifer mattered. On the other hand, taking her away from the flat, alive, wasn't the pattern of the previous killings. Of course, they might have taken Philippa Morgan away from the Clinic, alive, but he didn't think so. The doctor had said something about some of the blood having dried, and it would have been far safer and more convenient to butcher her at the Clinic. As they might be doing to Jennifer right this minute. If he could just get Lampson to obtain a search warrant! "All right," he said. "Figure this."

Lampson listened, more interested than Jonathan would have dared hope. "Anybody got a road atlas?" he asked when Jonathan was finished.

"There's one in that bookcase." Parton opened it before them, and Lampson did some measuring.

"That's quite ingenious, Rudder," he conceded at last. "If your mileage figures on the tachometer are correct."

Jonathan took the Honda Manual from his pocket. "There's the entry from the garage, there's the entry I made this afternoon."

Lampson cracked his knuckles. "If these figures are accurate, sir, the whole thing could start to fall into place," Parton ventured. "Surgical knowledge, surgical instruments . . ."

"But why?" Lampson demanded. "Tell me why?" He glared from Parton to Jonathan. "You are suggesting that this Dr Colley, the man who is taking care of your uncle, is a homicidal maniac, with links to . . ." he changed his mind.

"Links to what?" Jonathan asked.

"Forget it." Lampson couldn't see that telling Jonathan about the other twelve murders was going to help – telling Jennifer Brand might have been a serious mistake. "Give me a motive."

"I don't *know* the motive," Jonathan almost wailed. "But I believe Jennifer Brand found one. We know she visited the Clinic yesterday afternoon. We know she understood she was taking a risk, because she made those elaborate telphoning arrangements with Caunt. Ebershaw being around may have been another protective arrangement. She tried to get in touch with me, but I wasn't there. And now I have proved that Philippa Morgan *was* there, and probably murdered there . . ."

Lampson held up one finger. "You have proved that she *could* have been there."

"All right, that she could have been there. The point is, Jennifer *could* be there now, about to be murdered, and you are sitting here doing nothing about it."

"I think perhaps we have enough to get a search warrant, sir," Parton suggested.

Lampson cracked a last knuckle, and then snapped his fingers. "Right. You'll have to wake someone up."

"There's an all-night court sitting in Brixton. I'll get down there." He hurried from the room.

"And just how long is this going to take?" Jonathan demanded.

"We should have a warrant in a couple of hours."

"A couple of hours," Jonathan groaned. "She'll be dead by then."

Lois stopped outside the garage doors, and flashed her torch. The doors opened, and she drove into the interior. The doors closed, and the lights came on. This night, in addition to the several different models of car always available, there was also a large refrigerated truck, and piled on the floor beside it, a number of frozen lamb carcasses. "I was getting worried about you," said the foreman, Mr Bell, large and red-faced and perspiring. "This lot has to be on the road by two."

"We had to wait until dark," Lois explained. "Where are you going to put her? Colley doesn't want her frozen. Yet."

Bell nodded. "We have a special compartment."

"It must be somewhere she can breathe, and you can get at her on the journey," Marcus said. "How long is the drive to Antibes?"

"From here and including the crossing, fifteen hours. We don't stop, save for a leak."

"Then she'll need to be jabbed on the way. I'll give her a top up now, before you leave, and you give her one at eight o'clock tomorrow morning. Now, you have to be careful, Bell. I've mixed up the dose." Marcus handed over the phial of liquid and the hypodermic needle. "There's twelve ccs, but she's only to have six. The other six are for emergencies, just in case you get delayed. Remember, six ccs. Don't exceed that unless it is absolutely necessary."

"Or she'll be as stiff as the rest, eh?" Bell grinned.

"Oh, she won't die. But it'll take her a long time to wake up."

"Why do they want her alive?"

"You'll have to ask Colley that."

"Maybe I will. Well, let's get going." His assistants were standing by. From the freezers along the wall they took a dozen special aluminium containers, each about a foot square and eight inches deep, and these were packed on the bottom of the refrigerated body of the truck. A false floor was then placed over them and bolted into place.

Marcus had by now lifted the bodybag from the back of the car, and unzipped it. He dug his fingers into Jennifer's armpits and pulled her naked, crumpled body out of the bag, laid it on the stone floor of the garage, and pushed the needle into her arm. She remained inert and apparently unfeeling.

Bell stood above him, looking down at her. "You sure she's alive? Where did all that blood comes from?"

"It's not hers," Marcus said.

"Maybe I should wash it off."

"Your job is to deliver her, right?" Lois said. "When you stop, you jab her, not bathe her or fuck her."

Bell grinned, and beckoned two of his men. They brought forward a very plain wooden coffin. Into this they lifted Jennifer's body, arranged her on her back, and screwed the lid into place. A breathing tube extended from the lid, and two tubes from each end. Marcus and Lois watched with interest as the entire driving seat in the cab of the truck was lifted out, and the coffin placed in the aperture. The tubes were linked up to the coffin, the breathing tube being extended through a hole in the seat, while the other two were linked, beneath the truck, to the engine compartment. "Happy?" Bell asked. "She breathes the same air we do, and she gets the same heat we do, from the engine. While we can also hear if she happens to wake up."

"She won't, if you remember to jab her on time," Marcus told him."

"There's no risk of exhaust fumes getting in there?" Lois asked.

"That tube goes nowhere near the exhaust."

Marcus watched the men replacing the driving seat. "Do you have to take that whole thing out to get at her?"

"No problem." Bell demonstrated. "One end of the seat is hinged and lifts up, and, presto, this end of the coffin is a separate panel and lifts out. It's over the face, see? So all I have to do is move my cushion, lift the two lids, reach in, and prick." He obviously intended to enjoy his journey.

"Just make sure she gets there alive," Lois said. The mechanics were now loading the carcasses, filling every available inch of the refrigerated space. "Don't you ever worry," Lois asked, "about having an accident when carrying that load?"

"Not before today," Bell said. "What's a few spare organs scattered amongst a lot of dead sheep? But a human body now, that would be difficult to explain. We'll just have to make sure we don't have an accident."

"And the best of British luck," Marcus said.

"I suppose you're home to bed," Bell remarked.

"Chance would be a fine thing. We're on duty tonight," Marcus said. "I'd rather be driving down through France, with you." He and Lois got into the car they had left at the garage earlier the previous afternoon, and drove out of the back entrance. Bell watched them go, then signalled his men to close up the truck.

He took the wheel himself, with two others in the cab to spell him. They drove down to Dover just as the first fingers of dawn were beginning to flicker into the sky. They stopped at the dock gates, handed over their documentation to the customs officer. "I should look inside," the officer said.

"Help yourself, mate," Bell told him. He remained behind the wheel while one of his crew opened the back of the truck. "Don't be too long. You're letting all of our cool air out."

The officer peered at the sheep, then nodded. The doors clanged shut, and the truck rolled forward, down the ramp into the bowels of the ferry. "Time for breakfast," Bell said, as he locked the cab up and led them up the stairs to the saloons. "And then, heigh-ho for the Med."

"With a break to attend to our friend," one of the others said, with a grin.

CHAPTER 9

Detective-Sergeant Parton returned with the search warrant at four o'clock, and they set off with three squad cars to the Freedom Clinic just as the first signs of dawn were creeping into the sky. "I suppose you can come along," Lambson told Jonathan. "But keep your mouth shut. Understood?"

"Absolutely," Jonathan promised. He had been tempted to break out of the police station and proceed on his own, but he had been too carefully watched for that. So now he had no expectations of what they would find, unless they were very, very fortunate – and Jim Colley was very, very careless.

There was a black porter on duty at the reception desk, who looked duly scandalised at the arrival of a dozen policemen led by a Chief-Inspector. "I'll just get the duty doctor," he said.

"Tell him to come down here," Lampson said. "Nothing else."

The man obeyed, and after few minutes a tall young man appeared, eyebrows raised as he too took in the unexpected visitors. "Marcus Lowndes. Can I help you?"

"Chief-Inspector Lampson," Lampson told him. "I have a warrant . . ." he showed it, "to search this hospital."

Marcus's eyebrows climbed even higher. "This is not a hospital, Inspector. It is a clinic."

"You mean you don't have patients."

"Yes, we have a few patients. But these are simply

waiting for treatment in hospitals, to which they will be transferred in the next few days."

"I'd like to have a look at them."

"They are fast asleep, Inspector."

"Don't you wake them up at dawn?"

"Good lord, no. That went out with the ark."

"I'm afraid I must search the premises, Dr Lowndes."

Marcus hesitated, then shrugged. "I shall make a protest to your superiors. But if you must . . ." he turned. "Nurse Stanley, will you show these, er, gentlemen, whatever they wish to see."

Lois had appeared in the inner doorway. "Of course, doctor."

"Try not to disturb the patients more than you have to."

"Yes, doctor." She glanced at the policemen, who were looking more and more embarrassed. "If you gentlemen will follow me."

"Three of you stay here," Lampson said, and Parton pointed at three of the constables. "Are you coming?" Lampson asked Jonathan.

"Why not?"

"You'd better. Because if we don't find anything . . ."

"You aren't going to find anything," Jonathan said, and gave Lois a savage smile. "Is he, Nurse Stanley?"

Lampson's mood grew steadily worse as he was given a guided tour of the hospital by Lois Stanley. She was utterly helpful, even allowed the Chief-Inspector to tiptoe into the various occupied private rooms and look at the sleeping patients. "Of course, it would be a great help if you would tell me what you are looking for," Lois remarked.

"We'll tell you when we find it," Lampson grunted.

Jonathan trailed along behind the police, trying to think, to decide what had happened. The most likely scenario was that Jennifer was already dead. The pattern hadn't really been broken by her being removed alive – they had removed Philippa alive. Or had they? The doctor in Berkshire had been doubtful about that. But if Jennifer was still alive . . . but why would they want her alive? It would have been so simple to make it look like a murder and suicide, the end of an affair, as Lampson had suggested. But whoever had killed Ebershaw had wanted to make it appear that Jennifer had fled. Why?

Perhaps she had convinced Colley that she had evidence which might convict him of murder, and he wanted to find out what she knew. That thought, supposing Colley was indeed behind the murders of Angela and Philippa and Douglas Openshaw, made his blood run cold.

As they crossed another corridor, he looked to his right, and saw Marcus Lowndes, sitting at a desk and turning the pages of some kind of ledger. Jonathan dropped even further behind, and then turned away from the police group and hurried along the corridor. It was time to take the bull by the horns. Marcus looked up. "Oh, hello. You're with the police, aren't you?"

"With them, not of them," Jonathan said. "You must find this search business a terrible imposition."

"Frankly, I do. Have you any idea of what we are suspected?"

Jonathan sat down in the straight chair beside the desk. "As a matter of fact, yes. My name is Jonathan Rudder, by the way." He held out his hand. Marcus's head jerked, and Jonathan realised his instincts were guiding him in the right direction. "I was Angela Moresby's fiancé," he explained.

Marcus had got control of himself, but even so his eyes flickered as he shook hands; his flesh was moist. "Angela Moresby," he said thoughtfully. "The name is vaguely familiar."

"She was murdered, just over a week ago. Rather

nastily. Tied to her bed and then chopped into little pieces." He studied Marcus as he spoke.

"As you say, nasty," Marcus acknowledged. And frowned, very artificially. "This doesn't have anything to do with that, does it?"

"I suppose it does, indirectly. There have been two other murders, committed by the same people. There was more than one killer, you see."

Marcus snapped his fingers. "Of course. I remember reading about them. *Very* nasty. Real Jack the Ripper stuff."

"Oh, indeed. Even down to the surgical skill with which the murders were carried out. I thought of becoming a surgeon once. Couldn't stay the course. I was at medical school with Jim Colley though. He works here, doesn't he?"

"That's right. He's our senior registrar."

"Angela Moresby was a patient of his. Shouldn't you have known that?"

"I'm afraid I don't know all of Jim's patients, nor he all of mine. Look, Mr Rudder, I am very busy, so if . . ."

"Douglas Openshaw was another of Jim's patients. And so was Jennifer Brand," Jonathan said chattily. "At least, I suppose she was. She spent some time here yesterday afternoon."

"Jennifer . . . Jennifer Brand?" Now he was definitely rattled.

"Was she your patient, or Jim's?"

"We aren't allowed to divulge that kind of information, Mr Rudder. Now, if you will excuse . . ."

"That's who the police are looking for, you know," Jonathan said. "Jennifer Brand. She's disappeared, you see. After having spent an hour here yesterday afternoon. And after telling the police she had a lead connecting the Clinic to the death of her fiancé, Douglas Openshaw."

Marcus took a handkerchief from his pocket to wipe

his brow. "This is the most arrant nonsense I have ever heard," he declared. "This Clinic, connected with some sex murder . . ."

"Ah, there you are, Mr Rudder," Lois Stanley said, appearing beside his chair. "Chief Inspector Lampson is waiting for you. I'm afraid he isn't very pleased. He has found nothing at all, you understand. Whatever it is he was looking for, is just not here." She smiled at Marcus. "I think we will have to make an official complaint about police harrassment, doctor. Don't you?"

"Oh, you do that," Jonathan agreed. "It would be most appreciated." He got up. "Jim coming in today?"

"He'll be here at nine," Lois said. "And he's not going to be very pleased about what's happened here this morning, either. But I'm afraid he's leaving for a few days."

"Holiday? Or fleeing the coop?"

"It is a business trip, Mr Rudder."

"But you'll be seeing him before he leaves? Just in case I don't get back to him in time, will you give him a message?"

"Yes, Mr Rudder, I'll give him a message. What is it?"

"You tell him that I am going to find out the truth. And then I am going to come after him. And you tell him that if Jennifer Brand has been harmed in any way, I am going to break every bone in his body. Will you tell him that?"

Lois Stanley goggled at him. "Are you mad, Mr Rudder?"

Jonathan smiled at her. "Of course, Nurse Stanley. Aren't we all?"

"I ought to lock you up and throw away the key," Lampson growled as they drove away from the Clinic.

"I told you you weren't going to find anything," Jonathan pointed out. "Your due process of law takes just too goddam long."

"It was your idea," Lampson groused. "You made me

look like a fool. And they probably *are* going to file a complaint."

"Not them," Jonathan said. "They're as guilty as hell. You could tell that by looking at them."

"You must have X-ray vision, Rudder. Right now, I don't want you within a mile of me. Until we catch up with your current girl friend. She's going to have to answer a lot of questions."

"Then drop me off here," Jonathan told him. "I can walk to where my car's parked."

Marcus stood at the window to watch the police cars drive off. "Rudder knows," he muttered.

Lois frowned at him. "Knows what?"

"Everything. That girl must have told him, somehow. That's who they were looking for, you know."

"The police certainly didn't know anything," Lois pointed out. "You want to take a hold of yourself, Marcus. You could be cracking up."

"He knows, I tell you." Marcus sat down, picked up his phone.

"What the hell are you doing?" Lois asked, her voice sharp.

"Calling Jim."

"For God's sake, he'll be here in an hour."

"He has to know now," Marcus insisted. "This whole thing is on the point of blowing up in our faces."

"Well, just don't say anything that matters over the phone," Lois reminded him.

The moment Colley heard the Clinic had been searched he came right down. Nan Welldon arrived a few minutes later. They both listened to what Marcus had to say; by now he was extremely agitated, and Lois found it difficult to conceal her irritation. Colley filled his pipe. "The Brand woman *could* have told Rudder about her suspicions," he said.

“But they can only be suspicions,” Lois argued. “There is no shred of evidence anywhere in England that can be held against us.”

“If that is the case, why did we have to kidnap her?” Marcus demanded. “Damned risky. It's that what brought the police on to us.”

“It was Rudder brought the police on to us, looking for Brand,” Lois insisted. “And it backfired. But if you are going to do anything about anyone, it should be that great lout.”

“Oh, no,” Marcus snapped. “We've done our bit in London. In England, as far as I'm concerned.”

“You sound like a couple of squabbling schoolchildren.” Colley remarked, sucking vigorously and getting his pipe alight. “I'm inclined to agree with Lois; something does need doing about Rudder.”

“Then you'll do it yourself,” Marcus said.

Colley raised his eyebrows. “I intend to. There won't be a problem. I think it'll all work out rather well. From what you have told me, despite Rudder's efforts the police believe that Brand killed her boss-cum-lover and did a bunk, as we intended them to. If Rudder now also does a bunk, it'll look as if he's following her.”

“You are going to attempt to kidnap Rudder like we did Brand?” Marcus was sceptical.

Colley smiled. “That won't be necessary at all.” He picked up the telephone. “Mrs Malcolm? Get me the St Croix Clinic, Antibes, will you. Dr Schleyer.”

Jonathan regained his car, sat and thought for several minutes; as he had had no sleep he was very tired. He was also very hungry. He found a transport cafe and had a solid breakfast, with several cups of black coffee, and began to feel slightly better. But he still faced a very dreary day, unless his muttered threat to Colley produced any results.

Angie was gone. He had never loved her, but he had been very fond of her. And she had been cut to pieces. By Colley? Philippa was gone. He had not loved her either, but she had been a gorgeous hunk of womanhood. And she had been cut to pieces. By Colley? Jennifer was gone, almost certainly dead. He had never slept with her, but she had been growing on him, moment by moment; he had almost felt he *was* falling in love with her, and he hadn't felt that about any woman for a very long time. And now she too had most likely been cut to pieces. By Colley?

Then what about Marcus Lowndes and the woman Stanley? And the woman Welldon? And even that very pleasant Mrs Malcolm on the desk, or the black fellow this morning? Were they all part of a serial killing gang? And why? Try as he did, he could make no sense out of it. He only knew that he wanted action, against them all, in a big way.

He left the cafe to drive back out to Blessop, found himself frowning, and insensibly driving faster and faster. Where did the St Croix Clinic fit into the pattern? The Clinic where yesterday his uncle had undergone heart surgery . . . he had been supposed to call back last night, and had forgotten all about it in the excitement over Jennifer. Was the St Croix involved? He didn't want to believe that. He had liked Schleyer. He had liked the whole set up. And there was no *need* for them to be involved. Whatever his midnight activities, Jim Colley obviously maintained an entirely normal facade during the day – therefore his links with the French clinic had to be perfectly normal as well.

At the same time, it really was important that he find out how Uncle Eric had got on. He scattered gravel as he pulled to a halt before the manor house, and ran up the steps. Caunt opened the door for him. "Mr Jonathan, thank God you're back. There's a message for you."

"Hold it, Caunt. I have to call Antibes."

"The message is from Antibes, sir." Jonathan checked, turning slowly to look at the butler. "It was from a Dr Schleyer. He said it was most urgent he speak with you."

"How long ago?"

"Not long. Twenty minutes."

Jonathan ran into the study and called the French number. His heart was pounding and he was sweating. If anything had happened to Uncle Eric . . . "Clinique St Croix?"

"My name is Jonathan Rudder. My uncle . . ."

"Ah, Mr Rudder. Yes. It is most urgent. Will you hold, please? I will put you through to Dr Schleyer."

Jonathan drummed his fingers on the desk as he waited.

"Mr Rudder?" Schleyer's voice was massively calm, but there was an undercurrent of tension.

"Yes. What's happened? Didn't the operation work?"

"The operation was a success, Mr Rudder. Last night I was very optimistic. But this morning I am afraid a complication set in. You know that foreign tissue is sometimes rejected by the recipient."

"You mean the heart?"

"I'm afraid so."

"He's dead?"

"No, no, Mr Rudder. We have this rejection problem. I am attempting to combat it with drugs. If this fails, well, we shall have to try another operation."

"Oh, my God! Can he stand that?"

"I don't know. We shall keep him on support, of course, and make a decision in the next twenty-four hours. However, in all the circumstances, I feel that he would like you at his side."

"Tell him I'm on my way. And thanks for calling, doctor."

"I am only sorry it had to be on such a subject,

Mr Rudder. I shall look forward to speaking with you later on today."

Jonathan hung up, and then called Heathrow. "Nice," said the clerk. "There is a flight leaving at ten, but it is boarding now, sir. You won't make it. The next is at two."

"Ah . . ." Caunt was standing beside him. "Hold on a moment," Jonathan said. "What's on your mind, Caunt?"

"You haven't forgotten, sir, that today is the funeral of Miss Moresby?"

"Oh, Jesus Christ! I *had* forgotten. Christ, what a foul-up. What's it to be, Caunt? A dying uncle, or a dead fiancée?"

"Well, sir, I am bound to say that the living should take precedence over the dead. I'm sorry I mentioned it."

"You were right to mention it. And I agree with you." Jonathan said, and turned back to the phone. "The two o'clock. One open return. I'm on my way."

"Schleyer called," Nan Welldon said. She was wearing pants and a shirt, sandals, and carried a floppy hat. She was prepared for the sun.

"And?" Colley was still in his suit, but his bag was in the corner.

"Rudder is on his way."

"Right. Is Hanson standing by? Then let's be on *our* way." He picked up his bag.

Nan followed him out of the surgery. "What do you think about what Lois said? About Marcus?"

"Cracking up? I suppose it's possible."

"Shouldn't something be done about it?"

"I've told Lois to monitor the situation. But Marcus will have to wait. We need to be careful, just around now, you know. Let's get the Antibes business done first, and worry about Marcus after. 'Bye Mrs Malcolm," he called, as they went through the lobby to the car park.

"Have a nice day," Mrs Malcolm called back.

Jonathan threw some casual gear into an overnight bag. "When do you expect to be back, sir?" Caunt asked.

"Haven't a clue. I'm going to have to sit this one out."

"You'll keep us informed, sir."

"You bet. Well, I'm off."

But as he reached the door the telephone buzzed. "Blessop," Caunt said.

"Geizuntheid," the American voice replied. "Jonny there?"

"Who shall I say is calling, sir?"

But Jonathan had heard the conversation and come hurrying back. "Bruce!"

"Just thought I'd call to let you know I'm on my way."

"Well, I'm just off to Antibes."

"I thought you had problems?"

"I have several problems. And one of them is in Antibes. A very sick uncle."

"Not old Eric? Shit! You're surely having a rough time. What's the word on Philippa's killer? Have they got the guy?"

"Afraid not."

"Jesus! What the fuck are your police doing? They must have a suspect?"

"Sure they do. I told you. Me!"

"For Christ's sake! Don't you have any ideas of your own?"

"A few."

"Tell me."

"On a trans-Atlantic line?"

"Who cares? Come'n, Jonny, you know who did it, right?"

"I've an idea it might be a chap called Colley. He's a

doctor. who appears to be mixed up in a lot of shady business. For starters, I reckon he's kidnapped, and maybe murdered, a friend of mine named Jennifer Brand. But he could have done Phil as well."

"Colley, eh? A doctor, right? What's his first name?"

"James. Now, look here, Bruce . . ." Jonathan was only too aware of Bruce's American tendency to take the law into his own hands. "No funny stuff."

"Wouldn't dream of it. Say, how long are you gonna be down in Antibes?"

"As long as it takes to get Uncle Eric back on his feet, I suppose."

"Right. I'll switch my flight. See you tomorrow."

"In Antibes?"

"You betcha. Where are you staying?"

"Check with the St Croix Clinic. They'll know."

"Keep your peckah up."

"A friend of yours, sir?" Caunt asked as Jonathan replaced the phone.

"The best," Jonathan told him. With Bruce Hardy in his corner, he knew he couldn't lose – as long as he kept the crazy fool under control.

"Not a damned thing," Detective-Sergeant Parton said in disgust. "That woman has nose-dived out of existence. We now have descriptions of her at every seaport and airport, and I'm certain she hasn't tried to leave the country. She doesn't have that wide an acquaintance of friends, but using her address book, we've contacted them all, including these Holt people down in Cornwall. We've even been in touch with her mother in the States, getting any addresses which might not be in her book. There weren't any."

"How did the mother take it?" asked Lampson.

"Not very well. We didn't tell her the daughter is being sought in connection with a murder inquiry, just that she's gone missing. Anyway, she's catching the next plane over. That'll be some time this evening, so we can expect her on our doorstep tomorrow morning. Early."

"Well, you can handle her. She might turn something up, mind, you never know. So what have we got, altogether, Ned?"

Parton sat down with a weary sigh. "A whole mess of nothing. We have a bunch of serial killers to whom Rudder and Brand may or may not belong; we have four murders on our books, all of which may or may not be part of the serial murders; we have Rudder, who has close links to two of the murders but on whom we have no positive evidence; we have Rudder's latest girl friend, who just happens to have been Openshaw's girl friend as well, apparently shooting another of her lovers and disappearing; and we have the most tenuous links to the Freedom Clinic."

"What links are those?"

"Well . . . Brand . . ."

"Brand has some wild suspicions which she couldn't articulate, but which she may or may not have told Rudder. And the entirely co-incidental fact that both Openshaw and Moresby were, briefly, patients of Dr Colley. There is absolutely no link between either Morgan or Ebershaw and the Clinic."

"Rudder claims there is. Via that mileage compilation of his."

"Well, he would, wouldn't he? I still say, Rudder is the key to the whole business. I don't know what his part is in the Ebershaw killing, but sooner or later he is going to go looking for his girl friend, or linking up with her, and then we have the bugger. Both the buggers. We're going to put them away for the crimes we can nail on them, and worry about the rest later." He gave a savage grin. "Who knows, maybe the serial killings will then just stop." Parton said nothing, gathered his papers and stood up. There was a knock on the door. "Come," Lampson said.

DC Martin entered, looking somewhat diffident. "Sorry to interrupt, sir, but some items have just come in which I thought might interest you."

"Speak."

Martin took out his notebook. "Miss Brand's photograph has now been circulated to all stations, and we have a reasonably positive sighting."

"Where?" Suddenly Lampson was interested.

"At four o'clock yesterday afternoon."

"Oh, good God," Lampson snorted. "That was before Ebershaw died."

Martin was one of the few constables not immediately reduced to a jelly when in Lampson's company. "Yes, sir. But it is where she was sighted that is interesting; she was seen by a beat policewoman entering a car outside the Freedom Clinic off the Edgware Road."

Lampson frowned at him. "Is this WPC certain?"

"I said, reasonably positive, sir. Apparently she has a good memory for faces."

"They said she hadn't been there," Parton said.

Lampson cracked a knuckle. "Anything else?"

"Well, sir," Martin went on reading. "The car was not a taxi. It was an Alfa-Romeo, which is what attracted WPC Collinson's attention to it in the first place."

"Don't tell me: she's also interested in cars."

"As a matter of fact, sir, her husband is a used car dealer, yes."

"And naturally, she wrote down the number."

"No, sir, she did not. There was no reason. However, when pressed by her sergeant, she thought the first three letters were KFN."

"A K registration Alfa-Romeo," Lampson said thoughtfully. "Now, how many of those do you expect are in existence?"

"Well, sir, with the other two letters . . ."
"Which are not positive."
"No, sir. But the sergeant used them anyway. There is a Alfa, registration number KFN 100, which belongs to Mr Richard Ebershaw, of Maidstone Place, Epsom, Surrey. I have checked it out, sir, and an Alfa with that registration number is parked in Moleton Close, and seems to have been there since yesterday afternoon."
"A break at last," Parton said.
"What kind of break? We know Ebershaw must have been in Moleton Close yesterday. How he got there is immaterial."
"Well, sir, we now also know that Jennifer Brand *was* at the Freedom Clinic yesterday afternoon, and that she was picked up from there by Ebershaw . . ."
"Who then drove her home, had a row, and got himself shot."
"But suppose they didn't have a row, sir? Why did Ebershaw take time off work to meet Brand at the Clinic? It can only be because he shared her suspicions. Then they go off to digest whatever it is they learned. But the people at the Clinic, the murderers, perhaps, are now alerted and decide to do something about it."
"To do something like what they did, between four o'clock and at the outside five-thirty yesterday afternoon, in such a manner that we don't have a trace, when Ebershaw and Brand only left the Clinic at four o'clock, suggests an organisation on the lines of MI6," Lampson said.
"Well, sir, it's possible."
"And who are you suggesting? The entire staff?" DC Martin coughed. "Yes?"
"The other items, sir."
"What are they?"
"One is a routine report from Gatwick Airport, sir. We circulated Miss Brand's photograph there as well, amongst

the airport police and handlers, and it was also noted that she might be linked with the Freedom Clinic."

"Who the hell authorised that?" Lampson glared at Parton.

Parton cleared his throat. "Well, sir, she *is* linked with the Freedom Clinic. Isn't she?"

"Next time you want to do something like that, Sergeant, just remember I'm running this show." He turned his glare on Martin. "What did that turn up?"

"A report from Air Traffic Control, sir. A private jet, registered in the name of the Freedom Clinic, took off an hour ago bound for Nice Airport, France."

"I bloody well know where Nice is," Lampson snapped. "How many passengers?"

"Just two, sir." Another glance at his notebook. "Dr James Colley, and a Miss Nan Welldon."

"Colley!" Parton said.

"And Brand. And they were just allowed to leave?"

"The lady was not Miss Brand, sir," Martin said. "Miss Welldon has red hair, Miss Brand's hair is dark brown."

"Have you never heard of wigs, Constable?"

Martin continued to be unflappable. "Miss Welldon is also described as being five foot eight inches tall, and weighing about one hundred and forty pounds. Miss Brand is described as being five four, and weighing a hundred and twenty."

"I suppose it could be a perfectly normal business trip," Lampson decided.

"It could," Parton agreed, sceptically.

Martin did some more throat-clearing. "There is a third item, sir. A telephone call from DC Dickinson. An hour ago, Mr Jonathan Rudder left Blessop Manor and drove to Heathrow Airport."

"You'll be telling me next that he's going to Nice as well."

"That is absolutely right, sir. DC Dickinson followed him, and ascertained that that was his destination."

"Let's get this straight," Parton said. "You have positive information that James Colley and a woman left Gatwick for Nice an hour ago, and now that Rudder is checked-in at Heathrow for a flight there as well?"

"Yes, Sergeant. Dickinson waited until he could confirm the booking, with the help of the airport police, before calling. The flight boards in forty-five minutes. He wishes to know if you wish him to arrest Rudder and prevent him from leaving."

Both men looked at Lampson, who cracked a knuckle. "Something is happening, sir," Parton said.

"Yes," Lampson agreed. "And to hold Rudder might quash the whole thing. Do we know anyone down there, Ned?"

"Oh, indeed, sir. At least we did. Inspector Brouard was at Nice last time I heard."

"Brouard. That's good news. Get him on the line, explain the situation, and ask him to put a tail on both Rudder and Colley when they land. I don't want them arrested, unless they actually attempt to break the law; I just want them watched, and every movement noted. Then get us seats to Nice as well."

"You're flying out there?" Parton was taken aback.

"I'm not sitting here on my tod while these bloody people get away. I'll clear it at the top. You get us those seats."

"For today, sir?"

"Of course bloody well today."

"But . . . when would we come back?"

"How the hell should I know? When we've made an arrest. You can bet your bottom dollar that Jennifer Brand is also in Nice. The whole goddamed shooting match are in it together."

It occurred to Parton to ask his chief how Brand had

managed to get there, when every airport and seaport in the country was being watched, but he had more important things on his mind. Such as the fact that he was taking his fiancée to the theatre that night. "What about the Openshaw inquest, sir?" he asked. "That's tomorrow morning."

"Is it? Damnation. Well, someone else will have to handle that. This is more important. I'll sort it out."

"And Mrs Brand, sir? She's arriving from the States early tomorrow morning. You said you'd meet her."

"Bugger Mrs Brand. No one invited her. You just get us the first available flight to Nice."

Parton gave up. "You mean Rudder's flight?"

"No, it had better be the next one. We don't want to scare him off. Brouard's people can keep an eye on them all until we arrive."

"Time for breakfast and a look at the lady," Bell decided.

It was eight o'clock and the refrigerated truck was south of Paris and rolling along the A6 for Lyons. "There's a service area about four miles ahead," Lewis said, checking the map.

"No service areas this time," Bell told him. "That's why we brought those sandwiches and thermoses. We need somewhere private."

Hall grinned. "For looking at the doll?"

"That's right. We'll take the next picnic area. Shouldn't be too many people around this hour of the morning."

But it was over an hour before they found a picnic area. Bell turned off the road and kept going, past the toilets to the very end of the area reserved for trucks. Here they were close to a small wood, and it was very quiet and peaceful. There were three other trucks, but these were all French and parked some distance away, their drivers smoking and gossiping. They paid little attention to the English vehicle. "You keep an eye out, Bert," Bell told Hall.

"Why me? I want to look at her, too."

"You can, after," Bell promised.

Hall got down, lit a cigarette, and leaned against the side of the truck, gazing back across the park at the Frenchmen. Inside the cab, Bell moved into the middle of the driving seat, folded back the cushion and then raised the hinged bench, carefully sliding it over the air tube, and gazed at the head board of the coffin. "God," Lewis muttered, peering over his shoulder. "Suppose she's dead?"

"She won't be." Bell unscrewed the panel in the lid, and lifted it away. They looked at Jennifer's hair, pressed into a dark brown, silky mound. Bell grinned. "I'll just check, shall I?" He slid his hand over her head and touched her face, then reached further into the interior of the coffin, found her shoulders and breasts. "Oh, she's alive all right. Warm as toast." As if to confirm his words, Jennifer stirred and gave a little moan. "And she likes having her tits felt," Bell said with satisfaction.

"Christ, she's waking up," Lewis said in alarm. "We've left it too long. Do something."

"I thought you wanted to feel her tits?"

"You put her back to sleep, first." Lewis had always had a deathly fear of being buried alive; he didn't want to imagine what be this girl's reaction might be to waking up and finding herself in a coffin.

"Suit yourself," Bell said. He took out the dose Marcus had given him, inserted the needle and drew off the liquid. "Pull her arm out."

Lewis bit his lip, cautiously reached into the coffin, found Jennifer's left arm, and dragged it through the aperture. Jennifer gave another moan, and rolled, her face twisting although her eyes remained shut. Lewis gasped, and jerked on the arm. "Easy," Bell admonished. "We don't want to break it."

"What's going to happen to her, after?" Lewis asked.

"After Colley's finished with her? She'll wind up on a dump somewhere."

"Seems a crying shame. Doesn't he ever get turned on?"

"He gets turned on. Oh, she'll enjoy a minute or two before the end." Bell swabbed Jennifer's arm with antiseptic, then inserted the needle. "I think in all the circumstances, we'll give her the lot. There. That'll hold her until we get to the Clinic; they can have fun trying to wake her up. Go and tell Bert he can have a feel, then we'd better be on our way."

Lewis looked down at the face, now again serenely relaxed. "Seems a crying shame," he muttered. "She could warm up my bed any time she liked."

When Colley and Welldon landed at Nice Airport, the St Croix car was waiting for them, and they were at the Clinic just after one, local time. "We've held lunch for you, Dr Colley," said the receptionist. "Dr Schleyer is waiting."

Colley nodded, left the bags at the desk, and he and Welldon went upstairs to the private suite where Schleyer lived, and where he was waiting for them with Staff-Sister Haniff, who, Colley knew, was also Schleyer's mistress, and shared the apartment with him. "Hans!" The two men embraced, and then he kissed Brigitte Haniff as well.

Schleyer embraced Nan. "A drink?"

"We'd love an aperitif."

Brigitte went to the bar and mixed four Pernods. "Now I wish to be brought up to date," Schleyer said. "I do not like all this excitement. I also wish to know what you want done with Eric Rudder?"

"How was the operation?"

"A great success. He is still on support, but I anticipate a full recovery. Unless the machine is switched off."

"I see no reason why he should not recover. It is his nephew we must deal with. When do you expect him?"

"Some time this afternoon. He said he was coming right down. But I do not follow what the problem is."

"Simply this: his girl friend, an American woman, has managed to figure out what is going on. How, God alone knows. But I mean to find out. She's on her way here now. As far as the UK police are concerned, she's on the run from a murder charge, and has disappeared. She will stay that way. As far as they know, again, Rudder has also fled the country, somewhat more obviously. Now, he must die in an accident, as soon as is practical after he arrives."

"I do not like that, James. When he arrives, he is going to come straight here. The police will be able to learn that."

"Of course. But he has every reason to come straight here. His uncle is here, under your care. When he arrives, you will let him see his uncle, tell him that there has been a dramatic improvement since you spoke to him on the phone, that the drugs are obviously working, but that in all the circumstances you think he should remain here for a day or two, until the crisis is past."

"Here?"

"In Antibes. If he has arranged an hotel, that will be a nuisance, but still, you will find out where it is, and arrange an accident. If he has not booked an hotel, well, then it will be easier for you. You will simply send him wherever you choose; wherever it will be simplest."

Schleyer scratched his chin. Although he was the originator of the whole spare parts scheme, and the senior partner in the two clinics, he yet knew the Colley was the stronger personality. "And the woman, Brand?" he asked.

"I will look after Brand," Colley said. And smiled. "But you may give me a hand, if you wish."

Schleyer sighed, and glanced at Brigitte Haniff. Brigitte also smiled. "You may leave Rudder to me," she said. "He fancies me. He will not be difficult."

Jonathan touched down just after five, local time, and went to Hertz to hire a car. At the counter, however, he was met by Brigitte Haniff. "There is no need to hire a car, Mr Rudder," she said. "We knew you were coming."

"What a pleasant surprise," he said. "How is Uncle Eric?"

"He is responding to treatment," Brigitte said. "He is, what do you say in English? A tough old goose."

"Any bird will do, actually," Jonathan said. "Although I suppose he'd be hurt to think you didn't regard him as a gander. Can I see him?"

"Of course. That is why I am here." She led Jonathan to her Saab. She wasn't wearing uniform this afternoon, and looked cool and elegant in her summer frock, her straight yellow hair resting quietly on the shoulders. "I feel I was short with you, on your last visit," she remarked, as they drove out of the car park.

"I suspect I was jumping my fences a bit early."

"Jumping your . . . ah. Yes." She smiled. The windows were open and the breeze ruffled her hair as she increased speed. "Well, you must try again."

"I shall," Jonathan said, reflecting that he would never understand women.

"Your uncle," Brigitte said, gazing at the road. "You must understand, Mr Rudder, that we have not told him how ill he is. As far as he knows, the operation has been a total success, and recovery is just around the corner. This is necessary psychology, you understand. So when you see him, you will make no reference to any drugs. He is unaware that he is being given any additional treatment."

"Quite," Jonathan agreed. "I am most terribly grateful for all that Dr Schleyer has done. And yourself, of course."

"It is our job. You should be grateful to Dr Colley, for sending you to us."

"I am. Do you do a lot of business with Dr Colley?"

"Yes. He sends us many patients."

"Have you done business with him for a long time?"

Brigitte made an attractive moue. "I believe so. He and Dr Schleyer have worked together in the past, often."

"I see." It occurred to Jonathan that pumping this rather ingenuous woman might be very productive. As well as rather fun. But was he here to have fun? He was here to see Uncle Eric – and find out if the link between the Freedom and St Croix Clinics was criminal . . . and might involve Jennifer. They turned off the highway on to the drive up to the clinic, and found themselves behind a large refrigerated truck. "Dinner being delivered?" Jonathan asked, eyeing the number plates. "All the way from England? I believe some hospitals in London have their catering done in Wales."

"It is all a matter of cost," Brigitte agreed seriously. "But those will be surgical stores." They followed the truck through the gates; the truck then turned to the right to go round the back of the huge building, while Brigitte pulled to a halt on the forecourt. "You may leave your bag in the car, and I will drop you at your hotel later," she said. "Where are you staying?"

"I'm afraid I left in such a hurry I didn't have time to book in."

"And we are at the start of the season." She made a clicking sound with her tongue, and then smiled. "Never mind, I know a place which will find room for you. It is run by my brother. I will drive you there when you have seen your uncle."

Jonathan reckoned it was going to turn into a profitable evening – if he could just get Jennifer off his mind.

* * *

Eric Rudder was propped up in bed, his face virtually invisible behind nose masks and various drips. "You must not go too close," Brigitte said, although she had equipped Jonathan with gown and mask and cap of his own. "The slightest infection could be dangerous."

"Hello, Uncle," Jonathan said. "Can you hear me?" Eric raised his hand and then let it flop again. "How are you?" Jonathan called. Again the flop of the hand, more enthusiastically. "Dr Schleyer says you'll soon be up and about." Eric waved some more. "Well . . . I'll be back in tomorrow." Eric waved.

"I know it seems a long way to come for just those few words," Brigitte said, as she closed the door on them. "But it will be very good for his spirits, believe me."

"When will he be absolutely out of danger?"

"Another twenty-four hours should decide it. You are in no hurry to go back?"

"Well, actually, I am. There's a lot going on."

"Oh? Is there anything we can do to help?"

She was such an attractive woman, obviously experienced yet with a touch of vulnerability. Above all, he was sure she was a woman he could trust. But she worked for Schleyer, and Schleyer was Jim Colley's business associate. That didn't mean a thing. Even less could it mean that this woman was involved in anything as nasty as motiveless serial killings. But he still felt that pumping her might be at once interesting and informative; as she was Schleyer's chief assistant, she might even be able to put his mind at rest, and give him one or two answers.

"If you won't be bored," he said. "I'd like to talk to you about it over dinner."

CHAPTER 10

"I'm afraid Dr Schleyer is tied up right now," Brigitte Haniff told Jonathan as they left the ward. "I know he wants to see you, but it will have to be tomorrow morning. Anyway, I think we should do something about finding you that room for the night." She led him down the main staircase. "Tell the doctor I have gone out with Mr Rudder, but will be back in an hour," she told the reception clerk.

"Uh-uh," Jonathan said. "What about dinner?"

"It is only just after six."

"Well, then, what about aperitifs before dinner?"

Brigitte considered. "Tell the doctor I may not be in again this evening," she said, and smiled at Jonathan. "Is that satisfactory?"

Schleyer and Colley stood at an upstairs window to watch the Saab drive off. "That is the last we shall see of Mr Rudder," Schleyer said with satisfaction.

"Can you guarantee that?"

Schleyer nodded. "Sometimes Brigitte frightens *me*. Not like your Miss Welldon, eh?" Colley glanced at Nan, and raised an eyebrow. The phone buzzed; Schleyer picked it up. "Schleyer."

"There is a consignment here from England, doctor. Mr Bell says it includes a special item for Dr Colley."

"Jennifer Brand," Colley said. "We'll be right down."

Nan was already at the door, and Colley paused to look at Schleyer. "Coming?"

"I have work to do. You can check out the consignment as well, if you wish."

"My pleasure." Colley led Nan along the corridor to the elevator. "I feel quite excited about this."

"You mean to torture that poor girl?"

"Poor girl shit. She's an inquisitive little bitch who's too smart for her knickers. Yes, I intend to enjoy myself. Using the Morgan reminded me how much I have missed being in the field."

Nan said nothing, gazed at the numbers as the lift took them down into the bowels of the building. When she had first worked for this man she had fallen in love with him; he had been so calm, capable, for all his youth. So international in his knowledge, so sophisticated in his habits. She had slipped into bed with him without a moment's hesitation, had regarded her immediate promotion to Staff Sister at the Freedom Clinic as her due reward, and looked forward to working even more closely with him as the years went by. She had even considered marriage.

Then had come the day she had learned there was more to the Freedom Clinic than met the eye. When, towards the end of last summer, he had invited her to take a holiday with him in the south of France she had been delighted. She had not even been more than slightly amused when he had told her they would be staying at a clinic outside Antibes, run by an old friend of his, Hans Schleyer – presumably he was seeking free accomodation. And she had certainly been impressed by the St Croix, which also made a very comfortable hotel. But after two days of lounging on the beach, one morning Jim had said, "It's time you knew something more about the business," and had taken her down to look at the cold rooms.

She had not known what to expect. She could not possibly *have* known what to expect, and had been violently sick. But it had not occured to her to betray him, especially when he had explained that he and Schleyer, and the doctor in Spain, were really performing a great service to mankind. "What were these people?" he had asked. "They are none of them geniuses, whose mental processes are going to enhance and improve humanity in their old age. They happen to have been superb physical specimens, who have reached their apogee – in a few years time they will start to decline, and become progressively of less and less importance, merely cluttering up the stage, eating food and breathing air which others need more urgently. By removing them from the stage, now, we are enabled to prolong the lives of far more worthy men and women, people who can truly contribute to the future of mankind, were they granted a few extra years of life."

He had made it sound almost noble, and somehow logical. Besides, she would have done anything he wanted, anyway. Thus she had been hooked. Even when she had realised that the "people who can truly contribute to the future of mankind" had simply been those with the most money. Besides, in the early days, the victims had always been itinerants, hitch-hiking students or petty criminals whose disappearance had been accepted by the police as a matter of course. It had only been last summer that Schleyer had decided that, because of the high wastage rate – even with the most modern methods of controlled freezing and resuscitation, each organ had to be used within a very limited time – and as so many of their current spares were diseased or in too poor condition to use at all, they would launch a specific campaign, using only people who could be guaranteed to be in the best of health.

She supposed part of her defeat had been occasioned by the sheer normalcy of it all. She had trained as a nurse and now worked for a clinic. All her adult life she had been surrounded by the ill and the dying. And the dead.

To project that into a frame of mind where the clinic also carried out the killing had not seemed illogical, given the premise on which the murders were planned. Especially when the element of risk had been so totally eliminated. Or so it had seemed, until the appearance of Jennifer Brand. Then again, she had always supposed that murderers, or murderesses, were necessarily creatures apart, desperate men and women who would betray themselves by their looks or their behaviour. She had never met more normal people than Lois and Marcus. Lois had worked for Colley and Schleyer from the beginning; Marcus had been recruited in France. When they were given a name and an address, they had carried out their task with the simple efficiency of two top-class surgeons, which they were. They had never tampered with their victims; tying them to the beds and letting them bleed to death, as well as the superficial mutilations, had been dictated to them by Colley. He had said this was to confuse the police into assuming there was something ritualistic about the murders, although keeping the organs alive as long as possible – the heart was always the last to be removed – lessened the risk of disintegration setting in before they could be frozen. She had believed him, even though she knew he had been Lois' partner in the Spanish murders – and he had been right about confusing the police.

When the job had been done, Lois and Marcus would resume their normal lives, two happy, well-adjusted medics, eager to help the public in their ailments – as was Colley. And no one could be more happy and well-adjusted than Mrs Malcolm, or Davenport the porter. Mass murderers all, if only by association, carefully recruited by Colley over a period of time, just as Schleyer, presumably, had recruited his people here in France and they had jointly recruited the Spanish team. But the actual executioners had always been British, Colley and Lois, and then Lois and Marcus, and now

Colley again . . . and Nan Welldon. She had joined their ranks, almost without a backwards glance. She had never doubted, never allowed herself to doubt, until Philippa Morgan. She had told herself that Jim was right in his course of action with Philippa, right to carry out the dissection himself, because there simply wasn't time to call out Marcus and Lois . . . but then she had watched him standing over the unconscious woman, so obviously turned on by her, and by the thought of what he was about to do to her. When he had started to cut, it had no longer been clinical, detached, impersonal; he had wielded the knife like a fiend, had almost drooled over what he had been doing.

That had frightened her, made her wonder if she could have been wrong about him all of these years. And now he was on his way to launch an assault upon Jennifer Brand. Nan had no doubt he intended to kill her, when he was finished interrogating her to find out what she knew. Or just enjoying himself.

And she had no idea what to do about it.

The lift came to a stop, and the doors opened. Colley led Nan out and into the unloading bay situated in the garage beneath the Clinic; a ramp led up to the ground level, and down this ramp the refrigerated truck had been backed. Bell, Lewis and Hall were standing by the truck; the back had been opened, and half a dozen hospital orderlies were removing the sheep carcasses, attaching them to hooks, and pushing them along an overhead rail. Two more men stood by the open door to the cold room, and the carcasses, still attached to the rail, were sent into the sub-zero temperatures beyond. "Enough food to feed the hospital for six months," Bell remarked. "Evening, doctor. Nurse."

"All well?" Colley asked.

"Right as rain, doctor," Bell assured him.

The last of the carcasses was sent into the cold room, and now the orderlies were removing the driving seat from the cab. Nan glanced at Colley; his eyes gleamed with anticipation. Grunting, the orderlies dragged the coffin out and placed it on the floor. "For the special cold room?" one asked.

"No," Colley said. The men went back into the truck, and began removing the false floor. "Open it up," Colley told Bell.

Bell nodded to Lewis and Hall, who unscrewed the coffin lid, and lifted it off. Colley stood above the coffin to look down at Jennifer Brand, who lay on her back, absolutely still, her eyes closed; only the faintest flutter of her stomach indicated that she was breathing. "What have you done to her?" Colley asked, his voice suddenly sharp.

"Nothing, doctor. Nothing."

"You did not tamper with the dosage?"

"Who, me?"

Colley reached into the coffin, lifted Jennifer's left wrist, and took her pulse. "This woman is very heavily drugged. She should be on the point of waking up."

"Ah," Bell said. "Well, we were a little late giving her the last injection. Couldn't find a place to stop, see."

"When *was* she given the final injection?"

"Well, it would have been after nine."

"Then she still should be just about awake."

"Well . . . because we were late, and we didn't know if there were going to be any delays, I gave her the whole twelve ccs."

"Oh God damn! She won't be back with us until nearly midnight, and then she'll be too groggy to be any use. All right. Fetch a bed trolley."

Lewis hurried off. "Foiled again," Nan said, with a wry grin.

"I suppose we'll just have to be patient," Colley grumbled. The trolley was brought, and Lewis and Hall lifted Jennifer out of the coffin and laid her on it. Colley checked her pulse again, and took her temperature. "Ninety-six. That's far too low."

"That would be the drug, wouldn't it?"

"And the long period without consciousness, yes. But she mustn't catch cold. Blankets."

Blankets were brought, and Jennifer was wrapped up, and then strapped to the bed. "I thought she was for dissecting, when you'd finished with her," Bell commented.

"Perhaps she is. But I want her wide awake when I'm talking to her. Come along, Nan." He wheeled the trolley into the lift, and Nan pressed the button. They rose to the fourth floor, which was not in general use, and Colley wheeled Jennifer along the corridor to the operating theatre. Between them they transferred the inert body from the trolley to the table, and again strapped her in place, so that she could not move when she woke up. Nan then draped Jennifer's naked body in the blankets. "We may as well go out to dinner," Colley said.

Lampson and Parton landed at Nice just after six, and were met by Inspector Brouard. Brouard was a small man with hunched shoulders, who looked as if he was anticipating a blow on the back of the head at any moment. He and Lampson had worked together before, on a drugs case, and they respected each other; from Lampson's point of view, Brouard had the inestimable advantage of speaking fluent English. Now Brouard was excited. "Do you really suppose you have a lead on the serial killings?" he asked as they got into the police Citröen, where the fug left the Englishmen breathless. "I can at least smoke in my own car," Brouard explained, lighting a Gaullois.

"We certainly have a strong lead on a couple of them

in England," Lampson said cautiously. "What's the latest on our men?"

Brouard signalled his driver to move off. "Dr Colley and Nurse Welldon arrived this morning just before lunch. They were met at the airport by a car from the St Croix Clinic, and driven directly there. Up to now, they have not come out. I cannot see anything suspicious in that; it is established that the Freedom Clinic in London and the St Croix Clinic in Antibes do a great deal of business together."

"What about Rudder?"

"He arrived at five o'clock, and was met by the senior staff nurse from the Clinic. She also drove him directly to the Clinic. He remained there only a short while, however, and then Nurse Haniff drove him away again, into Antibes itself. We assume she has taken him to an hotel, but in any event, they are being tailed and we should get a report at any moment. Do you consider that Rudder and this Dr Colley are somehow linked?"

"I believe they may well be, although I don't know how, exactly at the moment. It was Rudder insisted we search Colley's clinic . . ."

"Could have been a ploy, sir," Parton suggested. "He knew we wouldn't find Brand there."

"And kept saying so," Lampson pointed out. "Besides, I can't escape the impression that he's keen on Brand. God, this case is getting me down. Everything seems to fit, but when you actually start to put things together, nothing fits. Maybe we'll turn up something down here, eh, Alexandre?"

Brouard looked sceptical. "You are aware that Rudder's uncle is in the Clinic, and has just undergone heart surgery?"

"So that also would be perfectly normal," Parton said. "If he came down to see his uncle."

"And there have been no other comings and goings from the Clinic?" Lampson asked.

"Only a refrigeration truck, which arrived late this afternoon. But this is too normal; that truck often delivers goods to the Clinic." The car turned into the police station.

"It's all just too bloody normal. Any chance of getting a search warrant?" Lampson asked.

"I do not think so, Chief-Inspector. As we have agreed, there is nothing suspicious in Dr Colley visiting a hospital with which he has professional links, in a delivery truck entering the hospital grounds, or in Mr Rudder visiting his sick uncle and then leaving again; if Mr Rudder senior had his operation yesterday, five minutes would be all the time a visitor would be allowed with him, in any event. There are no grounds for searching the Clinic, or for arresting Mr Rudder, unless you are prepared to charge him, or you have additional evidence." He led the way up the stairs to his office, leaving a trail of smoke behind him.

"Then as I said, we'll just have to hope the surveillance turns something up."

A sergeant was waiting for them, with a sheet of paper. He spoke briskly in French, and Brouard nodded. "Here is the latest report on Rudder. He has been taken to a small hotel in Antibes. It is run by Sister Haniff's brother. He has gone in, and Sister Haniff has come out. Leaving him there. I would say he is there for the night."

"Then I would say, so are we," Lampson growled. "Any chance of some tea and sandwiches?"

"Do you like the room?" Brigitte Haniff asked.

Jonathan stood at the window, looking along the street. "Would that be a glimpse of the beach over there in the distance?"

Brigitte smiled. "Between those two houses, yes. I am sorry, but this is all that is available."

"Who's complaining? Can we get a drink here?"

"You can."

"We?"

She shook her head. "Not right now. I must get home and change. I will see you later."

"And then?"

She shrugged. "I am yours for the evening."

Jonathan stood at the window again to watch her drive away. Presumably she *was* coming back, whereupon he was going to do his damndest to get her into bed – he did not think that was going to be dramatically difficult to accomplish. She was attractive, and attractively earthy as well. And he had never had a hospital sister. But the fact was that he was merely going through the motions, from sheer habit. He didn't want to be here at all. He wanted to be in England, grabbing Colley by the scruff of the neck and shaking Jennifer out of him.

He watched a man leaning on the wall opposite the hotel, smoking a cigarette. He had policeman written all over him. If this had been England he'd have said he was still being tailed. Well, maybe he was: Lampson could easily have contacted the Nice police. But what a waste of bloody time and money. He wasn't going anywhere tonight; it was a temptation to lean out of the window and tell the *gendarme* that. Instead he had a shower, changed his shirt, and strolled downstairs, to be greeted by the proprietor. He already knew this was Brigitte's brother, Edouard Haniff, but the resemblance between brother and sister was so strong he would have guessed it anyway. "You wish a drink?" Haniff said. "Let me make you a cocktail."

"Such as?"

"Rum, rum and more rum."

"Sounds interesting." He went into the lounge, which was empty, and a few minutes later the drink was brought by a pretty young woman he had not seen before.

"I am Françoise," she said. "Brigitte is my big sister."

"Pleased to meet you, Françoise." As with Edouard, it would in any event have been easy to decide who she was; she had the same straight golden hair and very similar features. He sipped the drink. "Did you make this yourself?"

"It is my brother's recipe. Did you know there is a man outside in the street, watching the 'otel? Brigitte saw 'im when she left. She has telephoned. She says 'e is a policeman."

"I imagine she's right."

"Is 'e looking for you?" She did not seem unduly concerned, merely curious.

"He knows where I am. He just wants to find out everything I do."

Françoise nodded. "Brigitte thought this. She thinks it would be better if you joined 'er on the front, rather than she come back 'ere."

"Why cannot she come back here? I'm sure the cooking is adequate."

"But 'ere, it is not romantic, monsieur. Brigitte is one for the romantics. The beach, and the moon, and the, 'ow do you say? The ambience."

"That sounds like fun, as a preliminary, certainly. However, won't the policeman just follow me?"

Françoise wrinkled her nose most attractively. "He will not, monsieur, if he does not know you have left the 'otel."

"Good thinking. Can I get out of here without him noticing?"

"Of course, monsieur. I will take you myself."

"The evening grows brighter by the moment."

"Finish your drink, and we will go."

"What about dinner?"

"We will dine on the front, monsieur."

"I think you had better start calling me Jonathan," Jonathan suggested.

He finished his drink. Françoise said goodbye to her brother – oddly, there didn't appear to be any other guests in the hotel, however crowded the town might be with tourists – and then led Jonathan through the kitchens and into the back yard. Here there was a gate in the fence which allowed them into an alley, before they climbed over another fence into another back yard, Françoise hoicking up her skirt as she did so to reveal very good legs and a pair of frilly knickers. The evening became more and more distracting. This back yard also belonged to an hotel, apparently, and a busy one, just serving dinner. No one paid any more attention to the two people who suddenly appeared in the kitchen other than to greet Françoise, who was apparently known to the staff. Then they were down a corridor and emerging on to a busy street. Françoise giggled with excitement, and tucked her hand into his. "Wasn't that good sport?"

"Excellent," Jonathan agreed. She led him on to the crowded front, and they found a table at a café, situated away from the lights. Jonathan bought exotic drinks, and Françoise sighed as she stirred her rum punch with her straw, and looked down at the beach. It was now past eight, and starting to grow dark, but there were still people on the beach, and even some in the water, suitably topless. "Where is Brigitte?" Jonathan asked, although as he watched the wind riffling through Françoise's golden hair, he began to wonder why he was still interested.

"We are to go to her, when we have finished our drinks," Françoise said. "She does not wish to be seen."

Jonathan raised his eyebrows. "Who is she hiding from?"

"Brigitte is engaged to be married," Françoise said

seriously, making attractive sucking noises through her straw.

"Ah! But . . ."

Françoise giggled. "She finds you attractive, Monsieur Jonathan. But it would not be good for her boy friend to find out, eh?"

"Absolutely," Jonathan agreed. "I have enough problems without jealous boy friends."

"You, 'ave problems?" She seemed surprised.

"Haven't I just. Tell me about the Clinic."

"I know nothing about the Clinic."

"You must know something. Your sister works there."

"Yes, but she does not live at the 'otel. She lives 'er own life. You wish to know about the Clinic, you must ask 'er. Shall we go?"

"Don't we eat, some time? There's an aching void down there."

"We eat when we are with Brigitte."

"Then let's get at it." She finished her drink, led him away from the café and the esplanade and the crowds, down to the beach just outside the town. Here there were low cliffs, and tumbled rocks, and no people. Françoise took off her shoes to wade as she rounded an outcropping of rock which went right into the sea, and Jonathan followed her example, rolling up his pants to the knees. On the far side there was more beach, a small area this, made private by the rocks. And here was Brigitte, naked, kneeling in the shallows.

"I thought you were never coming," she remarked.

Jonathan paused to admire the view as she stood up; even in the near-darkness it was spectacular. "I'd have hurried if I'd known you were waiting," he said.

"Come into the water."

He glanced at Françoise. But Françoise was also removing her clothes, rapidly. There was not a lot to choose between them, save that Françoise was generally on a smaller scale. "Why not?" He threw his clothes on the sand and went into the water with them. Brigitte came up to him, put her arms round his neck, and kissed him, rubbing her breasts against his chest. Françoise meanwhile clung to his back, holding on to his shoulders to raise herself up and wrap her legs round him and her sister.

Either I have discovered Paradise earlier than most, or these two superb young woman are trying to drown me, Jonathan thought – and suddenly realised it was almost certainly the latter. Even as he tried to decide what to do about it, the weight of the wriggling women threw him off balance, and he fell into the water, the girls still holding on to him. As he went under, he heard more splashes from near at hand: they had company. But the girls were still holding on to him, squealing with laughter as they wriggled against him. He got his head up to take a breath, and found that they had been joined by two men, also naked. One of these promptly seized Jonathan's head and forced it back under the water, while the other added his weight to the girls keeping him there.

Pennies began dropping in Jonathan's brain with great thuds: they *were* trying to drown him. And they were going to succeed if he didn't do something pretty damn quick. But that meant they were indeed connected with Angie's death, and Philippa's . . . and Jennifer's disappearance: that the St Croix Clinic was probably the hub of the whole thing. His brain boiled. He gave an almighty heave and rose to his feet. The men came up with him, with startled exclamations . . . in English! One of them got behind Jonathan and put his arm round his neck, seeking a strangling hold. The other hit Jonathan as hard as he could in the belly. Brigitte, on her knees beside him, reached for his genitals and squeezed. Françoise, on his other side, seized his left arm and bit it.

Jonathan gave a roar of mingled pain and fury. A sweep of his left arm scattered Françoise across the surface of the sea. The punch in the belly had not hurt too much, and his legs were still free. He brought one up with all the force he could muster in the shallow water. Brigitte gave a shriek and fell away from him, and the man in front of him also went backwards. The man behind him was throttling away as hard as he could, and Jonathan was beginning to see stars. He reached behind him, dug his fingers into the man's buttocks, pulled them apart and did a forward somersault in the same movement. He went down and over, beneath the water. The man went with him, and lost his hold. He landed on his stomach, but now Jonathan was the one behind. Jonathan seized his shoulders, bringing him up and pulling him backwards, at the same time as he drove his knee into the small of the man's back. There was a dreadful scream as a vertebrae snapped, and he subsided into the water.

The other man had fallen away again as Jonathan went under. Now he came forward, fists swinging. Jonathan caught the nearest fist and dislocated the arm as easily as he had done in the Marquis of Granby; the man collapsed in the water, moaning. Brigitte, re-emerging above the surface beside Jonathan, saw the destruction of her colleagues, and turned for the shore. Jonathan seized her hair, brought her back to him, lifted her out of the water, waded towards the beach, and threw her away from him, landwards. She uttered a despairing wail as she flew through the air, then struck the hard-packed sand with a terrible crunch, rolled a few feet, and lay still.

Jonathan looked left and right. One of his assailants lay inert in the water. He picked him up, and threw him also on to the beach. The other was still staggering and moaning as he pawed at his dislocated arm; Jonathan let him get on with it. Only Françoise was left, and she was making desperately for the land, attempting to swim in the shallows. Jonathan caught her ankle, and brought her back to him. "Please don't hurt me," she gasped. "Please!"

He held her by the throat with his left hand. "You had better tell me what I want to know, sweetheart," he said. "Or I am going to break every bone in your body." She gasped, and wriggled. "Who sent these goons?" he asked. "Who told you to get me out here?"

"Brigitte told me what to do," she gasped. "Brigitte always tells me what to do. You were to drown, playing with us in the water. The men would have gone. It was to be an accident. That was all she told me. I don't know who the men are."

Jonathan decided she was probably telling the truth. He released her throat, picked her up, and carried her ashore, enjoying her frantic kicks and wrigglings. He had enough to go on. If Brigitte had been giving the orders in the field, as it were, her orders had come from the Clinic. That had to mean not merely that the Clinic was indeed involved, but that if they were so desperate to be rid of him, they had something to hide right there on the premises. There was also the small matter of Uncle Eric's life, which now had to be in real danger, if the old boy wasn't already dead. He stood above Brigitte, but she wasn't moving. She was breathing, however. "You'd better join your sister," he told Françoise, set her on her feet, and hit her on the chin, with about half strength. She gave a little moan, and when he let her go, collapsed on the sand.

Jonathan dressed quickly, dragging his clothes over his wet body. There were voices in the near distance, to suggest that someone had heard the various screams. He picked up his shoes, and crawled into the shelter of the rocks, watched people splashing through the water to the stricken bodies on the beach.

He made his way up through the rocks, heading away from the esplanade, put on his shoes, and found the street leading out of town. Towards the Clinic. At last he had somewhere to go.

* * *

"I'm afraid it looks like being a quiet night," Inspector Brouard commented.

"Absolutely bloody damn all," Lampson agreed.

"Well, Chief Inspector, my wife is waiting supper for me. Do you have somewhere booked to stay?"

"I'm afraid we didn't have time."

"Ah. It is not easy, this time of year, in Antibes."

"We were sure you would be able to recommend somewhere. And for dinner."

"Ah," Brouard commented, and repeated. "It is difficult, at this time of year, you understand."

"Unfortunately, police work knows no time of year, Alexandre, as you are well aware."

"Absolutely," Brouard agreed. "I must telephone my wife." He began dialling.

"We're not spending the night with them, are we, sir?" Parton asked, anxiously, in a whisper.

"I think we probably are, Sergeant. Don't worry, I'm sure the Inspector has at least two spare rooms. He married money."

Parton did not look reassured, and a few minutes later Brouard put down the phone. "My wife says you are welcome to spend the night with us, Chief Inspector. And the sergeant, of course. And have dinner. It so happens, she is serving bouillabaisse tonight. You will like bouillabaisse, yes?"

"Oh, indeed, yes," Lampson said.

"I will call a car." Brouard picked up his phone.

"What is bouillabaisse, Chief-Inspector?" Parton whispered,

"Boiled fish heads."

"Sir?"

"It's in a sauce. Well, a kind of soup, really, with all manner of goodies added. You'll like it, sergeant."

"Sir, I am allergic to fish. Especially fish heads."

"Oh, Jesus Christ! Brouard . . ."

Brouard had replaced his phone, and stood up. "We go now, eh?" The telephone jangled. Brouard picked it up, listened. "I cannot be bothered with this now," he said. "Take their statements. What are we dealing with, some kind of monster? That is absurd." He replaced the telephone. "It is always like this in the summer months. Mayhem! If it is not young girls coming into the town wearing nothing at all, when they are only supposed to do this on the beaches, it is louts fighting. And I have to tell you, Chief Inspector, a lot of these louts are English."

"I know," Lampson said sympathetically. "Louts appear to be our chief export nowadays. Once, we enticed them with the Queen's shilling into the army, and sent them to Africa to fight the fuzzy-wuzzies."

"Now, you entice them with beer and send them abroad to fight anyone who will fight," Brouard said severely. "There are two of them in hospital, and they are saying that it was an Englishman who came out of the water, and started attacking people. He broke one man's arm, and another man's back, and a woman's hip, and there is another woman who is a gibbering wreck: you heard what I told them. Are we dealing with some maniac?"

"Too much booze," Lampson said.

"Sir," Parton ventured.

"We must go," Brouard said. "My wife's bouillabaisse, it must be eaten, when it must be eaten. Not a second later."

"Oh, quite," Lampson agreed. "My wife is entirely the same. Late for dinner, why, the entire week is ruined. And it is so good of her to have us, at all."

Parton hurried behind them down the stairs. "Sir," he said urgently. "Doesn't it sound as if what happened at the beach was the result of someone running amok."

"Very likely, sergeant," Lampson said over his shoulder.

"Well, sir, don't we know an Englishman who runs

amok? And who happens to be here in Antibes right this minute?"

They had reached the courtyard, and the waiting car. But Lampson checked, frowning. "You know, Ned, you could be right. Inspector? What is the latest on Jonathan Rudder?"

"Rudder?" Brouard picked up the car phone and made a call. "It is all right," he said, replacing the handset. "My man is still outside the hotel, and Rudder has not come out. I would say he is there for the night."

"Good thinking, bad idea, Ned," Lampson said. "You want to concentrate on your bouillabaisse."

When he was well away from the beach, Jonathan put on his shoes and straightened his shirt. There was a great deal of noise from down there, but somehow he did not feel either Brigitte or her sister, or either of the men, were going to be telling the whole truth of the matter. On the other hand, just as soon as they could they were going to get in touch with the Clinic to tell Colley and Schleyer that everything had not gone according to plan.

He debated the idea of calling a taxi, and decided against it: he probably could not get to the Clinic before it was warned, in any event, and it was more important for no one, and that included the police as well as Schleyer, to be able to find out just where he was. It was safer to walk, and keep them all guessing.

Colley took Nan to a little bistro close to the front, where they had a quiet meal. "You mustn't be agitated," he said. "There is nothing to be worried about, really."

"It all seems to have gone wrong, since the operation moved to England," she said.

"In what way?"

"Well . . ." she wasn't going to tell him that it was

he who had gone wrong. "The way Rudder and Brand linked up."

"That was always a possibility," he said reassuringly. "But it really isn't going to matter. Brand figuring things out was actually a stroke of luck. We know the police have Rudder firmly elected as the number one suspect for the deaths of Moresby and Morgan, and at least half a suspect for Openshaw. Equally, they obviously reckon he's involved in the Ebershaw murder, for which they want Brand. Now, he's going to wind up drowned, and she is going to disappear altogether, and there aren't going to be any more killings in England. I've talked it over with Schleyer. We're going to move to Holland next. So . . . Scotland Yard are going to be left with a bunch of unsolved and insoluble murders, and two dead or disappeared suspects. They are going to be happy to close the book. Believe me. I know the way the police think."

"Don't you think you're being just a little bit arrogant? What happens if they link up with Spain and France?"

"Why should they? They haven't so far."

"As far as we know they haven't." She cocked her head. "What's all that racket on the front?"

"God knows. There's always some kind of racket on the front in places like these. Trust me," he said, and called for the bill. "Let's go back and have an enjoyable evening with little Jennifer."

Nan shuddered.

They caught a taxi right outside the restaurant, and were at the Clinic in ten minutes. "Any problems?" Colley asked the woman at reception.

"No, doctor. The patient is still fast asleep."

Colley looked at his watch. It was just before nine. "She has another couple of hours to go," he said. "Dr Schleyer still up?"

"Yes, doctor. Shall I tell him you're on your way?"

They went up in the lift, to Schleyer's apartment. "Any word from Brigitte?" Colley asked.

"Not as yet. Brandy?"

"Please. Nan?"

"I think I'll pass." She stood at the huge plate glass window looking down the hill, at the lights of Antibes, and the darkness of the sea beyond. "Do you think she's done it yet?"

Schleyer looked at the clock. "Nine o'clock. I should think so. It is a matter of getting him drunk, and then persuading him into the water. Your men Lewis and Hall will do the rest. Then it will just be an unhappy accident. You know the sort of thing, tourist gets drunk and goes swimming, and drowns. Very straightforward."

The telephone jangled. Schleyer picked it up. "Schleyer."

"Doctor, there is an urgent telephone call for you. It is from Françoise Haniff."

Schleyer frowned. "Put her through. Françoise? What is the trouble?"

"Oh, doctor, doctor . . ." Françoise was panting. "It is terrible. The man Rudder . . ."

"He's dead?"

"No, doctor, no. He is alive, it is we who are dead."

"Look, calm down," Schleyer snapped. "Where are you?"

"I am in a callbox in the hospital in Antibes, doctor."

"The hospital?"

"Yes. It is very bad. Brigitte has a broken hip. One of the Englishmen has a broken back. The other has a broken arm. And I . . . I am all bruised, monsieur. He hit me on the chin."

"Rudder did all this?"

"Yes, doctor. Yes, it was the man, Rudder."

"Good God! And where is he now? Under arrest?"

"No, doctor. He has disappeared. He left us lying

on the beach and went off. That is why I am calling you."

"You think he is coming here?"

"I do not know, doctor. He has disappeared."

"Yes. Well, thank you, Françoise. I hope the others are being well looked after?"

"They are in hospital," Françoise moaned. "The police are here . . ."

"The police?"

"They wish to find out what happened."

"What have you told them?"

"That we were bathing, the four of us, and were attacked by this giant of a madman."

"Nothing more than that?"

"Oh, no, doctor. I did not wish to involve you."

"Françoise, you are adorable. Thank you again. Now you stay with your sister. I will get down to see her as soon as I can." He replaced the telephone, gazed at the anxious faces watching him, and repeated what Françoise had told him.

"Oh, shit!" Nan said. "Oh, shit, shit, *shit*! I just knew getting involved with Rudder was going to end in disaster."

"Explain it to me," Schleyer said.

"I think she's losing her nerve," Colley remarked. "It's simply that two of our recent subjects were girl friends of Rudder's."

Schleyer frowned. "Was that wise?"

"It didn't seem a risk at the time. And they were both magnificent specimens."

"And you sent his uncle to me for a transplant? Did you not consider *that* a risk?"

"I thought that was rather amusing. No, I did not consider it a risk, again, at the time. But then he got together with this bloody Brand woman, and I will admit they have been causing us some trouble, between them.

That's why we got them down here, so they could be dealt with quietly and efficiently. I must say, Hans, I'm disappointed in this woman of yours. You told me she was the perfect person to get rid of Rudder."

"He seems to be more difficult than I had thought," Schleyer admitted. "But your truckers . . ."

"They deserve everything they got, if two grown men couldn't handle a drunken layabout like Rudder. Well, we'll simply have to do it ourselves. We can be quite sure that Rudder is now on his way here; even he will have been able to figure out that if Brigitte Haniff was attempting to drown him she was acting on orders from you, Hans. Well, forewarned is forearmed, as they say. We'll be waiting for him. Because we also know that he ran away from the scene of the fight. That means no one, including the police, has any idea where he is. If, having disappeared from the Antibes waterfront, he just stays disappeared, then that's it. We can dispose of him any way we choose, once he breaks in here. I assume you have a gun, Hans?"

"Oh, I have a gun," Schleyer said thoughtfully. "You make it sound very easy."

"Killing is, when you make up your mind to it." Colley recalled that Schleyer had never actually performed one of the dissections.

"And suppose he doesn't come here, but goes to the police instead?" Nan asked.

Both men turned to look at her. "Rudder, go to the police?" Colley asked.

"We know the police have been tailing him," Nan said. "Nurse Haniff told us that when she telephoned. They would only be doing that if they had been asked to co-operate by Scotland Yard: Rudder hasn't committed any crime here in France. If he and Brand both share the same suspicions, he might well go to them and tell them enough to have them obtain a search warrant."

Schleyer stroked his chin. Colley knocked out his pipe and began to refill it. "Can they obtain a warrant?" he asked.

"It is not as easy as in England," Schleyer said. "But if Rudder were to go to the police, and because of what he told them they decided to interrogate the injured people . . ."

"That can hardly be immediate."

"Oh, entirely. It will not be before tomorrow morning, at the earliest. Yet I think it is something we must consider as a definite possibility."

"They'll have us on toast," Nan muttered.

"Of course they will not have us on toast, Miss Welldon. It is a possibility I have always had to bear in mind, and therefore I have taken certain precautions. The Number One Cold Room is in fact a detached chamber, rather like the car of an elevator, eh? Should I decide to dispose of it, a flick of that switch over there will send it plunging down its shaft, some fifty feet into the hillside. It is then replaced from above, immediately, by another empty chamber which is also capable of refrigeration. All of this happens within five minutes. Anyone searching the building, therefore, once I have been given five minutes notice, will find only an empty cold chamber. The set-up was expensive, but I believe in being covered against every eventuality."

"What happens to the full chamber afterwards?"

"That is up to us, James. Should we consider it necessary, the contents can be left down there to rot. However, should we decide that the danger is quite past, and I believe that is the decision we will take once the police have departed, suitably abashed and in line for a harassment suit against them, it will be a simple matter to return the chamber to its original position." He smiled. "The decision is not one that should be left indefinitely, as of course once the chamber is dropped it loses its connection to the cooling system, and in this climate disintegration will very rapidly set in."

"Sounds like you do have that one covered."

Schleyer smiled. "I have everything covered, Jim. I even have my own private escape route, should it become necessary. Come into the bedroom. This will interest you, Nurse Welldon." Nan glanced at Colley, who shrugged, and they followed Schleyer into a very elaborately furnished bedroom, dominated by the huge round bed itself; the drapes were red and purple. "My passion pit," Schleyer said. "Every man should have a passion pit. But over here . . ." he opened what appeared to be a walk-in cupboard. "My private elevator. It goes straight down to the basement garage." Colley and Nan made suitably complimentary noises. "That is why I say I have every angle covered. But there is, of course, the question of your little friend," Schleyer pointed out.

Colley nodded, and smiled himself. "I think we'll just go wake her up, find out what we want from her, and then, I tell you what, Hans, she can go into that Number One Cold Chamber with the other goodies. By the time I'm finished with her, she'll be fit company."

"You are both stark, raving mad," Nan shouted. "You have gotten away with murder for so long you think you can never be found out. What about those people in hospital? You don't suppose they are going to tell the police what is happening here?"

"Brigitte would never betray me," Schleyer declared. "None of my people would. They are absolutely trustworthy. So are little Françoise and her brother. Well, you have had evidence of that."

"Lewis and Hall are good men," Colley said. "They're in this as deeply as any of us. Anyway, what are the police going to question them about? Only Rudder. The police know nothing about our organisation."

"And us? Why are *we* here, when we know they are

already suspicious of us? There's no use us trying to hide. They'll know when we left Gatwick, and our destination."

"Why shouldn't we be here? Eric Rudder is our patient, and he has taken a turn for the worse. Jonathan will tell them that. We rushed to his bedside."

"And what about Bell?" Nan demanded.

"He's more reliable than any of them."

"I'm thinking of the truck. Suppose they take the truck away, for detailed examination. Don't you suppose they are going to find the false floor, where the coffin was stored, the vents for the air pipes and the heating pipes? Don't you think they are going to make certain deductions? They're not fools. The mere fact that that truck is not an ordinary refrigeration vehicle is going to make them suspicious."

"Hm," Schleyer said. "What do you think, Jim?"

Colley had got his pipe alight. "I think you have a very good point, Nan. But one that is easily remedied. Bell will take the truck out now, and start his drive back to England. There will be nothing unusual or suspicious about that. Time is money."

"Bell won't like it. He only arrived here a few hours ago."

"And has been sleeping ever since. He'll have to like it. I'll go see him. You go upstairs and get Brand awake. Give her a stimulant if you have to, but wake her up. Hans, you had better alert all of your people, and of course, we will wish instant knowledge of any appearance by the police."

"Of course. What about Rudder? Suppose he does not go to the police, but instead comes here on his own? I know you feel we can deal with him, but it might be better to keep him out."

"Can you do that? Guaranteed?"

"Of course. The entire boundary fence is electrified. It

has six thousand volts. Not a rabbit could get through that without burning to a cinder. I had thought of switching it off, to entertain Rudder. But now . . ."

"Yes, maybe that would be the best idea. Keep him out. *Make* him go to the police. By the time they get here, they won't find a thing."

"And Eric Rudder?"

"Everything must be normal, Hans. You keep Eric Rudder alive and well. And when Jonathan does show up with his escoct, tomorrow, we'll be as nice to him as we can." He grinned. "It should be an exciting day, tomorrow."

CHAPTER 11

Bell had been happily dreaming when Colley woke him up. He sat up, and listened to what had happened, rubbing his eyes and scratching the back of his neck. "Shit!" he commented when Colley was finished. "What about the lads?"

"They are receiving hospital treatment. We'll have them transferred up here just as soon as possible," Colley assured him. "Right now, and until Rudder is finally laid to rest, we have to make sure the police can't lay hands on the truck."

Bell got out of bed and began to dress. "I knew I should've gone down there myself," he said.

In which case, it's very likely you'd be in hospital as well, Colley thought – but he didn't say it. "You weren't to know this fellow behaves like a madman when pushed."

"And you reckon you'll be able to deal with him when he busts in here, Jim?"

"Yes. But he's not going to bust in here, except as a cinder. You just get out. With the truck."

"I can't drive non-stop all the way back home, by myself," Bell pointed out.

"Do what you can. If you have to have a couple of hours sleep, do it down some quiet lay-by. When you get home, report the situation to Marcus and Lois. Remember, there is absolutely no need to panic. Right?"

"Right." Bell finished dressing. "You're quite sure you can manage here?"

"Quite sure. Just take care of your end."

Bell nodded, and went down to the car park at the rear of the Clinic, where the truck waited. It had been thoroughly hosed and cleaned by Schleyer's people, but he knew Colley was right: any competent police search would turn up all manner of refinements in the cold coach which would need explaining. There was a watchman on duty all night in the park. Bell told him what he was doing, in poor French, and the man telephoned Dr Schleyer to check it out, then nodded, and released the inner gates. Bell drove through into the outer park, beyond the chateau, and up to the outer gates. Here he paused, and a few moments later these gates too swung in. He drove through, in his rear view mirror watched the gates swing to again; the Clinic had been turned back into an electrically guarded fortress.

He drove slowly down the twisting lane towards the coast road, aiming to get to the motorway just as quickly as possible; four hours of fast driving would put five hundred kilometres behind him, and then he could sleep for an hour or two and hope to be at Calais in time for a lunchtime boat to Dover. He had not travelled more than a quarter of a mile from the Clinic – although the building and its lights were out of sight behind him – when he saw a body lying in the road. Hastily be braked, coming to a stop only a few feet from the inert form.

"Christ," he muttered. The last thing he wanted was to get involved with the police. He was very tempted simply to drive over it. But then blood might spurt on to his wheels, and even if he went through a car wash he could be spotted by some keen-eyed mechanic or policeman or customs officer. And the body looked at least unconscious, if not dead. If he just rolled it down the ravine on his left it would probably lie there for hours, undetected, and he'd be in England this afternoon. He put on the hand brake, stepped down from the cab, and bent over the man. He was a big chap who looked as if he had lived a fairly rugged life, even if he did not appear to be very old. Bell grunted, grasped the man's shoulder, and all hell broke loose.

Jonathan seized Bell by the ankles and upended him, got to his feet and kicked him several times, and when Bell tried to sit up, knelt beside him and wrapped his fingers round his throat. "You drive this truck for Schleyer, or Colley?" he asked. Bell goggled at him, face twisted with pain, and Jonathan closed his fingers. "You going to talk, or am I just going to throttle you?"

He allowed his hand to relax, fractionally, and Bell inhaled, noisily. "I work for them both," he gasped. "They work together."

"And you've just delivered a load of goods to the Clinic," Jonathan reminded him. "I saw you drive in, this afternoon. What was in it?"

"Frozen lamb carcasses."

Jonathan tightened his grip again. "You'll have to do better than that, old son."

Bell panted, and made a sudden writhing movement. With his free hand Jonathan hit him again, in the stomach. He moaned, and vomited. It was some seconds before he could speak. "I have a broken rib."

"Only one? I intend to improve on that. Tell me what you know about Jennifer Brand."

"Jennifer . . . God, I'm in agony."

"It's going to get worse," Jonathan promised him. "Jennifer Brand."

"She was in the truck. I brought her down. Colley wanted her brought down. He wanted to talk with her."

Jonathan was afraid to believe his ears. "You mean she's alive, and in that Clinic?"

"You'll never get at her," Bell said.

"Watch me," Jonathan told him. "On second thoughts, you won't be able to." He stood up, picked Bell up, and threw him into the ravine, listened with satisfaction to the despairing scream and the sound of the body bouncing on the rocks and stunted tree trunks. He was in that sort of mood. He was also pleased with himself. He had been up to the perimeter fence earlier, thrown a stick at it, and watched the sparks flying. That had told him he had to be patient, until someone opened the gate – and he had made the decision that in view of everything that had happened, the gates would be more likely to be opened for someone leaving, at this time of night and in view of the reports likely to be coming out of the town, than arriving. Thus he had waited a quarter of a mile from the gates, and this lout had driven straight into his arms. That the man might not have stopped seemed irrelevant in the context of recent events.

He got into the truck, drove on down the narrow road until he found a cross lane into which he could reverse, and then drove back up to the Clinic.

Colley left Bell's bedroom and took the elevator up to the fourth floor; there were no other patients on this floor, which was why he had chosen it. Nan Welldon was already in the operating theatre, standing above the unconscious woman. "Still out."

"Well, we are going to wake her up. But first thing, prepare her for dissection."

"Eh?"

"That's what I said. Don't worry about any sheeting; if we make a mess in here it can easily be cleaned up before morning."

"I thought you were going to interrogate her, try to find out who else shares her theory?"

"I *am* going to interrogate her. Can you think of a more persuasive argument than to be told that if you don't spill the beans you are going to be dissected, before your eyes?"

Nan swallowed. "Then you don't actually mean to do it."

Colley grinned. "She has to believe I mean to do it, Nan. Now let's get to it." She wished she could believe him – after his remark about cleaning up the blood. But she pulled off the blankets. "She's actually an attractive little thing," Colley remarked. "It would be amusing if we decided to use some of her organs after all."

"You said . . ." Jennifer gave a little moan, and stirred.

"Progress," Colley said. He placed his bag on the table, took out a needle. "We'll just tickle her up a little." Nan cleaned the forearm, and Colley injected the stimulant. "Wakey-wakey, Jennie."

Jennifer's eyes opened, blinked, and then stayed open. She gave a slight tug on her arm, frowned, and then tried to move a leg. Then she raised her head to look down at herself and the straps holding her in position. "You are a shit," she commented, and glanced at Nan. "Two shits."

"How do you feel?" Colley asked. Jennifer turned her head again, to and fro, and then let it fall back on to the mattress. Colley held the little toe of her right foot, and jabbed it with his needle.

"Ow!" Her leg jerked against its bonds.

"I'd say you're wide awake," Colley commented. "Now, Jennie, you came to my office yesterday and made some very provocative suggestions. Amazingly, you were spot on. Everything. Well, you can imagine that was fairly disturbing for my colleagues and myself." Jennifer gazed at him, her eyes filled with loathing. "Now I imagine the last thing you remember is being put to sleep yesterday afternoon in your flat, just after Ebershaw had been killed. Since then you have been under sedation, so that we could move you to a safe place. The police think you killed Ebershaw, you see, and then fled the scene of the crime. Should you never turn up again, they will no doubt be secretly relieved, however many motions they may go through, pretending to look for you. That is, providing no one else prods them. So, what I want you to tell me is, with whom did you share your interesting theory? Rudder? The police? I really do need to know, Jennie."

"Jennifer," she muttered. "The name is Jennifer." Think, damn you, she told herself. Find out where you are, for a start. Well, it seemed obvious that they would have taken her to the Freedom Clinic. Except that she had a vague impression of travel.

"Ah, yes," Colley said. "You don't really like diminutives, do you. But you know, Jennifer, you are going to become a diminutive yourself, if you don't cough up. I told you, your theory was right. So, if you won't co-operate willingly, I intend at least to use parts of you, unwillingly. In the first instance, I am going to open you from . . ." he took a piece of blue chalk from his pocket, placed it at the base of her throat, and drew it slowly downwards to her pubic hair, raising the chalk to pass over the straps. "There to there!" She gave a start. The chalk felt almost like a knife itself; all her muscles were tensed and her knees had instinctively tried to draw up. "See what I mean?" Colley asked with grin.

"You bastard!"

"But first, I'm going to . . ." he circled each breast with the chalk. "Cut these off. While you watch,"

"I hope you choke on the blood," she retorted.

"All in a day's work. Now, the point is, any of your organs we do decide to use have got to be absolutely free of germs. So it has to be a proper operation. You do understand? So what we are going to do is, I am going to have a wash and change into my gear, and my nurse here, Sister Welldon . . . you remember Sister Welldon? Of course you do. Well, she is going to shave you, and get you all ready. Okay?" He beamed at her, and she wanted to spit at him. Then he bustled from the room.

Nan Welldon took his place beside her. "He means what he says, Miss Brand," she said. "For God's sake, tell him what he wants to know. Listen, you're in a clinic in the south of France. No one in the world knows you're here, and no one in the world is going to come to get you. If you co-operate with him, I promise I'll do everything I can to keep you alive."

Jennifer had read enough spy novels to remember the carrot-and-stick routine. But although she would never have admitted it, even to herself, she was deathly afraid . . . and humiliated. Yet she was not going to surrender to them. "Do you take me for a fool?" she asked. "I told Jonathan Rudder all about it. You remember Jonathan?"

"We know Mr Rudder," Nan said, grimly.

"Well, you can bet your bottom dollar he's doing something about it, right now." Nan gulped. "I also told the police," Jennifer said. "That man Lampson. I should think he's tearing your Freedom Clinic apart right this minute."

Colley returned, wearing gown and cap and gloves. "What, not shaved? Whatever have you been doing, Nan?"

"Talking to her," Nan said. "She says she has told both Rudder and the police about her theory. I believe her."

"You are too gullible, Nan. Rudder may know something, but the police don't have a clue. We saw that last night. Anyway, it doesn't matter now. We are going to operate."

"For God's sake, Jim. If she must die, just cut her throat."

Jennifer swallowed. These people were talking about *her*.

"Where would be the fun in that? This little bitch has damn near ruined our operation. Well, I want her to get every last second of satisfaction out of her detective work.

I am going to dissect her. And there is going to be no pre-med. She is going to feel every cut."

"You're mad," Jennifer said. "You have to be mad."

"Are you going to shave her, or not?" Colley asked. "Or shall I do it myself?" Nan Welldon stared at him, willing herself to resist him, to defy him . . . and the telephone buzzed.

Colley picked it up. "Yes?"

"It's Hans. I am sorry to interrupt your operation, but your man Bell has returned. He is at the gate. He is saying that something is the matter and he wishes to be allowed in."

"What the hell . . .? All right, Hans. Let him in. I'll come down to talk to him." He replaced the phone, pointed at Nan. "When I've sorted Bell out, I am coming back. And you had better have her ready by then."

The door closed behind him, and Jennifer and Nan gazed at each other. "Please," Jennifer said. "He's mad. You know he's mad. Let me up."

"He'd kill me," Nan said.

"So are you just going to stand there and watch him kill *me*? God, have you any idea what he did to those others?"

"I helped him," Nan said. "With Philippa Morgan."

Jennifer's mouth opened, and then closed again. Her head fell back on to the mattress. Oh, God, she thought. I am going to die. Horribly. Oh, if only Jonathan were here.

"That was a most delicious dinner, Madame Brouard," Lampson said, wiping his lips with his napkin. "I'm sorry. I meant, ah . . . *trés bien. Délicieuse.*" He looked hopefully at Brouard.

"My wife has a few words of English, Chief Inspector. And you, Sergeant? Did you enjoy it?"

"There's a bone stuck in my throat," Parton whispered, hoarsely. He had been unhappy even before the meal, having discovered that the Brouards after all only had one spare room, and that contained a double bed.

"Oh, really, Ned," Lampson protested.

"I'm sure of it, sir."

"Then you must roll up a piece of soft bread, so," Brouard demonstrated. "And swallow it. The bone will go down with it, wrapped up in it, eh? And then there will be no trouble."

Parton took the piece of bread, his expression reminiscent of Socrates accepting his cup of hemlock. "What happens at the other end?"

"The bread will take care of that too, sergeant." Parton swallowed, and the telephone rang. "Brouard." The Inspector listened, alternating between frowns and raised eyebrows, and flicks of his cigarette; his wife did not seem to object to the large amount of ash being deposited on her carpet. "Yes," Brouard said at last. "I will call you back." He replaced the receiver, lit a fresh cigarette from the stub of the old. "That was my sergeant at the hospital."

"Something devolved?" Lampson was eager.

"It may have," Brouard said carefully. "The injured people are sticking to their story that they were attacked by an unknown assailant who came out of the sea, but my sergeant has learned that three of them are employees of the St Croix Clinic. The two men are English, who drive the Clinic's truck to and from England, delivering food and medical supplies. One of the women is the Head Sister at the Clinic. The other is her sister."

"Jesus!" Parton commented.

"Coincidence?" Lampson asked. Parton raised his eyebrows. "Well, if Rudder hasn't left his hotel . . . can you check that out, Inspector?"

"Of course." Brouard dialled, asked, listened. "No one

has gone in or out of the Haniff Hotel this evening," he said.

"I don't like it, sir," Parton said. "It's just too *much* of a coincidence that the people we are interested in should be mixed up in a fight with a man who sounds very like Rudder."

Lampson grunted; he had been looking forward to sampling some of Brouard's excellent Calvados. But there might still be time. "Right," he said. "Tell your man to go in to the hotel, Inspector, and ask to speak with Mr Rudder."

"He will have no right to insist, you understand, Chief Inspector."

Lampson nodded. "If Rudder refuses to speak with him, then we can assume he isn't there."

"Suppose he is there?" Parton asked.

Lampson gave him a pained look. "Aren't you arguing against yourself, Ned?"

"No, sir. But he has had the time to beat up those people, and return to his hotel, and go to bed, or whatever, presenting a picture of perfect innocence."

"Sergeant, two of the people he has assaulted and hospitalised, if it was Rudder, are the sisters of the hotel proprietor. You're not going to tell me he'd be welcome back. No, no. He is either there, having never left, in which case your theory is wrong, or he has left and he isn't coming back. In which case . . ." he turned his gaze on Brouard. "We had better get out to the Clinic."

"Again, Chief Inspector, we have no right to force an entry."

"Then let's get a warrant."

"On what grounds?"

"If Rudder isn't at the Haniff Hotel, then I'll bet my last cent he's at the Clinic."

"Do you wish to place him under arrest?"

Lampson hesitated for a last time. "Yes," he said. "We have enough to arrest him. If only on suspicion of causing the fracas at the beach tonight. And if we also have reason to believe he is sheltering at the Clinic, or has gone there, for whatever reason . . ."

Brouard still looked doubtful. "Let us first of all discover if he has left the hotel. It will not be possible to obtain a warrant before tomorrow morning, anyway."

Jonathan watched the gates swing in, resisted the temptation to gun the motor. He didn't know what other obstacles might lie between himself and getting into the Clinic. He followed the drive, turned into the forecourt; as he got there, the inner gates also swung in. For a moment he hesitated, then he reflected that it was probably easier for Schleyer to seal off the front of the building than the back, and drove through these as well. A man was standing in the centre of the inner yard, waiting for him. Jonathan had never seen him before, but it seemed obvious that he would know the truck driver who had left only a few minutes earlier. He swung the truck to a stop only feet from the man, who hastily jumped out of the way – but not far enough. Jonathan slid down from the cab, reached him with swinging fists in the same movement. The man hit the ground without a word.

Jonathan looked left and right. He was entirely surrounded by the hospital buildings; most of them were in darkness, but there were lights in the larger block, backing on to the chateau itself. He ran at the door in front of him, and it opened, to allow four men to come out. They shouted at him in French, then he was in their midst, again swinging his huge fists from side to side. They scattered around his feet and he reached the doorway, blinked in the sudden light, and saw a flight of stairs in front of him. He went up these, reached a landing, looked to his left, and saw Colley and another man coming towards him; Colley was wearing a green operating robe. "Shit!" Colley snapped. "How did he get in here?"

Jonathan ran at them. The orderly attempted to stop him, Colley turned and ran the other way. Jonathan blocked the orderly's punch, picked the man up by the thighs, and hurled him against the wall; he slid down it to the floor, unconscious. Adrenalin was pumping through Jonathan's arteries; he wanted to fight the world, and it seemed as if he might have his wish. He pounded along the corridor, reached the end, and looked left and right. Colley had disappeared, but a nurse was peering at him round the corner. She also tried to run away, but he reached her in three long strides, grabbing the back of her gown and bringing her against him. "Aaagh!" she screamed. She was middle-aged and wore glasses; these fell to the floor and shattered.

"Listen," Jonathan told her. "If you don't speak English, you're done."

"I . . . I speak English," she gasped.

"Is there an Englishwoman in the hospital? A woman named Brand?" She licked her lips, and he shifted his grasp to her neck. "Make it quick," he suggested.

"I do not know. There is a patient on the fourth floor. I believe she is English. I do not know her name."

"When did she come in?"

"Today. This afternoon."

"That's the one. Fourth floor." He threw her aside and ran for the lifts.

Colley took the lift to the top floor, burst into Schleyer's apartment. Schleyer was sitting in an armchair, looking out through the plate glass windows at the lights of Antibes and the invisible sea beyond, and listening to Elgar's *March of the Moghul Emperors*. He turned his head at the intrusion. "James? Whatever is the matter. You look as if you've seen a ghost."

"Rudder!" Colley gasped. "He is in the hospital. He's tearing the place apart."

Schleyer frowned and got up, walking to the music centre and switching of the CD player. "Rudder? How did he get in?"

"God knows. Your place isn't as foolproof as you thought. Where's that gun of yours?"

Schleyer opened his desk drawer and took out a Browning automatic pistol. "Where is he now?"

"Looking for his little friend, I suspect. Well, they can go to perdition together." Colley checked the magazine, slammed it back into the butt.

"Do you wish me to come with you?"

"Yes."

"Then I had better be armed too." Schleyer took out a second pistol, and grinned. "I think, between us, we can cope even with your Mr Rudder. Before he destroys my clinic."

Brouard's man telephoned back only ten minutes later. Brouard gazed at the phone as if it was someone he disliked very much, then looked at Lampson, who was sipping his Calvados with immense enjoyment, smiling at Madame Brouard. Parton was eating more bread. "Rudder is not at the hotel. In fact, the man Haniff says he has not been there since just after eight tonight. He spotted my man outside, and went out the back way."

"Shit," Parton commented.

"You were right all along, sergeant," Lampson said. "Well, now, we can be pretty damn sure what he did with his evening, and where he is now." He finished his drink, got up. "Let's get out to that clinic."

"Without a warrant?"

"I have never yet needed a warrant to get into any self-respecting hospital," Lampson told him. "If they refuse us entry, then they are not on the up, and we'll have a reason for a warrant. Let's go."

* * *

Jennifer watched Nan Welldon move the clippers over her groin; the metal was cold, but that wasn't what kept making her shiver. The woman had seemed so nice, still seemed so nice, but she was carrying out Colley's instructions with cold-blooded dispassion. Yet she had to try. "Listen," she said. "Don't you realise that you're going to be sent to prison for the rest of your life? Hell, no, if we're in France, you'll be sent to the guillotine."

"Only if I'm tried and found guilty," Nan said. "And to do that, they have to find out exactly what is going on. And they'll never do that." Nan had finished with the clippers. Now she turned her attention to the lather. "Please don't wriggle," she requested. "I don't want to cut you."

"You don't want . . . for Jesus' sake, is *everyone* in here mad?" A straw! "Listen you agreed with me that Colley is mad. You did, remember?"

Nan finished lathering and selected a safety razor from the tray. "Lie still." Jennifer's nerves cracked. She threw back her head and screamed to the fullest extent of her lungs. Nan frowned at her, then put down the razor and slapped Jennifer's face, crisply. "Stop that."

Jennifer panted. "Don't you think I'm going to scream when Colley starts to cut me?" she shouted. "Or are you going to slap my face then too?"

Nan looked as if she might hit her again, then checked, and half turned. The windows were shut in the ward, and so was the door, yet even so there was a sudden surge of distant sound, men shouting, someone screaming almost as loudly as Jennifer had done.

"The police!" Jennifer breathed. "Oh, God, the police."

"Don't be stupid," Nan admonished. But she went to the door, opened it, and listened. The distant noise persisted, but did not seem to be coming closer. "Jim will explain it when he comes back." She closed the door, and returned to the bedside. "Now, please do not scream again, or I shall have to gag you, and as I said, keep still." Her tongue peeped between her teeth as she carefully moved the razor blade over the smooth white flesh.

God, it has to be the police, Jennifer thought. It has to be someone. Something. I can't be going to die like this, cut to pieces before my own eyes. I can't. She realised she was very near the brink of a total breakdown. But mightn't that be better than trying to be brave, trying to think of some way of resisting them, some way of escaping?

"There we are." Nan dried her with a towel and removed the last of the shaving foam. "Jim will be pleased with that. Now . . ." Again she checked, frowning, as there came the bang of a door, close at hand. Immediately the sound was followed by another.

"There's someone on this floor," Jennifer said. "Looking in all the rooms. The police! Help!" she shouted. "In here! Help!" Nan ran at her, but before she could shut her up the door burst inwards. "Jonathan!" Jennifer shrieked.

"Well, hello there," Jonathan said. "Nurse Welldon! Now, just what are you doing to my little friend."

Nan reached for the tray of surgical instruments and found a scalpel. But before she could use it, Jonathan had closed his hand on her wrist. He didn't twist, just squeezed. Nan gave a gasp of pain and the scalpel clattered to the floor. She kicked him on the ankle and swung her free hand at his face, but, still holding her right wrist, he merely thrust his other hand between her legs, gripped her thigh with such force that she squealed with pain, lifted her from the floor, and threw her across the room; she struck the wall and fell to the floor in a crumpled heap. "My God!" Jennifer gasped; she had never seen anyone quite so ruthlessly destroyed.

He untied her. "Do you have any clothes?"

"Apparently not." She got off the bed, hugged herself. "They were going to cut me up, Jonny. Like Angie. And Doug."

He wrapped her in one of the blankets. "First thing is to get you out of here." Nan stirred, and Jonathan stepped across to her, grasped her by the bodice, and lifted her to her feet. "We may need you." He threw her over his shoulder, peered through the door. "Come on." He stepped into the corridor, Jennifer immediately behind him, and walked to the lifts.

"Does anyone know you're here?" Jennifer asked.

"Everyone in the hospital, I should think."

"Then . . ." she looked left and right.

He nodded. "It's too quiet. They're waiting for us. And they can tell where we are by watching the lights. So . . ." he laid Nan on the floor.

Nan stirred, opened her eyes. "God," she muttered. "What happened?"

"You ran into my friend and a brick wall," Jennifer told her with pleasure. "They're virtually synonymous."

"They're going to kill you," Nan said. "Both of you. You don't have a chance. They've got guns."

"Then you'd better hope they don't start shooting," he told her. "Because I intend to hold you in front. Come on."

He picked her up again, as if she were a sack, Jennifer thought. "Listen," Nan said urgently. "I can get you out of here."

"Oh, yes?"

"Go up, not down. Above us is Schleyer's penthouse. He has a private lift to the basement. They won't expect you to be using that."

"Won't there be people waiting for us in the basement as well?" Jennifer asked.

"Not if you're quick enough."

"If we can make the yard, the truck's there waiting for

us," Jonathan said. He took Nan from his shoulder, now handling her as if she had been a doll and peered at her. "Tell me why."

"I want to survive. And . . . she said she could get me off if I helped."

"That was some time ago," Jennifer reminded her. "But get us out of here, and it's a deal."

"He's staying on the fourth floor," Colley said. "We'll have to go up."

"I think not," Schleyer said. "He has to come down, eventually." He picked up a wall telephone. "Is every floor guarded? Good. I think we'll wait for him to make his move. But when he does, he'll go for the basement. You and I will go down there, Jim."

"What about Nan Welldon? She was in the room with the Brand woman, preparing her for dissection. If Rudder has regained Brand, he has Nan as well."

"Do you think he has killed her?"

"He's not that sort of chap. Although when he really gets aroused he can be very violent."

"I have observed this. Well, she will have to take her chances. If, as you say, Rudder is not a killer, the odds are that she will survive. But Brand and Rudder must come first. We will use the stairs, so as not to interfere with his plans." He went along the corridor, and after a moment's hesitation, Colley followed him.

The lights were on in Schleyer's apartment. "Stay away from the windows," Jonathan warned Jennifer.

"There should be a fire escape, shouldn't there?"

"They'll have that covered. Where is this private elevator, Sister?"

"In the bedroom." Nan led them into the ornate bedroom, and opened the cabinet in the corner to reveal the lift shaft and the waiting car.

"Looks kind of small," Jennifer said. "You reckon it'll take three people?"

"No," Jonathan said. "You'll have to stay behind, Nan. On the bed." She looked from one to the other. "We're not even going to shave you," Jonathan told her. "Sadly."

Nan climbed on to the bed, lay down. Jonathan opened the wardrobe, found Schleyer's tie rack, took out a handful. He rolled her on her face, tied her wrists, then her ankles, and then pulled her legs up behind her and tied wrists to ankles, so that she was utterly helpless. He then manhandled her up the bed and tied her wrists to the bedpost. They were both gasping by the time he was finished. "You enjoyed that," she said.

"As a matter of fact, I did. Shame we can't have round three."

"A gag?" Jennifer suggested.

"Good thinking." He opened one of Schleyer's drawers, and found a handkerchief. "Open wide." Nan glared at him, but obeyed. Jonathan stuffed the handkerchief into her mouth. Jennifer was standing by with another necktie, and this was secured round Nan's mouth.

"I have the strangest feeling that I should want to *do* something to her," Jennifer said.

"But you can't think what. I suppose that's the essential difference between people like them and people like us. Let's get out of here."

Schleyer and Colley ran down the stairs, arrived in the basement, panting, and found three men waiting for them. One pointed at the control panel, where a red light glowed. Schleyer grinned. "Your Nan has told them about the private elevator. I hope you will speak to her about that, James. But it makes it that much easier." He signalled his men to follow him to the far side of the huge garage.

* * *

There was just room for the two of them to stand against each other in the elevator. Jonathan pressed the button, and they shot downwards. "Are we going to make it, Jonathan?" Jennifer asked.

"Haven't a clue. If we can reach that truck . . ." The lift stopped, the door opened, and they gazed at Schleyer and Colley, and several other men.

They also gazed at the two automatic pistols. "No trouble now, Mr Rudder," Schleyer said. "You have caused enough mayhem for one evening."

Jonathan's muscles tensed, and Jennifer clutched his arm. "Where's Nan?" Colley demanded.

"Upstairs," Jennifer told him. "We didn't hurt her. Well, not seriously."

"I'm sure she's looking forward to hurting *you*, now." Colley gestured with the gun towards the regular lift shaft. Jennifer glanced at Jonathan, and stepped away from him. Her brain felt numb. But she supposed there had never been any chance of their escaping this place. Yet the thought of having come so close, and now to be returned to that bed, tied down to await slaughter, was unbearable.

"What about Rudder?" Schleyer asked.

"Bring him along. He always wanted to be a surgeon. And we may even find that he has something worthwhile inside that whisky-sodden frame."

"Rudder!" Schleyer also pointed with the pistol. A telephone buzzed. "Answer that," Schleyer said to one of the other men. Jonathan and Jennifer waited, hearts pounding.

"It's Sister Marianne, doctor," the man said. "Inspector Brouard is at the gate, with several men. He wishes to come in."

"Shit!" Colley snapped. "Those people of yours at the hospital must have shot their mouths."

"They would not do that," Schleyer objected.

"Well, send them away."

"The police?"

"They have no right to come in without a warrant."

"If we send them away," Schleyer spoke as if he were addressing a small child, "they will simply obtain a warrant, and then return. Filled with suspicions. We must let them in. Tell Sister Marianne to open the gates and allow the police to come in," he said. "I will be there in a moment."

"And what are we going to do with these two?" Colley demanded.

"As I told you, the solution is very simple. Turn round, Mr Rudder, and walk the other way, if you will. But I think, James, that you should hurry up to my flat and release Miss Welldon."

Colley hesitated, obviously reluctant to let Jonathan out of his sight, then nodded, and went to the lift. Jonathan attempted to assess the odds; one of the pistols had been removed. But there were still four men present, and a gun, and this time he lacked the element of surprise. He glanced at Jennifer. He didn't know how good she might be in a fight – he had the impression she was about at the end of her tether. "Oh, you take Miss Brand with you," Schleyer said. "I am going to lock you up until after we have seen the police."

While there was life, there was hope, Jonathan decided. "We'd better do as they say, darling," he told Jennifer.

"Through that door," Schleyer pointed. The wall behind them had opened, giving access into what looked like a large lift car, out of which there came a blast of cold air. "Do not worry," Schleyer said. "I will turn off the cooling system while you are in there."

"Joanathan . . ." Jennifer's voice was quavering.

"We have to trust him," he muttered, held her arm, and propelled her across the garage floor to the doorway.

Inside was brilliantly lit, and he saw that the interior of the car was actually very narrow; on either side there were a mass of shelves, stretching from the floor to the roof. They stepped into the car.

"Now, Mr Rudder," Schleyer said. "When I turn off the cooling system I must also switch off the lights. But as I understand you are a squeamish fellow, I would not wish you to feel uncomfortable in the darkness." He snapped his fingers, and one of his men came forward with a flashlight. "Use it carefully," Schleyer recommended.

It was a good, solid, rubber-cased torch, and could, Jonathan thought, be handy as a weapon. But before he could act, the door slammed shut. Almost immediately the whirr of the cooling system ceased, and the light went off. "There, Mr Rudder," Schleyer's voice came through a tube. "I am a man of my word. It will now steadily grow warmer, and you should be quite comfortable. But I should pray, if I were you, that the police do not make a nuisance of themselves, or you will find it quite uncomfortable after a while. We will be back as soon as we can."

"Jonathan," Jennifer muttered, clutching his arm.

The "room" was moving. It *was* a lift car. And they were going down. It wasn't a very deep shaft, and after only a few seconds they came to rest again. "Smart," Jonathan said. "He probably has another car above this one, made to look like a room. This way he can conceal us from the police for as long as he likes, while still letting them search the building."

"Jonathan! It's not us he's concealing. He could easily have shot us and dumped us down this shaft. Put on the flashlight." Jonathan switched it on, sent the beam round the car. Jennifer released his arm, slowly, reluctantly, as if she was afraid to lose contact, but as if, too, she was being drawn to the shelves on either side as if they were magnets and she a piece of iron.

Jonathan watched her with a frown. The shelves were

laden with what looked like pre-packed food, only the containers were all made of aluminium. Each was labelled, and some of them were quite large, about a foot square. It was now perceptibly warmer in the car, and he became aware of a peculiar smell. An incredibly human smell! Jennifer was standing before the shelf. She stretched out her arm and took down one of the containers, looked at it, and put it back; a tremor ran through her entire body. "So what are they hiding?" he asked.

Jennifer turned to look at him; her face was almost green.

"Jennifer?" He reached for her, and past her, to pick up the container. The lid was transparent, and he looked at a human heart, frozen in its own blood. He gulped, picked up another. Another heart. He released Jennifer, and she slid down his body to the floor, where she remained, kneeling. Jonathan took a container from a lower shelf, and looked at a human liver, also frozen in its own blood and liquid. "Jesus Christ!" he muttered. Schleyer had reminded him he was squeamish – and had given him the flashlight to make sure of it.

"There's your motive," Jennifer whispered from the floor. "I worked it out . . . but I hadn't thought . . . God! What are we to do?" Jonathan inhaled, and realised the room was warmer yet. Schleyer had said they had better pray he didn't leave them down here for too long. Already he had a gagging sensation at the back of his throat. He looked up and down the shelves; there were twelve on each side, each shelf two feet deep, and each shelf laden with containers. They were surrounded by human organs, all of which were going to start disintegrating in a matter of hours. Probably a lot less.

CHAPTER 12

"Mr Jonathan Rudder," Hans Schleyer said thoughtfully; he had received the police officers in the library, a vast, quiet room with book-lined walls. "The young man whose uncle has just had a transplant? Yes, of course, Inspector. He was here this afternoon. I had to ask him to come down, I'm afraid, because his uncle's condition suddenly took a turn for the worse. Although the operation was a success, you understand, his body began to show signs of rejecting the heart."

"Where is this uncle now, doctor?" Brouard asked.

"In his room. I immediately began treating him with drugs, and I am happy to say he showed a rapid recovery. Young Mr Rudder was very relieved. But he is not here. He went off with one of my staff sisters; she had promised to find him a room for the night. Antibes is very crowded at this time of year."

"So we gather," Lampson said, and glanced at Colley, who had just appeared, looking distinctly hot and bothered. "Who are you?"

"This is Dr James Colley, of the Freedom Clinic, in London," Schleyer explained. "Chief Inspector Lampson and Detective Sergeant Parton, of . . . you did say Scotland Yard, didn't you, Chief Inspector? And Inspector Brouard of the Nice police." He exuded urbanity.

"Colley!" Lampson said.

"Odd we've never met," Colley agreed. "I believe you searched my Clinic, last night."

"Just what are you doing here, Dr Colley?"

"Eric Rudder happens to be my patient," Colley explained. "When Hans called me to say there were complications setting in, I came right down. However, as he says, happily it appears to have been a false alarm."

"Right," Lampson said. "Now, Jonathan Rudder. We know he left here with your staff sister this evening, Dr Schleyer. Are you aware that the lady is now in hospital?"

"I heard there had been an accident, yes," Schleyer said, and frowned. "But I was told it was not serious."

"She has a broken hip. And two other men, also employees of yours, are badly injured. We think this was done by Rudder."

"One man?"

"He is violent when aroused. We also think that having assaulted your people, he would have come here."

"Here?" Colley appeared astounded. "But why?"

"That is something we have to find out. As we will, when we find Rudder."

"But you will not find him here, Chief Inspector," Schleyer said. "As you know, Inspector Brouard, our fence is electrified and the gate can only be opened from inside the Clinic. There is no way he could have got in."

"We are quite sure he will have come here, doctor," Brouard said. "I have men searching the perimeter now. Are you certain there is no way in apart from the front gate?"

"Absolutely."

"There is no such thing as an absolutely foolproof security system," Lampson asserted.

"You make this man Rudder sound like a demigod, Chief Inspector," Schleyer pointed out. "But I cannot understand why you should think he needs to break in. Mr Rudder is welcome here. His uncle is a patient of mine. Young Mr Rudder was here this afternoon, as I have told you. If he wishes to see his uncle again, all he has to do is telephone from the gate and it will be opened for him."

"He might not feel he is welcome, after putting three of your staff in hospital," Parton suggested.

"Well, of course, I am very upset about this," Schleyer said. "But I cannot see what it has to do with me. I observed both on Tuesday and this afternoon that Mr Rudder has an eye for the ladies, and especially Sister Haniff. In fact, I wondered if I should warn her. But she is a grown woman. Now . . . I am afraid there has been some kind of tiff with another of her boy friends. However, as regards Rudder, I assure you that should he turn up here, I will telephone you immediately, and endeavour to hold him here until you return."

Lampson looked at Brouard; he still wanted to search the Clinic. But Brouard seemed quite happy with the situation. "In that case, doctor, we will withdraw. We . . ." he turned.

Sister Marianne had emerged from the reception area. "It is the gate phone, Inspector. One of your men wishes to speak with you."

"Do you mind, doctor?"

"Of course not, Inspector."

Brouard hurried off, and Parton watched Schleyer and Colley exchange quick, and he felt, anxious glances. Not everything was quite as it seemed here. "Well," Lampson said regretfully. "It looks as if we shall have to say goodnight, Doctor. Colley."

Parton also nodded to the two doctors, and followed his boss to the door, which was suddenly filled by a returning, agitated, Brouard. "My men have found a body," he said.

"A what?" Lampson shouted.

"A man. He is alive, just. He appears to have been thrown down the ravine. My men say they do not think he could have fallen that far."

"Good God! Rudder!"

"You think it is Rudder?" Schleyer asked.

"I am damn sure it *isn't* Rudder. But whoever it is, I'm pretty damned sure it was Rudder put him there. Has he said anything, Alexandre?"

Brouard shook his head. "He is unconscious. My men are bringing him in now. I told them not to worry to call for an ambulance . . ." he looked at Schleyer.

Schleyer glanced at Colley. Now he turned back to the police. "Of course, we will look after him here."

"Odds are he's one of yours," Lampson said. "Has any vehicle entered or left the hospital this evening?"

Schleyer hesitated. The man in the ravine could only be Bell . . . and if Bell were to say anything before he could get to him . . . he could almost feel Colley's gaze boring into his back, willing him to make the right decision.

"Why, yes, Chief Inspector," he said. "Our refrigerated truck, which brings us food as well as medical supplies from England, left this evening, and then returned. The driver said he had a small problem."

"So he was re-admitted. Where is this driver now?"

"I have no idea. I do not deal with that sort of thing. I assume, as he told the desk he did not intend to leave again before tomorrow morning, that he has gone to bed."

"No one saw him?"

"Why should they?"

Lampson cracked a knuckle. "Then there's our answer. The man in the ravine is your driver, doctor. And Rudder is loose, and inside this complex. Has been, since that truck returned."

"Oh, really, Chief Inspector. I cannot accept that."

"Accept it or not, we'll know in five minutes, when the injured man is brought in. If he is your driver, I would like to search your hospital."

"Search the Clinic?"

"It is for your own safety, doctor. And that of your

staff, and patients, I may add. You have a lunatic loose on the premises. We have to get him before he does any more damage."

"Well, of course, Chief Inspector. You must do what you think best. But the truck came back over an hour ago. Where do you think Rudder has been all this time?"

"Hiding somewhere, waiting for the Clinic to settle for the night. We'll begin with the truck, and then I wish to see the driver's bedroom."

"Of course. Sister Marianne, please show the Chief Inspector whatever he wishes. You'll excuse me a moment; I must alert my people that there may be a lunatic loose on the premises." He hurried from the room, Colley at his heels.

They gained Schleyer's office, and Schleyer immediately picked up the phone. "Jules," he snapped. "Those people hurt by Rudder, when he first broke in. You will tell the police that it was an accident in the handling room." Quickly he brought Jules up to date on what was happening. "Make sure they all tell the same story." He replaced the phone. "How the hell did Scotland Yard policemen get here?"

"I would say our plan worked just too well. They obviously had a tail on Rudder, and have decided he's the man they want more than any other."

"Where is Nurse Welldon?"

"Still upstairs. She had a set-to with Rudder, and is a bit shaken up."

"You had better get up there and put her in the picture."

"What about Rudder and Brand? They've been down there half an hour."

"Not so long. But I agree, we should get them up as rapidly as possible. Not for their sake, but because of the spares. They are well frozen, but it is very warm in that shaft, and should they even begin to disintegrate . . ."

"Rudder will go stark raving mad."

"And we will lose several months work. But there is nothing I can do about that while the police are on the premises."

Colley stroked his chin. "How long will they have?"

"Before disintegration becomes a serious problem for them? Oh, several hours yet. But they will suffer severe psychological problems, I would estimate, just by being locked up with so much dissected humanity. It will be interesting to observe, when we fetch them out. But for now, let us cease worrying about Mr Rudder and Miss Brand, and attend to the police."

"Jonathan." Jennifer's voice trembled. "What are we going to do? This stuff . . ."

"Is going to be a problem, I agree. Let's see if we *can* do anything about it." He surveyed the car in the beam of Schleyer's flashlight. There was an inspection hatch in the roof above his head, and he could just reach it by standing on tiptoe and with his arms fully extended. He peered at it. There were a dozen screws holding it in place. He looked at Jennifer. "You wouldn't happen to have a screwdriver on you, by any chance?" She hugged the blanket more tightly round her shoulders. "I didn't think you would. Well . . ." he looked at the aluminium trays.

"Oh, God," she said. "You can't."

"I don't think we have any choice," he pointed out. Carefully he took out one of the trays; it contained a kidney. Feeling his mouth fill with saliva, he opened it, emptied the contents on the shelf; it was just beginning to thaw. Jennifer turned away. Jonathan began to work the aluminium base, twisting it and cracking it, until he was able to tear it and then shape it some more. "*Voilà!* One screwdriver." His hands were wet with melting blood and serum, and his fingers were ice cold.

"It won't last twelve screws," Jennifer pointed out.

"Well, we have a lot of spares, right? I don't suppose you'd care to start work on number two?"

"I don't think I could, Jonathan."

"All right. Take it easy." He stood on tiptoe, inserted the tip he had created into the first screw head, and began to turn. The aluminium buckled and snapped, and he patiently fashioned a new tip, and resumed work, arms aching now. The head moved, just a little. "Got the bugger!"

The screw fell to the floor, but the improvised screwdriver was now useless. And the heat inside the car was increasing every moment. So it seemed was the smell. Jonathan knew this was pure imagination, but it was going to become real soon enough. Jennifer realised this too, and forced herself to help. They worked with furious concentration, trying to ignore the mess with which they were surrounded. And now the disintegration process had definitely begun. The pile of discarded, bent and broken aluminium grew, as did the pile of discarded organs. Jennifer panted and tried not to breathe, and watched Jonathan, working away with a single-mindedness she had not known him to possess.

They had been working for over two hours when the eleventh screw came out. Jonathan looked round for another tool, and saw Jennifer collapse in a heap on the floor, her hands to her face: the atmosphere in the car was foetid. For the first time he was glad he hadn't had any dinner, and realised that Jennifer couldn't have eaten for well over twenty-four hours. But there could be no doubt that in another couple of hours the car was going to be untenable.

"Shit!" he muttered, and leapt up at the hatch. Now held by a single screw, it moved under the impact, and he was able to lodge his fingers on the rim, then get his other hand up. Hanging there, he worked the lid so that it slowly rotated away from the hatch. Then he could get his shoulders through, and a moment later was on top of the car. He looked back down. "Come on up."

She looked up at him, and got unsteadily to her feet. "How do I do that?"

"Chuck me up the blanket." She hesitated for a moment, then took off the blanket and threw it at the roof. It fell well short of his reaching hand. "Come along, darling, make an effort," he told her. "If I lie here long enough looking at you I'll be as weak as a babe."

"Fuck you," she commented, rolled the blanket into a ball, and hurled it.

"That's the general idea," he told her as he caught it. He wrapped one end round his wrist, then lowered it back into the car. "Can you hold on to that for a matter of five seconds?"

Jennifer grasped the blanket in both hands, and took a deep breath, going red in the face as Jonathan drew the blanket and her up through the aperture. "God!" she panted. "Close it up."

He replaced the lid; it was heavy enough to sit quite tightly on the opening. Then he took the torch from his belt and looked around him. The car filled the shaft almost exactly. He looked up. The torch beam just picked out the floor of the car above, some forty feet away. "Can we get up?" Jennifer asked.

Jonathan shone the beam on the walls of the shaft. "Too smooth to climb. And it wouldn't do us any good. We can't get through the floor of that car."

"Then what are going to do?" Her voice was beginning to quaver again.

"Wait. Sooner or later Schleyer is going to want to find out how we're doing. And how his spare parts are doing as well. Look at it this way: we're warm as toast, and if we sit on this lid, there won't even be any smell."

"I'm so hungry I could eat anything," she muttered.

"Well," Jonathan said. "We'll just have to think of some way of both passing the time and distracting your mind."

"I just do not understand it," Lampson said, standing, hands on hips, in the centre of Hans Schleyer's library. It was well past midnight, and he and Parton, together with Brouard's men, had scoured every inch of the hospital.

"Searching hospitals just doesn't seem to be your forte, Chief Inspector," Colley remarked.

Lampson glared at him. "We know Rudder came in here." Bell, although still unconscious and now in a bed in the Clinic, had been identified. "There is no one else who could have done what he did. No one else could have driven the truck in. Yet he has disappeared as if he never existed."

Schleyer looked puzzled. "He must have found some way back out."

"Through your foolproof security system?"

"As you said earlier, Chief Inspector, no system is foolproof. I stand corrected for my over-confidence."

"But why should Rudder go to all the trouble to break in, just to break out again?" Parton asked.

"I formed the impression, when he first visited here with his uncle last Tuesday, that he was not entirely stable," Schleyer said.

"Why, do you know, so did I," Colley agreed, "when he first came to the Freedom Clinic. Mind you, poor Jonathan has never been a very stable character. I knew him at medical school, you know, Chief Inspector."

Lampson looked about to explode.

"And now, Inspector Brouard," Schleyer said. "If you will excuse me, I really would like to get into town and see my injured people. I wish to transfer them up here, you understand, where I can treat them myself."

"Of course," Brouard said. "Shall we leave, Chief Inspector?"

"What about Rudder?"

Brouard turned his hands outwards; as the Clinic was plastered with No Smoking signs he had been growing increasingly agitated over the past three hours. "He is not here."

Lampson looked at Parton. "Well, sir," Parton said. "Perhaps someone should stay on the premises. I'd be quite happy to volunteer." Anything to avoid sharing a bed with Lampson.

Lampson apparently felt the same way. "Why, that would be the answer. I'm sure Dr Schleyer can offer you a bed for the night, eh, doctor?"

"Certainly," Schleyer agreed. "If you feel it necessary, Chief Inspector." He looked Parton up and down. "Sister Marianne," he said. "Will you provide the sergeant with a pair of hospital pyjamas, a toothbrush, and a razor. You may sleep wherever you wish, Sergeant." He smiled genially. "As long as it is not with one of my patients, of course. Now, Chief Inspector, if you will excuse me, Sister Marianne will attend to everything." He nodded to them, and left the library. Colley hurried behind him. They got into the lift to the fifth floor.

"What the hell are we going to do?" Colley demanded.

"About what?"

"This idiot Parton."

"I don't think we need to do anything about the sergeant, James."

"But Rudder and Brand are still down there."

"And they are going to have to stay down there until the police get fed-up and depart for good. I'm afraid the spares we have stored in that chamber will be lost, but I think they are already lost – disintegration will certainly set in very soon. There is no use crying over spilt milk. We will have to replace them from Holland." The lift stopped, and he led the way into his apartment. Nan Welldon sat in front of the picture window, feet drawn up on the sofa, staring out at the night, a glass of brandy in her hand.

"She really was shaken up by Rudder's assault," Colley explained. "Seems he threw her against a wall."

"He's no gentleman. Well, there is a spare room. I suggest you take her in there, put her to bed, and get in with her, if you wish. And stay there. There is absolutely nothing to worry about. I am going into town to see Brigitte. I will be back in an hour. Then I too will have a good night's sleep, and tomorrow, once the police have gone, we will deal with Rudder and Brand. I am quite looking forward to that. To seeing what condition they will be in, after a night in that cold chamber . . . which by now I would say is warming up very nicely indeed."

"Jonathan," Jennifer said. "What time is it?"

He peered at the luminous dial of his watch. "Ten past four."

"We have sat here for more than three hours."

"Doesn't get any softer, does it. Did you really work out what they were doing?"

"Yes. I was stupid not to have realised it before. I mean, Doug more or less spelled it out in his diary, but it took me so long to force myself to read it."

"But are those organs really any good, after they've been frozen?"

"I imagine they lose a lot. But with all the new techniques they have, using electric shock treatment once they are thawed out and put in place, there's no reason why they shouldn't work."

"God damn! I wonder whose heart Uncle Eric has."

She was silent for some minutes, then she asked,

"Jonathan, suppose they never come for us? Just leave us here to die of starvation?"

"They'll come for us," Jonathan said. "They won't be able to resist it. They're just trying to make sure we're past caring by the time they open up."

"When they open up, what are you going to do?"

"Take this whole bloody place apart," Jonathan promised.

"Just time for a cup of coffee between flights," Bruce Hardy said, stamping along the corridor from the aircraft to the transit lounge in Heathrow's Terminal Three.

"This ticket says we leave for Nice from a different building, boss," Lem remarked.

Aware of both kidnapping and harrassment possibilities, Bruce never travelled abroad without his two minders, Lem and Albert, who happened to be the gorillas in his yachting crew; they also doubled as his valet and butler. Walking between the two very large young men he was nearly invisible. "Shit," he commented. "Well, let's get over there. What about the bags?"

"I guess they get transferred across."

"You'd better hope so."

They waited while their passports were checked, passed through the Green Channel, made inquiries of a baggage clerk, and were told that if they were in transit and their luggage was properly labelled, it would be waiting for them in Nice. "Seems okay, boss," Albert said.

"Yeah, coffee." Bruce turned abruptly, and nearly fell over a small, elderly lady who was standing at the customs exit blinking at the crowd of waiting people. "Oops, sorry, lady."

"Say," the woman held his arm. "You're American."

"Ain't we all?"

"Could you help me? Do you know what an English policeman looks like?"

"They're different," Lem pointed out.

"Why do you want a policeman?" Bruce asked. "You lost something?"

"One was supposed to meet me," the lady explained. "An inspector person, named Lampson. A detective," she added importantly.

"A detective would be in plainclothes, ma'am," Albert explained. "You'd better check at Information."

"Hold on just one minute," Bruce said. "Let me get this straight, Miss . . ." he cast a hasty glance at her left hand. "Mrs . . .?"

"Brand," the lady said. "Olive Brand."

"Holy shitting cows! I beg your pardon, Mrs Brand. And you say some policeman named Lampson is meeting you here? It's to do with your daughter going missing, right?"

Olive Brand looked somewhat alarmed. "How did you know about that?"

"You come with us, and I'll tell you."

Olive Brand looked more nervous yet. "Are you kidnapping me?"

"Sure. To find your daughter. Listen, we're going to Antibes. We're going to pick up a friend of mine who's also trying to find your daughter. You'd better come along with us."

"I don't have a ticket to Antibes."

"Lem, get the lady a ticket to Antibes, on our flight."

"You'll never do it, this time of year," Olive protested.

"We always travel First," Bruce told her. "No hassle."

"But the cost . . ."

"You're my guest."

"What about the police?"

"You don't want to worry about them, Mrs Brand. I never do."

* * *

Colley awoke with a start, looked at his watch: it was half-past eight. He glanced down at the head of auburn hair nestling on his shoulder. "Christalmighty!" He leapt out of bed and ran for the shower.

Nan was thrown on to her back by his sudden departure, and sat up, scratching her head. "What's the problem?"

"We've overslept," he shouted above the noise of the water. Well, he supposed they had had a pretty exhausting day yesterday. But to oversleep today . . . he dragged on his clothes and went into the lounge, where Schleyer was sitting before his picture window, having breakfast. "For God's sake, Hans."

"Coffee? I'm afraid the croissants have gone cold, but I can heat them up."

"You're just sitting there, as though nothing had happened!"

"Nothing has, save that my poor Brigitte has a broken hip, and one of your people is very badly injured."

"What about Parton?"

"I expect him to leave, soon. We will attend to that as soon as we have eaten."

"And Rudder and the woman?"

Schleyer smiled. "I hope your stomach is good and strong, James. It could be a very nasty business."

Detective Sergeant Parton was being served breakfast in his room by one of the nurses. He looked embarrassed to be visited by the two doctors, as if he were a patient. "The fact is, Sergeant," Schleyer explained. "Even you must concede that if Rudder is inside the Clinic, he is playing a very odd game."

"I suppose so, sir." Parton was in an excellent humour; he had slept like a log, and was having a very good breakfast.

"So, if you'd like to get dressed and report to your superiors . . ."

"Of course, sir. It has been very good of you to put up with me."

Forty-five minutes later Colley, Nan and Schleyer watched Parton being driven away in the taxi Schleyer had called for him. "There goes the end of our worries," Schleyer said.

"When are we going to open that chamber?" Colley asked.

"As soon as I've seen how Brigitte is."

"May we see her?" Nan asked.

"I think she would like that." Schleyer escorted them to the room where Brigitte lay propped up on pillows. "How are we this morning?"

"Hurting like shit." She was encased in plaster and bandages from the waist down. "Where's Rudder?"

"We are about to deal with him."

"I want to be there."

Schleyer smiled, and kissed her on the forehead. "I do not think it would be wise for you to get up. We want that hip to knit just as quickly as possible. But I will bring him up to see you, if he is in any fit state to see anyone." He went back downstairs, accompanied by Nan and Colley. "How many men have we fit for duty?"

"Six," Sister Marianne told him.

"Then get them together in the garage. Tell them they must wear protective gear and face masks."

She reached for her phone even as the gate phone rang. She listened for a moment, put her hand over the mouthpiece and looked at Schleyer. "Don't tell me the police are back?" Colley asked.

"No, no, doctor. There is a Mr Bruce Hardy at the gate. He wishes to come in. He says he is a friend of Mr Rudder."

"Oh, Jesus Christ!" Colley snapped.

"Softly," Schleyer said. "Which Mr Rudder?"

Marianne spoke into the phone. "Both."

"Well, let him in."

"Are you crazy?" Colley demanded.

"I am trying not to be crazy. Eric Rudder will have made no secret of the fact that he is undergoing treatment here. He is obviously a man with a wide circle of friends. He certainly cannot be visited for more than five minutes at a time. We will soon get rid of this Mr Hardy. But everything must at all times be normal." He went into the reception hall, and watched the hire car pull up before the front steps. There were several people in the car, but only one got out, a somewhat small man wearing casual clothes. "Mr Hardy? Hans Schleyer!" Schleyer shook hands. "You are a friend of Mr Rudder, I believe?"

"Right first time. Is he about?" Bruce stepped past him into the foyer, as if expecting to find a Rudder waiting for him.

Schleyer followed. "Didn't you know that Mr Rudder has just had a serious operation? You can see him, of course, but only for a minute."

"But the old geezer's alive, right? Great! Where's Jonathan?"

"You mean young Mr Rudder? I'm afraid I don't know."

"He said he'd meet me here. Or you'd know where he is."

"He's a somewhat disorganised young man," Schleyer said. "He was here yesterday afternoon, visiting his uncle. Then he went off. I have to tell you, Mr Hardy, that there is a rumour going around that he's in some kind of trouble with the police."

Bruce grinned. "Wouldn't surprise me. But you're expecting him back here, right?"

"I simply do not know. One imagines he will come to see his uncle again . . ."

"Odd." Bruce looked at Colley, who had come down the stairs to see what was going on.

"My colleague," Schleyer explained. "James Colley."

Bruce had been turning away. Now he checked. "Did you say Colley?"

Colley came across the room. "Have we met?"

Bruce looked him up and down. "I don't think so. Something about the name. Well, if Jonny isn't here . . ."

"Don't you want to see Mr Eric Rudder?"

"Not really. You give him my love. And if Jonny shows up, tell him I'll be seeing him."

Schleyer walked to the door with him, watched him get into the car, and turned back to Colley. "He seemed to know your name."

"Well, he would. If he's a friend of the Rudders, either Jonathan or Eric would have mentioned that I was the one arranging Eric's op."

"Yes, I suppose so." The car had vanished round the bend in the drive. "Are the men kitted up, Sister?"

"Yes, doctor."

"Then we'd better do the same. I don't want to be interrupted for the next hour, Sister, unless it really is an emergency."

"You look kind of bothered, boss," Lem remarked, as he started the engine.

"We have action," Bruce told him. "Stop this crate right in the middle of the gate. There's a guy in there I want to have a chat with." Lem stopped, exactly in the centre of the open gateway. Here they were out of sight of the chateau, although undoubtedly the nurse at reception would know the gate was still open. "Say, Olive, can you drive?" Bruce asked.

"Sure I can drive. I wish you'd tell me what is going on."

"I want you to get behind the wheel and drive this car into Antibes. Go to the police station, and tell them there's trouble at the St Croix Clinic, and to get up here, quick. Think you can do that?"

"Sure I can. Is this going to help us find Jennifer?"

"Those guys in there know where she is. That's what we're going to talk to them about. Off you go now. Quick as you can. But remember not to get a ticket for speeding. At least they drive on the right side of the road over here."

He watched the car go through the gates. Immediately they swung shut, but then there was a shout, and a loud barking. The three Americans turned, to see a man approaching, armed with a shotgun, and accompanied by an Alsatian dog. The dog continued to bark, and the man shouted at them in French. "You understand what he's saying, Albert?" Bruce asked.

Albert had been to college. "Something about *défense d'entres* . . . that's trespassing."

Bruce led them forward. "No savvy," he explained. The man came closer yet, waving the gun, still shouting. "No savvy," Bruce repeated.

"*Je ne comprends pas*," Albert said.

"Say, that's great," Bruce said admiringly. "I reckon he's close enough. I'm going to grab the gun. Lem, you hit him. Albert, you hit the dog. Let's move it."

"Jonathan," Jennifer whispered urgently. "Listen." From above them came a whirr, as the lift mechanism started.

Jonathan stretched, painfully. "God! I was dreaming of steaks."

"You mean you were asleep. Oh, shit, we're going up! If the other car doesn't move, we're going to be squashed flat."

"It'll move," Jonathan promised, peering up into the gloom. He daren't risk using the flashlight, just in case someone was looking down the shaft. "Now, remember: you stay here."

"What are you going to do?" she whispered.

"Give them the shock of their lives," Jonathan said. "But you may have to hold your nose." He crouched above the hatch, while the car continued its ascent. Above them the reserve car, as he had prophesied, had risen into the shaft, and now the cold car was coming to a halt. "Remember, hold your breath," he told her. "And the moment I'm gone, push the lid back shut and sit on it. Right?"

"Oh, Jonny!" She held his arm. "I'm so scared."

He kissed her. "That's because you're hungry." He opened the hatch, and dropped through.

"What do you expect to find?" Colley asked as he and Schleyer, together with Nan and the six men, watched the car slip into place.

"Two pretty distraught human beings. I don't think there'll be any problem." Schleyer pulled his face mask into position, and Colley did the same. The lift came to a halt. Colley and Schleyer both drew their pistols. "Switch on the interior lights," Schleyer commanded. One of the men obeyed. "Now open the door."

The man pressed a button and the door opened. Nan Welldon gave a little gasp through her mask, as she gazed at the scattered, bloody, disintegrating mess which covered the car, it seemed from floor to ceiling. She turned away, leaning against the wall. Schleyer was frowning. "Where the hell are they?" he demanded.

Colley also took a step backwards. He had never anticipated seeing his handiwork reduced to this. The men weren't looking too happy, either. "They can't have disappeared," Schleyer snapped. "Get in there and find them."

"In there, doctor?" the first man asked. "I would never sleep again." He sounded very shaken, and there could be no doubt that his companions were equally upset.

"I'll do it," Colley snapped, pulling himself together; he knew it had to be ended, now. He stepped into the doorway, his pistol thrust forward, looking right and left, and was engulfed in a mound of human organs, descending from the upper shelf. "God!" he screamed. "God!" And then discovered that immediately behind the mound was a huge, bloodstained figure, which seized him by the arms, wrenched them both out of their sockets, twisted the gun from his grasp, and then hurled him out of the door at the horrified people beyond. Jonathan levelled the gun he had taken from Colley's hand and fired twice. Colley hit the floor with a sickening crunch. Jonathan was no great marksman, but at that range he couldn't miss; one of the orderlies gave a shriek and fell backwards.

"Hit the switch!" Schleyer shouted, and fired his gun. The bullet slammed into the car, missing Jonathan but checking his advance. Before he could recover the doors, had closed and he was plunged into darkness and falling again.

"Jonathan!" Jennifer had opened the hatch. "Jonny, are you there? God, the smell . . .! Ouch!" The car had come to a thundering stop, making them both bounce. "Jonathan?" A beam of light seeped up through the opening. "Oh, thank God."

"I'm coming up." He leapt for the opening, swung himself through, and closed it again. He was covered in blood and guts and too much of the stench had escaped the car.

"Are you all right?" Jennifer asked.

"I'm fine. Colley's done for the foreseeable future, and one of the goons."

"So what do we do now?"

"Wait for Schleyer to make his next move."

"Jonny . . . how long are we going to be able to stand it down here? With . . . those?"

"They say one can get used to anything," he reminded her.

"Jim! Oh, Jim." Nan Welldon knelt beside the moaning Colley. "Both his arms are dislocated."

Schleyer stooped to jerk them back into place, and Colley screamed, and again; bloody froth appeared in his mouth. "He also has broken ribs," Schleyer said, "and perhaps a punctured lung. You and you, get a bed trolley and take him upstairs. Quickly!"

"What about Jules?" asked one of the porters, standing above the man who had been shot.

Schleyer gave the man a quick examination; the front of his white overalls were covered in blood. "He is dead."

Nan gave a little sob. "Those bastards," an orderly snapped. "What are we going to do about them, Dr Schleyer?"

"We are going to settle them," Schleyer said. "Fetch me all the oxygen cylinders we have. That is a sealed shaft. We'll pump it full of oxygen until their lungs burst."

"Yes, sir," the man said enthusiastically, and hurried off, followed by two others. The remaining two had wheeled a bed trolley in from the stairs, and were carefully lifting Colley on to it. Colley moaned and twisted in agony. "He needs a sedative," Nan said.

"As soon as we get him upstairs. Réné, you remain here and keep an eye on that shaft. Not that there is any way they can get up. I'll be back in half an hour to finish the business. Take my gun." The orderly grasped the pistol and stood in front of the doors to the cold chamber, as if willing Jonathan to appear and be shot. Schleyer himself wheeled Colley to the main lift shaft, Nan at his side. They had just reached it when an alarm bell rang.

"Oh, my God!" Nan screamed; her nerves had reached breaking point.

Schleyer grabbed at the telephone beside the lift. "Marianne?" There was no reply. "I must get up there," Schleyer snapped. "You stay here, with James. You must. If it is the police, how do we explain his injuries? I will let you know the situation in one minute."

He stepped into the lift, and sent it up. Nan bit her lip, looked down at the moaning Colley, then at Réné, and listened to the sound of feet on the stairs. A moment later Bruce Hardy was in their midst, followed by Lem and Albert. Nan goggled at them in horror. Réné turned, but was too late; Lem was also armed and sent the orderly crashing to the floor with a single shot.

Bruce glanced at Colley. "Looks like our boy has been around. That's a shame; I wanted this one for myself." He grabbed Nan by the arm. "Where is he? Give, or you'll wind up looking like your friend."

Nan was not prepared to argue any further. "They're down the shaft," she said. "In a lift car. It's . . ." Bruce leapt at the controls, and pressed the buttons. "It's dreadful!" Nan shouted. "Oh, my God, it's dreadful."

Bruce glanced at her, frowned, and reached for the controls again and pressed stop. The mechanism whirred to a halt. Bruce pressed the button to open the doors, and recoiled. "Christ, what do they have down there?"

"Bruce!" Jonathan shouted. "Brother, do you sound good. Get us up. But stop as soon as the roof of the car is level."

Bruce pressed the button, peering down. Feet clattered, and the four orderlies returned, each carrying two oxygen cylinders. Lem pointed his gun. So did Albert; he had taken Réné's. "Stop right there," Albert commanded in French. "And put down those cylinders." The men hesitated, then obeyed. Without Schleyer they lacked leadership.

The lift car roof reached ground level, and Jonathan

and Jennifer scrambled out. "Jesus Christ!" Bruce commented. "Just what have you guys been rolling about in?"

"Don't ask." Jonathan glanced at Colley, and Nan, and the waiting orderlies. "Where's Schleyer?"

"Haven't a clue," Bruce said.

"Then how did you get in?"

"Just walked in. Girl on the desk did a bit of screaming, but when we shook her up a little, she told us the action was down here. We didn't see anyone else except for these goons."

Jonathan looked at Nan. "Give."

"When the alarm went off he dashed upstairs," she said. "I don't know where he was going."

"Uncle Eric!" Jonathan snapped, and ran for the stairs; he couldn't afford to trust the elevator.

"Catch!" Bruce snatched the gun from Lem's hand and tossed it. Jonathan caught it and went on his way.

"He'll need help!" Jennifer said.

"I doubt that," Bruce said. "Say, your name wouldn't be Jennifer Brand?"

"It is."

"Your Mom's looking for you; she'll be here in a little while. But say, what's that you're wearing?"

"It used to be a blanket." Jennifer looked at Nan. "I need a shower. Where is there one?" Nan pointed at the washrooms in the far corner of the basement. "I'll also need clothes."

"Yes," Nan said vaguely. "What about Jim? He's very badly hurt."

"We'll take care of him, until the police get here," Bruce said. "You look after Miss Brand. And lady, any funny stuff and we'll put you down that shaft, right?"

* * *

Jonathan took the stairs three at a time, and reached the second floor in a few panting seconds. There was no one in sight, but as he turned down the corridor he saw Schleyer emerging from Eric's room. They stared at each other, and then Schleyer fired. Jonathan dropped to his hands and knees and returned the shot, but he knew he had also missed, and before he could aim again Schleyer was gone, along the corridor to the second flight of stairs. Jonathan regained his feet, ran into his uncle's room, and found a shambles. Schleyer had not merely switched off the life support machine, he had wrecked it; loose tubes lay all over the floor. Jonathan stood at the bedside, gazing at Eric. But Eric was already dead.

The deep anger which lurked in Jonathan's psyche began to well close to the surface. But he needed to save it all for Schleyer. He ran along the corridor to the back flight of stairs, looked up, and heard voices, one sharp with pain. Of course, Schleyer was getting Brigitte. But there was no place for them to go. He ran up the stairs, pistol held in both hands and thrust forward, reached the corner into the corridor, looked round, and a bullet slammed into the wall behind him. He returned fire, heard footsteps, and looked again. Schleyer was running along the corridor, Brigitte in his arms. Jonathan sent a shot above their heads; he knew Brigitte deserved to die as much as any of them, but he was not in the business of killing women. He followed to the inner staircase, and listened to footsteps above his head. Certainly by now Schleyer knew that his career was over, but no doubt he still hoped to make the basement garage and escape.

Jonathan went up, and again, to the top floor. He waited at the landing, listening, and heard Brigitte give a scream of agony as she was brushed against something. He ran forward, bursting into the apartment.

Schleyer had laid Brigitte on the bed, and was filling his pockets with money taken from his bureau drawer. "Game's up," Jonathan said, and stepped back.

Predictably Schleyer fired, the bullet hitting the door. And again. Jonathan stepped inside, and Schleyer levelled the gun again. "Bastard," Schleyer said, and squeezed the trigger.

But there was only a click. Jonathan grinned at him. "You've been wasteful," he said. "Now lie on the floor, hands behind your head."

Schleyer glared at him, then looked at Brigitte, then lowered his head and charged like a bull. It was Jonathan's turn to listen to the click of a hammer on an empty chamber. He threw away the gun, and took Schleyer's charge. They staggered together, Schleyer's arms wrapping themselves round Jonathan's waist, pressing with all his enormous strength, forcing Jonathan back against the wall, while his shoulder ground into Jonathan's chest. Jonathan saw stars, and then remembered that he was as powerful as this man – at least in the short term.

He brought his hands together and chopped on the back of Schleyer's neck, and again, with no result. In the bedroom, Brigitte was attempting to drag herself up, moaning with pain. Jonathan struck down again, and at last felt the paralysing grip on his body begin to slacken. He brought up one knee, and Schleyer grunted. Jonathan hit him again, and the doctor fell away, almost to his knees, before recovering and straightening.

"Fitter than I thought," he grunted, half smiling, and threw a punch. Jonathan did his fist-catching trick, but this time when he tried to twist the arm it didn't move, and instead he was hit with the other fist, a savage blow in the ribs which left him gasping. Schleyer now grinned, pulled his right hand free, and struck again. But Jonathan saw this one coming, realised he had to change his tactics, and went down in a deliberate fall, grasping Schleyer's shirt front as he did so. The doctor flew over his head and struck the floor, heavily.

Jonathan turned on his knees, seized Schleyer's leg, and twisted it. As he had surmised, the doctor was less powerful from the waist down. Schleyer grunted with pain, and tried to check, but found himself on his face. Before he could recover Jonathan was astride his back, kneeling just above his buttocks amd twining his fingers in Schleyer's hair. "Move and I'll break your back," he said.

Schleyer attempted to jerk his head free, and they both listened to the sound of police sirens coming up the hill. Insensibly Jonathan slightly relaxed his hold, and a moment later Schleyer was rolling again, carrying him with him. They reached their feet together, panting, Schleyer's shirt torn and now stained with the blood which still covered Jonathan from head to foot. But Schleyer was the more exhausted; daily workouts in a gymnasium were not quite the same thing as crewing for Bruce Hardy, or playing a hard game of rugby. "Want to call it a day?" Jonathan asked.

Schleyer stared at him. "I never killed anyone," he said. "Your uncle was going to die, anyway."

"Yeah?"

"Listen. All the murders were done by Colley and Nan Welldon, and the other English couple, Marcus Lowndes and Lois Stanley. They killed your fiancée."

"That's nice to know," Jonathan said, and ran at him again. Schleyer got his hands up, but was too exhausted to do more than parry the first couple of blows. He went down under the third, a tremendous right-hander to the stomach.

Bruce and Lem appeared in the doorway. "Shit," Bruce commented. "You're always one step ahead of me."

"He's yours now," Jonathan said. "Where are the police?"

"Swarming all over the place, downstairs."

"Take Schleyer down and hand him over, but keep them out of the basement for the next half hour," Jonathan said. Bruce raised his eyebrows. "I have some unfinished business," Jonathan explained. "And it can't be done by anyone save me."

He used Schleyer's shower to clean himself up, then put on some of Schleyer's clothes – they were much of a size. By then the entire hospital was humming with noise. He kissed Brigitte on the forehead. "Most prison hospitals are pretty well equipped, nowadays," he told her, and took the private elevator to the basement garage. Thanks to Bruce's delaying tactics, this was deserted, save for the discarded oxygen cylinders and the body of the man Jules . . . and the stench as the spare parts really began to disintegrate . . . But it was open to the morning, and the truck was waiting for him. He ran up the ramp, got into the driving seat . . . and found Jennifer beside him.

She wore a borrowed nurse's uniform, and looked most attractive; her hair was still wet. "Bruce told me you were making a run for it," she said. "I thought I'd better come along."

"I'm not making a run for it. I want Angie's killers, before they get word of what has happened down here. They're Doug's killers, too."

She nodded. "I thought that might be the case."

The inner gates stood open. He drove through. Two gendarmes waited beside several cars in the front courtyard. They waved him to a halt, and spoke to him in French. Jonathan jerked his head at the nurse beside him. "I'm being taken to another hospital," he said. "Go check with Chief Inspector Lampson." He drove on.

* * *

others," Jonathan explained. "But you don't have any more arms, do you? Well, then . . ." he picked up the weeping Marcus from the floor, walked to the window, and threw him out.

Marcus fell the twenty odd feet from the first floor to the concrete of the car park, and lay there, screaming. Jennifer and Mrs Malcolm ran outside to stare at him, and then look up. "Oh, my God!" Jennifer shouted. "Jonathan!"

"Is he alive?"

"Yes. But I think both his legs are broken."

"So are both his arms," Jonathan told them. "Mrs Malcolm, you may use your telephone, to call an ambulance. I don't suppose there's anyone left around here capable of straightening him out."

"You can't just go around the place breaking people's arms," Lampson pointed out.

"And legs," Parton added.

"Do you realise you have put eight people into hospital in the last twenty-four hours? I should lock you up and throw away the key," Lampson said.

"The point is," Jonathan said. "Are you going to lock that crowd up and throw away the key?"

"I would say, yes. When they come out of hospital. And when we are finished with them, the French and the Spanish are waiting to get their hands on them. Stick around, Rudder. You're a witness."

"Well, the fact is . . ." Jonathan looked at Bruce.

"He's coming back to the States, with me," Bruce announced. "I need him for the season. There won't be any trial before the fall, right, Inspector? I'll see he's back then."

"I'll have to be back, looking for a job," Jonathan added. "What I am likely to pick up from Uncle Eric isn't going to last that long."

"What about you, Miss Brand?" Lampson asked.

"I have to start looking for a job, right now."

"Can you cook?" Bruce asked.

"Sure."

"Do you get seasick?"

"Never have."

"Then you have a job, for the summer, anyway. You can also keep an eye on the boy, here."

Jennifer looked at Jonathan. "Do I want to do that?"

"Sure you do," Bruce said. "He's in love with you. He told me so. Then when the summer is over, you can start looking for a job, together."